Inspired by the life of Irena Golcvegaite

Finding Home - Book I

Displaced

A Family Without a Country

Sue Stewart Ade

DISPLACED
Copyright © 2025 by Sue Stewart Ade

ISBN: 979-8-88653-359-0

Melange Books, LLC
White Bear Lake, MN 55110
www.melange-books.com

Published in the United States of America.

Cover Design by Ashley Redbird Designs

This book is dedicated to Irena Golvegaite for her brave spirit and for trusting me with her story, as well as other Lithuanians who were caught between the Soviets and the Germans.

PROLOGUE

July 27, 1943
Hamburg, Germany
(Operation Gomorrah)

rena fisted her hands and raced through the crowded street to the bunker. Her bare feet slapped against the cobblestones as her pigtails flopped behind her.

Eeeoooeeeoooe.

The high-pitched screech of the air-raid siren sent chills slithering down her spine. She wasn't going to make it. She wasn't going to make it. She squinted through the fog of smoke. Her eyes burned. "Mama, Da, where are you?" The wind carried away her words.

Screams surrounded her and footsteps pounded against the pavement. She pumped her legs harder. She had to reach the bunker before the door closed.

The sky rumbled. Her head jerked up. Airplanes. Lots of enemy planes, one after another, cut through the clouds.

Why was Hamburg being attacked again? The smoke and soot hadn't cleared from the bombing two hours ago. And what was the target? Didn't the British know this was where the workers and their families lived?

The siren changed to the *Fliegeralarm*, fifteen four-second wails, warning only minutes until the attack. Sweat prickled on her brow. She was only eight years old. She didn't want to die. She just wanted to go home to Lithuania.

Jutting out her chin, she fisted her hands and charged through the smoke and wind.

Boom! Boom! Boom!

The ground rolled. In the distance a bomb exploded. A yellow ball of fire illuminated the night sky. Lying on the street were mounds of soot from the previous raid. Her foot hit something solid. Her arms shot out to break the fall. Her knees slammed against the jagged stones, ripping the skin as her hands landed in the black soot. Only it wasn't soot. None of the black mounds lying lifeless in the street were soot.

She screamed.

1940

Before the beginning of World War II, Hitler and Stalin signed the German-Soviet Nonaggression Pact, a secret protocol that divided Eastern Europe into German and Soviet spheres. The Soviets were given the Baltic countries.

When the Soviet Union invaded Lithuania in 1940, Irena Golcvegaite was six years old. This is the story of Irena and her family, plus the thousands of other Lithuanians who fled from their homeland.

Two thirds of them died.[1]

CHAPTER
ONE

April 1940
Kaunas, Lithuania

The river whispered over the rocks, calling her name. Harriet quickened her step as she lugged the basket of laundry through the marshy reeds. Their leaves rustled against her long skirt. Shoes hurt her bunion, so she was barefooted, but she enjoyed the grass tickling her toes.

After the harsh Baltic winter with its bitter winds and blinding snow, she basked in the sun, warming her body like a welcome embrace of spring. The air scented with pine trees and wildflowers was a respite from a world that seemed on the brink of war.

"Hurry, Mama," called Irena, dashing toward the riverbank, her brown pigtails flying behind. Bridget, only four, tried to keep up with her older sister.

As Harriet followed the girls, she flushed with motherly pride. In the fall, Irena would turn six and start school. Letting her oldest daughter go out into the world would be hard. Irena was a good girl, but spirited, and the world might crush her spirit.

When Harriet reached the river, the girls were on the bank, dangling their bare feet into the blue water. She set the basket down next to them. "Stay here while I gather rocks."

"Maybe you'll find some gold," Irena said. "Then we'll be rich."

Amber, which was called Lithuanian gold, had been fossilized thousands of years ago. The gems occasionally washed up from the river, although Harriet had never found any. Her humble home, loving husband, and precious daughters made her feel rich.

Lifting her skirt, Harriet tiptoed into the shallow water. The coolness sent a refreshing shiver through her. She reached down, searching for rocks to scrub the clothes. From the bottom of the riverbank, she dug through the silt. Scooping up a fistful of sand, she opened her hand, letting the water sluice through her fingers. No Lithuanian gold glistened in the sunlight, only ordinary gray rocks. She rolled them around in the palm of her hand, keeping some and discarding others. When she had what she needed, she waded back to the girls and led them to a flat boulder, where they stuck their hands into the water mining for treasures.

From the clothes basket, she pulled out her husband's T-shirt and dipped it into the river, swishing it around. Then she slapped the wet shirt against the rocks before she laid it on the flat stone and scrubbed it with the small rocks she'd gathered. Next, she washed the girls' plaid jumpers—one green, one blue. As she worked, she established a rhythm—the swishing of the clothes, the slapping of the wet garments, the clicking of the rocks. The sounds created a soothing melody. *Swish-swish-swish, slap-slap-slap, click-click-click.*

"Look what I found, Mama." Irena opened her fisted hand.

6

A heart-shaped rock rested on her palm. "I'm going to add it to my collection."

Nearby, a train whistled. Harriet turned toward the trestle spanning the river. A steam engine chugged across the tracks, its wheels clickety-clacking against the steel rails.

"Wouldn't it be fun to ride on a train?" Irena asked, stretching out her arms. "Just cross the river and fly away."

Harriet didn't answer. She didn't like change. In her life, change had meant unhappiness, except for marrying Oskar and having her own family. She leaned back and tilted her chin up. A cool breeze lifted her wavy brown hair off her neck. A trickle of unease rippled down her back, hinting at a change to her peaceful world.

Last fall, Germany invaded Poland, claiming the western part. Sixteen days later, the Soviet Union invaded Poland, claiming the eastern part. Lithuania was a tiny country, but rich in natural resources, which made it appealing to both Germany and the Soviet Union. Harriet pushed away the troubling thought, not wanting anything to intrude on her idyllic corner of the world.

After she finished the laundry, she hefted the basket of clothes and headed toward home. Irena and Bridget skipped ahead, meandering through the meadow dotted with wildflowers. Irena stopped and picked a cluster of Lithuanian blues, their azure petals dancing in the breeze. Bridget gathered a bouquet of white-centered daises with lemon-yellow heads. The girls rushed back to Harriet, shyly curtsying as they presented them to her.

Smiling, Harriet dropped her basket and clutched the flowers against her chest, trying to hold on to this day of wildflowers and joy.

CHAPTER
TWO

August 9
1940-Kaunas, Lithuania

Harriet stood at the stove and plopped another handful of dumplings into the boiling broth. The savory scent of chicken and dumpling soup wafted through the room, giving it an inviting aroma. Yesterday she had turned twenty-five. Today was Irena's sixth birthday, and they would celebrate tonight with Irena's favorite soup.

Harriet glanced down at her and Bridget sitting cross-legged on the floor, playing house. Irena stirred rocks in a pan while Bridget dipped in a spoon to taste.

"It needs pepper." Bridget shook her clenched fist over the pan, pretending to add the spice.

The innocent joy on their scrubbed faces contrasted with Harriet's turmoil. Oskar was late. An evening breeze ruffled the printed curtains at the open window above the sink. She peered out, hoping to see Oskar riding his bicycle. The sidewalk was empty. Below the window grew her herb garden and in the apple tree hung a wooden swing Oskar had made for the girls. Both were simple pleasures that made the two-bedroom rented flat feel like a home.

Harriet's stomach twisted. Last night, she and Oskar had argued. He had suggested this crazy idea that they leave Lithuania. She couldn't imagine giving up her home and her country.

She moved away from the window and checked the soup. Her mind continued to worry, swirling like the dumplings floating in the broth. In June, Soviet troops had settled in Lithuania, supposedly to protect them from Germany, which had invaded most of the surrounding countries. Then last week the Soviets announced they had annexed Lithuania, making it part of the U.S.S.R., Union of Soviet Socialist Republics.

"It's still Russia," Oskar said. "You remember what it was like living under the communists."

Harriet nodded. When she was a child, Lithuania had been controlled by Russia. The communists had tried to wipe out anything Lithuanian. They had burned books written in Lithuania, and Harriet had to learn to speak Russian. She was afraid of what might happen now. She didn't want her daughters to grow up under communism, but there had to be a better solution than leaving.

Finally, Oskar's boots thudded up the stairs. "Girls, your father's home."

As the door opened, Irena and Bridget jumped up from the floor. "Da," they squealed, greeting Oskar with outstretched arms.

He wasn't a handsome man. His forehead was too high and his nose was too wide. Sometimes he could be gruff, but he was a good provider and fiercely loved his family, which showed in his smiling face as he leaned down and hugged the girls. "Something smells good," he said as he took off his plaid newsboy cap and raked his fingers through his thick brown hair.

Irena pointed to the table with a glass jar of blue-and-yellow wildflowers. "Mama let us pick them for our birthdays." She rocked on her bare heels, obviously pleased.

As Oskar smelled the flowers, he looked up at Harriet. "They're almost as pretty as my girls." Irena and Bridget giggled while Harriet blushed as if she were the young school girl instead of her daughters.

The family gathered at the table, and Harriet said her usual prayer, thanking God for their food and blessings. As they ate, Irena and Bridget babbled about going to the meadow. Harriet smiled, content to have her family around the table, enjoying their food and each other. She ignored any troubling thoughts that the Soviets might disrupt their lives. The troops had been stationed in Lithuania all summer and little had changed. Why did Oskar want to leave?

"Something happened at the candy factory when I was closing up," Oskar said. The lines in his forehead deepened, making him appear older than twenty-nine, and his serious tone alarmed her. He had said the communist government might seize all the industries in Lithuania. Had they taken over the candy factory?

"When I started to turn off the light in the supply closet, I spotted a rat hiding on the top shelf, his head peeking out from behind a bag of sugar."

Harriet relaxed. Oskar was merely entertaining the girls with one of his stories.

Irena squealed. "What did you do?"

Rising, Oskar rolled up his long sleeves and pantomimed his actions. "I grabbed a pitchfork." He raised his muscular arms over his head, pretending to wield a weapon. "Then I jabbed at the rat." He lowered his arms and stabbed into the air.

"Did you kill it?" Bridget asked.

Oskar poked with the imaginary prongs. "He tried to get away and jumped right at me."

Irena covered her face with her hands as if the rat had jumped on her.

Chuckling, Oskar patted her hair. "Don't worry, little one. The rat landed on the points of the pitchfork."

Rising, Harriet gathered their empty bowls. "I wish the Soviets were as easy to get rid of as that rat."

Oskar hurried to the open window and banged it shut. "Be careful what you say, Harriet. We no longer live in a free country."

"Da, did you bring me something for my birthday?"

"Close your eyes," he said.

Irena giggled and squeezed her eyes shut.

"Happy birthday," said Oskar.

Irena opened her eyes. Oskar had placed a wrapped piece of candy on the table in front of her. Snatching it up, she unwrapped it and popped the chocolate into her mouth.

"Candy," cried Bridget, putting out her hands to Irena, but she was already wallowing it in her mouth.

"Irena, you should have shared with your sister," Harriet scolded.

"It's my birthday." She reached over and patted Bridget's back to console her. "Da will bring you candy for your birthday, won't you?"

"If I'm still working there." He lifted his eyes to Harriet's, and she knew he was thinking about leaving.

That night, after Harriet tucked the girls into their beds, she returned to the kitchen and sat with Oskar at the table while he smoked a cigarette he had rolled. All week he'd talked about leaving Lithuania. She loved her country—the pine forests, the meadows, and the meandering rivers. It was home. But like him, she was worried about staying in Kaunas. Her grandmother had lived through the Russian reign of terror before the

Great War. Men had been separated from their families, sent to Siberia, or even killed.

Oskar laid his cigarette on the canning jar lid he used for an ashtray. "Have you thought any more about what we'll do if Lithuania is attacked?"

"That's all I have thought about." She was pulled in two different directions. How could she leave her homeland, her friends, and the rest of her family? But if she convinced Oskar to stay, the Soviets might drag him away like they had done to her grandfather. Stay...leave. Stay...leave. The words swirled in her head. Maybe they could wait to see what the Soviets planned to do. "It might not be the right time. Irena will start school next week."

"What if this is the only chance to leave? We'll be safe in Germany. Look what Hitler has done. The Germans were destitute after the Great War. Now they're thriving."

"But Germany invaded Poland."

"Before the war, part of Poland belonged to Germany." Oskar lifted his cigarette and took several long puffs. The scent of tobacco filling the kitchen did not ease the tension. "The Germans only took back what once belonged to them."

He ground the butt of his cigarette into the jar lid, twisting it until it crumbled. His gray eyes changed, and his hands, calloused from years of swinging a pick in the coal mine, reached across the table and clutched hers. His voice was softer, but his words were as rough as his hands. "I never told you the things I saw during the Great War, unimaginable things."

His words frightened her, and yet she had to hear them. "Like what?"

"I don't remember how old I was, maybe six, close to Irena's age. Pa and I were sneaking down an alley, searching for scraps of food. We stopped behind the bakery and peeked around the corner. Men were lined up in the street, their hands behind their heads. Two Russian soldiers with their backs to us pointed their rifles at the men. Pa pulled me into the shadows of the building, but I heard their rifles—*pop, pop, pop.*

"Sinking to my knees, I covered my ears, but I couldn't shut out the shots or the screams. It went on and on for so long that I thought I would go mad. When it finally ended, Pa inched forward to look out. I sidled up beside him. Bodies littered the street and blood ran down the cobblestones. One of the soldiers leaned over the men, opening their mouths. I thought he was checking to see if they were dead, but he reached into a man's mouth and yanked out his gold tooth."

For a long while Oskar didn't speak, and when he did, she understood what was driving his fear. "I never want our daughters to go through anything like that."

Harriet choked back a sob for the young boy Oskar had been. Now she understood his fear, and it became her fear. "If you say we should go—"

Irena screamed. Harriet jumped up and rushed to the girls' bedroom. Irena was propped up against a pillow, wailing. She had woken Bridget across the room in her own bed.

Harriet sat next to Irena and hugged her. "What's wrong?"

Irena fisted her hands and rubbed her eyes. "I opened a box of chocolates. Inside was a rat with two big front teeth. He pounced on me."

"It was just a bad dream." Harriet hoped her words were true.

CHAPTER
THREE

August 1940
Kaunas, Lithuania

rena twirled around the living room in her new red dress, her pigtails flying out to the sides and her waist ties flapping behind her. She danced faster, soaking up the sunshine streaming through the open window. The comforting aroma of the freshly baked rye bread wafted from the kitchen, making her mouth water.

Last night she had lain in bed, listening to her parents whispering about their plans. They were in the kitchen, so she couldn't make out all of the words, only 'Soviets.' The worry in their voices had scared her. In the daylight, however, those fears seemed foolish as she made her own plans.

Next week she would start school and wear the new red dress Mama had sewn for her. The bread Mama had made was also for Irena to eat at school. Poor Bridget. She sat across the room, rocking in the small wooden chair their grandfather had built. She was too young to go to school, so she would have to stay home.

Irena liked going places, especially to the market. When she was good, Mr. Livergood, who ran the store, would let her reach into his big glass jar and get a peppermint stick that she would lick all the way home.

Bridget stopped rocking and clapped her hands. "Pretty."

Irena knew Bridget was talking about the dress. Da called Irena cute, but he called Mama pretty. Mama had lots of curves, not a twiggy body like Irena's, and Mama's brown hair was silky because she washed it in rainwater from the barrel. What Irena liked best about Mama was her mouth, the way her lips curved up in a smile, like they were doing now.

"Come here," said Mama. "I'll tie your dress."

Irena spun to Mama, who sat on the couch with her sewing basket at her feet. As Mama fixed a bow in the back, Irena fingered the five rosebud buttons down the front and tried to stand still.

"All done," Mama said as she patted Irena's back.

Springing into action, she threw out her arms and circled the room again, flipping her skirt one way and then the other. Dreams of school and making new friends filled her head.

The door to the flat flew open. Da burst in. Mama jumped up, knocking over the sewing basket at her feet and spilling the contents. Irena stopped in mid-circle. Why was Da's cap crooked? Why were his eyes darting around?

"The Soviets. They're coming." Dad sounded like he was out of breath. "They're sending more troops to take over Kaunas right now."

Irena's heart drummed. She scurried to the window, expecting to see soldiers on horseback charging down the street. Instead, the sunshine that had brightened the sky was now hidden under the gray clouds, casting shadows on the sidewalk from the flocks of people rushing around. Some carried suitcases; others gripped lumpy pillowcases flung over their backs. A few cradled possessions in their arms. One woman squatted on the ground, clawing the dirt with her long fingers as she dug a hole and filled it with her china plates and cups.

Irena turned from the window. "Mama, why would anyone bury their dishes?"

Kneeling on the floor, Mama gathered the spilled spools of thread. "They're hiding their valuables so the Soviets won't steal them."

Oh, no. Irena didn't want the Soviets stealing her treasures. She dashed into her room and from under the bed slid out a glass jar filled with her prized rocks. She clutched the jar against her chest and carried it into the living room.

Mama's hand, usually so steady when she sewed, shook as she dropped the scissors into her sewing basket. "What do the Soviets want?"

Irena gripped the glass jar tighter. "They're not getting my rocks."

She expected Mama to reassure her, but Mama was listening to Da. "I heard they're rounding up Jews and rich Lithuanians, then shooting them."

Mama banged her sewing basket closed. "But we aren't Jews or rich."

"No, but they might make me join the Soviet army or exile me." Da removed his cap, and his dark hair sprang up in clumps. "I should join the Lithuanian resistance."

Mama rushed to him, throwing her arms around his neck. "Oskar, I won't let you do that. You said the Soviets were too powerful for Lithuania to win."

"I have to do something." Da stepped back and pounded his fist into the palm of his hand. "How can I protect you and the girls if they send me to Siberia?"

Putting down her jar of rocks, Irena rushed to Da and

grabbed his trouser leg, holding on tightly. "I won't let them take you," she said with all her determination.

Da brushed her away and wiggled free. "We have no choice, Harriet. We have to go through with our plan."

Tears streamed down Mama's cheeks. "What time is the train?"

"Train?" Irena wanted to stomp her foot and protest. On Monday, she was going to start school, make new friends, and learn to read. But Mama was crying and Da was pounding his fist. Irena twisted the rosebud button on her dress. "Why do we have to leave?"

Mama wrapped her arms around Irena and whispered, "It's the only way to keep our family together."

Irena snuggled closer to Mama. "Where-where are we going?"

"Germany," Da answered. "We'll be safe there."

———

At the train station, Irena was seized with panic. She had never seen so many people—babies crying, mothers yelling, fathers shoving to reach the ticket window. The hot air stunk like the pigpen at Papa's farm.

She clutched her stomach. She was suffocating. Sweat soaked into her polka-dot dress beneath the wool coat Mama had made her put on. At least she hadn't worn her red dress and gotten it dirty.

Irena's lower lip quivered. School. When would she start school? She peered up at Da and asked, "Will we be back on Monday?"

He didn't answer. He righted his felt hat and wedged through the packed station to secure their train tickets.

When he returned, his face was flushed as he patted the pocket of his long coat. "Four round-trip tickets."

Round trip. That meant they were coming back.

He led them outside, where they were pushed onto a platform with another mob of people. In the distance, the shrill whistle of the train alerted the crowd. They jostled forward. A big steam engine with billowing clouds puffing from the smoke stack roared toward the station. Its iron wheels hissed as the train screeched to a stop.

The word 'soldiers' whirled around them like winds of a storm. The sea of bodies shoved her and her family from the platform and onto the train. Irena's legs went rubbery. There were no seats, only more people with suitcases and bundled possessions elbowing for a space to stand.

Mama stopped as if unsure of what to do. A man in a suit, standing near the window, waved, offering her a place. Mama gripped Irena's hand and squeezed around a big woman, straining to hush the crying baby in her arms.

When Mama was close to the man, she tried to smile, but Mama's red lips barely turned up, and her wavy hair had wilted onto the shoulders of her winter coat.

Irena glanced back, checking for Bridget. Her little sister would be scared without her, but she was with Da in the center of the train car. Their suitcase rested next to them on the floor.

The train whistled and lurched forward, jolting Irena, and causing her feet to shift for balance. She had never ridden on a train before. She pressed her nose against the soot-streaked window.

People running alongside the train waved their hands and yelled, "Stop! Stop!" Others at the station screamed as Soviet soldiers on horses galloped toward them.

Irena felt queasy. The train picked up speed, rocking the car back and forth. Beneath her feet the floor vibrated, making it difficult to stand. What if the train tipped over? What if the soldiers caught them? Trying not to cry, she buried her head against Mama's winter coat and rubbed the soft wool between her fingers.

"We must be brave," Mama whispered in her ear.

After a short time, Irena's stomach settled. Lifting her head, she peeked out the window. Ahead was city hall. She looked for the Lithuanian flag with its yellow, green, and red stripes flying from the tall steeple. Instead, a red flag with a hammer and a sickle like the one Papa used to cut wheat flew above the white building.

Mama gasped. "The Soviet flag."

The train passed the blue-domed Catholic Church. Next year, she would be seven and make her first communion there. She would wear a white dress, and after church, they might go to one of the eateries along the street. Today the street was empty and the familiar shops—the market, the bakery, and the dry goods store—blurred as the train sped out of town, leaving her with a sense of longing.

The steam engine reached the trestle above the river where Mama washed their clothes. Irena gazed down at the muddy banks where she had stood on the rocks, watching the train speed across the tracks. She had thought it would be a wonderful adventure to ride the train and disappear into the unknown. Now she didn't think it was so wonderful.

Stuffing her hand into her pocket, she ran her thumb over the smooth edges of the heart-shaped rock. "When can we go home?"

A tear spilled down Mama's cheek. She wiped it away with the back of her hand. "Don't think about that. The important thing is we're together—and safe."

The big woman, who had quieted her baby, clucked. "Safe? No place is safe. We're at war."

CHAPTER
FOUR

Harriet stood near the window on the train, her breathing ragged as her beloved Lithuania flickered by. Irena clung to her coat while Oskar, holding Bridget in his arms, had wedged closer to them.

The train rumbling on the tracks picked up steam. Tears filled Harriet's eyes. She splayed her fingers against the window as the countryside streaked by, a quilt of green thick pine forests, emerald pastures dotted with sheep, and grassy rolling hills. She wanted to hold it all in, but they were speeding away too fast, leaving her entire world behind.

The train entered Poland with its low-land plains, Baltic Sea coast, and dense forests. The country where her grandparents had lived seemed much like Lithuania. During the Great War, when Russia seized Poland, her grandparents had not fled. One night at supper, Russian soldiers barged into her grandparents' house, dragging her grandfather away. The Soviets were capable of doing the same thing to her family, or worse. So, she'd accepted Oskar's decision to leave, but she didn't know leaving would feel as if that Soviet sickle on the flag flying from city hall was ripping out her heart.

A man on the train whispered, "There's one of them Jew camps." He said *Jew* as if he were spitting out sour milk.

Harriet squinted through the soot-streaked window. Sprawling red-brick buildings were surrounded by barbed wire. Under her black wool coat, she was clammy with sweat, but the barbed-wire fence sent chills down her spine. She'd heard rumors of camps where Jews were imprisoned, but she hadn't believed them. Maybe the brick compound was for war prisoners or criminals.

As the sun set, the view out the window faded. Lulled by the darkness, she leaned against the window. Her bunion throbbed as Irena curled up at her feet. The wheels hissed and the train jerked to a stop. They shuffled off with the other passengers for a brief break.

The night air cooled her body. She inhaled a deep breath. "How much farther?"

"We just crossed the German border," answered Oskar.

The stars twinkling in the night sky lit the way to an outhouse that stood beside the tracks. They waited in line and afterward, followed another group to a table with kettles of steaming soup and hot tea.

Harriet ladled small cups of familiar-smelling cabbage soup and weak tea for her family. As they sipped the liquid that warmed their bellies, Harriet's legs steadied and her fear eased.

They boarded the train again, and she whispered to Oskar, "You were right to insist we come to Germany."

They didn't have a place to live, Oskar didn't have a job, and she didn't speak the language, but they'd be together until the war ended. This time on the train, she leaned into the swaying rhythm and nodded off, dreaming of the day they could return home.

The wheels screeched, lurching the engine to a stop. She jolted awake. Daylight streamed through the sooty window. Careful not to wake Irena at her feet, Harriet rubbed her stiff neck and peered out, hoping to be greeted by more warm soup and tea.

Strutting toward the train were two soldiers wearing belted tunics and red armbands with swastikas. One soldier held a leash, restraining two barking German shepherds. The other pointed his rifle at the train window—and her. She jerked away, searching for Oskar. Catching his eye beneath his felt hat, Harriet frantically pointed to the soldiers.

A grin lit up his face, making him look years younger than twenty-nine. Nodding, he answered her unspoken question. "We're in Hamburg. We're safe."

CHAPTER
FIVE

F rom the moment Harriet stepped off the train, she did not feel safe. She pressed Irena against her chest.

"Don't look." Harriet didn't want her to be frightened by the soldiers and dogs, even though she reminded herself these weren't barbaric Soviets. They were German soldiers, and Oskar had assured her they'd be welcomed here.

Latching onto Oskar's coat, she shuffled behind him as he inched forward, carrying their suitcase and Bridget. Heat slapped Harriet's face. She fought down bile. The soldier with the rifle pointed it at the disembarking passengers, shouting something in German.

Other passengers balked. She tugged on Oskar's coat sleeve. "What's he saying?"

"This is the Registration Department. He's saying they're checking identification and travel documents." But Oskar was no longer smiling.

Weighed down by her heavy winter coat and Irena, Harriet followed Oskar to a line leading into a red brick building with a barbed-wire fence jutting out from the corners. The front of the building was guarded by more soldiers with guns and German shepherds restrained by leashes.

The camp in Poland flashed through her mind. She wanted to turn around and board the train. She wanted to go back to the welcoming stop with the warm soup or speed ahead to another town. Other passengers must have also wanted to flee. The man in front of Oskar, hefting a lumpy pillowcase over his shoulder, slipped out of line, moving several families behind them. The soldiers at the entrance didn't seem to notice. Then the tallest one straightened. He stretched his mouth taut, revealing large teeth, and pointed his rifle in the man's direction. "Halt."

The German shepherds, sensing something amiss, strained against their leashes, barking and baring their teeth. Irena jerked up. Harriet pressed Irena's head down so she couldn't see.

The man bolted from the line toward a bank of waiting buses beyond the barbed wire. His unbuttoned coat flew open and his pillowcase flopped against his back. The tall soldier bared his teeth in the same way as the dogs and repeated, "Halt."

The man continued running. The other soldier unleashed the dogs. They charged the man. The first shepherd pounced on his back, knocking the man forward. For a few seconds, he stayed suspended in mid-air. Then his whirling feet stopped, and he thudded to the ground. The pillowcase fell next to him, spilling out a rumpled white shirt and sock.

The second dog latched onto the man's leg, ripping through his trousers and sinking sharp canines into his fleshy calf. Blood spurted from his leg, soaking into the once-white sock lying on the ground.

Harriet's chest tightened. Others shrieked and called out. She clamped her mouth, gritting her teeth to keep from screaming, so she wouldn't pass her fear onto Irena, who was already whimpering. Harriet blocked the view with her hand, but she didn't turn away from the dogs mauling the man, their mouths dripping with blood.

As if nothing had happened, a soldier motioned the line forward. Oskar nudged Harriet. She followed him, shaking with each step. At the entrance to the red-brick building, Oskar handed a soldier their identification papers. The man studied the papers, grunted, and returned them before pointing to the doors behind him.

The creases on Oskar's high forehead smoothed. He opened the door and gestured for her to enter. She recoiled. Oskar said this was the Registration Department, but what if it was some sort of camp? He continued to wave for her to follow.

Her feet remained rooted, and his gray eyes locked on hers. "Go ahead, Harriet. I'll stay with you."

He prodded her and Irena through the door. It slammed behind them. They were confined with others in a small foyer with a black-and-white tiled floor and two soldiers. The burly one separated the people—the men and boys to the left door and the women and girls to the right door.

"Take Bridget," Oskar said.

Harriet feared being separated. She didn't know the language and was afraid she couldn't protect the girls or herself. She pressed Irena against her chest and locked her other arm through Oskar's. "You said you'd stay with me."

"They're only checking to make sure we're not sick or undesirables," explained Oskar.

"But what if that's not true?"

The huge soldier grabbed Oskar, jerking him and Bridget away. He twisted, trying to free himself, but the man was too strong. Harriet lunged forward, but the other soldier stepped in front, blocking the way.

Fear exploded through her. What would they do to Oskar and Bridget?

Harriet screamed at the line of men and boys across the

room. "Help us!" They kept their heads down as if she and Irena were invisible. Harriet appealed to the line of women and girls on the other side. They, too, ignored her.

Across the room, a familiar voice yelled, "Mama!" She turned. Bridget was standing near the men's door, alone and shaking.

The soldier still obstructed Harriet. She whispered into Irena's ear, "Get your sister."

Choking back sobs, Irena wiggled loose and dropped to the floor. She dashed to Bridget, grabbed her hand, and pulled her across the tile.

"Good girls. Keep coming," Harriet said under her breath.

The huge soldier returned, stomping toward the girls. He scooped Irena under one arm and Bridget under the other. They dangled from his arms like helpless puppies. "Mama, help us."

Harriet couldn't let the soldiers hurt her babies. "I'll go with you. I'll do anything. Just don't take my girls away from me."

It was too late. A middle door opened. The soldier carried Irena and Bridget, kicking and screaming, through the door and disappeared.

CHAPTER
SIX

August 1940
Registration Department, Hamburg, Germany

"Mama!" screamed Irena as the door shut. She was suspended in the air, hanging under the soldier's arm. She struggled to free herself. At least she wasn't alone. Bridget was trapped under the man's other arm, screaming, too. Her little sister couldn't help much, but she would be counting on Irena. Fear swelled up in her, beating against her temples like a drum. *Fight! Fight! Fight!* David had fought Goliath and won. The soldier holding her was as big as Goliath.

The drumming changed to anger. Goliath had grabbed them from Mama. Irena fisted her hands and punched Goliath, battering him over and over. The blows bounced off his steely side and hurt her knuckles.

She yelled, "Hit him, Bridget!"

Bridget slapped his other side. He grunted as if she were a

pesky fly. Unexpectedly, the giant opened his wings like a chicken hawk and dropped them. Irena stuck out her arms, landing on her hands and knees. Bridget fell next to her, rolling on her side. Irena crawled to her sister. They huddled together, clinging to each other, shaking.

Goliath's heavy boots thudded across the floor. He opened the door, slamming it after him. Instead of silence, voices behind them cried out. Irena looked over her shoulder. About a dozen girls were scattered around the brightly lit room, which had no windows or furniture and smelled like sweat. One wall was filled with coats of various sizes and colors, hanging on hooks like pelts stripped from helpless animals. Across the room from the sad-looking coats was a mountain of discarded clothes—dresses, blouses, and skirts in all sizes and colors, along with socks, slips, and undies.

Irena's arms prickled with goosebumps. Two large women, standing at the entrance to a hallway, were stripping off the girls' clothes. If the women had not been wearing green uniforms with skirts that covered the tops of their knee-high black boots, Irena might have mistaken them for men. The flat-chested women had wide shoulders and short, brown hair. The woman with wavy hair and the other with straight hair worked as a team.

The woman with straight hair held a girl, maybe about twelve, in an armlock. The girl kicked and screamed while the other guard ripped off her clothes and tossed them into the growing pile. When they freed the girl, she hunched over, crossing her arms to hide her nakedness. The guard with the wavy hair gripped the girl's shoulder and shoved her down the narrow hallway to join the line of other naked girls.

Even though Irena was hot in the winter coat that Mama made her wear, she didn't want to be naked. She reached into her coat pocket and rubbed her fingers over the heart-shaped rock. Turning her back to the women, Irena searched for a way out.

Unexpectedly, she was whisked off her feet. The guard with straight hair hoisted her up. The other guard grabbed Bridget.

Irena kicked and screamed, but it didn't help. The guard removed Irena's coat and pulled her polka-dot dress over her head. Next, her slip and undies were stripped off. If Mama were here, she would protect them, but they were alone. Irena blinked back tears, but the white dots in her dress lying atop the pile of discarded clothes blurred together.

She crossed her arms over her nipples, trying to cover them. Bridget stood beside her, naked, too.

From behind, someone shoved them into a long hallway with other naked girls. Irena swung her arm back for Bridget to latch onto. Together, they were pushed forward, down the hall, and into a round, tiled room. The humid air became steamy. She squinted through the mist at a dozen showers hanging from the walls, all spraying out water. A female guard stood near the door, handing out small brown bars of soap and assigning each girl a specific shower.

The guard gave Irena a bar of soap and directed her to an empty space. Irena pulled Bridget with her so they wouldn't be separated and stood under the shower, letting the warm water wash over her. She lathered the soap onto her body. It smelled like the lye soap her grandmother made in a metal pail on the back porch. After scrubbing away the grime from the train, she helped Bridget wash.

Too soon, the water shut off. Irena blinked, searching for a towel. Not seeing any, she shook like a dog after a bath to remove the water from her body and out of her hair. She waited for the door to open. Nothing happened. Irena tittered nervously.

The pipes above her creaked. She tilted her chin up,

expecting more warm water. Instead, something that looked like white flour sifted from the pipes and landed on her. Irena yelped and danced around, shaking her hair, and batting the white powder with her hands. The snowy substance continued to fall and stick to her body. She was caught in a blinding snow-storm, only whatever spewed from the showers wasn't melting.

She tried to move away. Too many girls were jammed into the room, and the powder was swirling everywhere. The floury stuff caked on Irena's lashes and landed in her eyes, stinging them. Screaming, she squeezed her eyes closed. Thick white flakes coated her lips and slid onto her tongue, tasting bitter. Irena clamped her mouth shut, but the powder flew into her nose and ears.

It reminded her of the rat poison Mama set out in a canning lid and warned Irena never to touch. Her nose was clogged, but she forced her mouth to stay closed. Her lungs were on fire. She swayed. The room dimmed. Darkness closed in.

She groped for Bridget's hand. She wasn't there. Irena was alone. She couldn't hold her breath much longer. She had to open her mouth and breathe, but if she did, her lungs would fill with poison—and she would die.

CHAPTER
SEVEN

rena continued to clamp her mouth and eyes closed to stop the rat poison spewing out of the showers from getting inside her. She couldn't breathe. She was going to die. A tiny hand slipped into hers. Poor Bridget. Irena couldn't let her little sister die. But what could she do? Bridget tugged on Irena's hand, pulling her forward with the other girls.

She slit her eyes, wincing from the stinging pain. Ahead was another door. Something worse might be behind it. Bridget yanked her through the door and into a room with no tiled walls or showers.

Irena's eyes teared. She opened her mouth and sucked in a deep breath. Her lungs filled with air and white poison. Coughing, she spit it out. Bridget and the other girls coughed and spat, too. Irena and Bridget helped each other, using their hands to dust off the floury stuff clinging to their bodies and sticking in their hair.

Along the far wall near an exit were rows of shelves stacked with neatly folded clothes. A line of girls waited as a stocky guard handed each of them something to wear. Irena didn't want to be naked. She nudged Bridget, and they joined the line.

The guard handed Irena a brown dress and panties. Irena clutched them to her chest, thankful to have something to cover up her privates. She slipped on the undies, relieved they fit, and pulled the brown dress on. It wasn't her polka-dot dress, but a straight sack that sagged almost to the floor.

Bridget's dress, a green print, didn't fit either. The full skirt stopped inches above her knees, and Irena had to tug to fasten the black buttons down the front. "It's too small," cried Bridget.

Irena wondered if their parents would recognize them in these strange dresses. She wanted to ask the guard for their own dresses, but a girl pushed them forward, propelling them through the exit. Irena grabbed Bridget's hand and shuffled behind the others into a room with bunk beds lined against the walls. Some girls sat on the bottoms, while other girls dangled their legs from the tops. She and Bridget were assigned an empty bunk in the middle. Irena climbed to the top, and Bridget dropped to the bottom.

A stocky guard entered, pushing a wheelbarrow piled with coats. She steered the wheelbarrow into the center of the room and dumped the contents onto the floor. Tumbling on top of the coats were dozens of shoes. Both were covered in what looked like the same white powder that had sprayed from the showers.

As soon as the door banged behind the guard, a swarm of girls dived from their bunks toward the coats and shoes. Only then did Irena realize the pile on the floor was *their* coats and *their* shoes. She and Bridget joined the skirmish.

Clawing through the heap, Irena plucked out her shoes and coat. She raced back to their bunk and dug into her coat pocket. Her fingers fisted around her heart-shaped rock. She breathed easier. They hadn't stolen her treasure.

That night, Irena lay stretched out on the top bunk, clutching her rock. Moonlight beamed through the window, casting dark shadows onto the floor. Her body was slick with sweat as she worried if the guards would come back, yank her out of bed, and take her clothes.

Bridget was in the bunk below, but Irena felt alone. A tear leaked from her eye. She used her coat as a pillow and kept her hand in the pocket, gripping the rock. Her stomach growled. The last time she had eaten was when the train stopped, and she'd sipped some warm cabbage soup and tea.

Her ears perked up. The room stilled. A noise outside. She held her breath. Something or someone was scurrying in the grass. A rat, a cat, a girl sneaking under the barbed wire to escape, or...

Bang! The gunshot echoed through the room. Irena and the other girls screamed. Who or what had been shot?

"Irena!" cried Bridget, sounding terrified.

Irena grabbed her coat and climbed to the bottom bunk. Bridget lay curled in a ball. Irena sat on the bed and rubbed small circles on her sister's back the way Mama did to comfort them.

Irena whispered, "Think about something fun, like flying high on the swing in the apple tree."

She thought her voice was too low for anyone else to hear, but a dark shadow outlined by the moonlight appeared in front of their bunk. "I speak Lithuanian, too."

Irena straightened. Her language sounded like music.

The girl curtsied. "I'm Mia."

Irena couldn't clearly see the girl, but she was tall with dark hair that frizzed around her narrow face, making her forehead look high like Da's. Irena patted the bed beside her and Mia joined them. "I'm Irena." She nudged her sister. "This is Bridget." Irena pulled on her baggy shift. "Why did they take our clothes?"

"To get rid of the bugs."

"What bugs?" Irena asked.

"The bugs you brought with you."

"I didn't bring any bugs."

"They gave you a shower to get rid of the bugs," Mia said.

Irena shivered. "They showered us with poison."

"That wasn't poison. It was disinfectant to kill the bugs."

Irena fingered her hair. "I told you I don't have any bugs."

"Me, either," said Bridget.

"That's because the disinfectant killed the bugs that live in your hair, like head lice, and bugs from your mattress, like bedbugs."

"Will it kill us?" Irena asked.

"It didn't kill me," answered Mia.

Irena wiped her brow. At least she wouldn't die from the poison. "When will we get our clothes back?"

Mia moved closer. "After they rip out the hems to find the money."

"What money?" Irena asked.

"The money you hid in your clothes."

"I didn't hide any money. I only brought a rock." Irena opened her hand to show Mia her heart-shaped rock. "When will we see our parents?

"First, a doctor has to examine you."

A trickle of hope tingled through her. "A doctor examined me when I was sick with a tapeworm."

"It was so big." Bridget held out her hands to show how long the tapeworm was. "They kept it in a jar to show everyone."

"It wasn't that big," said Mia.

Irena was offended. "Uh-huh. The doctor said it was the longest tapeworm he'd ever seen."

Mia didn't seem convinced, but she continued, "The doctor here will ask you lots of questions."

Irena chewed her lip. She didn't know German. What if she couldn't answer correctly? "What questions?"

"Basic ones like your name, your parents' names, and where you lived, but whatever you do, don't mention anything about being Jewish."

"Why would I?" Irena asked. "I'm not Jewish."

"And don't talk about Hanukkah."

"What's Hanukkah?"

"You're very good. Keep answering like that and they won't think you're a Jew and they'll let you go."

"How long have you been here?" Irena asked.

"Five days. Every day they ask more questions."

Irena quit listening. *Five days, five days, five days* pounded in her head. How could she live five long days without Mama or Da?

CHAPTER
EIGHT

August 1940
Registration Department, Hamburg, Germany

H arriet lay on the metal table in a white-washed room, naked. Instinctively, she crossed her arms over her bare breasts. A warm flush spread through her as a doctor hovered above her. His wire-rimmed glasses magnified his bulging eyes that raked over her body. She was paralyzed, a monarch caught in his net. She wanted to be free and fly away. Panic bubbled up. She hadn't seen Irena and Bridget since yesterday when they'd been snatched from her, nor had she seen Oskar. Her heart ached for her family.

The doctor's bony fingers pushed against the side of her neck and then ran down her arm, stopping at her wrist to check her racing pulse. Each touch sent ripples of repulsion through her, but she would let him poke and prod every part of her body if she got her daughters and Oskar back.

The doctor said something to a nurse, standing next to him,

dressed in a starched blue uniform with a white cap and apron. If Harriet understood German, she would know what the woman was writing down on her clipboard.

Harriet was jolted when the doctor pressed a cold stethoscope onto her chest. She tried to breathe normally, inhale...exhale, so he wouldn't hear her hammering heart. The doctor's attention focused lower. He slapped her thigh, motioning for her to spread her legs in a wide 'v,' and insert them into the stirrups at the end of the table.

Shuddering, she slipped her feet into the cold iron rings. He moved between her legs and lodged himself there. Shutting her eyes, she gripped the sides of the table and willed herself away. She was no longer a butterfly spread out like a specimen on a cold metal table. She was in Lithuania, flitting through the meadow. Lemon-yellow daisies with snow-white centers bobbed their heads, and Lithuanian blues waved their azure petals. Water from the river trickled over the rocks as a cool breeze tickled her skin. The beautiful August day was Irena's sixth birthday. The day before, Harriet had turned twenty-five. She hadn't felt old then but had danced with a childish glee. Irena and Bridget ran ahead to gather fistfuls of wildflowers. They raced back to her, presenting them with curtsies and shy smiles. Harriet lifted the yellow and blue flowers to her nose.

An antiseptic odor assaulted her. Her eyes popped open. The doctor's long fingers probed inside her. She ground her teeth, praying for the examination to end. Finally, he slid out his fingers and grabbed her arm, brushing against her breast as he pulled her into a sitting position. She blinked against the glare of the bright lights. No matter how white the room was, it could not obliterate the evil surrounding her.

They had taken her dress, replacing it with a sleeveless red flapper decorated with fringe. Feeling cheap, she wiggled into the red satin dress and ran her fingers through her wavy hair, wishing for a brush to tame her unruly locks. How long would the war go on? A few months? A year? And how long would it be before she and the girls experienced another carefree day romping in the meadow?

She stepped toward the door, hopeful she'd surrendered enough that she would be reunited with her family. Instead, the nurse gripped her elbow, steering her into another room. She pointed to a single chair in front of a desk. Harriet rubbed her damp palms down her red dress. The interrogation wasn't over.

CHAPTER
NINE

A nurse in a spotless blue uniform with a white cap and apron led Irena and Bridget into a brightly lit room with a single chair in front of a large desk. A *single* chair. What did that mean? In the last room, a doctor had laid her and Bridget out on a hard metal table, stripped off their clothes, and inspected them with cold instruments. He'd examined every inch of their bodies, even their privates. Then he smacked their fannies, which she thought meant they'd passed inspection. Instead, the nurse approached with a long needle. Irena knew what was coming and fought, but the doctor pinned her down while the nurse jabbed the needle into her arm, which really hurt. Then they had attacked Bridget.

Standing in front of the desk, Irena swayed. The shot or not eating must have made her dizzy. After the examination, she hoped they'd be rewarded with food, but the single chair worried her. She whispered to Bridget next to her, "Don't let them split us up."

Bridget grabbed her hand just as the side door opened. Another doctor, wearing a long white coat and carrying a medical bag, strode in. He had a protruding forehead and thin black hair that swept up to his crown, making his head look pointed.

Why did they keep examining her? After yesterday's shower, she couldn't have bugs. Did they think she was ill? She puffed up her chest, determined her voice wouldn't quiver. "I am not sick."

Without replying, the man placed his medical bag on the desk and settled into the chair behind it.

Irena mustered up her courage and tried again, "My sister is not sick."

The nurse moved to the doctor and handed him their charts. He pulled a pair of wire-rimmed glasses from the pocket of his white coat, planted them on his nose, and studied the papers. When he finished, he peered over his glasses, his stare sliding down their bodies.

Then the nurse opened her mouth and sang with gusto, but her voice cracked. She wasn't a very good singer. She motioned with her hands for them to sing.

Irena frowned. Mama hummed when she was happy. Irena wasn't happy and could not remember a single song.

Bridget's clear voice filled the silence. "Away in the manger..."

Recognizing the Christmas carol, Irena joined in, "No crib for a bed."

Their singing must have pleased the doctor because he clapped his hands, stamped their charts, and waved to the side door where he'd entered.

Irena's mouth went dry. Her feet wouldn't move. What would they have to do in the next room? Bridget grabbed Irena's hand and pulled her through the door.

Irena balked. Tacked across the front wall was a huge red flag with a white circle and some kind of symbol inside. Beneath the flag was a gigantic gold-framed portrait of a man.

His slicked-back hair and bushy black mustache made him look mean.

Bridget nudged her and pointed to the long rows of wooden tables with benches that lined the room. All were empty, except for the first row where a lone woman in a red dress sat, eating.

"Mama!" cried Irena.

The woman turned and jumped up. Irena sprinted forward, but her whirling legs were slowed by the long shift.

Mama opened her arms. Irena and Bridget launched themselves at her, almost toppling her over. "My babies." Tears streamed down Mama's cheeks as she pulled them to her. Irena didn't even mind being called a baby. She was just happy to be in Mama's arms.

Irena kissed Mama's wet cheeks. "Why are you crying? Are you hurt?"

"I'm crying because I'm happy." She swiped away the tears. "Did they hurt you?"

Irena stiffened her quivering lips. "They looked at our privates, but didn't hurt us."

"Yes, they did," said Bridget. "They gave us shots."

Irena touched her sore arm. "Well, not too bad." She spied Mama's bowl on the table. "I'm hungry."

"I can take care of that. Follow me."

"Are you taking us to Da?" Irena asked.

As if he'd heard his name, the side door opened and Da walked in, carrying their suitcase. She ran to him. He dropped the suitcase and pulled her, Bridget, and Mama into his arms. Irena soaked in the comforting feel of Mama and Da.

Then she stepped back and looked up at her parents. "Can we go home now?"

CHAPTER
TEN

September 1940
Hamburg, Germany

H arriet followed Oskar off the bus and stared at blocks of two-story red-brick apartment buildings. "What is this?" she asked.

"It's called the projects," said Oskar. "It's where we'll live."

Before the family left the Registration Department, they had been given a number, their clothes, identity papers, photographed, and assigned an apartment.

Oskar entered a single-story white building near the arched entrance where the bus had let them off. Inside they waited in more lines. Oskar was given a key to an apartment and a box of basics—cookware, towels, and other necessities—that eased a little of Harriet's worry about how they would manage on what they had been able to stuff into a suitcase.

Oskar led the way, holding a large skeleton key in front of him like a standard and pumping the suitcase back and forth.

Harriet, weighed down by the box and her worry, trailed behind with Irena and Bridget.

Irena tugged on Harriet's coat. "Which one will we live in?"

Before Harriet replied, Oskar held the key higher. "Number 303 B." As they passed each block, Oskar read aloud the numbers until he announced, "This is it. The building has four apartments. The 'B' means ours is on the second story."

Anticipation fluttered through her as she climbed the stairs behind Oskar. He unlocked the door, threw it open, and stepped inside. "Just like home."

Harriet crossed the threshold. A sour smell and mossy green walls greeted her. Except for being on the second floor, nothing was like home. No sunny-yellow walls or ruffled curtains. Just one big room with black curtains that dimmed the light, along with her hopes.

On one side were a sink, stove, and square table with four wooden chairs; on the other were a brown divan, which sagged in the middle, and a faded green chair with white stuffing springing from the seat. As she set the box on the table, she pushed away the image of her own fragrant kitchen and cozy living room.

Oskar stood at the door, waiting for her reaction.

It was not what she had hoped for, but then she realized if they'd stayed in Lithuanian, the Soviets might have seized their apartment and taken Oskar away. At least here they were alive and together. "I'll make do," she said as much for herself as for him.

"Let's see the rest." Irena tugged on Bridget's hand and pushed open the door between the kitchen and living area. Harriet followed them. The smaller room had two iron-railed beds, a double and a twin. Pillows, sheets, and blankets were stacked at the ends of the thin mattresses. In between the beds stood a three-drawer dresser.

"I'm older. I get the big bed." Irena plopped on the double bed.

Bridget threw herself on the smaller one. "Just my size."

Irena's head swiveled around. "Where are you and Da sleeping?"

Harriet looked for another door that might lead to a second bedroom but didn't see one. Another thing she would have to 'make do' with.

She plastered on a smile. "I guess we're all sleeping here, which means the double bed is for Da and me."

Irena frowned. "I don't want to share a bed with Bridget."

Harriet didn't want to give up her privacy either, but she was relieved her family had a place to stay and they would be together.

Irena hopped off the bed and started jigging. "I have to pee."

Harriet hadn't seen any other doors. Taking Irena's hand, Harriet led her into the first room where Oskar was slumped onto the green chair. "Where's the water closet?"

He waved toward the kitchen door. "Try the hall."

Irena tugged her out of the apartment and down the hall where Harriet pulled open the door at the end. A sink and lavatory, but no shower or bathtub. The relief of having their own place faded. Sharing a bedroom and a water closet might not be all she would have to 'make do' with.

That night, after Harriet had unpacked the box, she went to the bedroom and opened the suitcase. Oskar sat propped up on the bed, smoking. She held up her green housedress with the capped sleeves. Like her other dresses, the hem in the skirt was gone. "Why did they rip out the hems in our clothes?"

Staring up at the puffs of smoke swirling above him, he merely shrugged as if it wasn't important that she would have to rehem most of their clothes.

She finished unpacking the suitcase and returned to the

kitchen. She gave the girls some nuts and cheese left from what she'd squirreled in her pockets for the train ride and began the familiar bedtime routine—only now when she washed the girls at the kitchen sink and brushed their hair, they sat in the kitchen chairs. With each stroke of the brush through their wavy brown hair, she silently reassured them. *See, everything will be all right.*

Trying to believe those words, she shepherded the girls into the bedroom where Oskar still lay on the bed, smoking. The girls kneeled on the floor and folded their hands. "Be sure to pray for Nana and Papa and everyone left in Lithuania and thank God for providing us a..." She couldn't say *home*. "A place to stay."

They silently said their prayers and scrambled into bed without bickering. Harriet leaned over, tucked them under the thin sheet, and kissed each girl's cheek. She hoped her loving touch would reassure them.

The girls didn't close their eyes, and Irena burst out with the question that had haunted Harriet all day. "How long do we have to stay here?"

Harriet stroked Irena's forehead. "Until the Soviets are gone."

Irena's lower lip trembled. "Will we be back by Christmas to go to Nana and Papa's?"

Harriet hadn't had time to say goodbye to her parents. What if she never saw them again? She choked back a sob and stretched out her hand for Oskar to comfort them—and her.

He cleared his throat. "Possibly a year or more."

How would she manage for a year without knowing the language? How would she feed her family if Oskar didn't have a job?

"Now go to sleep," Oskar said firmly.

Instead of climbing into bed with Oskar, she crossed the room and took his hand, pulling him into the larger room. He sank onto the couch, and she settled in his lap. She snuggled into the familiar curve of his shoulder, expecting him to pull her closer and reassure her.

He remained wooden. Drawing back, she searched his face. "What happened to you at the Registration Department?"

His gray eyes hardened. "The same as you. They checked my papers and me."

He didn't sound upset. But she was upset. "I-I didn't know it would be like this."

"Like what?" Oskar gestured with his hand around the room. "We've been given a place to live and we're safe."

"Safe? The soldiers had guns and dogs. They ripped the girls away from me, and I didn't even know where you were."

"You could have made it easier on yourself, Harriet."

She squinted at him. "What do you mean?"

"If you'd obeyed, you wouldn't have been separated from the girls."

"You think it was *my* fault?" She pulled away and stood. "Look what they gave me to wear." She ran her hand down the red satin dress, her fingers shaking the fringe across the bodice.

He reached out and drew her back onto his lap. "I'm only saying we're in a foreign country. We have to do what they tell us."

"But I don't speak their language. Do you know how scary that is?"

He wrapped his arms around her. "It's over and we're here."

Was he so unfazed by the interrogation? He sounded as if he expected her to put it behind them. Well, if that's what he wanted, she would try. "Promise you won't leave me alone again."

He squeezed her reassuringly. "I'm right here. I'll help you settle in."

She breathed easier, and when she went to bed, she drifted off thinking tomorrow would be better.

Hours later, she was awakened by pounding on the door. A deep male voice shouted, "Oskar Golcvegas."[*]

Beside her, Oskar jerked up. "Stay here, Harriet." Pulling on his pants and shirt, he shuffled to the kitchen.

The door creaked open. A man's voice said something in German she didn't understand, but she recognized his authoritative tone.

Oskar called into the bedroom, "Harriet, I have to go with these men."

"Go? Go where?" Not caring she was wearing a thin nightgown, she jumped out of bed and raced into the kitchen.

Oskar stood in the doorway, slipping on his shoes. "Lock up behind me."

The door shut. She sprinted across the room and threw open the door. Two men in brown uniforms led Oskar down the stairs.

"Oskar, where are you going?" she cried.

He twisted to look back at her, his eyes wide with terror. The men dragged him forward, pulling him down the steps and out the door.

---

[*] *Note on Lithuanian surnames. A daughter's name has a different ending than either of her parents and a woman's married name has a different ending than her husband's.*

CHAPTER
ELEVEN

Harriet dropped into a kitchen chair. Oskar was gone. She and the girls were alone in a foreign country. She didn't know the language or how to get around. Oskar had promised he would not leave her, but he had no choice. The men had dragged him away. Where had they taken him? And more importantly, when would he be back?

She began to shake. Crossing her arms over her chest, she tried to hold herself together. Last week, her most pressing problem was letting Irena start school. Now her family's life had been upended, and she had no idea when it would be normal again.

Harriet had endured loss—first her brother, and now her parents and friends. She couldn't lose Oskar. She just couldn't. He was more than a provider. He was her emotional support and love. She needed him.

Maybe her imagination was rampant. Being in a foreign country that was at war didn't mean something bad would happen to him. At home, she had a weekly routine. Monday was washday. Tuesday was ironing. Here she would establish a new routine. She glanced at the faded wall calendar tacked next to the sink. The months and days were written in German. She groaned. The Lithuanian calendar was based on the seasons. The German words reminded her of how hard it would be to adjust to her new life.

Sewing calmed her nerves, and she had plenty of clothes to hem. As she tiptoed into the bedroom, the wood floor creaked beneath her bare feet, but she didn't wake the girls. She gathered her sewing supplies and three dresses—the pink baby doll with the smocked bodice for Irena, the blue seersucker for Bridget, and the green housedress with capped sleeves for her.

Back in the kitchen, the black curtains shut out the light, filling the room with the gloom that had settled in her since she had arrived. Determinedly, she pushed open the curtains. Dawn filtered into the room, lifting her spirits. If the family stayed long enough, she would sew bright curtains with ruffles and paint the walls a homey yellow like in Lithuania, although she couldn't imagine this bleak apartment as home.

She returned to the couch, and as she whip-stitched the hem on Irena's dress, she forced herself to think of something pleasant—the first time she'd met Oskar. She'd finished her work as a domestic for the Greenbergs, a Jewish family who had employed her. It was Monday, and she'd labored over the laundry for hours. On the way home, she stopped at a well and took off her shoes because they bothered her bunion.

As she rubbed her aching feet, a man with thick, dark hair approached and sat beside her on the rim of the well. "I have the perfect cure for sore feet."

She gazed into his friendly gray eyes, hoping he wasn't about to suggest he rub her feet. She didn't like anyone touching them.

Reaching into the pocket of his coat, he pulled out a wrapped piece of chocolate and handed it to her. She opened the candy and popped it into her mouth. The creamy sweetness melted on her tongue.

"I'm Oskar." He stood and took her arm, carrying her shoes as he walked her to the farm. She had enjoyed his stories so much she forgot about her throbbing bunion, but her parents had not been happy when they discovered he was Lutheran, not Catholic.

A different image flashed through her mind. Oskar slumped in a chair, two men beating him with batons. She forced the image away and continued hemming Irena's dress.

By the time she'd finished the dresses, sleepy groans sounded from the bedroom. She didn't want the girls to be frightened by the unfamiliar surroundings. She rushed into the bedroom and sank onto the bed, pressing the girls against her. Their warm bodies smelled of the rose-scented soap she'd used last night. Too quickly they drew away. Happily chattering, Irena and Bridget seemed oblivious to their new surrounding and the danger. She hoped their innocence would not be destroyed.

Rising, Harriet pushed open the black drapes in the bedroom to check for Oskar. Gray clouds cast shadows on the desolate street below. She started to pull the curtain closed, but two German soldiers with grim faces under their hats marched on the sidewalk in front of their building. Their polished black boots high-stepped with precision. Her heart slammed against her chest. A few more meters and the soldiers would reach their door.

She jerked the bedroom curtains closed. Her legs buckled, and she sank to the floor. Soldiers had dragged Oskar away. Were they coming for her and the girls? Her stomach twisted into knots.

The girls stared at her. Harriet had to remain calm. Irena and Bridget were counting on her, but she was paralyzed by fear. She needed Oskar. He would know what to do. She took several deep breaths, lifted her head, and peeked out the curtains. The soldiers had marched past their building. Her stomach unwound.

"I'm hungry," said Irena, her voice breaking the tense silence.

"Me, too," said Bridget.

Harriet felt queasy. She couldn't keep any food down, but eating might distract the girls. Rising, she led the girls to the kitchen. Her eyes darted to the lock on the door. She had chained it after Oskar left, but she didn't feel safe. Another image of Oskar flicked through her mind. He was lying on the ground, blood pooling from his head, as two men kicked him with their black boots.

She shook away the vision and focused on the food she had brought—tins of porridge, flour, beans, plus dried herbs from her garden and the loaf of rye bread she'd baked for Irena's lunch at school. Had that been only four days ago?

Her hands trembled as she broke off two small chunks of bread. "Sit at the table."

Irena and Bridget scampered onto the chairs. Harriet joined them as they automatically folded their hands and bowed their heads. "Thank you for another day. Watch over Oskar and keep him safe. Bless this food you have provided for us. Amen."

Reaching for the bread Harriet had set on the table, Irena asked, "Where's Da?" Her eyes searched the kitchen for some sign of him.

"He had some errands."

Thankfully, Irena seemed to accept her vague answer.

Bridget gobbled down a bite of bread. "Mama, you forgot the butter."

Of course, they would expect butter. That's what Harriet usually spread on their rye bread. "We don't have butter." Her voice caught in her throat. "Eat it plain."

Irena nibbled hers, but Bridget frowned. "Go to the store and buy some."

The fear Harriet had pushed away since they'd arrived in Germany overwhelmed her. She couldn't stop the words. They flowed out. "How can I go to the store? I don't know where it is. I can't speak German, and I can't buy anything because we don't have much money and your da..." she trailed off, her voice cracking.

The girls stared at her, their eyes wide. She'd said too much. She tried to choke down her sobs, but they gushed out. Giving in, she laid her head on the table and burst into tears.

She couldn't control the large wracking cries. Irena's small hand patted her on the back. "It's okay, Mama." Irena tried to comfort her in the same way Harriet comforted them when they were upset. "We don't need butter, do we, Bridget?"

Bridget didn't answer.

Harriet was the mother. Falling apart would frighten the girls. Sniffing back her tears, she swiped her hands across her wet cheeks and lifted her head. Fear churned in Bridget's and Irena's eyes. Harriet gathered them close and silently vowed she would not break down again.

"We don't have butter and other things," Harriet said, "But we have a place to stay, and we have each other." Her voice was filled with renewed determination.

Late that night, after she'd put the girls to bed, she stayed in the kitchen, continually looking out the window for Oskar. She opened the curtains again when a knock sounded at the door. "Harriet, let me in."

Oskar. Relieved, she rushed to the door and unhooked the chain. "Where have you been?" Her high-pitched voice sounded desperate.

He didn't answer. His shirt was stained, and his face was drawn tight. He wasn't bloody or didn't have broken bones, but something had happened to him. He had been gone from morning to night, but he looked years older.

She drew him to her to make sure he was there. He smelled

of sweat and dirt but having him in her arms didn't ease her fears. She locked the door and led him to the table. "What happened?" She steadied her nerves. He needed to know she was capable of confronting whatever it was, and they would work through it together.

As he slumped in the chair, his head turned toward the window. Bolting up, he shot past her and yanked the blackout curtains closed. "We could be arrested or killed for that."

"For what? I merely opened the curtains."

Oskar gripped her shoulders as if to shake her like a child. "Keep the blackout curtains closed. If you don't, the bombers will see the light, and we'll be a target."

She wiggled free. "Is Hamburg being bombed? I thought you said we were safe here."

"Hamburg is a major industrial city. It's where most of Germany's manufacturing plants are. They took me to a factory and forced me to work all day."

Harriet's bloody visions vanished. "I was worried you might be harmed. But a factory job is good." She tried to hide her fear. "You worked at a candy factory in Lithuania."

"This isn't a candy factory," Oskar returned to the table, weighed down by his new reality. "It's an armament factory."

She didn't like the job, and it wasn't one Oskar would choose. "What do you do? Make bullets?"

"Not bullets."

Harriet looked down at him. His head was drooped, and he didn't answer.

Something was wrong with the job, but she didn't know what. "Is it dangerous?"

Oskar's gray eyes lifted to hers as if searching for under-standing. "I'm building bombs."

The word exploded through the kitchen. Harriet crumpled into an empty chair. Now she understood why the lines in his forehead seemed deeper and his mouth was stretched taut, making him appear older.

He reached across the table, his palms turned up in supplication. "It's what they expect me to do. One man refused to work, and they shot him." His voice trembled with what sounded like desperation. "I feel the way I did when I went down in the mines."

After his pa was killed, Oskar went to work in the coal mine to support his mother. Harriet didn't want him to be caught up in a nightmare again to support their family. She tried to sound hopeful. "We can save money and move."

"I'm a guest worker. I'm not paid the same wages as German workers. They provide a place for us to live and food, but few extras."

"That's not fair, especially if you're doing the same work." Frustrated, she crossed her arms tightly over her body.

"It's better than the slave laborers." Reaching into his trouser pocket, he pulled out a handful of zinc coins and dropped them onto the table. His voice filled with bitterness. "I earned a few *Reichspfennig*s." From his shirt pocket, he slipped out a red card and handed it to her. "They issued me a ration card. They said, 'No work, no food.' I have to provide for our family. I have no choice. I have to do what they tell me. I have to make bombs."

CHAPTER
TWELVE

The next morning at dawn, another knock on the door, and Oskar left for work. Still in her nightgown, Harriet stood in the kitchen, alone. The reality of her new life slammed against her, sucking out the air and suffocating her. Last night her mind had whirled, plotting ways for her family to leave. Now those plans seemed dangerous. If they were caught, Oskar and she might be sent to one of those camps or killed. That would leave Irena and Bridget at the mercy of the Nazis.

A wave of homesickness washed over her. They'd had to flee from the Soviets so quickly, she hadn't been able to tell her parents goodbye. What were their lives like now? Had the Soviets confiscated their land? If so, had they been shipped to Siberia or somehow escaped?

She would write them a letter. If they were still at the farm, maybe they would receive it. Pulling open the kitchen drawer where Oskar kept the important documents, she found paper and a nubby pencil. From the living room, she carried the kerosene lamp to the kitchen table and lit it. The yellow glow illuminated the red rations card on the table and cast shadows on the walls, intensifying her fears. Last night, Oskar had given her directions to the market. They needed food, but she feared the soldiers or getting lost. They had some food—rye bread, porridge, beans, plus cheese and nuts left from the train ride. Maybe Oskar wouldn't have to work late tonight, and they'd go to the market together.

She placed the blank sheet of paper over the red card so it wouldn't stare up at her accusingly and began to write.

Dear Mamuska and Tata, (Her parents were Polish, so she used her childhood names for them. Mamuska was Mother and Tata was Father.)

We made it safely to Germany and live in a flat in Hamburg. Oskar already has a job. (She would not tell them what the job was or how scared she was for him.)

Oskar admired Hitler for bringing the country out of poverty after the Great War. Oskar had been told since he was Lutheran, he would be welcomed into Germany, not forced to make bombs to feed his family. Maybe she could persuade her parents to come here. How much better her life would be if Mamuska and Tata had come with them.

If you decide to leave Lithuania, you can live in Hamburg, and we'll all be together again. (Tata would never give up the farm voluntarily, but he might be forced off the land.)

As Harriet ended the letter, she squirmed, no longer able to ignore her basic needs. Her bladder was full. If she used the chamber pot, she'd wake the girls. Rising, she lifted the key from the nail beside the wall calendar and slipped into the hall. Locking the door, she tiptoed past the flat on the other side and hurried to the water closet at the end.

She reached for the door. It swung open. Standing in the door frame was a short man with a thick neck and wide nostrils. He wore a zipped-up jacket and tan trousers. His mouth was surrounded by a dark wiry beard that made him look menacing.

Harriet, still in her nightgown, was paralyzed with fear. The key slipped from her hand and onto the wooden floor near her bare feet. The clattering reverberated through the empty hall. Bending, the man stretched out his huge hand to grab her key. She bolted into action and plucked it up first.

Straightening, he moved to step around her.

The girls. They were in the apartment, alone. The door was locked, but if the man was determined to get inside, a locked door wouldn't stop him. Whirling, she raced past him to the flat. As she fumbled with the key in the lock, reason set in. Somebody lived in the apartment across the hall. They would use this water closet, too. The man could be her neighbor, not some interloper ready to attack, but why would he wear a coat to walk down the hall?

Footsteps thudded behind her. She listened for the creak of the door opening on the opposite side. His steps didn't stop. If she unlocked the door, he could push her inside and the girls would be in danger, too. She fisted the key, pointing the jagged end out, and spun around, ready to defend herself.

Without looking in her direction, the man mumbled something she didn't understand then stomped down the stairs and out the door.

Harriet sagged against the hall in relief. Her bladder screamed at her, demanding attention. Unlocking the door, she quickly shut it and hooked the chain. She was going to lose control. She couldn't wait. No longer worrying about waking the girls, she rushed into the bedroom and pulled the ceramic bowl from under the bed. Squatting over it, she released her muscles, letting the warm liquid gush out. Just as she predicted, Irena and Bridget woke up.

Harriet stayed over the chamber pot until her legs were steady and her body no longer shook.

Bridget called out from across the room. "I'm hungry."

Food might distract the girls, but she was too shaken to eat. In the kitchen, she pinched off two small chunks of rye bread and sat at the table. Not trusting her voice, she asked Irena to pray.

"Bless Mama, Da, Sissy, and our food. Amen." Irena was obviously in a hurry to eat. She and Bridget grabbed for the bread.

Bridget popped hers into her mouth, gulping it down. Irena, chewing slowly, pointed to the lamp and the letter in the center. "What's that?"

"A letter to my parents."

Irena leaned in closer. "Something red is under it."

Harriet automatically answered, "A ration card to buy food."

Bridget clapped. "We can get butter."

Irena scooted back in her chair. "Let's get dressed."

Why hadn't Harriet put the ration card away? "The store's not open," she said. She didn't know if that was true, but she wouldn't be taking them to the store today.

The girls begged to go outside, but after much haggling, Harriet convinced them to play in the bedroom.

As soon as they slammed the door, she snatched the ration card. She didn't want it lying on the table for Irena and Bridget to see again. She carried the card to the cupboard above the sink. Standing on tiptoes, she slid it onto the top shelf. The front edge stuck out. She pushed against it, expecting the card to slide in. Instead, it buckled, as if blocked.

Searching the kitchen, she grabbed a worn-looking broom propped in the corner. She hoisted it over her head, handle first, and poked into the cupboard.

Clank. The handle hit something. She slid the broom from side to side. A small, flat can tumbled out and rolled across the floor. She bent over, snatching it up. The label was in German, but from the shape of the tin and the image of a fish on the front, she guessed it was tuna. She pressed the can against her chest and said a prayer of thanks. The tuna was their safety net.

Angry voices rose from the bedroom. The girls were already squabbling. Harriet pushed the can and card onto the top shelf and rushed into the bedroom.

Irena stood facing the window, the blackout curtains open. Bridget stood nearby and whined, "Irena won't let me look out."

Harriet panicked. "Get away from that window."

Startled, Irena jumped back, knocking over Bridget, who began to cry.

Ignoring Bridget, Harriet marched to the window and yanked the curtains closed. "Why were you at the window?"

Irena cowered. "I saw a girl about my age in the apartment across the street. She has pigtails, like mine, except blonde." Irena stepped toward the window. "She lives—"

"Don't open the curtains," snapped Harriet.

Irena flinched. "I want to see if she's still there. If she is, can we play outside today?"

"No." The word came out angrier than Harriet intended.

Tears sprang to Irena's eyes. Now both of the girls were crying. Harriet hadn't meant to be so harsh, but Irena and Bridget needed to understand not following the rules was dangerous. Harriet also had to find a way to keep them inside and not argue all day. "Get dressed and I'll comb your hair."

Irena sniffed. "Where are we going?"

Harriet plastered on a smile. "Today you're going to start school."

"You said we had to stay inside. Is the teacher coming here?"

"I'm going to be the teacher."

Irena frowned. "That doesn't sound like fun. There won't be other kids there."

"That sounds like fun to me," said Bridget, wiping her eyes.

Irena stomped her foot. "That's not fair. Bridget's not six."

"No, but she's as smart as some six-year-olds."

"We don't have any books," argued Irena.

Lord, give me patience.

"Can I wear my new school dress?"

Harriet was tempted to say 'yes,' but then Irena would ask to wear it every day. "Let's save it for when you go to a German school."

Irena's frown disappeared. "When will that be?"

Harriet wasn't sure Irena and Bridget would be able to enroll in a school in Germany. "Ask your da."

Irena plopped onto her bed. "Playing school is dumb."

"No, it's not," said Bridget.

Harriet took Bridget by the hand and tried to sound cheerful. "Let's go into the kitchen. I'll teach you how to write your name. Then you can sign the letter to your grandparents, and they'll see how grownup you are."

Irena jumped off the bed. "I want to write my name on the letter, too."

Smiling like a Cheshire cat, Harriet added. "One other thing. Today we have to use the chamber pot."

That night, Oskar did not come home early. He dragged himself into the kitchen, hunched over as if he didn't have enough energy to pull himself upright. Telling him about the man in the bathroom would add to his burden, but she had to protect the girls. Pulling Oskar to the couch, she sank onto his lap. Not caring how grimy he was, she pressed herself against him, trying to draw from him whatever strength he had left.

"Harriet, you're shaking. Did something happen at the store?"

She pulled back, reluctant to admit it. "I didn't go. Right after you left, I ran into a man coming out of *our* water closet."

Oskar frowned. "It was probably one of the men who live across the hall. It's *their* water closet, too."

"I thought of that, but he was wearing a jacket and didn't go into the apartment. He bolted down the stairs and out the door."

"This happened after I left?"

Harriet nodded.

"The two men who live across the hall ride in the same truck that picks me up for work. This morning, we had to wait because one of them was late."

Oskar's explanation sounded reasonable, but it didn't settle her. "What do you know about them?"

"They look alike, and I think they're brothers from Albanian. Lots of people from that region fled when Mussolini attacked."

Not having a woman living across the hall was more upsetting than she expected. Two additional flats were on the first floor, but she hadn't been brave enough to venture downstairs. "Do you know anything about our other neighbors?" she asked.

"I haven't seen them, but they won't be Lithuanian. Guest workers come from all over Europe, but they aren't assigned apartments near people from their own country."

"Why not?"

"The Nazis don't want us fraternizing."

Harriet felt even more alone. She'd hoped to find someone who would help her navigate her new life. But with Oskar gone at least twelve hours a day, she was on her own, and any mistake she made might be deadly.

CHAPTER
THIRTEEN

Harriet, with her pocketbook dangling from her arm, led the way down the apartment stairs. She stopped at the bottom and glanced back at the girls clattering behind. Irena's pink baby-doll dress billowed around her thin legs, and Bridget's pleated jumper swayed from side to side. Both wore sweaters and headscarves, tied under their chins, that covered their hair except for their brown pigtails, which flopped on the sides.

"Button your sweaters," Harriet said. She cracked open the door and peered out, checking for the soldiers, who patrolled the street. During the five days the family had lived in the second-story flat, a pair of soldiers had marched by their apartment building daily, but at various times.

Yesterday, a group of men, who wore brown shirts, ties, and carried batons, had run by. Oskar called them Brownshirts and said many of the men were ruffians or former soldiers disgruntled by Germany's loss in the Great War.

"Let's go," said Irena, tugging on Harriet's arm.

Irena and Bridget were eager to be outside, but Harriet was

petrified. What would happen if the soldiers or the Brownshirts confronted her?

Harriet tried to keep her voice steady but failed. "Remember, we're in a foreign country and don't know the language. Keep your head down and don't talk." She led them outside the safety of their apartment building. An empty sidewalk stretched ahead. She gripped the girls' hands and turned in the direction of the store.

"Can we talk to you?" Irena asked.

Harriet shook her head. "It will only draw attention, and people will know we aren't German."

"Can I wave at the girl in the window?"

Harriet ignored the longing in Irena's green eyes. "No, and stop talking."

"But you're talking."

Exasperated, Harriet tightened her grip on Irena's hand and lowered her head as she towed the girls beside her. Irena lagged, her shoes scuffing on the sidewalk. Harriet looked over. Irena had raised her head, and her hand was in the air, waving to the girl in the apartment building across the street.

"Irena, put your head down," Harriet whispered through gritted teeth.

"There's the girl." Irena pointed to the second-story window. "Can I play with her?"

"If you mind." Harriet's tone was firm.

"Yes, Mama." Irena immediately lowered her head and stopped talking.

Harriet glanced over at Bridget, who had her head down. At least one daughter was behaving.

The dreary gray sky was filled with clouds of industrial fumes spewing from the smokestacks that shot up on the horizon. Hamburg was a manufacturing city, but she hadn't expected the acrid scent of the factories to permeate their life.

The street, which cut through projects, was lined with more

identical red-brick buildings, but she didn't see any place for the girls to play—no green lawns or trees, only a few patches of brown grass that matched the bleakness of the surroundings. No birds chirped, singing their melodious songs, and no river rippled over rocks, calling her name. Instead, slicing through the eerie silence was the tapping of their shoes against the concrete sidewalk and the distant rumble of automobiles.

They passed through the arched-brick entry, connecting the projects to a street, bustling with bicycles, wagons pulled by horses, and automobiles. Here, other women in their market dresses, similar to her full-skirted, purple paisley, swished past them. A few children walked beside the women, but no one greeted them or spoke.

Harriet paused to orient herself as she silently repeated the directions to the store that Oskar had given her. "After the arch, go one block and turn at the street sign. The market will have a red flag flying above the door."

No soldiers were in sight, so Harriet led the girls down one block, turned the corner, and froze. On both sides of the street, all of the stores were flying red flags with black swastikas that proudly displayed their allegiance to Hitler. Harriet's chest constricted with a chilling unease.

Irena tugged on Harriet's hand and gazed up questioningly. Bridget stared up, too. The girls were counting on her. At the end of the block, a line of women, some with children, waited to get inside a store. That must be the right one.

Resolutely, she marched toward the store and lined up behind a woman with three children younger than Bridget. Two of the girls with blonde hair clung to the woman's long checked skirt. The third girl, a baby pressed against the woman's shoulder, gazed at Harriet, giving her an adorable toothless grin.

"Oh, how sweet," Harriet automatically said, her voice softening.

The woman didn't turn. Harriet glanced over her shoulder

to see if anyone had heard. A barefooted boy, no bigger than Irena, stood behind them. He had a dirty face and shaggy hair that flopped into his eyes. His drooping knickers held up by one suspender revealed scrawny arms and legs. Harriet hoped her girls would never get that thin. She wondered who the boy was with because the woman behind him wore a stylish belted dress, hat, and gloves.

When the line moved forward, Harriet stepped inside the crowded store. Posters that looked like propaganda signs were tacked above food she didn't recognize, reminding her of how ill-prepared she was to navigate this new life. Along the walls were barrels filled with flour, oats, and other staples. On the shelves were canned goods stacked to the ceiling and labeled in German. In the front, a gray-haired man, wearing a vest stretched across over his large belly, stood behind a cash register. Her cheeks flamed. The ration card allowed her to purchase items, but she still needed money to pay for them. Oskar had explained the currency, but the prices were written in German.

She searched for another customer who might help, but the women weren't chatting or clustered in groups, like at her neighborhood market. Here, no one spoke and each time she approached a woman, she would avert her eyes and hurry away, making Harriet feel even more isolated.

Dropping the girls' hands, she reached into her pocketbook and pulled out a pillowcase to use for a shopping bag. "Stay close behind me."

She maneuvered through the other shoppers, as she selected potatoes, onions, turnips, and cabbage. When they stopped near a bin of apples, Irena reached in and swiped a shiny red apple. "Can I have this?"

An apple was a healthy treat, but Harriet hesitated. "If I have enough money—and you're good. First, I have to get butter, cheese, milk, and meat."

Irena obediently returned the apple to the bin.

Harriet continued to squeeze through the store, searching for the items. When she didn't find them, she turned toward the front. The clerk, who had been busy checking out customers, was alone at the counter. Harriet stepped toward the gray-haired man. She kept her voice low but spoke distinctly as she asked for the food in Lithuanian.

Glaring, the man waved his hands in front of him, not seeming to understand. Harriet tried again, this time in Polish.

The man raised both arms above his head and boomed, "*Deutsch! Deutsch!*"

Harriet did not understand the word, but the man's tone made it clear that he didn't want to be bothered. She shrunk back, floundering in the aisle, unsure what to do.

The woman with the three little girls approached and pointed to the corner of the store. Harriet followed the woman to a bucket filled with ice. She pointed to a pale yellow rectangle wrapped in milky paper and said in Polish, "Butter substitute, margarine."

Leaning down, Harriet picked up the square white stick and examined it. She had never heard of margarine. It didn't look like the creamy yellow butter they churned on the farm, but she dropped it into the pillowcase and then looked up to thank the woman, but she'd scurried away as if she were anxious to separate herself from Harriet.

Since she hadn't found the other items on her list, she should have money to buy an apple. She turned to Irena. Only Bridget stood behind her.

Harriet's heart stopped. She couldn't breathe. *Don't panic. Irena's somewhere in the store.*

"Where's your sister?" she asked Bridget.

Bridget pointed to the front of the store, where a line of customers waited at the counter to pay for their food.

Harriet grabbed Bridget's hand and, trying to be unobtrusive, scooted toward the women. Scanning the line, Harriet searched for Irena. Not finding her, Harriet stepped closer. She wanted to approach the man behind the counter, but she was afraid he would yell at her again.

Sweat beaded on her forehead. What if Irena had run outside? What if soldiers had found her and whisked her away?

As if she had conjured them up, two soldiers in shiny black boots marched through the front door. The man at the counter immediately stood at attention, saluted, and said, *Heil Hitler*.

The soldiers clicked their boots together, raised their arms, and repeated, *Heil Hitler*.

They approached the man, their boots pounding against the wooden floor, reverberating through the uneasy stillness that had settled through the store.

Harriet stepped back, shoving Bridget behind her, out of the view of the soldiers. Bridget bumped a shelf, sending cans clattering to the floor. The soldiers whirled around, pressing their hands on the guns at their belts, and focused on Harriet and Bridget.

CHAPTER
FOURTEEN

Cans clattered across the floor. Irena was wedged between the fruit bins to hide from the soldiers who had entered the market. She took several ragged breaths, whiffing the odor of a rotting apple.

She peeked out at Mama. Behind her cowered Bridget, next to the shelves where the canned goods had fallen. Did Bridget knock over the cans?

Goosebumps prickled up Irena's arms. She couldn't stop shaking. This was all her fault. Why hadn't she minded Mama? She'd told Irena to stay close behind. Instead, when Mama had followed the Polish woman, Irena had slipped away—just for a minute—and planned to return before anyone noticed. She was curious to see if the clerk hid a jar of candy underneath the counter.

Back home, Mr. Livergood kept a big glass jar filled with peppermint sticks near the cash register in his market. When Mama took her and Bridget to the store, Mr. Livergood would pull out his jar of red-and-white striped candy and let them take one. Once, Irena had reached in and wrapped her fist around two sticks. Mr. Livergood had waggled his finger at her until she slid the second one back. On the way home, Irena always enjoyed licking the peppermint stick and letting the sugary sweetness melt on her tongue.

But when she had sneaked behind the German clerk and peered under the counter, no candy was there. The man's belly was so big that he must have eaten the whole jar of sweets himself.

She had started to slink back to Mama, but light beaming through the window of the market had cast shadows of two soldiers onto the wooden floor. Their boots had thudded into the market, filling the air with fear.

If Irena ran toward Mama, the soldiers would spot her, so Irena had backed up and hid behind the fruit bins. When the cans toppled to the floor, the soldiers moved toward Mama and Bridget. A sick feeling spread through Irena. The soldier with the jaw that jutted out past his mouth looked angry. His red face made him seem like a bomb ready to explode. As he paced in front of Mama, he kept his hand near his holster. With each step, his fingers inched closer to the gun.

The younger soldier with closely cropped blond hair barely visible beneath his hat was bent down gathering up the cans and stacking them on the shelf in precise order. Finishing those, he lined up the cans in the next row and the next. Then he turned his attention to Mama, snatching her pocketbook from her arm and pulling out some papers.

Irena had heard Da tell Mama, "You have to take your iden-tification papers with you when you go out. They show we have permission to live here."

What if Mama didn't have the right papers and the soldiers took Mama and Bridget away? Irena swiped her sweaty hands on her pink dress. All of her breath came gushing out. The soldier pacing, whirled toward the apple bins. She ducked. Had he seen her? What if he marched to the bins and pulled her out by her pigtails? Would he reach for his gun and shoot her and Mama and Bridget? Would they be left to rot with the apples?

Mama's voice, pleading with the soldiers, cut through Irena's fear for her own safety. Mama and Bridget were in trouble. Irena had to help them. If she stood and ran from the store, the soldiers might chase her and leave Mama and Bridget alone. But then what would happen? Irena didn't know the area and would get lost. Or if the soldiers caught her, they might cart her away. She needed to quit acting so impulsively. That's what had put Mama and Bridget in danger.

The boy who had been in line behind them as they waited to enter the store streaked by the apple bins and out the door. Clutched under his thin arm was a long loaf of crusty brown bread. The soldiers must have seen the boy with the bread. Dropping Mama's purse and papers, they rushed out the door after him.

As soon as they were out of sight, Irena dashed to Mama. Before Irena could say how sorry she was, Mama grabbed her, pressing her close. Irena reveled in Mama's warm arms and comforting scent. Too quickly, Mama pulled away, gathered her papers, and folded them into her purse. The other women in the store went back to shopping as if nothing had happened.

Irena had to apologize. She needed Mama to know how sorry she was. Shifting from one foot to the other, she whispered, "Mama, I didn't mean to—"

"We'll talk later." Mama snapped her pocketbook closed.

Irena had promised to be good. Instead, she had broken another rule: do not talk.

On the way back to the projects, Irena was relieved Mama and Bridget were safe, but she dreaded her punishment. She didn't even have a peppermint stick to lick, although she didn't deserve one. Following the rules all the time was hard, but she held onto Mama's hand, didn't talk, and kept her head down. Irena hoped Mama wouldn't punish her—at least not too hard.

After walking and walking, Irena's shoes pinched her feet. She peeked up, just to see where they were. They had reached the entrance to the projects. The Polish woman and her girls were ahead. Mama pulled her and Bridget through the archway and called out in Polish, "*Czekac!*"

The woman glanced over her shoulder, but instead of waiting, she walked faster. She had helped Mama in the store. Why didn't the woman stop now? Irena wanted to talk to the girls, but she had learned her lesson. She would not disobey again.

Trying to catch up with the woman, Mama quickened her pace, but the woman rushed ahead, dragging her daughters with her. They disappeared into the apartment building next to the one where the girl in the window lived.

Back in their apartment, Mama made Irena sit on a hard wooden chair. "Stay here until your da comes. When he finds out what you did, he'll want to talk to you."

Da didn't do much talking, but he really spanked hard.

CHAPTER
FIFTEEN

October 1940
Hamburg, Germany

The following week at breakfast after Irena and Bridget finished their oatmeal, Bridget slid her bowl toward Mama. "More."

Irena kicked Bridget under the table. She didn't want to go to the store again.

"That's all we have," Mama said.

Irena was still hungry, too, but she willed her stomach not to growl. Being outside no longer seemed fun. There were no shade trees or a river or meadow to play in, but plenty of soldiers.

Mama had already put on her paisley dress and pinned her wavy hair off her neck. "Girls, get ready to go to the store."

"I'll stay here and watch Bridget," Irena said.

"I wanna stay," agreed Bridget.

At least Irena had an ally.

"I'm not leaving you here," said Mama. She opened the cupboard. Except for tins of spices, the shelves were empty. "And we have nothing left to eat."

"I'm not hungry," lied Irena.

"I am," said Bridget, climbing down from her chair to get dressed.

Traitor.

"You promised to be good," Mama said.

Irena's stomach knotted. She had no choice but to go with Mama.

Mama, however, seemed scared, too. At each corner, she slowed to check for soldiers ahead. When they stepped inside the store, the smell of apples made Irena's stomach hurt. As Mama searched for milk, cheese, butter, and meat, she kept turning around to make sure she and Bridget were behind her.

Irena was relieved that nothing bad happened that day or the other days they went to the market. Still, her fear did not go away, and she couldn't shake the image of the soldier with the gun yelling at Mama.

When they went to the market, Mama quit trying to talk to other women. Most days she stayed in the flat, cleaning, cooking, and sewing. She was a really good seamstress, that was the word Mama used, but when she sewed, Mama didn't hum the way she did back home. It was as if she were afraid to make a sound and wanted to be invisible.

Da was different, too. He left for work before sunrise and returned after sunset. Sometimes she and Bridget didn't see him for days unless Mama let them wait up. Then he would shuffle into the apartment and smile at them, but his gray eyes didn't twinkle, and he didn't tell them funny stories about where he worked.

Their meals weren't the same either. Mama fixed whatever she found at the store. Da quit asking about meat, and Mama quit looking for butter. They ate mostly soups, gravies, and bread. The bread was so hard that even spreading it with 'margarine' didn't help. The only food that tasted almost the same was potato pancakes. At home, Mama used leftover mashed potatoes, but here they never had leftovers. Mama would grate a potato, add a little flour, and fry them in margarine. Sometimes she made gravy to pour over the potato pancakes. That was so yummy.

At the table, Da kept his head down, sipping his soup or sopping up the gravy. Mama didn't babble on about their day. Instead, they shoveled in their food, which was never enough, and if they talked, it was always about the same thing—going home.

Irena soon discovered doing what Mama said all the time was hard. One day Irena stood in the bedroom longing to see the girl at the window. What would it hurt if she just peeked out the curtains?

She slid the blackout curtains open, just a sliver. The bedroom door swung open. Irena yanked the curtains closed and jumped into bed.

"Whatcha doing?"

It was only Bridget, who sat on the bed beside her. "Wanna play hide-n-seek?"

"There's no good hiding places."

Bridget held her stomach, pretending to be sick. "Wanna play nurse?"

Irena shook her head. She enjoyed being the nurse, but Bridget would want to switch roles. Irena didn't like getting shots, even pretend ones.

"What about the train?"

Irena and Bridget had made up the game after they had ridden the train to Germany. "Okay."

Bridget pulled the empty suitcase from under the other bed. Irena ached to go home. She didn't like Hamburg. She didn't like staying inside, she didn't like the soldiers, and she didn't like going to bed and waking up scared.

Bridget struggled to open the suitcase. "Help me."

Sliding off the bed, Irena crossed the room and flipped open the latches. "Hurry. We have to leave before the Soviets catch us."

She and Bridget rushed around the bedroom, opening drawers and pretending to pack their clothes. When they finished, Irena snapped the latches. Then she and Bridget gripped the handle and lugged the suitcase into the kitchen.

From the couch, Mama looked up from her sewing. "Are you playing train again?"

Irena nodded. "We packed clothes and lots of food."

"Be careful with the suitcase. We'll need it when we return home."

Mama always sounded like she wanted to go home, too.

Irena and Bridget scooted the four chairs into a line. "The table is the depot." Irena liked being the ticket man—selling the tickets, boarding the train, and walking down the row of chairs to collect them.

Bridget bought a ticket at the 'depot' and slid into the second chair. Irena strolled down the row of chairs, stopping beside Bridget, who pretended to hand her a ticket.

"Now I get to be an engineer." Bridget raced to the first chair and plopped down. Irena wiggled into the last chair.

"Choo-choo. Chuga-chuga-chuga." As Bridget imitated train noises, Irena closed her eyes. Memories of their train ride flooded back. During the night, she'd swayed to the rhythm of the wheels clickety-clacking on the tracks as the train took them farther and farther from home.

"We're here," Bridget announced.

Irena didn't open her eyes. When she and Bridget played train, their roles switched from ticket taker to engineer to passenger, but their destination always remained the same. Home.

The next night, Irena knew she wasn't at home. An ear-splitting siren screeched through the flat.

Eeeoooeeeoooeeeooo.

She and Bridget jerked awake and screamed.

Eeeoooeeeoooeeeooo.

Da jumped from the bed and sprinted across the room, grabbing Irena. "Air raid." He yelled at Mama, "Get Bridget. Head for the basement."

Eeeoooeeeoooeeeooo.

Da had warned them about the possibility of an air raid, but Irena still cried as Da carried her through the kitchen and out of the apartment. Mama was close behind with Bridget. They clambered down the steps, following the other people in the flat.

Eeeoooeeeoooeeeooo.

In the basement musty air slapped against Irena's flushed face. Startled, she hitched back sobs and squinted into the darkness, trying to make out the furnace and coal bin she knew were there. Mama had taken them to the basement and shown them where they would go in case they were attacked. Irena hadn't been scared then because Mama said, "It probably won't happen."

But it was happening. They were being attacked. Irena couldn't quit shaking. The siren changed. Instead of one solid wail, the screech stopped and started, stopped and started. After several similar blasts, the sound ended.

Da bent down to set her on the floor. She screamed and clung to his neck. He pried her fingers loose. "It's okay. The air raid will be over soon."

Her bare feet hit the cold floor. Chills raced down her back. She curled into a ball, sucking in short breaths. Mama and Da had talked about bombs destroying London. They hadn't said anything about bombs destroying Hamburg.

Fear pulsed through her. After several minutes, her uneven breathing stopped. She listened for planes, but the only sounds were whispers from the other families crouched in the dark.

A match sparked under the steps, lighting up the two brothers who lived across the hall. The squat men with full bushy beards looked like twins. Da called the man who lit the cigarette Big Angelo and the other one, Spyros. Mama always knocked on the bathroom door to make sure one of them wasn't inside.

Before the match died, Irena glimpsed two other couples, who probably lived below them, whispering. She couldn't make out their words, only the foreign sounds.

Irena choked back a sob, and Mama, who held Bridget on her lap, whispered, "Sh-sh. We're safe here."

Irena didn't feel safe. She wished she had her rock. When she ran her fingers over the smooth heart shape, she remembered home. Water dripped from above and hit her bare feet. She tucked them under her nightshirt and stayed curled up. She wanted to be in bed, not the bed upstairs, her old bed at home.

Eee eee eee eee eee eee eee.

She screamed and scurried to Da, trying to climb up his leg. He reached down and hoisted her into his arms. "Listen."

Eee eee eee eee eee eee eee.

"This siren is different. You need to learn the meanings. The first *Kleinalarm* that woke us signaled enemy planes nearby. The second is the *Fliegeralarm,* fifteen rapid, four-second wails, that warns us to get ready. That's the one we heard down here. It means take cover immediately."

Eee eee eee eee eee eee eee.

"The third siren signals all clear. The air raid is over."

"But I didn't hear any planes."

"That's good," said Da. "It means the planes never made it here."

As Da carried her upstairs and tucked her into bed, she couldn't think of anything good about the air raid. She reached under her pillow and held her rock. Even rubbing the familiar edges didn't make her feel safe, and it was a long time before she was calm enough to sleep.

The following night when Irena climbed into bed, she kept her shoes on and the rock clutched in her fist, in case they had another attack. She was afraid the bombers would come, and she wouldn't know which siren was sounding. But no sirens went off. The following night, the sirens were silent again. The third night, Irena didn't wear her shoes. She closed her eyes and drifted off to sleep.

Eeeoooeeeoooeeeooo.

She and Bridget woke up screaming.

CHAPTER
SIXTEEN

November 1940
Hamburg, Germany

After the air raids, Irena added a new request to her prayers. *Please, God, don't let the bombs hit us.* Each night that no siren sounded, Irena awoke and thanked God for answering her prayer. She hoped God would answer her other prayers—going home, making friends, and starting school, a real school, not one with Mama as the teacher and Bridget as the only other student.

But when Irena gazed at her red dress hanging on a hook near the door, she became discouraged. "Please, Mama, can I wear my school dress?"

"*Nein. Nein,*" answered Mama. Irena didn't like hearing 'no.'

One morning Irena stared at the red dress. She was tired of waiting. She slipped it on, working the rosebud buttons into the right holes.

Bridget's eyes widened. "You'll be in trouble."

"I'll take it off before Mama comes in." Irena twirled around, flipping her skirt. "You can choose one of my dresses, and we can play princess."

"I want to wear your baby-doll dress." Bridget pulled it off the hook and wiggled into the pink dress with the high waist. The skirt was so long, she had to hold it up as she danced around the bedroom.

The knob on the bedroom door turned. Irena and Bridget raced to their bed, jumped in, and pulled the blanket up to their chins.

Mama stepped into the room. "What are you girls doing in bed?"

Irena closed her eyes. "Resting."

Bridget made loud snoring noises. "Zzzzzz."

"That's too bad. The sun's shining. We won't have many warm days before winter. I'm going to hang the clothes on the line, but if you girls want to stay in bed—"

Irena threw off the blanket and hopped up. Playing outside was different from going to the store. If the soldiers came, they could run inside.

Mama's mouth dropped open. "I see you're already dressed to go out."

Irena forgot she had on her red school dress. Her cheeks turned warm.

Bridget pointed to Irena. "It was her idea."

Mama shrugged. "Wear your sweaters. It's nippy outside."

Irena ran outside before Mama could scold her about wearing her school dress. The November air was cool, and Irena was glad she had on her sweater. She ran around the clothesline, flapping her arms like a red bird set free from its cage. When she got tired, she glanced up at the window where she'd seen the girl. The curtains opened.

The girl stood at the window, waving. Irena waved and then

motioned with her hand for the girl to come outside. She nodded and closed the drapes.

Irena sprinted to Mama, who was hanging Da's work shirt on the line. "The girl across the street is coming." Unable to stand still, Irena ran in circles until the door to the opposite apartment building opened and the girl, holding her mother's hand, stepped out.

The girl was tall and had blonde pigtails. She wore a gingham dress with a sweater buttoned down the front. Irena was glad she'd worn her new red dress, even if her itchy sweater covered most of it.

After they crossed the street, the girl dropped her mother's hand and dashed to Irena, stopping close enough for Irena to touch the freckles scattered across the girl's nose and cheeks. But that would be rude, so she clasped her hands behind her back.

The girl pointed to herself. "Hi, I'm Hanna. That's my mother, Audra."

The girl spoke Lithuanian, but Irena couldn't get her tongue to work, so she unclasped her hands and waved.

The girl blinked. Her eyes were the shade of Lithuanian blues, the flowers that grew in the meadow.

Irena worked her tongue loose. "My name is Irena."

Bridget butted in. "I'm her sister."

"She's only four." Irena stood up straighter. "I'm six."

"I'm eight." Hanna's blue eyes lost some of their brightness. "You're lucky to have a sister."

"I am?" Irena didn't think having a sister was anything special. "Sometimes Bridget can be a pest."

Bridget scowled. "Am not."

"But you always have someone to play with," Hanna said.

Irena didn't know how to explain that playing with her sister wasn't the same as playing with a girlfriend. "Do you go to school?"

Hanna shook her head, whipping her pigtails around.

"Me either. Mama just teaches us," said Irena. "Let's play school."

Bridget whined. "I wanna play house."

Annoyed, Irena turned to Hanna. "You're the oldest. You decide."

Hanna coughed several times before she answered. "Let's play rock, paper, scissors. Whoever wins can choose."

Irena scrunched her nose. "I don't know how to play."

"It's easy. I'll teach you."

"Hanna," called her mother, who was talking to Mama near the clothesline. Hanna's mother was as tall and straight as Mama's broom handle. Her hair resembled dry bristles, and like Hanna, a spray of freckles ran across her nose. "Time to go."

The sparkle in Hanna's eyes faded. "I want to play with my new friends."

Hanna's mother glanced around. "The soldiers might see you."

"Can my friends come inside?"

Hanna's mother turned to Mama. "Would you like to have a cup of tea while the girls play?"

Irena waited for Mama to say 'yes.' Instead, she twisted her lips at the corner the way she did when she was thinking. What was Mama thinking about? They never got to do anything. Irena rushed to her. "Please Mama, we'll be good, won't we Bridget?"

Bridget nodded.

Mama glanced up and down the street. "It might be safer inside."

Irena rushed to Hanna and hooked her arm through hers. Bridget latched onto Irena's other arm. The three girls, linked arm-in-arm, dashed across the street and into the flat as if they had been friends forever.

———

"I'll heat some water." Audra put on the teakettle while the girls hurried into the bedroom to play.

Harriet slipped into a kitchen chair with an upholstered flowered seat. It felt strange being in an apartment like theirs—one room for the kitchen and living room, both painted the same mossy green. Yet, this apartment looked different. The furnishings were more elaborate. She rubbed her fingers over the polished mahogany table, fine enough for a dining room. Spoiling the effect was a saucer in the center filled with ashes and dirty dishes piled into the sink.

In the living room was a large maroon divan and matching chair. Crocheted dollies decorated the arched backs and rounded arms. Between the divan and chair was a small end table scattered with newspapers. Against the far wall, a three-shelved hutch was jammed with books arranged haphazardly. And on the floor was what appeared to be an expensive Oriental rug. Harriet admired the furnishing, but the clutter made her want to set things right.

Audra set a porcelain teapot embossed with clusters of pink roses, along with two matching cups and saucers, onto the table. As she poured hot water into it, steam-scented peppermint rose from the curved spout, evoking memories of enjoying a fragrant cup of tea with friends. Since coming to Germany, she'd never had the luxury of spending time with a friend. She was as hungry for adult conversation as the girls were to have a friend.

Although Audra had said 'a cup of tea,' Harriet had expected a cup of hot water like she often drank. "Where can you even get tea?"

Audra reached into the hip pocket of her flowered shirt-waist dress and pulled out a tin of cigarettes and matches. Her hand shook as she lit the cigarette and inhaled. "My husband has relatives in Germany. They help us with little luxuries—tea, cigarettes, and sometimes things for Hanna." She pushed the tin of cigarettes toward Harriet, offering her one.

Harriet shook her head. She'd tried smoking once, out in the barn with her friends. She hadn't liked the taste but had forced herself to finish the whole cigarette to fit in with the group. Her dad, who'd found the cigarette butts in the barn, had been upset. "Women don't smoke, at least not good women."

Audra seemed like a good woman, certainly not a floozy. She poured the steeped tea, and Harriet took a sip. "This is wonderful."

Audra waved her cigarette dismissively. "If you need something, I'll try to get it for you."

The offer surprised Harriet. Oskar worked more than twelve hours a day, six days a week, and still, she could buy only the necessities. A few extras would relieve their hardship. She considered real coffee, instead of the chicory or ground acorns called *esckat* she sometimes bought for Oskar. Then she remembered Bridget's request. "I'd like some butter."

Audra let out a braying laugh. "Wouldn't we all? I can't get you butter or meat. Maybe a few extra potatoes and turnips."

Harriet's spirit rose as she picked up her cup of tea. "Thank you. We'd appreciate anything."

Audra's pencil-thin eyebrows formed a straight line. "Of course, I'd want something in return."

Tea sloshed into Harriet's saucer. "Like what?"

Audra held up the tin of cigarettes. "My husband smokes, too. We never have enough tobacco rations."

Oskar smoked cigarettes, mostly when he was upset, but they had so little money that she'd only bought tobacco once since they'd arrived. She wanted to agree immediately, but it should be Oskar's decision. "I'll have to talk to my husband." Already Harriet was thinking of everything they needed. "How much would yard goods be? I'd like to make dresses for the girls."

"Clothes from resale shops or the black market are easy to get." Audra flicked ashes into the already full saucer on the table. "My husband has German relatives here, but he's not German. His family was originally French. Konstantin was named after his great-grandfather, who fought in Napoleon's Grand Army during the 1812 invasion of Russia. Of course, as you know, the French were defeated."

Harriet's schooling had been sporadic, and she remembered little about Russian history, but she nodded as if it was a well-known fact.

"Our Baltic winters are bad, but Russian winters are worse. When the French retreated, they were hit with Arctic winds and blinding snowstorms. The men tromped through knee-high snow with little rations. Konstantin's great-grandfather made it as far as Latvia and stayed."

"What does your husband do?"

"He's a printer. In Latvia, his grandfather owned his own printing company. During the Great War, those bloody Bolshevik pigs confiscated all his presses and made him print their Russian lies." Audra waved her cigarette, gesturing toward the scattered newspapers. "The German papers aren't much different. They're full of propaganda. All the headlines are about the *Blitz*."

"The *Blitz*?" Harriet had never heard the word.

"*Blitzkrieg*. Since September, Germany has been bombing England every day. According to the newspapers, we've flattened the entire city of London." Audra's voice rose. "But there's never any mention of the air raids here." She took a long sip of tea that seemed to calm her. "What about your husband? What does he do?"

Harriet didn't want to admit that he made bombs. "Oskar's a good man. In Lithuania, he was a coal miner, like his pa." She looked down and stirred her tea. She didn't tell Audra that Oskar's pa wasn't such a good man. He'd started as a trapper—red squirrels, foxes, and occasionally a prized deer. He used the meat and tanned the hides, but income was sporadic and with five kids, he turned to the coal mine for steady money. Laboring underground had revealed his dark side. After the mine whistle blew, he'd stop at the pub to treat himself to a pint or two and worries about putting food on the table or shoes for his children were sloshed away.

Audra stubbed out her cigarette. "Mining is dangerous."

Harriet nodded. "The mine where Oskar's pa worked collapsed. He was trapped inside. They tried to dig him out, but they never found his body. Oskar's brothers and sister were older and had left home. Oskar was just thirteen. He quit school and worked in the mines to provide for his ma."

"Doing his duty," Audra said matter-of-factly.

"I don't think Oskar thought of it that way. Providing gives him a sense of purpose. He didn't like going down into the mine, but he worked there for five years until his ma passed on. The day after her funeral, he quit the mine and went to work at a candy factory."

Audra let out another braying laugh. "That's a switch. I bet Adolf doesn't have him making candy here."

Audra's use of Hitler's first name surprised her. Oskar always referred to *Der Führer* as Hitler. Harriet sipped her tea, enjoying being with Audra. In Lithuania, she'd always had friends. Those lifelong ties were irreplaceable, but Audra might be someone Harriet could share her problems with, and she wouldn't feel so alone.

She rose and squeezed Audra's hand. "Thank you so much for the tea. I hope we can be friends."

Audra returned her squeeze. "Hanna needs a friend, and so do I."

CHAPTER
SEVENTEEN

That night after the girls were in bed, Harriet sat on the divan, patching Oskar's flannel shirt. She was anxious to tell him about Hanna and Audra. Finishing his shirt, she tucked her needle and thread into the pillowcase with her other sewing supplies. With Audra's help, Harriet hoped to get material and more sewing supplies.

Oskar's boots sounded on the stairs. She tossed his shirt on the divan and rushed to the door. Unchaining it, she threw it open. "Today we met a woman and her daughter from Latvia, but they speak Lithuanian."

Oskar dragged in, acknowledging her words with a nod as he hung his coat and cap on the hook by the door.

Undaunted, she continued to chat as she walked to the stove and heated the potato soup. "Audra, that's the woman, said they've been here almost two years. Their flat has expensive-looking furnishings, and she offered me real tea. She even smokes cigarettes." As she stirred the watery potato soup, she kept her back to Oskar. She wasn't sure how he would feel about giving up his tobacco rations, and she didn't want to crush his pride by letting him see how eager she was to have more than he provided. "She offered to get us some extras if we would...trade some tobacco rations."

His chair scraped the floor as he sat. "Go ahead. I don't want you to squander our rations on tobacco while you and the girls do without." He was an unselfish man, and she should have known that would be his answer, but was relieved to hear him say it.

Turning, she carried his soup to the table and sank into the chair across from him. Although agreeing, he hadn't shown enthusiasm about her new friend or possibly more food. Of course, he spoke German and talked to other men every day. Also, he was a proud man, and it must hurt his pride that he didn't make enough to provide for them. She'd hoped he would be relieved that she'd found a way to help the family have more. "Can we invite them over on Sunday? I haven't met Audra's husband, but it might help you to have a friend, too."

Oskar's words were flat. "I have to work Sunday."

Harriet frowned. "But you need some rest."

"Supposedly the mother country needs bombs more."

"Because of the *Blitz*?"

He put his spoon down. "How do you know about that?"

"Audra said it's in all the newspapers. I'm still not exactly sure what it is, except Germany is bombing London every day."

"*Blitzkrieg* is lightning war. That's the way Germany conquered France and Poland, quickly striking by land and air."

"I hope Germany wins, and the war is over soon."

"They should win. The guards are always bragging about bombing the British every night, dropping as much as five hundred tons of explosives. Last week, on the fourteenth, the Germans bombed Coventry for ten hours and lost only a single bomber."

"No wonder the British are bombing us. Audra said that Adolf never says anything about the damage the Allies do here."

Oskar bolted out of his chair, all signs of tiredness gone. He pointed his finger at her and shook it. "Never say that again."

Shocked, she sat up straighter. "What-what did I say?"

"Never call Hitler, Adolf. People who disagree with his policies use his first name to show disrespect."

Harriet wrung her hands on her apron. "Audra used it, so I assumed others did."

"You can trade our tobacco rations but be careful what you say around this Audra. She might repeat something to the wrong person or she might even be a spy planted in the projects to see who is loyal."

Harriet's hands stilled. "Do you think the Germans would do that?"

"Since I've been here, I've discovered Hitler will do anything to promote his master race."

While Oskar returned to the table and ate, she thought about the war. Now that she knew where Germany was bombing, the war was harder to push away. She'd never been to London, only seen pictures of the city—London Bridge, Trafalgar Square, and Buckingham Palace. Had they been destroyed by German bombs? And what about the people? How many families in London were forced to go to their basements? And what about those who didn't make it to a shelter before the bombs exploded? A shudder rippled through her.

Oskar finished his soup and pushed his bowl away. "Hitler isn't reporting the bombings here because so far the British have not damaged much, but if America enters the war—"

Eeeoooeeeoooeeeooo.

He jumped up from the table. "Get the girls and head for the basement."

As they rushed to the basement, Harriet understood. This was war, and as a mother, she would do whatever it took to keep her family safe.

CHAPTER
EIGHTEEN

December 24-25, 1940
Hamburg, Germany

rena, still in her long underwear, parted the curtains and squinted through the glass frosted with ice crystals. She sighed. Hanna wasn't at her window. The only fun part about Germany was having a friend. The three girls had played together several times until Hanna became too sick.

Irena's shoulders slumped. No one understood how lonely it was here. She was trapped inside all the time. She had Bridget to play with, but Irena wanted to play with Hanna. At night when Irena prayed, she poured out her longing to God and prayed for Hanna to get well.

The door creaked open. Mama stood in the doorway, smiling. "Today is *Kūčios*."

Christmas Eve. No wonder Mama was smiling.

Bridget threw off the blanket. "Why didn't you tell us Germany had Christmas?"

Mama's smile disappeared. "It's hard to keep track of the days."

Irena thought about the wonderful Christmases at home. "Will we have a tree and food and go to church?"

"Will we get presents?" Bridget asked.

"We can't attend Mass, but for good girls, there might be presents."

"Can we see Hanna?" Irena asked.

Mama shook her head. "When she's well."

Poor Hanna, being sick for *Kalèdos*. Irena was glad she wasn't sick for Christmas. "Will we have special food?"

"*Ja*. Come see."

Mama had been using a few German words like *ja* for 'yes' and *nein* for 'no.' Irena wanted today to be full of *ja's*.

In the kitchen, the warm yeasty aroma of bread reminded Irena of home. Longing washed over her. Then she spotted the food on the counter—beets, potatoes, carrots, a tin of herring, a head of cabbage, a shiny red apple, celery, and onions. "Are we eating all that?"

"Do you remember how many dishes of food we eat on Christmas Eve?" Mama asked.

"Twelve, for the number of Jesus' disciples."

Mama patted Irena's head. "That's right. I will make the beetroot soup so it will be cool for tonight, and you girls can help by making the beetroot salad."

Irena scrambled to the table. Beetroot soup was a beautiful dark red, and the salad greens mixed with cooked beets were pretty, too. But the best part was eating them.

"Break off the leaves for the salad while I clean the beets to roast."

As Mama stood at the sink, cleaning the beets, she started singing, the way she used to when she was happy. "Silent night, holy night." The familiar Christmas carol carried Irena home. Days before *Kalèdos,* Da cut a tree from the forest and set it in the living room. The family spent hours decorating it. On Christmas Eve they attended Mass, and on Christmas Day, Papa would come with Dolly hitched to the wagon to take the whole family to the farm for more food and presents.

"We don't have a Christmas tree," Irena wailed.

Mama stopped singing. "Don't think about what we don't have. We're together and we have all this food."

"Will you make those special cookies?" Irena rubbed her hand over her tummy. "They're my favorite." She didn't remember the name. "They have black seeds and you dip them in milk."

"*Kūčiukai,* Christmas biscuits. They're made with poppy seeds, but we won't have milk."

"I don't care," Irena said. "I love the sweet cookies."

The morning flew by, the kitchen alive with eager hands, as Irena and Bridget helped Mama prepare the Christmas Eve meal. When they finished, she didn't rest. "Now we clean."

Cleaning didn't sound as fun as cooking.

"Having everything clean on Christmas will protect us from getting sick during the year."

By the time Da's work boots thudded on the stairs, Irena had changed into her red school dress and Bridget wore her blue-plaid jumper. As usual, Da's face and clothes were dirty, but as he entered, he had an extra bounce in his step and a bundle of straw in his hand. "Something smells wonderful."

Irena beamed with pride. "We helped Mama cook."

Mama took the straw from Da. She pointed to his black trousers and white shirt on the chair in the living room. "I laid out your clothes."

Da strode to the chair. "I'll wash up so we can eat."

While Da went down the hall, Mama gave the girls handfuls of straw. "Scatter them on the table."

Bridget wrinkled her nose. "Straw isn't clean."

Irena remembered the tradition. "It's because baby Jesus was born in a stable."

After they finished, Mama covered the straw with a white tablecloth she'd got from Audra and placed a candle in the middle.

As Da returned, he rubbed his hands together. "Is anyone ready to eat?"

Irena and Bridget both clapped and said, "*Ja.*"

Da crossed to the window and pushed open the curtain. "I don't see a star. I guess we'll have to wait."

Irena rushed to the window. A bright light blinked in the dark sky, like the star that had guided the wise men. She hopped up and down, pointing to it.

Da swooped her up and carried her to the table, depositing her into a chair. "I guess that means it's time to eat...after we pray."

Irena hoped Da didn't pray too long. She was starving.

Da looked at her. "Irena, will you say the blessing?"

Irena sat up straighter. She'd never been asked to give the blessing at a holiday meal before. She gathered her thoughts. "Thank you for baby Jesus and Father Christmas. Thank you for Mama, Da, Bridget, and me. Make Hanna well so we can play together. Keep Nana and Papa safe and everyone else in Lithuania like—"

Ouch. Bridget kicked her shin underneath the table.

"And bless all this delicious food. Amen."

Da picked up his fork. "Let the feast begin."

The soft candlelight cast a warm glow on the family enjoying the food. After they finished, Irena asked, "Where are the special wafers."

Mama was no longer smiling.

"The wafers have to be blessed by a priest, but we can still observe other traditions, like the straw." Mama smoothed her hand over the white tablecloth. "Oskar, you go first."

Da reached his hand under the tablecloth and pulled out a thin straw.

"What does it mean?" Irena asked.

"It means this year my wallet will be flat."

Mama nodded. "That's true."

Da laid the straw on the table. "Harriet, you're next."

Mama reached under the tablecloth. Her straw was thick in the middle. She turned to Da. "That's not happening."

"What?" Bridget asked.

Da beamed. "Another baby."

Irena giggled. "A brother or sister would be fun."

Mama blushed. She did not look happy.

"Irena, it's your turn," Da said. "Remember, take the first straw you touch."

Slowly Irena stuck her hand under the tablecloth. She didn't want a flat one like Da's or a thick one like Mama's. Touching a piece of straw, she pulled it out. She frowned at the bent straw and dropped it on the table. "This one is broken. I want to try again."

Da stayed her hand. "A bent straw means you'll have a turn in your life."

"Is that bad?" Irena asked.

Mama patted Irena's shoulder. "I'm sure it will be a good turn." But Mama and Da shared a look that Irena didn't understand.

"Now me." Bridget reached under the tablecloth. She pulled out a long slender stalk and waved it. "Does mine mean something good?"

Da nodded. "It's the longest straw so you'll live a long life."

That night as Irena lay in bed, she thought about her bent straw and all the things that could happen. The war could end. They could go home. She could start school. She could...

"Bridget, Irena, wake up," Mama called through the door. "It's *Kalėdos*."

Kicking off the blanket, Irena and Bridget hopped up and raced into the kitchen. Irena skidded to a stop. In the living room, stood a beautiful pine tree, stretched from floor to ceiling. She must be dreaming. She tiptoed across the room and touched a branch. Needles pricked her fingers. She wasn't dreaming. She twirled around. "A Christmas tree."

Da stood next to it smiling. "Father Christmas left your presents under the tree."

Irena squealed in delight at the red-and-green hats and mittens under the tree. She leaned over to snatch the red ones and spotted something near the back. She dropped to her knees. "Galoshes!" She scooted on the floor. "Now we can go outside and build a snowman."

Irena slipped her feet into the galoshes and smiled. The boots were too big, but Mama could stuff the toes. Christmas in Germany was almost as fun as at home.

1941

On June 22, 1941, Germany reneged on their nonaggression pact and attacked the Soviet troops in Lithuania. The Lithuanians greeted the Germans as liberators and hoped the Germans would re-establish their independence. They did not. [1]

CHAPTER
NINETEEN

March 1941

H arriet added an extra swish to the broom as she swept the kitchen floor. Happiness. She hadn't realized how long it had been since she'd felt a spark of joy. From the time they'd fled to Germany, almost eight months ago, she hadn't been living, but surviving the week, the day, the hour. Now, she'd made a friend. Audra had helped her get some extras, and Christmas had been happy.

The girls had beamed on Christmas morning when they spotted the Christmas tree and their presents. Oskar was right to bring them to Germany. Their family could do more than survive. Maybe they could even have a good life here.

But the holidays had been a respite, and her happiness waned now that the harsh winter had arrived, bringing cold winds and freezing snow that trapped them inside. She drew her cardigan tighter as the wind snaked in around the blackout curtains and whistled down the stovepipe, intensifying their isolation.

Unexpectedly, her stomach heaved. She swayed, hit with a wave of nausea. Closing her mouth, she fought the queasiness from the lingering odor of last night's cabbage soup. She neared the scrap bucket, and her stomach heaved again. Her eyes darted to the wall calendar marked with black X's to keep track of the days and months.

The broom slipped from her hand. The handle banged against the floor as she sank into the nearest chair. The date couldn't be right. That would mean she had missed her menstrual period for February. Occasionally, she was a few days late, but only twice had she been more than a week late, and both times she'd been pregnant.

Irena burst into the kitchen. "What was that noise?"

Harriet pointed to the broom lying on the floor. Irena picked it up and set it in the corner. "Phew. The scrap bucket stinks."

Irena was right. The waste from last night's cabbage soup smelled. Possibly the odor, and not her late period, had made Harriet queasy. She dreaded going out, but she couldn't put it off. Steadying herself, she rose and walked to the coats hanging near the door. "Watch your sister. I need to empty the bucket."

"I'll go," Irena said.

Harriet's hand stilled on her coat. Being trapped inside affected Irena the most. She became restless and cross, almost as if she needed to be outside to live. The dumpster was across the street between Audra's and the Polish woman's buildings. Could Irena go alone?

As Harriet hesitated, Irena lifted the bucket and dragged it to the door. "I'll be right back."

Harriet didn't want anything to happen to Irena. "What if the soldiers come?"

Irena shrugged as if it were a minor problem. "I'll run inside."

On the farm, Harriet at age six, which was Irena's age, had started doing chores—grinding corn for chicken feed, gathering eggs to sell at the market, and dumping scraps for the pigs to eat. The chores had given Harriet a sense of responsibility and might do the same for Irena. "Okay, but come straight back."

As Irena slipped on her coat and galoshes, Bridget darted out of the bedroom. "Where're you going?"

Irena straightened and puffed out her chest. "I'm taking out the slop bucket."

Bridget, who usually followed her sister everywhere, ducked back into the bedroom.

Harriet unchained the door. "I'll watch from the window."

Irena shuffled out of the flat, lugging the bucket down the stairs. Harriet hurried to the window and inched the curtains open, peeking out. Irena stomped through the crusty snow, dragging the bucket, which wiped out her footprints. When she crossed the street and reached the large metal dumpster, she hefted the bucket, dumping it. Then she turned. A big smile stretched across her face.

Harriet's heart raced. She checked for soldiers. Seeing none, she waved for Irena to come back. In less than three minutes, Irena was inside with the door chained behind her. Her cheeks were flushed from the cold and her boots left puddles on the floor. "That was fun."

Harriet didn't scold her for tracking in snow. Her cheeks flushed with chagrin. Irena seemed braver than Harriet. Another wave of nausea hit. She rushed to the sink and heaved.

"Are you sick?" Irena asked, her voice sounding worried.

Harriet avoided the calendar. She didn't throw up because her period was late. It was the odor from the garbage. She turned to Irena, forcing a smile. "I'm fine."

The following morning, Harriet stood at the stove stirring the buckwheat porridge while the girls waited at the table. The nutty aroma of the groats filled the air. Harriet's stomach rumbled. I'm just hungry, she told herself. Her stomach cramped and began to swell. She bolted from the stove, hung her head over the sink, and vomited.

Irena rushed to her side and patted her back. "Are you sick again?"

Harriet couldn't answer. She continued to gag until nothing was left. Finally, when the heaving stopped, she rinsed her mouth of the sour taste. She turned to Irena, who stared at her with round owl eyes.

Harriet squatted down and hugged her. Bridget nudged into the circle. Harriet drew them closer, inhaling their sweet, little-girl scents. "I'm fine. Finish your breakfast and go play."

After the girls had eaten, Irena asked, "What about school?"

Although Irena had complained at first, now she was eager to learn.

"We'll do it tomorrow," Harriet said.

They didn't argue but scampered into the bedroom. Harriet sat at the table, taking deep breaths. Her eyes strayed to the calendar. She couldn't be pregnant. She just couldn't. Her body wouldn't betray her like that. Having a baby would be different if they weren't living in a foreign country and being bombed. But she couldn't bring a child into a world of hunger and fear.

The first time she'd been pregnant, she'd been scared, but she'd stayed with her parents for the last few weeks. When she delivered, her mother and the local midwife had been at her side. Who would help her with this birth? And how would Oskar feel about providing for another child?

When Harriet told him she was carrying their first child, his gray eyes had sparkled with pride and he'd swooped her up, twirling her around. He'd been just as happy when Bridget was born.

"You're not disappointed I didn't have a boy?"

He smiled down at their daughter cradled in her arms, his

eyes twinkling with that same gleam. "How can I be disappointed with girls as beautiful as their mama?"

She glanced at the calendar again. She still wasn't used to the names of the months on the German calendar. Possibly, she was reading the date wrong. She would talk to Oskar tonight.

That night, Harriet paced the kitchen, anxious for him to return. The initial shock was over. She was rational now. She wasn't sure she was pregnant. Her cycle might be late. It would start tomorrow. But even if she were carrying a child, by the time the baby was born, their circumstances might be different. The Germans were bombing London every night. The *Blitz* must be working. They hadn't had an air raid since the middle of November, almost four months ago. Maybe the war would be over before the baby was due—if there even was a baby.

Oskar stomped up the stairs. Harriet rushed to the door and unchained it, greeting him with a false cheerfulness. The dark circles under his eyes and his stooped posture showed the strain of his job. He would be thirty this year, but he looked like an old man. She didn't need to add to his burden by telling him about some silly suspicion. She heated the left-over cabbage soup and joined him at the table, talking about Irena and what a big help she was with the garbage.

In bed, Oskar fell asleep, but Harriet lay awake, her thoughts circling the possibility of a baby and how Oskar would react. All his life, he worked to provide for his family. When his pa died, he'd quit school to support his mother.

When Oskar proposed, he'd said, "I'll make sure that you and our family never go without."

Since coming to Germany, he worked twelve-hour days, six or seven days a week, and still, their family had to go without. His greatest fear was that he would become like his father—a failure. Oskar wasn't a failure, and she didn't want him to feel that way. She wouldn't tell him until she was sure.

Eeeoooeeeoooeeeooo.

The screeching of the air-raid siren jolted her out of bed. She rushed to Irena and Bridget, who were sitting up in bed, crying.

Oskar was beside her. "Hurry, head for the basement."

CHAPTER
TWENTY

Harriet huddled in the dark basement, leaning against the concrete wall. The damp coldness sent a chill through her. She held Irena, and Oskar sat beside them with Bridget. Four months without an air raid had convinced her that the *Blitz* had wiped out most of Great Britain's resources and the war would soon be over. Tonight's raid must be a fluke or a drill. The routine was familiar. After the sirens sounded, they hunkered in the basement, listening for planes and waiting for the all-clear siren.

Even the families from the other apartments were predictable. The brothers, Big Angelo and Spyros, from across the hall, lay sprawled under the steps, smoking. Sometimes Harriet thought she heard a wireless playing from their apartment, but the government forbade owning radios, so the Albanian brothers were either fool-hardy or brave.

The two couples from the first floor crouched in opposite corners. The younger couple, tall and blonde, were possibly Scandinavian. From the window, Harriet watched them leave each morning together, but return later in the day, separately.

She assumed the woman worked, possibly as a domestic, a clerk, or even a factory worker. Harriet had heard of women working with men in factories. When she'd asked Oskar about it, he said Hitler didn't want women in the factories. Their role was at home.

The gray-haired couple talked the loudest. The man was almost deaf and held a horn-shaped hearing tube to his ear and spoke in guttural tones that sounded Hungarian. His wife was feeble and hobbled down the stairs with a cane.

After an hour on the basement floor, Harriet's body stiffened. She imagined sitting on concrete, cross-legged and several months pregnant. She shook away the image. The all-clear siren would soon blare, and they'd return to their warm beds.

In the distance engines hummed. The sound grew louder. The rafters shook. Fear exploded through her. Airplanes. Tonight's raid wasn't a fluke. Planes, probably carrying bombs, were flying over their flat.

The girls screamed. Harriet was shaking. From under the steps, the brothers yelled something. She didn't understand the words, but she understood the sound of fear.

The humming changed to a rumble. She silently prayed, *God, keep us safe.* Her teeth chattered and the familiar words of the rosary slipped away. She didn't want to die. She wanted to see Irena and Bridget grow up. They deserved a chance to live. She thought about the baby. She wanted to see her baby, too.

It was probably only minutes before the rafters stopped shaking and the rumbling faded, but that was long enough to frighten Harriet and to remind her they were living in a country that was at war.

Irena snuffed back her cries. "Is it over?"

Oskar cleared his throat. "It sounds like the planes are gone, but we have to wait for the all-clear siren."

They stayed another fifteen minutes before the siren sounded. Then Harriet and Oskar carried the girls up the stairs and tucked them into bed. Oskar and the girls fell asleep, but Harriet lay on her back, staring into the darkness. To calm herself, she conjured memories of growing up. During the early years, her childhood had been ideal. In the summer, she'd enjoyed climbing trees, playing with the barn cats, and feeding the animals. In the winter, she built snowmen and ice skated on the pond. Then her brother died, and everything changed. She had not lost just her brother, but her parents, too. She had needed them, but Tata handled his grief by working long hours in fields, and Mamuska became so depressed that she didn't seem to have enough energy even to say Harrietta's full name, so it had been shortened to Harriet.

She vowed her children would have a better childhood than she had. But would Irena and Bridget even remember their peaceful life in Lithuania? And what would her baby know except hunger and fear?

The memories faded. Tomorrow would be better.

Tomorrow was not better. Her cycle didn't start, and at night they were awakened by the shrieking air-raid siren.

Eeeoooeeeoooeeeooo.

Again, they hunkered in the basement, waiting for the all-clear siren. Instead, airplane engines roared, shaking the rafters above and the ground beneath them. Irena and Bridget scrambled into her lap. Harriet embraced them, holding them close and praying they wouldn't die. They huddled in the basement for an hour before the all-clear siren sounded and they could return to their beds, but no one slept.

The following day was miserable. The wind howled and freezing rain pelted the windows. The girls were cross during their school time and spent most of the day bickering. Harriet couldn't take their squabbling. She put them to bed early and returned to the kitchen. Too keyed up to sit, she paused at the sink and peeked out the black curtains.

The rain splattering on the window reminded her of the day Oskar had proposed. They'd been out in the field, digging potatoes, and hadn't noticed the gathering clouds until the rain pelted on them. Leaving the bucket of potatoes, they raced into the barn and climbed the ladder to the hayloft. He tackled her, knocking her on the soft mound of straw. His wet hair fell onto his forehead, curling in wavy locks. Bending over, he lowered his face and pressed his soft lips against hers. This time, his kiss was different, and she reveled in his tenderness. The kiss made her feel as if she were someone to be cherished, someone special.

He propped himself up on one knee and proposed. "If you marry me, I'll take care of you and our children. I'll make sure you never go without."

"I'll marry you," she said, although truthfully, she was disappointed in his proposal. He hadn't said, "I love you." Like most girls, she wanted to hear those three special words. Later, when he told her how he had taken care of his mother after his pa had died in the mine, she understood Oskar showed his love by providing for his family.

Since fleeing to Germany, Oskar worked from sunup to sundown and did not provide what they needed. Each day, she saw the toll on him, so she still had not told him she was pregnant. She was afraid of how he would react.

As she gazed out the window at the foul weather, an ugly word surfaced. *Abortion.* Oskar wasn't Catholic, but Lutheran. What if he decided they wouldn't be able to feed another child? What if he insisted she get rid of it?

She had heard eating carrot seed or Queen Anne's lace would expunge a child. In Lithuania, back-street doctors or immoral midwives did a procedure—for a fee. Harriet let out a cry as lightning zigzagged across the dark sky. She grabbed her belly, trying to protect the baby, and collapsed onto a kitchen chair, keeping her hand covering her flat stomach. She yearned to talk to Oskar about her fears, but what if he told her to get rid of the baby? In her marriage ceremony, she'd vowed to love, honor, and obey. She'd reluctantly agreed to Oskar's decision to come here. But a baby. She looked down at her belly. He wouldn't ask her to harm their baby, would he?

That night when Oskar returned, lack of sleep from the air raids had left dark circles under his eyes. She greeted him with a hug and as usual, warmed up his supper. The bowl of onion gravy shook as she carried it to the table and sat across from him, considering how to broach the subject of the baby. He seemed so tired from working at the factory that he struggled to lift his spoon to his mouth.

When Oskar finished the thin gravy, he pushed back his bowl. "I heard some rumors at the factory today." His voice was weak, and Harriet leaned forward. "Supposedly, in last night's raid, at least two hundred British planes attacked Hamburg."

"I thought the British were ready to surrender."

Oskar leaned back in his chair. "That's what Hitler has been saying, but last night's raid was the deadliest yet. Fifty-one people were killed."

She crossed herself as she tried to absorb the deadly news. "Do you think the war will ever end? I can't bear the thought of living like this forever."

Oskar raked his fingers through his hair. "I'm afraid it's getting worse. I keep working and working and yet..." He waved his hand at the sparsely furnished room. "And yet we have so little."

"We have each other and the children."

His head drooped and his words were even softer. "I'm such a failure."

This was his greatest fear. She had never seen Oskar so

distraught. He was a proud man, but his spirit seemed broken. Reaching across the table, she gripped his hand and squeezed it reassuringly. "We'll find a way to get through this, together."

Now was not the time to mention the baby.

CHAPTER
TWENTY-ONE

April 1941

rena peeked out of the blackout curtains in the bedroom, hoping to see Hanna. During the winter when Irena had asked to go to Hanna's, Mama would say, "It's too cold or it's too windy or Hanna's too sick." Now it was spring, and Mama said, "Another day." Mama probably thought Irena would give up, but she wouldn't. Playing with Hanna was way more fun than playing with Bridget.

Irena shuffled into the kitchen where Mama was sweeping the floor and asked her usual question, "Can we go to Hanna's?"

Mama didn't even stop sweeping. "Another day."

Something inside Irena snapped. She shouted, "This *is* another day."

The broom stilled. Mama stared at her. "*Ja,* you're right." She set the broom in the corner and unpinned the apron. "We'll go but promise to be on your best behavior. No fighting with your sister."

Irena crossed her heart and ran to tell Bridget.

Outside, the air reeked of coal and oil from the factories. She didn't like being cooped up in the flat, so she lagged behind until Mama grabbed her hand. "Hurry, before the soldiers come."

That got her moving. She scampered across the street and up to Hanna's flat. Mama knocked several times before the door cracked open, and Hanna's mother peeked out. She pulled them inside, bolting the door behind her. She wore a shiny black dress that hugged her so tightly she didn't look as if she would be able to sit down, and her shoes were those spikey heels. Mama never wore shoes inside.

"Don't open your door without checking," Hanna's mother warned. "The Germans are rounding up people and hauling them away."

"What people?" Mama asked.

"Jews, gypsies, sick people—"

"Irena, you came," exclaimed Hanna from the doorway. She wore a red dirndl dress with a checked vest and her braided hair rested on the shoulders of her white blouse.

Irena gaped. "You look so…so German." She wished she looked German, but she had on the ugly brown shift they'd given her at the Registration Department.

Crossing the room, Hanna tugged on Irena's and Bridget's hands. "Let's go play."

"Don't overdo it," cautioned Hanna's mother, "and don't open the curtains."

Hanna pulled them into the bedroom and shut the door. The room was dark, but Irena didn't need the light to know what the bedroom looked like. She remembered it from the last time she'd played there, plus it was the same as theirs—two beds and a dresser, only the dresser had an oval mirror hanging above it and the beds were covered with fancy quilts.

"You haven't been at the window all week," Irena said.

"Mommy doesn't want me to open the curtains."

Irena's eyes adjusted to the dim light. "I'm not supposed to open the curtains either, but I do it when Mama's in the other room."

Hanna plunked onto the bed. "I overheard Mommy and Daddy talking. They're worried the soldiers will find out I'm sick and take me away."

Irena sat on one side of Hanna and Bridget on the other. "Take you where?" Irena asked.

"Someplace not nice."

"What would they do to you?"

"One time the doctors said they would cure me. But the medicine and shots made me worse."

"A doctor gave me a shot when we came to Germany. I didn't like it." Irena showed Hanna the scar on her bare arm.

Bridget pushed up the sleeve of her blue seersucker dress and pointed to her arm, too.

Hanna's cough was like a loud rattle in her throat.

Irena scooted away. "You sound awful."

Hanna spit phlegm into her handkerchief. "I'm not as bad as Mrs. Roka."

"Who's she?" Irena asked.

"The lady in the wheelchair. She can't walk, but she has lots of shoes."

Irena had seen the pretty woman in the wheelchair being pushed by her tall husband. "Why does she need shoes if she can't walk?"

Hanna was coughing too hard to answer.

"Let's play nurse," Bridget suggested. "We can use a chair and push Hanna around like Mrs. Roka."

Hanna managed to say, "I can walk."

A sliver of light streamed in between the pulled curtains and landed on the dresser. Perched on top was a baby doll with rosy cheeks and bright red lips. The doll's painted-on blue eyes matched the dress under her white sweater. Irena hadn't seen the doll before. She pointed to it and asked in awe, "Is she yours?"

Hanna nodded. "I got her for Christmas."

Irena stuck out her bottom lip. She'd asked for a doll for Christmas. "Can I play with her?"

Hanna hesitated. "It's hot. Open the window."

"Your mother said to keep the curtains closed."

Hanna coughed again. "I can't breathe. I need air."

Irena didn't want to get into trouble.

"I'll let you play with my doll if you open the curtains."

Irena ached to play with the doll, plus Hanna's breathing sounded as if she needed more air. Maybe Hanna's mother wouldn't find out. Irena tiptoed to the window and raised it.

Flopping onto the bed, Hanna gulped in air. "If you hear Mommy, close it."

Irena scurried to the dresser and pulled down the doll, cradling her in her arms. "What's her name?"

"Gertrude."

Bridget raced to Irena and jerked the doll out of her hands. "I wanna hold her."

Irena grabbed the doll back and darted to Hanna. "Wait your turn."

Hanna snatched the baby and tossed her onto the bed, her legs flopping into the air, showing her pantaloons. "Let's play hide-n-seek."

Bridget grabbed the doll from the bed. Irena glowered. She'd opened the window. She should have the doll. But she'd promised Mama she wouldn't fight with her sister, so she tried to distract her. "Bridget, you're *it*."

"Why do I always have to be *it*?"

"Because you're the youngest."

Bridget laid the doll on the bed and stomped to the door. Facing it, she counted, "One, two, three, four—"

"No peeking," Irena warned, her eyes straying to Gertrude.

Hanna, however, picked up the doll and wiggled under the bed with Gertrude. Irena rushed to the window and hid behind the long blackout curtains.

Bridget called out, "Here I come, ready or not."

Footsteps creaked across the wooden floor toward the bed. Irena silently snickered. Bridget always checked under the bed first.

"Got you," shouted Bridget to Hanna. "Now you're *it*."

Irena slid back the curtains. Hanna was bent over, gasping for air. Irena rushed to her and patted her on the back. The door swung open. Hanna's mother marched in. She placed her hands on her hips.

Irena turned toward the window. Too late.

"Who opened the curtains?"

Irena knew she was in big trouble.

Before she fessed up, Hanna's mother looked around. "Where's Hanna's doll?"

Irena scurried to the bed and pulled the doll from underneath it.

Mama stood in the doorway, scowling. "Girls, you promised to be good."

"We'll be good." Irena handed Gertrude to Hanna, who had stopped coughing.

Mama used her I-mean-business tone. "If there's any more trouble, we'll have to leave."

Hanna's mother lowered the window and shut the curtains. "Hanna, play something quiet, like cat's cradle. That won't wear you out."

Irena didn't know how to play cat's cradle, but she let out a breath of relief when Mama and Hanna's mother walked out of the bedroom and closed the door behind them.

———

While Audra heated a kettle of water, Harriet sat at the table. She was surprised that after months of medicine, Hanna hadn't improved. "Hanna's cough seems worse."

"That's why we keep her in." Audra sat across the table and stared at Harriet. "You seem a little peaked."

This was the opening Harriet had wanted. Taking a deep breath, she let the words spill out. "I might be pregnant."

Audra didn't congratulate her as Harriet expected. "We always wanted more children, and it finally happened about two years ago. A little boy."

Harriet had never seen Audra with any child except Hanna. "Where is he?"

"I don't know. I went—" The kettle whistled, and Audra hurried to the stove. She poured hot water into the teapot on the table and then reached for the cigarettes next to it. Her slender fingers shook as she struck several matches before her cigarette lit.

Audra paced across the kitchen, blowing smoke. "When it was time for my baby to be born, my husband took me to a hospital here in Hamburg. I was in labor almost twenty-four hours."

A swell of womanly sympathy washed through Harriet. "That must have been awful."

Audra waved her hand, pushing the cloud of smoke and Harriet's concern away. "It was the same with Hanna." Audra stopped pacing and tapped her cigarette ashes into the sink filled with dirty dishes. "After I delivered, I saw my baby—a boy. I heard him cry and expected the nurse to put him in my arms, but she said I was exhausted and gave me something to rest. I didn't wake until the next afternoon. That's when the same nurse told me my baby had died."

"Oh, Audra, I'm so sorry." Harriet longed to reach out to Audra, but she looked as if the slightest touch might make her disintegrate like the ashes falling into the sink.

"I asked to see my baby, but the nurse wouldn't bring him to me. She said, 'If you don't look, it won't hurt.' But that's not true." Audra clutched her stomach as if still in pain.

"You never saw him again?"

"No. They wouldn't let my husband see him either." She took several more puffs, lowered her gaze, and stared at Harriet. "My baby cried. I heard him, but the nurse said he was stillborn. If that were true, why wouldn't they let us see him?"

"I don't know." Harriet felt compassion for Audra and her loss but was skeptical about her story. "Why would they lie to you?"

"Maybe they wanted my baby for a German family."

Harriet's hands flew to her chest. "What?"

"Later, I talked to several women, refugees like us, who went to the hospital to deliver babies and came home without them."

"Would they take a baby from its mother?"

Audra flicked her cigarette butt into the sink and let out one of her braying laughs. Picking up the teapot, she poured the steaming liquid into Harriet's cup. "The Nazis can do anything they want. Everyone's too afraid to stop them."

Harriet had planned to ask Oskar to take her to the hospital to deliver. Now she couldn't chance it.

"How far along are you?" asked Audra.

"I'm not sure I'm pregnant. My last cycle was in February, but with so little to eat, my period might have just stopped."

Audra arched her thin brows. "This is April, so less than three months. That's good."

Harriet picked up her cup and took a drink of tea as Audra asked, "Are you keeping the baby?"

Harriet swallowed. The hot tea burned all the way down. "Of course. Why wouldn't I?"

"You have two children. How are you going to feed a third?"

This was one of her concerns and the reaction she worried that Oskar might have, but she had not expected another woman to question her choice, especially a woman mourning the loss of her child. "The extra food you give us for tobacco rations is a big help."

"I don't know how long I can continue to do that. Food is getting scarcer. Even I have to fix an *Eintopf* more than on Sunday."

Harriet had learned only a few German words. "What's that?"

"A one-pot meal. On Sundays, we're supposed to give up our pork roasts and sausages to cook a meal in one pot. It's a Nazi idea—everyone eating the same thing at the same time—a common sacrifice for a common good."

"We don't have meat to give up," Harriet said. "What kind of meal can you make in one pot?"

"Sauerkraut and beans are quite good."

It didn't sound good. "How does this help the Nazis?"

"The money saved from eating a cheaper meal is donated to the war effort. If you don't give, you're stealing from your neighbor. The newspaper wrote an article about it with a picture of Adolf eating stew without meat." Audra rose and walked to the end table. She sifted through the newspapers. "Here it is. The article says, 'Just as faithful Christians unite in the holy sacrament of the Last Supper in service of their lord and master, so, too, do National Socialist Germans celebrate this sacrificial meal as a solemn vow to the unshakeable people's community.'" [1]

Harriet stifled a gasp. The German government was comparing its sacrifices to those of the church and Jesus.

"There's another article you might be interested in. It encourages people to supplement their rations by foraging for food in the forests."

Harriet was interested. "What kind of food?"

"Nuts, berries, mushrooms. Even a lot of greens are edible."

"At Christmas, Oskar cut down a tree from the forest. He might know where to go."

Audra dropped the newspaper on the end table. "My husband's aunt gave me a sweater that's too big. I'll give it to you to make something for the baby."

"Thank you. And if I'm not pregnant, I can use the yarn to crochet sweaters for the girls."

Audra disappeared into the bedroom, and Harriet sipped her tea. For weeks she'd been worried that she might be pregnant. Now she wanted this baby. She just needed to know where to have it. Maybe the Polish woman with three children knew the name of a midwife.

Audra returned carrying the maroon sweater, and Harriet thanked her before asking, "Do you know the Polish woman who lives in the next flat? I don't see her out much."

"You mean Mrs. Novak? Poor woman. I can hear her husband yelling at her all the way over here. Have you noticed how she usually wears a hat that covers her face?"

Harriet had noticed.

"I think her husband drinks and then knocks her around. One time when I was talking to her, I peeked under the brim of her hat, and her face was bruised."

Harriet said a silent prayer of thanks that Oskar wasn't that kind of man.

CHAPTER
TWENTY-TWO

April - May 1941

Harriet settled on the couch, unwinding the yarn from the maroon sweater. April was almost over, and she no longer doubted she was pregnant. Her body was already changing—her breasts were tender, her hips wider, and her belly rounder. By her calculations, the baby was due in November. She needed to tell Oskar. He wouldn't insist on her getting rid of the baby when she was this far along, would he? They'd never discussed abortion, so she didn't know his beliefs.

As if she had conjured him up, Oskar knocked on the door. "Let me in."

The ball of yarn slipped from her hands and rolled across the floor. The last time Oskar had come home from work early was when the Soviets invaded Lithuania.

She hurried to the door and unchained it. Her voice squeaked. "What's wrong?"

"Nothing." Oskar entered, not with the usual stooped shuffle, but with a spring in his step. Leaning over, he balled up the yarn and handed it to her. "They let us off early. Tomorrow is a national holiday."

Harriet checked the wall calendar. Tomorrow was April twentieth. Last Sunday had been Easter, and she'd wanted to go to Mass. They'd lived in Germany for more than eight months, but Oskar discouraged her from attending the Catholic Church.

"Go to the Reich church," he'd said.

"What religion is that?"

"The Nazis started it."

She didn't like the Nazis, so she didn't think she would like their religion. She waited for Oskar to explain the holiday.

"It's Hitler's birthday. Two years ago, when he turned fifty, they made it a national holiday." He took her hands, pulling her up from the couch. "I have better news. I have Sundays off, and my workdays will be shorter."

The girls came out of the bedroom and ran to Oskar, shrieking with the same delight that she felt. He scooped them up and spun them around. Even after he put them down, they clung to him, starving for his attention.

"Will you take us outside, Da?" Irena begged.

"Have you girls been good for your mama?"

The girls squealed, "*Ja, ja,*" and Harriet nodded in agreement.

After Oskar herded them out the door, she tucked the yarn into her sewing bag and laid her head on the couch. She'd just rest for a few minutes. She drifted asleep and was awakened two hours later when Oskar and the girls clattered back into the flat.

That night, Oskar tucked the girls in bed. He was a good father. Tonight, when he wasn't mentally and physically drained, might be the time to tell him she was pregnant. Eventually, he would notice and would be angry she'd kept it from him.

On the other hand, telling him tonight might drag him down. Why not give him time to relax and enjoy his family? A few extra days wouldn't matter.

A few extra days turned into a few extra weeks, and still, she had not told Oskar about the baby. Over the winter the heat from the coal stove had streaked the kitchen walls with soot. She washed down three walls and started on the fourth.

After finishing, she sat and examined the clean walls with satisfaction. If only she were able to wipe away her problem as easily as the soot. During the day, she was afraid of the soldiers, and during the night, she was afraid of the air raids. So far, the planes had dropped their bombs on other sites, but the attacks frightened her and kept Oskar from sleeping.

He'd tried to reassure her. "They're bombing industrial sites, not the projects." But months earlier he'd said, "The air raids are nuisance attacks. We'll never actually be bombed."

Why had she been so naïve? When they fled to Germany, she thought their family would be safe. The fighting would be in other countries, the ones Germany was attacking, but never on German soil.

She added another worry to her list. The baby. She counted the months on the calendar. Her brother had been born in November. Agne with his stubborn cowlick and dimpled cheeks. She was seven years old when he came along. He was like a cuddly doll. She loved feeding him, bathing him, and even changing his nappy. When Agne took his first steps, he had toddled right into her open arms.

She placed her hand on her belly. This child might be a boy. Most men wanted a son, but she still hadn't told Oskar. Last week, during the night, he'd turned to her for comfort. Instead of giving herself to him the way she should have done, the way she ached to do, she'd pretended to be asleep. But soon she would begin to show.

Before she told Oskar, she needed a plan. She'd always found answers at church. She didn't know where a Catholic Church was, but she knew the route to the market and could ask for directions.

The following day, the girls were excited about venturing out. At the store, she approached several women. They all turned away. Then a squat woman holding a bag of produce and a little girl's hand was brave enough to direct her to a Catholic Church. "Walk several blocks that way." She let go of the girl's hand and pointed. "Look for the twin steeples."

It sounded easy. Harriet kept her head up, as she hurried in the direction the woman had pointed. The only steeple spiraling above the buildings was that of St. Nicholi, the Lutheran church, which had once been the tallest building in the world. As she searched, Irena and Bridget complained, but Harriet coaxed them on, wandering a few more streets. The surroundings changed. Store windows had been shattered, and shards of glass lay scattered on the sidewalk. Scrawled on a brick building was *JUDE*. Jew. Another store had its window boarded up and a star of David was painted on the wood.

After she married Oskar and before the girls were born, she was a domestic for the Greenbergs. The Jewish family worked her hard and paid her little money for cooking and cleaning. Sometimes she hid under the dining room table for a break. Still, the job was better than the back-breaking work in the fields with Tata.

She walked barefoot to the Greenbergs and slipped on her shoes before entering their house. One day as she left, Mrs. Greenberg handed her a pair of women's brown leather flats and said, "Throw these away."

Outside, Harriet slipped her feet into the shoes, amazed

they fit. She wore those shoes, even had them resoled several times until finally, she did throw them away.

Where were the Greenbergs now? Before she left Lithuania, she'd heard rumors about the Nazis rounding up thousands of Jewish shopkeepers and killing them. At the time, she'd thought it couldn't be true, but she could not ignore the businesses in this block that had been destroyed.

"Are we there yet?" asked Irena.

"I'm tired," said Bridget.

Harriet prodded them on. "It can't be much farther." After a few blocks, she spotted twin steeples spiraling above the buildings. "There it is." She pointed it out to the girls and walked toward the two steeples until a red-brick cathedral came into view. Next to it stood a smaller brick building, probably the convent.

She paused at the steps leading to the church and glanced around to make sure no one was watching before she withdrew three white handkerchiefs from her pocketbook. "Cover your heads with these."

Irena placed one of the handkerchiefs on her head. "Are we going to church?"

After covering Bridget's head and her own, Harriet said, "Not to Mass. I want to light a candle."

"I want to light one, too," said Irena. "Then Hanna will get well."

Harriet climbed the steps and tugged on the door, relieved it wasn't locked. She waved the girls in. At the font of holy water, she dipped her fingers, crossed herself, and motioned for Irena and Bridget to do the same.

When they finished, Harriet walked into the domed sanctuary. The high cathedral ceiling and massive marble columns were embellished with gold, but it wasn't the ornate surroundings that moved her. It was the holiness that enveloped her, giving her a sense of peace. For the first time since coming to

Germany, she'd found a place where she felt as if she belonged.

Gripping the girls' hands, she led them down the side aisle. Their footsteps tapped on the marble floor, echoing through the empty church. She stopped in front of a life-sized statue of the Virgin Mary. Her head was covered in a white cloth and her body was adorned in a light blue robe. Her outstretched hands welcomed them, and as Harriet gazed at Mary, the holy Mother's eyes bore into her soul.

Dropping to her knees, Harriet pulled the girls down with her, bowing at Mary's sandaled feet. A few of the votive candles that surrounded the base of the statue were lit. From her handbag, Harriet removed a knotted handkerchief that held a precious coin and dropped it into a small collection box. When she struck a match and lit a candle, the flame sputtered, dancing in the air.

Closing her eyes, she folded her hands and silently prayed, *Mother Mary, intercede on my behalf. Help me deliver my child safely into this world.* Harriet had always felt close to Mary. She'd birthed a child and understood the joys and sorrows of motherhood. But Mary had also suffered the pain of losing her child.

Harriet had two daughters. She already thought of the baby as her third child, and she couldn't lose it, not after she had lost her brother.

Harriet had been eleven when she and most of her schoolmates had contracted measles. She was quarantined to her room, but Agne, who was four, sneaked in. She warned him, "Go away. I have measles."

Agne crawled into her bed. "I want measles, too."

"No, you don't. They hurt." Light sent shards of pain shooting through her eyes, and her body itched from the welts of red rash.

Two weeks later, Agne got his wish. He broke out in

measles. "Take them away. I don't want them anymore." He was a mass of red spots. Even his head and ears were covered, and he developed a hacking cough.

After ten days, Harriet's measles had vanished. On Agne's tenth day, his fever spiked. Her mother made him sip water, spoon-fed him chicken broth, and wiped his forehead with a cold rag. When that didn't lower his fever, Mamuska immersed him in a tub of cold water. Still, his fever rose.

Mamuska begged Tata, "Fetch the doctor."

He was reluctant. "Let the measles run their course."

Several hours later, Agne's fever worsened. "Please, you have to do something," Mamuska pleaded.

Finally, Tata saddled Dolly and rode into town for the doctor. It seemed like hours before horses galloped up the lane. Mamuska laid Agne in Harriet's arms. "Hold him while I hurry them in."

As soon as the door slammed, Agne's head flopped back, and his eyes closed. Harriet rocked her brother's limp body and bargained with God. *I'll be good, do everything Tata and Mamuska ask, if only you'll make Aggie well.*

Harriet believed God and the doctor would save her brother. But after the doctor examined Agne, he shook his head. "He's slipped into a coma."

When her brother died, Harriet blamed herself. She had given him measles. His death was her fault. She had never experienced death before and didn't understand how life could go on. Rye was planted and harvested. Goats were fed and milked. Chickens roosted and laid eggs. Only Harriet remained stuck. She would glance over her shoulder, expecting to find Agne nipping at her heels. Sometimes she imagined his voice calling, "Wait for me, Harriet."

During planting and harvesting season, Tata kept her home from school to help in the fields. Farm work was back-breaking labor. While Tata plowed, she guided Dolly down the rows and checked for rocks in the soil. After her father cut the rye or hay with a scythe, she gathered the bundles and tied them with wire. She didn't mind the work. She enjoyed watching the crops spring up in the fields and felt the satisfaction of a bountiful harvest. And even though the sun baked down on her and the wind cut into her cheeks, she stoically accepted it as punishment for being alive while Agne was dead.

As she kneeled in front of Mary, she still ached for her little brother. A tear trickled down her cheek, followed by another and another. She'd promised herself she would not let the girls see her cry. Turning her head, she wiped her face on her sleeve. She waited for her heart to quit racing and the tears to stop flowing. Finally, she opened her eyes and reached for Irena's hand. It wasn't there.

Bridget was kneeling beside her, but where was Irena? She scanned the church and let out a breath. Irena was sitting in the front pew next to a nun.

Harriet gripped Bridget's hand and hurried to Irena and the nun, who sat with their heads together, whispering. Harriet interrupted, "I'm sorry, Sister. I hope my daughter isn't disturbing you."

The nun glanced up. Light from the stained-glass window illuminated the Sister's face, giving her a brilliant glow. Her rosy cheeks and fresh-milk complexion made her look as young as a schoolgirl. "Your daughter tells me this is the first time you've been here."

Harriet was surprised and delighted that the nun spoke Lithuanian. "Yes, we came to light a candle. But how is it you know our language?"

Longing clouded the nun's blue eyes. "Lithuania is my homeland. I'm from Jovana but fled when the Soviets closed our church."

"Jovana. That's north of our town, Kaunas. We also fled when the Soviets invaded."

"So sad for Lithuania." The nun reached out and took Harriet's hand, pulling her down onto the pew beside her. A connection passed between them. "I'm Sister Anne Lian. Do you have a special prayer request?"

Harriet glanced at Irena and Bridget. "Could we speak in private?"

The nun nodded and rose.

"Girls, stay here. I need to talk to Sister."

Sister Anne led the way. They stopped near Mary's statue, and Harriet confessed she was pregnant and afraid to have the baby at a German hospital because of what she had learned from Audra.

"I suspect your friend is right," Sister Anne said. "I know of several women who went to German hospitals and came home without their babies." The nun reached out and held Harriet's hand. "I will pray for you and your baby."

When Harriet left the church, her steps were lighter. She felt as if God had answered her prayers. She just didn't know what His answer was.

CHAPTER
TWENTY-THREE

That night Harriet sat on the divan in the living room, crocheting booties for the baby. As she worked, she rocked forward and back, the motion calming her. Today was Saturday. For the girls, Saturday was like other days. After breakfast, Harriet taught them lessons and then gave them homework that she would check later in the day. Irena and Bridget were so bright, she flushed with pride. But they didn't look forward to Saturday the way she did when she was young. On Saturdays, Tata would load the filled egg crates onto the bed of the truck, and the family would pile into the cab to drive to town. Their first stop was Livergood's General Store, where Mamuska would barter eggs for sugar, flour, and other staples.

When Harriet was older, Saturdays still meant going to Livergood's, but not to barter eggs. Instead, she secretly met Oskar. After her parents found out he was Lutheran, they forbade her from seeing him. They'd picked out what they considered a nice Catholic boy for her to marry. Oskar wasn't Catholic, but he was a hard worker, and she finally convinced Tata and Mamuska Oskar's religion didn't matter, but she and Oskar had never discussed abortion, and she couldn't keep the pregnancy from him any longer. The girls would tell him about their visit to the church, and he would ask why she had gone. Besides, eventually, he would notice the changes in her body and be angry she hadn't told him.

On the other hand, he had little time to spend with the girls. Why not let him enjoy the weekend before she added to his worries?

As she crocheted, her mind flipped back and forth. Tell him. Don't tell. Tell him. Don't tell.

The door opened and Oskar came in.

Harriet berated herself for not chaining the door when she'd gone to the water closet. As she hastily put the booties into her sewing bag, she pricked her finger on a needle. "Ouch!"

Oskar hurried to her. Kneeling in front of her, he grabbed her hand and brought her bleeding finger to his lips, kissing it tenderly. "You look tired, Harriet. Did the girls give you trouble today?"

She was touched that as hard as he worked, he was concerned about her. She opened her mouth to say the girls weren't a problem, but his compassion undid her. "I'm pregnant. I didn't plan it. I thought I was careful."

She looked for that glint of pride to shine in his eyes. She didn't see it. A lump formed in her throat. "I'm sorry, Oskar. I know this makes it harder on you."

He let go of her hand and slid onto the couch next to her. He hunched forward as if he shouldered the weight of her words and stared at her stomach. "How far along are you?"

Instinctively, her hand moved to her small pouch. Maybe she should say two months instead of over three, but she'd never lied to him before. She already felt guilty for her duplicity. He deserved the truth. She swallowed the lump. "More than twelve weeks."

He lowered his head and shook it. "Why didn't I notice?"

She didn't want him to blame himself. "Oskar, we barely see each other or have time to talk."

He lifted his head. "You could have found time to mention you're pregnant."

The anger she'd expected earlier sounded in his voice. She hurried to explain. "At first I wasn't sure and didn't want to worry you."

"And later?"

She steeled herself and didn't answer. She didn't want to say the word and give it more power over her.

He touched her face and tilted it up. His gray eyes weren't swirling with anger. They seemed puzzled. "Do you think something's wrong with the baby?"

She shook her head. "Nothing like that."

"Then what?"

She would have to tell him. She forced herself to say the vile word aloud. "Abortion."

He bolted off the couch. "You're considering an abortion? Have you taken something?"

Each word struck her. She shook her head in disbelief. "No, no." Why would he think she would even consider an abortion? He surely knew it was against her religion. "I was afraid *you* would want me to have an abortion."

"Me?" He stepped farther away from her.

At that moment, she understood how her deceit must feel to him. She needed to make this right. Standing, she took his hand, pulled him back to the couch, and sank onto his lap. "I'm sorry, Oskar."

She wrapped her arms around his neck and laid her head on his shoulder, soaking in the factory's smell that now was his. She'd married a good man. The war and the air raids and all her worries had tangled her thoughts until she expected the bad. "I should have told you sooner. I should have known you wouldn't want me to get rid of our baby. But it's—it's another mouth to feed."

He placed his hand on her stomach. "I admit our life in Germany isn't what I expected. But we have to work together, not keep secrets from each other."

"You're right. I just didn't know how much the war had changed you."

"I can't deny it. The war has affected me. Each day Hans Weber, one of the German guards, struts about like a peacock, spouting Nazi philosophy and bragging about how many people the bombs we make have killed. And for what? What did the British do to the Germans?"

It always came back to the war. "How much longer do you think it will go on?"

"I'm not sure. At the factory, the guards seem jubilant, as if something good is about to happen. Maybe it will be over soon. Maybe even before the baby is born." Possessively, he moved his hand onto her stomach. "Until then, we have something to look forward to. A new baby will bring us joy."

She wanted the baby to be a joy. "But how will we manage?"

"Our rations will increase. In Germany they have this saying, 'Women are created for the three K's: *Kirche, Küche, Kinder* ' meaning church, kitchen, and children. Hitler honors women who have four children with a *Muttercreuz,* a Mother's Cross."

"What if a woman has more children?"

"A silver cross symbolizes six, and a gold cross is for eight or more." His gray eyes softened. "After this baby is born, do you want to try for more?"

She playfully shoved him away. "How will we manage even one more?"

Oskar's gray eyes twinkled with that glint of pride. "God

blessed us with another child, so as you always say, God will provide."

CHAPTER
TWENTY-FOUR

June 1941

After Harriet told Oskar about the baby, he became more attentive, even suggesting she might want to take a walk on Sundays, something they'd done with her other pregnancies.

As she descended the stairs, she placed one hand on the wooden railing and the other on her round belly, which barely was visible in the wrap-around purple paisley. She wanted to feel the baby stir. Nothing, not even a twinge. By her calculations, the baby would be over four months along. Irena and Bridget had moved in the second trimester. Was it unusual for the quickening to happen later?

At first, Harriet was worried she *was* pregnant. Now she was worried something was wrong with the baby. The image of the three tiny crosses, Agne and the two babies who had been born later, was seared into her memory. If she were in Lithuania, she'd talk to her mother and her friends. She'd written to her parents telling them about the baby. The letter had been posted weeks ago, right after she'd told Oskar she was pregnant, but she hadn't received a reply to that letter or the previous ones.

At the bottom of the stairs, Oskar held the door open for her and the girls. She walked out into the gray day filled with the factory fumes that made it difficult to breathe. Summers in Lithuania were sunshine and cool breezes from the river. She pushed her longing for home away and hooked her arm through Oskar's.

The girls walked hand-in-hand behind them. "Where are we going?" Irena asked.

"Just for a walk," Oskar answered.

Since fleeing to Germany, Oskar had changed. In Lithuania, he enjoyed his work at the candy factory and entertained the family with his stories. In Germany, Oskar didn't tell stories. Each morning, he clenched his jaw and resolutely walked out the door. At night, he shuffled into the flat, his head low. He rarely complained. He thought providing for the family was his responsibility.

They strolled through the brick archway of the projects and down the sidewalk a few blocks before he turned the corner. He jerked to a stop. Harriet glanced up. Halfway down the block, German soldiers with guns barked out orders to a gang of men digging a huge hole. The men wore gray-striped pants and no shirts. Heavy chains wrapped around their ankles, binding them together.

Oskar stepped back, inching toward the corner, pulling Harriet with him. Silently she prayed the soldiers wouldn't see them. Too late. One soldier glared in their direction and pointed his gun at them. Oskar let go of Harriet's arm and moved in front of her. She grabbed Irena's and Bridget's hands, pushing them behind her.

Two soldiers marched forward. The thumping of their boots

on the brick sidewalk matched the thumping of her heart. The soldiers stopped in front of Oskar, towering over him as they barked at him in German. He reached into his shirt pocket and removed the family's identification papers. The younger man with flushed cheeks snatched the documents. His eyes swept over Oskar. Then he passed the papers to the other soldier, who had a thick mustache that covered most of his upper lip.

Harriet swallowed. Was something wrong with their documents? She remembered the day in the store that she had been questioned, and she had witnessed soldiers stopping other people on the street, questioning them, and then whisking them away. One day, two soldiers had halted a family of four, but had seized only the man, leaving his wife and two children kneeling on the street, wailing his name. What would she do if the soldiers took Oskar away? She wouldn't know where he was or how to find him. She didn't have her amber rosary, but she silently prayed the familiar words, *Hail Mary, full of grace…*

The soldier with the mustache tromped around Oskar and stared at Harriet. He ran his finger along the line of black hair above his sneering mouth, eyeing her up and down as if she were a tasty piece of meat. Her legs went limp. She squeezed the girls' hands, hiding behind her, and forced herself not to cower. She needed to appear strong for them.

Oskar moved closer to her. He said something to the soldier in German, his voice taking on a concerned tone. The soldier stumbled backward, flinging the papers at Oskar and waving them on. Grabbing the papers, he put his arm protectively around her waist. She held Bridget's hand, and Oskar held Irena's as they followed well behind the retreating soldiers.

Even with her head lowered, Harriet sensed when they neared the prisoners digging. She peeked out the corners of her eyes. The men's bare chests were slick with sweat. More prisoners were at the bottom, shoveling dirt into buckets that were hoisted up by ropes. The depth of the hole surprised her.

The family walked in silence for several blocks before Oskar stopped to rest under a shady oak. Irena peppered him with questions. "Who are those men? Why are they wearing leg chains? Why are they digging?"

Oskar held up the palm of his hand for her to stop. "They're digging an air-raid shelter, probably for us. Thousands are being built in Hamburg."

Harriet gasped. "Is the bombing going to get worse?"

"Not necessarily. We'll just be better protected in a bunker rather than our basement."

Harriet understood his logic, but she wasn't convinced. To her, more bomb shelters meant the Germans expected the Allies to drop more bombs. "What did you say to those soldiers?"

"I told them we were taking a walk because my wife was ill, and I hoped the air would make her better."

Irena rushed to her. "Mama, are you sick?"

"No." She placed her hand on her round belly. "Da was just tricking the soldiers."

Irena looked up, her chin quivering. Harriet wasn't sure Irena believed the little white lie. Harriet hadn't told her and Bridget about the baby yet. The image of the three little crosses worried her. She didn't want the death of a child to shroud their childhood, too.

CHAPTER
TWENTY-FIVE

On the last Sunday in June, the family took what was now their usual walk and stopped at the open-air market. Oskar led Harriet to the cheese vendor who, despite the heat, wore a leather vest over a sweat-soaked shirt that made him smell as ripe as his cheese.

"Send the girls to look at flowers," Oskar said. "I want to buy a little snack for you and the baby."

Harriet shooed the girls away. The baby hadn't moved yet. Oskar must be concerned, too, if he would spend money on food for her. Hungrily, she eyed the display of cheeses set out on the table—pie-shaped wedges, white and yellow wheels, and rectangles as big as bricks. She pointed to Limburger. It smelled, but the odor would linger long after the taste was gone. Even the stinky cheese man turned up his nose as he cut a slice and placed it in her palm.

She nibbled on the cheese, letting it melt in her mouth. Growing up, she had often eaten Limburger between thick slices of rye bread. The taste sent a wave of homesickness through her, making her side quiver. Or had the baby kicked? She waited. Nothing happened. Had she imagined the baby moving? She rested her hand slightly above her hip. Another small nudge. It was not her imagination. The baby was alive. Excited to share the news, she turned to Oskar, who was talking to the vendor.

Even after ten months in Hamburg, she had learned only a few German words. "*Litauen*," Lithuania, followed by "*Sowjetunion,*" the Soviet Union, caught her attention. The cheese man's voice boomed as he repeated, "*Deutschland. Deutschland.*" Harriet knew that was Germany, but couldn't understand the conversation, only the pompous pride in the man's voice.

The more he boasted about Germany, the more animated he became. His dark bushy eyebrows lifted and fell while his rotund chest in the leather vest puffed in and out like a wheezy accordion.

On the way home, Oskar threw his arm around her shoulder. His gray eyes locked on her. He was that young man at the well, smiling at her in a way that made her feel special. "I have good news."

"So do I," said Harriet.

Oskar glanced back at Irena and Bridget. "Let's wait until the girls are asleep."

That night, after Harriet put the girls to bed, she sat on the divan next to Oskar.

"What's your news?" he asked.

She placed his hand on her stomach. "The baby moved today."

Oskar's face lit up and his eyes twinkled. "That's wonderful."

"What did you want to tell me?"

"Last week, Germany drove the Soviets out of Lithuania."

She threw up her hands. "My prayers have been answered." Until this moment, she hadn't admitted how much she hated living in Germany. She'd felt as if she were trapped in a dark cave and now was free to step into the light. She slid off the divan and kneeled on the floor. "Thank you, God, for keeping us safe and freeing our country." As she struggled to rise, Oskar put out a helping hand. "I thought we might have to live in Germany for years, but this means we can go home."

Oskar's smile slipped. "I'm not sure we should leave yet."

Harriet's joy plummeted. "Why not?"

"The man at the market didn't say anything about Lithuania gaining its independence. Instead, he boasted about how Lithuania belongs to Germany."

"That's better than the Soviets. We live under German rule here."

Oskar pulled her next to him on the divan. "It's not that simple. We can't just pick up and leave."

"Why not? We have our train tickets."

"But we need travel documents. Besides, we came here without knowing what was ahead. When we go back, I want to have a place to live, a job, and most of all, I want to be sure it's safe for you and the girls."

"We can live with my parents, and you can help Tata with the crops."

"We considered living on the farm before fleeing to Germany, but we were afraid the Soviets would seize it. Maybe they already have."

She wanted to ignore the possibility that her parents were no longer on the farm and might have been exiled, but what if Oskar was right? "I'll write my parents again about the baby and work in some questions asking if it's safe."

Oskar rubbed his chin. "Okay. But don't tell the girls. I don't want them getting their hopes up about going home."

Harriet's mouth crinkled in a smile. She already had her hopes up. The Germans had ousted the Soviets. Her family was going home.

CHAPTER
TWENTY-SIX

The next day, Harriet peeked out of the blackout curtains. She wanted to talk to Audra and find out what she knew about the Germans driving the Soviets out of Lithuania. When Audra and Hanna emerged from their apartment, Harriet rounded up the girls and dashed across the street.

Before Harriet greeted Audra, a tall man in a double-breasted gray suit and Fedora rounded the corner, pushing a tiny woman in a wooden wheelchair. The suit hung on the razor-thin man, making him appear too frail to be able to push the woman, who looked like a child except she wore dangling earrings and had a dark braid coiled on top of her head. Even in the scorching heat, the woman's lap and legs were covered by a colorful block afghan.

Harriet had seen the couple before but was surprised when the man spoke in Lithuanian. "The soldiers are coming. Get into your flats."

After scooping up Hanna, Audra glanced back at Harriet. "Come with us. You might not have time to cross the street."

The thump of the soldiers' boots grew closer. Harriet

shooed the girls up the stairs and into the flat. She chained the door while Audra carried Hanna into the bedroom, followed by Irena and Bridget. "Play quietly," Audra said to the girls, "and don't open the curtains."

As soon as Audra returned to the kitchen, Harriet asked her about the frail man and the woman in the wheelchair. "Who are they?"

Audra lit a cigarette. "The Rokas. I think they're from Lithuania, too."

"Do you know what's wrong with her?"

Audra puffed on her cigarette, blowing out smoke. "Jonas, that's the husband, mentioned something about Rosa having polio. It's a shame they don't have children. Rosa is so good with Hanna, always taking time to talk to her and show off her shoes. Poor Jonas. They were assigned a flat on the second floor, and he has to carry her up and down the stairs."

The way his suit had hung on his sharp bones made him appear weak. "He must be stronger than he looks," said Harriet.

"They don't go out much now. They probably don't want the soldiers to see Rosa in a wheelchair."

Harriet was interested in the Rokas, but she was desperate to find out information about Lithuania. "Is it true? Have the Germans freed Lithuania?"

Audra continued to smoke before she answered. "The Germans have claimed Lithuania, Latvia, and the other Baltic countries for themselves. This time it's not just Hitler's propaganda."

Tears streamed down Harriet's cheeks. Her prayers had been answered. She didn't have to worry about the baby being born in Germany. They were going home.

"When will you return to Latvia?" Harriet asked.

"I'm not sure we will. The doctor here thinks he can help Hanna."

Hanna didn't look like she was getting better, but Harriet

didn't want to upset Audra by asking why Hanna was still so sick.

"Latvia isn't our home anymore," said Audra.

The comment puzzled Harriet. Audra had said they were from Latvia. Why didn't she consider that Baltic country her home?

"I received a letter from my cousin in Lithuania. Before the Germans arrived, the Soviets tried to wipe out as many Lithuanians as possible. One night in June, they rounded up over fifteen thousand Lithuanians, including women, children, and infants. They packed them into cattle cars and shipped them to Siberia."

"Those poor Jews," Harriet said.

"Not just Jews. There were Poles and Lithuanians, too. It didn't matter to the Soviets. They wanted to send a message to anyone resisting Soviet policies, and they wanted free labor."

Harriet felt dizzy. Had her parents been seized and herded away? Is that why they hadn't answered her letters? She vowed to write them again.

"Except for my cousin, I don't even know who's left in Lithuania or Latvia," said Audra.

"Other family members and friends must still be there. And your city."

"In Latvia, we lived in Riga. German tanks rolled in and heavily damaged the town. My cousin said that St. Peter's Church, where Konstantin and I were married and where Hanna was baptized, is nothing but ashes."

Harriet had never considered that the Kaunas she left might not be the Kaunas she would return to.

Audra ground the butt of her cigarette into the ashtray with such force it seemed as if she were trying to squash the Soviets herself. "At least this time the Soviets won't come out on top."

Harriet wanted to believe the Germans would be victorious. "How do you know?"

"Konstantin prints the news. According to sources other than Hitler, the Germans are close to Moscow and the German troops are expected to be home by Christmas."

Home by Christmas. Harriet and her family would be celebrating Christmas in Lithuania with their new baby.

CHAPTER
TWENTY-SEVEN

That night Harriet sat at the kitchen table, writing a letter to her parents. The kerosene lamp cast a yellow glow on the single sheet of paper. When she had previously written them, the Soviets had been in charge. Now that the Germans controlled Lithuania, she was more hopeful that her letter would be delivered.

As she wrote, her hand jerked, messing up the word 'home.' She erased the crooked letters and wrote it again, but her fingers, like her mind, had a will of their own. Ever since she'd heard the news that Germany had freed Lithuania from the Soviets, she was determined to have the baby at home.

When Oskar told her Hitler was a great leader and was improving Germany, she didn't agree, especially after their treatment at the Registration Department. She didn't like the way Jews and other groups were labeled inferior, but now she understood why many Germans revered Hitler as if he were a god. She didn't agree with all of Hitler's policies, but she admitted he deserved praise and adoration. Hitler and the German army had saved her country. She and her family could return to Lithuania, and they would be safe from those barbaric Soviets.

Harriet scribbled her name at the bottom of the letter and stuffed it into an envelope. The baby needed clothes, but she couldn't concentrate on the tiny stitches, not when her hormones were raging. One minute she wanted to dance around the apartment, sure that she would have the baby at home. The next she was battling tears, afraid that Oskar would remain adamant about not leaving.

Each day, the war became more real. When they'd arrived in Germany, the air raids had been just a few planes that Oskar called 'nuisance raids' because they deprived him of his sleep. Recently, the air raids seemed to be dozens of planes—with bombs. Still, the explosions had been far away. But that could change. And she didn't want to be here when the projects were bombed.

The war, with its terrible hardships of bombs and food shortages, had stripped away Irena's and Bridget's childhoods. Harriet wanted better for them and the new baby. Tomorrow she would post the letter, but a reply might take weeks or even months. She logically understood why Oskar wanted to wait. He needed to know they would have a safe place to live, and he would have a job.

In the past, she would have accepted his decision. He was her husband, and she respected him, but now she wasn't thinking logically. She was thinking emotionally. She had a new life to protect, and she couldn't do it in Germany.

For the next several days, Harriet tried to persuade Oskar to leave. He still refused, although he'd agreed to apply for their travel documents in case a letter arrived, assuring them it was safe to go home. She hated this tension between them. As she waited for him to return from work, she took deep breaths. Stress wasn't good for the baby. Maybe she should give in. She would have done that before. But was she too weak to stand up to her husband for what she felt in her bones was right for her and her family?

"Harriet," Oskar called from the hallway.

She unchained the door and Oskar walked in, waving papers in his hands. "Our travel documents."

She danced over to him. Her prayers had been answered. She touched the papers. The documents were real. This wasn't a dream. Now they could go home. "How were you able to get them so quickly?"

Reaching down, Oskar placed his hand on her stomach. "Because you're pregnant." He walked to the table and sank into a chair. "And because Lithuania is now part of Germany."

Harriet moved to the stove and warmed Sunday's *Eintopf* of sauerkraut and beans. She hadn't dwelled on Lithuania belonging to Germany. Surely that wouldn't matter. What was important was that the Germans had driven out the Soviets. An image of the soldiers in the store questioning her and another image of soldiers dragging a man from his family flashed through her mind. But those injustices wouldn't happen in Lithuania.

To the Lithuanians, the Germans were heroes. They'd saved their country from the Soviets. Harriet kept her back to Oskar as she stirred the one-pot meal. "At least the Germans aren't as barbaric as the Soviets." Harriet thought any occupiers would be better than the Russians, who had ruled Lithuania for over a hundred years until the WWI treaty had granted Lithuania its freedom. Perhaps Germany would occupy Lithuania for a short time and then give them independence. She glanced over her shoulder at Oskar. Now that they had the travel documents, maybe Oskar would soften. "When can we leave?"

"I still want to wait until we receive word from your parents."

She couldn't hide her frustration. "I just mailed the letter to my parents last week. A reply might not come for months." She vigorously stirred the beans and sauerkraut. They were repeating the same arguments. Harriet wanted to leave Germany as soon as possible. Oskar wanted to stay until he had more facts. She didn't want to worry Oskar, but she was concerned about the lack of food and stress on the baby.

After her brother had contracted measles and died, her mother wanted more children. A year later, she became pregnant. The baby was a tiny girl born prematurely. Sofije weighed barely a kilogram. Mamuska didn't produce enough milk, so they tried to feed little Sofije goat's milk, but in less than a week she wasted away, and the family buried a second child.

For months Mamuska was despondent. Then she became pregnant a third time. The baby was a boy, Tomas. He was born blue and never took a breath. After Tomas, her mother gave up. She said she couldn't bury another child.

Harriet was haunted by her siblings. She still could hear little Sofije's cries and see the unnatural color of Tomas's face. One day Oskar had noticed the three wooden crosses, and she told him about Agne and the babies.

The plate of sauerkraut and beans shook as she carried it to the table and set it in front of Oskar. She slipped into the seat across from him and reached for his hand, squeezing it. "I don't want to go through what my mother experienced with the babies who came after me. I don't think I could survive if I lost this child."

Oskar jerked his hand away and began to eat. Surely, he hated their life here as much as she did, and yet he wouldn't leave. Her voice trembled as she asked, "Is there something you're not telling me?"

He raised his head. Despair swirled in his gray eyes.

"What is it? Whatever it is, we can get through it together."

"That's just it. We won't be together."

She drew back. "Why not?"

"You and the girls can return to Lithuania, but they won't let me leave my job."

"You're a guest worker, not a slave laborer. We came here to flee from the Soviets, but they're gone, so why can't you leave?"

"If I could have left, Harriet, I would have when they first forced me to work in the bomb factory. I would have moved to a different city or a different job. But in Germany, you do what you're told."

All her hopes and plans ended. She couldn't leave without Oskar. The main reason she had agreed to come to Germany was to keep the family together. She fingered the documents on the table, tempting her. She had to give up her dream of having the baby at home. "I won't leave without you. Besides, the girls and I can't travel that far alone."

"You wouldn't be alone. I can have four days' leave, enough time to accompany you to Lithuania and return."

Relief flooded through her. "Once we're home, you can apply to stay. Or my parents can hide you." Oskar didn't respond. She wanted to return home, but not without him. "If the girls and I go back, promise me you'll stay with us."

Oskar shook his head. "I can't promise, but I'll try."

The next day, Harriet vacillated. Home—stay. Home—stay. Life would be better for the girls and the baby if they returned to Lithuania. But what would their life be like without Oskar? And what about his life? Would he take care of himself? He had to work at the factory and then come home and cook and clean. Another question surfaced. Was their love strong enough to survive the separation?

Staying seemed unfathomable. The rations, the air raids, the constant surveillance. Staying wasn't living. It was surviving.

On Thursday night, Oskar returned from work with a railroad schedule. "A train leaves Hamburg at seven a.m. on

Saturday morning. It travels through Kaunas. If that's what you and the baby need, we can leave Saturday."

Her heart leaped. She was going home, yet she was conflicted. What if Oskar was sent back to Germany? What if he wasn't there when the baby was born?

Oskar cocked his head at her. "I thought this is what you wanted. I thought you'd be happy."

Harriet hugged him, already dreading the possibility they might be separated. "It is, but I don't want to go home without you."

"I'll try to stay with you and the girls," he said. "I just can't promise."

On Friday, Harriet made Irena and Bridget take an afternoon nap. When they were asleep, Harriet pulled the suitcase from under the bed and began packing their clothes. She hadn't told the girls they were going home. They would be too impatient to leave. Even Harriet was impatient. She couldn't wait to see her parents and make sure they were safe. She wanted them to see how much Irena and Bridget had grown and tell them about the baby.

Harriet pushed away thoughts that her parents might not be at the farm as she packed her sewing bag, plus the few garments she'd made for the baby. She considered what else they would need. She wanted to be better prepared than when they'd come, but since they would live with her parents, they wouldn't need much.

In the kitchen, she opened the cupboard and gathered the staples and a few canned goods. Her hand fluttered as she reached for the last can. Tuna fish. The day she'd found the lone can of tuna on the top shelf of the cupboard had given her hope. It was foolish, but instead of pulling the can down, she stood on her toes and planted it on the top shelf for the next poor family to find.

The door to the bedroom opened. Irena walked in, yawning.

She stared at the suitcase on the table. Her green eyes widened in fear. "Where-where are we going?"

Unable to hide her excitement, Harriet beamed. "Home."

Irena jumped up and down. Then she stopped and her body deflated. "What about the Soviets?"

"The Germans ran them out."

With all the enthusiasm of a six-year-old, she dashed into the bedroom yelling, "We're going home."

"We're going home," echoed Harriet as she latched the suitcase and pushed away the niggling fear about what awaited them.

CHAPTER
TWENTY-EIGHT

June 29, 1941

Before dawn, Harriet stood in her bedroom, wearing her winter coat, too tight to button. Her hair was rolled at the nape of her neck and secured with bobby pins. She had put on her oldest dress, the green checked, because now that Lithuania was part of Germany, they might have a Registration Department to enter the country.

She hurried into the kitchen where her family waited. Oskar opened the door. "Let's go."

"Oh, no," cried Irena. "I forgot my rock." She darted into the bedroom.

"I have to pee." Bridget raced down the hall to the water closet.

Oskar scowled. "I thought they were ready."

Harriet shrugged. "We have a little extra time. The train doesn't leave until seven a.m."

Oskar stepped into the hall while Harriet stood in the

kitchen. She wouldn't miss these mossy green walls or waking up each day to fear. She wouldn't miss listening for the air-raid siren and huddling in the basement, praying they wouldn't be bombed. Resting her hand on her round stomach, she tried to conjure up good memories of her life here. The baby, and it was for the baby and the girls that Harriet had fought so hard to leave.

Irena ran past her. "Come on, Mama."

Harriet took one last look and walked out of the apartment, closing the door behind her. That life was over. They were going home.

The night was dark, and the overcast sky obscured the moon and stars. She followed the shape of Oskar and the tapping of his shoes as he carried their suitcase and led the way under the archway and onto the cobblestone street.

Every time they turned a corner, one of the girls would ask, "How much farther?"

Oskar finally snapped. "Be quiet. We're out after curfew."

Harriet had been so overjoyed about returning home, she hadn't considered the danger. What if they were stopped? They had their travel documents, but the Brownshirts didn't need a reason to harass people, and if soldiers stopped them for questioning, they'd miss the train.

Sweat trickled down her back as she conjured a plethora of problems. *What if the train is full? Or it's late? Or it never arrives?* She drew in deep breaths, trying to shake off the night terrors. Oskar had the tickets, and they'd left in plenty of time to reach the station before seven. She squinted through the darkness, searching for the depot. Nothing. No train station, but no Brownshirts or SS either.

After walking for more than half an hour, her feet hurt and, like the girls, she wanted to ask, "How much farther?"

The clop-clop-clop of horses' hooves on the cobblestones cut through the ebony darkness. Were those soldiers on horseback ready to arrest her family for being out after curfew? The clop-clop-clop was followed by the rattling of a wagon. In the distance, a locomotive whistled.

Harriet whooshed out a breath of relief. The railway station must be close. She quickened her pace. Within the hour, they'd board the train and begin their journey home.

Hope swelled in her chest. Everything was going to be all right. They would live in Lithuania. Oskar would not return to Germany but stay and work for Tata. The girls would go to school, and Harriet would birth a healthy baby. As if to agree, the baby bumped her side. Almost giddy, Harriet chuckled. Even the baby was kicking with joy about leaving.

Eeeoooeeeoooeeeooo.

The air-raid siren screeched. Harriet's heart slammed against her chest. The girls screamed and clawed at her coat. Their family was alone in the dark street. Unprotected. Vulnerable.

Eeeoooeeeoooeeeooo.

An air raid couldn't be happening now. Not when they were so close to leaving.

"We have to find shelter," said Oskar, as a searchlight turned on. Beams, like long steel sabers, cut through the overcast sky, lighting the street beneath. The blades crisscrossed, rotating back and forth, searching for enemy planes.

People rushed from the tall apartment buildings along the street. The basements wouldn't be large enough to hold all the residents, so they needed to seek additional shelter.

The searchlights swayed back and forth across the street, illuminating the people running. Some were dressed as if they hadn't gone to bed. Others wore nightshirts and slippers. Several carried lumpy pillowcases slung over their shoulders or valises swinging from their arms. One woman pulled a wagon with two toddlers. A girl with blonde corkscrew curls sucked her thumb while a younger boy peeked out from under a blue blanket.

The searchlights turned in the opposite direction, plunging the street into darkness. Harriet stumbled, caught her footing, and raced ahead. The pattern continued as the beams swayed across the sky. Light. Darkness. Light. Darkness.

More people stampeded forward, shouting words she didn't understand. Someone jostled her arm. Irena's hand slipped from hers. Harriet grabbed for it. Dear God, Irena was gone. Everything turned black.

"Mama! Da!" Irena sounded far away, her cries stifled by the screaming people.

Harriet shouted back, "Irena!" Others called out to their loved ones.

Oskar's voice cut through the chaos. "I'll find her. You carry Bridget."

Harriet picked up Bridget, swaying under the weight and terror. They had to find Irena.

Light.

Ahead was Oskar, his arms wrapped around Irena. Harriet wobbled through the crowd, trying to reach them.

Eeeoooeeeoooeeeooo.

The siren ended, followed by buzzing. The bombers were coming. The crowd pushed forward.

She staggered along the cobblestones, holding onto Bridget and trying to stay upright. Then the searchlights scissored the sky. Oskar and Irena were running toward a three-story building with the alley door ajar. Green light glowed from the opening as people rushed inside. A shelter. They would be safe there.

The beams turned in the opposite direction. Darkness surrounded her. The planes grew louder, paralyzing her with fear. She had to move. They had to reach the shelter. Harriet forced her quivering legs forward.

Light.

In the distance, enormous guns on wheels fired shots into the air. *Tha-thump. Tha-thump.* The cannon-like artillery shells hissed through the night sky, aiming at the planes. The sky exploded with light.

There was Oskar. He stood near the alley door to the department store. Irena was in his arms, waving. "Mama! Bridget!"

Bridget waved back. "Da! Sissy!"

Harriet wiggled through the dense crowd. Oskar grabbed her arm and moved her into the line with him. They shuffled behind the other people entering the shelter. She silently prayed, *Please, God, let us make it inside.*

The sky rumbled. She couldn't see the planes, only hear them. Their engines roared, vibrating the air. The people in the alley shot down the steps and into the shelter. Oskar started to follow. A civil defense worker in a green uniform and hard helmet stepped in front of him. The guard didn't have a gun, but he had wide shoulders and spread his legs, blocking their way.

Oskar pulled out their papers, showing them to the burly man. He scanned the documents, but his big black boots remained planted as he growled something to Oskar in German.

Tha-thump. Tha-thump. The guns fired toward the planes. Harriet looked back. Shells aimed at the unseen planes streaked through the sky, leaving a trail of green. What if they were outside during the attack? She frowned at the guard, still questioning Oskar.

Tha-thump. Tha-thump.

She had to protect the girls and the baby. She wiggled around Oskar, pushing past the guard. His hand shot out, grabbing her shoulder. She wrenched free and bolted down the stone steps, her heart racing. When she reached the bottom, she glanced back. Oskar and Irena clattered down the stairs behind them.

Harriet lurched into the basement. She was assaulted by the musty odor of water dripping down the brick foundation. Light bulbs hung from the ceiling and green fluorescent strips lined the long walls, illuminating the mass of people, possibly two hundred, crammed into the store's basement. The musty odor mixed with the smell of fear made her stomach heave. She forced down the bile.

From behind, Oskar nudged her along a narrow path between the people sitting on the floor, three deep on each side. She zig-zagged down the center, searching for a place to sit or another way out.

Oskar pointed to an empty area. "We can squeeze in there."

Harriet lowered her head and weaved through the people, careful not to step on any fingers. Oskar sank onto the floor with Irena, who was crying. Clumsily she folded next to him and placed Bridget on her lap. Leaning over, Harriet whispered to Oskar, "Why wouldn't the guard let us in?"

"This isn't our shelter. He needed to be sure we weren't Jews."

If the Jews weren't allowed into a public shelter, where would they go? She pushed the question aside. This basement was congested and noisier than the one beneath their flat that they shared with the three other couples from the building. Here, children whined, babies cried, and tempers flared. Yet, she was thankful not to be out in the street.

Oskar lost his temper with Irena. "Stop that crying." His gruff tone made her sob more.

Harriet handed Bridget to him and placed Irena on her lap. She rubbed Irena's back and whispered in her ear. "You're safe now." If only Harriet believed her own words.

Irena must have sensed Harriet's fear because her crying persisted, along with the other children and babies. Outside, the guns continued to fire their shells, only now the *tha-thumping* was followed by whistling as the enemy planes dropped their bombs.

Boom! Boom! Boom!

The floor shook. The walls vibrated. Irena screamed and covered her ears. Black specks fell from the rafters into Harriet's hair and onto her coat. She brushed the dirt from her shoulders, and tried to calm the girls as she whispered, "It'll be all right." But the bombs kept coming and coming and coming.

Boom! Boom! Boom!

What would happen if a bomb hit the department store? The bricks were old and cracked. Would the walls give way, trapping them beneath the rubble? Or what if an incendiary bomb hit, setting the building on fire? Would they be burned alive?

Harriet shook away the terrifying images and silently prayed. *God, keep us safe. Let my baby be born healthy. Let Irena and Bridget grow up, unscarred by the war. Let Oskar stay with us in Lithuania.* Harriet prayed, but her pleas did not stop the bombs.

She lost track of time. It seemed like hours before the drone of planes faded, the bombs stopped, and the guns quieted. They needed to be on that train and leave. Oskar pulled out his pocket watch. He turned the dial toward her. It was after seven a.m., their departure time. She grew impatient, but they had to remain in the shelter until the all-clear siren sounded.

Ten minutes later the siren went off. Harriet wanted to run out of the basement, board the train, and travel to a place where her family would be free of war and bombs and fear. Instead, her legs quivered as she stood and gripped Irena's and Bridget's hands. They followed Oskar, inching toward the door and what she hoped was freedom.

As they neared the steps, the air was cloudy. Then she smelled it. Smoke. "Cover your mouths, girls."

The girls put their free hands over their mouths. Holding her breath, Harriet lowered her head and climbed up the narrow stone steps. She expected to see daylight, but as they emerged from the basement and into the alley, the air was filled with a gray haze. A renewed urgency shot through her. They needed to board the train. She shouted to Oskar, "Hurry!"

Oskar increased his stride, his arm swinging back and forth with their suitcase. The crowd thinned, most of them rushing in the opposite direction to return to their apartments. Harriet followed Oskar, but each step moved her toward the smoke instead of away from it. She squinted into the haze. A large plume of gray rose above them. Harriet's legs almost buckled. What if the train station had been bombed? What if the station was burning?

Then Oskar pointed ahead. "There it is."

The red-brick train station was standing. The cloud of smoke was farther away. They could board the train. Her legs steadied, and she practically ran forward, pulling the girls with her.

As they neared the depot, her steps slowed. Something looked odd. The peak of the railway station sloped down, not up. Oskar had stopped running and was staring at the building. Harriet inched closer and gasped. The front and one side were standing. The bricks on the back and opposite side had tumbled into a deep crater cut in the ground by what must have been a bomb.

Harriet let go of the girls' hands. She crossed her arms over her stomach, trying to hold herself together.

"Where's the train, Mama?" Irena asked.

Harriet had heard the whistle of the train. A bomb had hit the station, but maybe the locomotive wasn't damaged. Maybe they could still leave. Her eyes watered as she peered through the smoke. A small crowd huddled near the tracks. The steam engine should be there.

She took another step. The engine, coal car, passenger cars, and caboose weren't standing on the tracks, but lying on their sides on the ground as if they were pieces of a toy train that some petulant child had picked up and tossed aside. Clouds of smoke still puffed out of the engine and the large metal wheels turned round and round, refusing to quit.

Even if the train was righted, it wouldn't be going anywhere, at least not on these tracks. The rails, once spiked into the ground, now rose—bent, twisted, and melted.

Luggage that must have been blown from the train was strewn along the tracks. One suitcase lay open, the clothes covered with soot. Farther down was an overturned wagon with a blue baby blanket. Beyond were mounds of what she suspected were bodies. Harriet scanned the handful of people near the tracks, gaping at the wreckage. No curly-haired girl or baby boy was there.

What if Irena hadn't gone back for her rock? What if Bridget hadn't needed to pee? Would they have made it onto the train? Would they be lying along the twisted tracks with the others?

Oskar stepped back and grabbed her hand, squeezing it. She covered her mouth to check her scream. But the tears welled up in her eyes and spilled down her cheeks until she could no longer clearly see the derailed locomotive—or a way to return home.

CHAPTER
TWENTY-NINE

July 1941

Harriet lay curled up on the couch. She didn't want to get up. She had been determined to return to Lithuania and have the baby, but she and her family had almost been killed.

For the first few days after their attempt to leave, Irena and Bridget had followed her around the apartment, from the kitchen to the living room, then the bedroom, and back. At night, they slept with her. Almost every night, one or both woke with a nightmare.

Oskar said he didn't blame her, but ever since they'd tried to leave Germany, his gray eyes had been evasive. Was it possible he blamed himself for failing to provide enough for them? She didn't know. Whenever she brought up that night at the train station, he stalked into the bedroom and when she suggested returning to Lithuania, he was adamant. They would not go back until they received a letter confirming Lithuania was safe.

Even though Oskar didn't blame her, old feelings of guilt arose. She thought of her brother's death. All her life, she had tried to take care of the ones she loved. She had failed Agne. She couldn't fail her girls.

Along with her guilt was the lethargy. Her spirit seemed to have been crushed under the weight of the train, and she didn't know how to get it back. The Harriet who had raced toward the train was a different Harriet than the one who had trudged back to the flat.

She forced herself off the couch and felt a little spark of hope. She would walk to the mail office to check for a letter. On the way, she hurried the girls along, convinced a letter would be waiting telling them to return to Lithuania. But when she stepped into the office, and the little man behind the big desk merely waved her away, her hope plummeted. She trudged back to the apartment and collapsed onto the couch while the girls retreated to the bedroom. Almost eight weeks had passed since she'd posted the letter about the baby and three weeks since she mailed another one. She had to face facts. Either the letters hadn't been delivered or her parents were no longer at the farm.

What if Oskar was right? What if the Soviets had seized the land? She closed her eyes. A gruesome picture flashed in her mind. Soviet soldiers riding to the farm, barging into the house, and forcing Mamuska and Tata to leave. From there, they would be loaded on a train headed to Siberia. It was a repeat of what had happened during the Great War, when the Soviets had invaded Lithuania and dragged her grandfather away.

A loud bang startled her. Harriet jerked up from the couch.

Irena had slammed the bedroom door and stood in the kitchen, her eyes wide. "Mama, what's wrong? Are you sick?"

Harriet was grieving the loss of home. But she couldn't pull away from her girls like her mother had done when she had lost her babies. Harriet gave Irena a wane smile. "Just tired."

Irena inched closer. Her eyes focused on Harriet's stomach. "But-but your tummy keeps growing."

Harriet's hand rested protectively over the green house dress pulled across her stomach. She wanted to wait until Oskar was here to tell the girls about the baby, but they were usually in bed when he returned from work. Irena continued to stare at her, obviously concerned. Maybe letting the girls know about the baby would brighten everyone's spirits. "Get Bridget and sit on the couch with me."

Harriet settled in the middle while the girls sat on each side, fidgeting as if they expected something bad. She reached for their hands and squeezed them. "I have good news." Smiling, she placed their stubby fingers on her stomach. "You noticed my tummy has been growing."

Each girl stared at her round pouch and nodded. "Irena, remember when you asked how you were born and I told you I carried you in my tummy?"

Irena's hands flew to her mouth, but her words tumbled out. "A baby!"

"A baby?" Bridget scrunched her nose. "Irena, are you tricking me?"

"No, your sister is right." Harriet ran her hand over her stomach. "I'm going to have a baby."

Irena beamed. "Just like the straw predicted, we're getting a new baby brother or sister."

Mama nodded. "You'll have to help me take care of it."

"I'll help," Bridget said.

"You're too little," complained Irena.

"Am not."

Harriet interceded. "Both of you can help, but you have to know how to care for a baby. Go to the bedroom and bring back a pillow."

The girls raced into the bedroom and returned, each carrying a pillow.

163

Harriet patted the couch next to her. "Sit down and pretend the pillow is your baby. Put your hands under the pillow to support the baby's head."

Irena and Bridget sat and listened as Harriet instructed them on how to hold a baby, feed a baby, burp a baby, and rock a baby.

For the remainder of the day, the girls carried their 'pillow babies,' laughing the way they used to at home. They even named their babies. Irena named hers Mia, after the girl she met at the Registration Department. Bridget named hers Oskar because she wanted a brother. The girls bombarded Harriet with questions. "When will the baby be born?" "How will it get out of her tummy?" "Will you go to the hospital?"

The mention of the hospital made Harriet's joy fizzle. She still didn't know where she would deliver the baby. She was scared to have the baby at a German hospital. She could deliver the baby here and Oskar could help, but Bridget had been breach, and the midwife had worked for hours to turn the baby to keep her from coming out feet first. Harriet needed to find a midwife.

For supper, Harriet made potato pancakes, and as the girls ate, they pretended to feed their babies, too.

"Time to put your pillow babies to bed."

The girls were asleep when Oskar knocked. She unchained the door and pulled him into the kitchen, giving him a hesitant kiss on his whiskery cheek. He washed at the sink while she warmed three leftover potato cakes. The potato crop was so plentiful this year that the government had stopped rationing potatoes. She set his plate with the pancakes on the table and sat opposite him.

Oskar must have noticed her lively mood. "Did a letter arrive from your parents?"

"No, I told the girls about the baby. Oh, Oskar, they're so excited."

He pushed the plate across to her. "I ate lunch at the factory. You eat these."

Harriet hungrily eyed the pancakes. "You said they only feed you watery pea soup."

"Today, we had hunks of potatoes in our soup."

She wasn't sure he was telling the truth. "I'll eat one." She picked up the fork and eagerly ate. Then she returned his plate. When he finished, she carried it to the sink. She kept her back to him so he wouldn't see how desperate she was. "Something might have happened to the letter. We could still go home." She didn't mention the changes in Lithuania that she'd heard from Audra. It might give Oskar another reason to stay. When she turned, Oskar was frowning.

"Yesterday a new man started at the factory."

Was Oskar changing the subject because he didn't agree with returning home? She moved to the table and waited for him to continue.

"We have to speak German at the factory because the guards don't want us to say anything they can't understand. This new man, Lukas, jammed his machine. When that peacock Hans Weber yelled at him, Lukas mumbled, *'U siki k, uzsikishk.'*"

Harriet's mouth flew open. "He told the guard to shut up?"

"He whispered it. But the words were Lithuanian."

Harriet raised her hands in joy. "Talk to this Lukas. If he's from Lithuania, maybe he can tell us what's going on at home."

"I don't know." Oskar stroked his chin. "The guards always watch us. It'll be dangerous."

She reached across the table and put her hand over his. "Please Oskar, for our baby." Even as she said the words, she disliked what she was doing. She didn't want to put Oskar in more danger, but she wanted—no, needed—the baby to be born at home.

The next day dragged, and the girls weren't as excited

about their 'pillow babies,' but that night Harriet was touched when Irena kneeled beside the bed and added to her prayers, "Bless our new baby, who I really, really hope is a sister."

Bridget prayed, "Please, Jesus, bring me a baby brother."

Harriet chuckled. At least one girl would be happy.

After they were asleep, she paced the kitchen waiting for Oskar, who was later than usual. What if he'd talked to Lukas, and the guards overheard? What if they'd dragged Oskar away for questioning? A cramp in her stomach doubled her over.

She sank onto a chair, cradling her belly. Too much stress might make the baby come early. Then what chance would the little thing have? She inhaled slowly until the pain went away. God had given her a precious gift. She must protect this child.

Footsteps sounded on the stairs. Rushing to the door, she fumbled with the chain several times before she unhooked it. Oskar's face was covered with soot. Only the rings around his eyes were white. "What happened?"

Not waiting for an answer, she pulled him inside and latched the door. He moved to the sink and pumped water, splashing it onto his black face. "Instead of cleaning up, I followed Lukas and talked to him."

Harriet's heart beat faster as she handed him a towel. "What did he say?"

Oskar dried off and returned the towel. Deep frown lines furrowed across his forehead. "It's not good, Harriet." He dropped onto the nearest chair.

She sank beside him, wringing the towel. "Tell me."

"When the Germans invaded, they promised Lithuanians if they fought alongside them against the Soviets, they'd get their freedom. Lukas joined the Germans and helped drive the Soviets out."

"The Soviets are really gone?" She wanted to wave the towel as a victory flag, but she couldn't ignore the lines on Oskar's forehead. "So, what's the problem?"

"Once the Germans gained control, they set up their own government."

The words didn't crush Harriet's hope. "We live under a German government here. What would be so bad about living under German rule in Lithuania?"

"The killing hasn't ended. In Kaunas, the Germans rounded up thousands of Jews and herded them to the Fortress."

"Why did they take them there?"

"The Fort used to protect the border. Now it's a prison."

"So they've locked the Jews up?"

"Worse." Oskar paused. The words seemed to stick in his throat. "They lined them up and shot them."

Harriet crossed herself. "Why?"

"The Germans said the Jews helped the Soviets." Oskar balled his hands into fists. "The bear and the eagle. Lithuania is caught between them. One swoops in and the other charges. The Germans are no better than the Soviets."

"But why can't we go back?"

"Hitler's philosophy is *lebensraum*, manifest destiny."

"What's that?" Harriet asked.

"The Germans believe they are the superior race and have the right to seize the land they need for expansion. They justify it by saying it's what America did to the Indians."

"But what does that have to do with us returning to Lithuania?"

"We would not be welcome. Germany is seizing Lithuanian land and resources for their own people. We would be looked on as a liability and possibly killed."

———

The following week, as Harriet, Irena, and Bridget returned to their flat from the market, the man in the Fedora walked ahead, pushing his wife in the wheelchair. Harriet wanted to thank him for warning them about the soldiers. Pulling the girls with her, she hurried down the street and caught up with him. "Excuse me," Harriet said.

The man stopped and glanced over his shoulder. Harriet rounded the wheelchair and introduced herself, adding, "We're from Lithuania, too."

The man tipped his gray Fedora. "I'm Jonas Roka and this is my wife, Rosa."

Rosa's poppy-red lips spread in a beautiful smile, revealing gleaming white teeth. Her hair, coiled into a thick braid on top of her head, bobbed as she nodded. Then she pointed to the girls. "Who are these pretty ones?"

Harriet laid her hand on Irena's shoulder to introduce her, but she curtsied and said, "I'm Irena. This is Bridget." Irena's hand flew to her mouth. "Oops. I'm not supposed to talk."

"It's all right," said Jonas, his blue eyes glistening. "We're from Vilnius, which once was the capital of Lithuania."

"And we live...lived in Kaunas, which was the capital, although I'm not sure now," said Harriet. "I've heard the Germans have driven the Soviets out. Do you have any news about our country?"

Jonas' head swiveled as if checking to see if someone might be near enough to hear. "I suspect it's worse in Lithuania."

Harriet's hopes plummeted. That wasn't the news she'd hoped to hear. "Are you going back?"

Jonas and Rosa exchanged wary glances.

"Audra said Latvia is bad, and her family is staying. She thinks the doctors here are good for Hanna."

Rosa's smile disappeared. "Poor Hanna. She's too young to be so sick. I'm glad you visit them."

"Hanna's cough seems worse," admitted Harriet. "I wonder when she'll get better."

Rosa frowned and gazed up at her husband. Another look passed between them that Harriet couldn't read. If something was seriously wrong with Hanna, Harriet needed to know. "Is it more than a cough?"

Rosa nodded to Jonas. "I want to show your girls my pretty shoes." She lifted her colorful afghan and revealed blue velvet flats fit for a princess.

As the girls stepped closer and admired her shoes, Jonas took Harriet's elbow and pulled her aside. "I'm not sure if you know, but I think I should tell you." He cleared his throat and looked around. "Hanna has tuberculosis."

Harriet grabbed Jonas's arm to keep from collapsing. Her heart broke for Hanna and her family, but Audra's betrayal stung. Harriet thought Audra was her friend. How could she have kept Hanna's illness from Harriet? Tuberculosis was contagious. Children and adults died from T.B.

Audra had lured Harriet in with her supposed friendship and extra rations. Audra had endangered Irena and Bridget, encouraging them to be friends with Hanna, knowing her daughter had a contagious disease. Harriet had noticed Hanna's cough was worse and had accepted Audra's vague answers about the illness.

Harriet did everything possible to keep the girls away from the Brownshirts and the Nazis. She hadn't expected danger to be lurking in her friend right across the street.

A new fear exploded through her. What if Irena or Bridget had already contracted T.B.? For the rest of the day, Harriet watched the girls closely. When Irena coughed, Harriet felt her forehead for a fever. When Bridget was tired and took her nap early, Harriet fretted Bridget was infected with T.B.

By nightfall, Harriet was convinced that one or both of the girls had tuberculosis. When she unchained the door for Oskar, she didn't wait for him to wash up or sit at the table. She blurted out, "Hanna has T.B. I'm afraid the girls might have caught it."

He headed toward the bedroom. "How high are their fevers?"

She put a staying hand on his arm. "They aren't feverish now. They're sleeping."

Changing directions, he walked to the sink and pumped some water. "I'm sorry about Hanna, but I doubt if the girls have T.B."

"How can you be so sure? They've played with Hanna for months."

After Oskar dried his hands and face, he pulled open the drawer with the documents from the Registration Department. He flipped through Irena's and then Bridget's inoculation records. "Just as I suspected." He showed her the books. "The girls were vaccinated against tuberculosis at the Registration Department."

Harriet collapsed into the chair. Then she wondered about herself. "I had a shot. Was it for T.B.?"

Oskar checked her documents and shook his head. "Stay away from Hanna and her mother, for your sake and the baby's."

His words struck her. "The baby? Do you think our baby could get it?"

"The doctors don't know exactly how tuberculosis spreads."

She'd never considered her friendship with Audra would endanger her unborn child. Those three tiny wooden crosses in the field flashed in her mind. Harriet placed her arms over her stomach as if to shield the baby, but the harm might already have been done.

CHAPTER
THIRTY

July - August 1941

rena gripped the sides of a wooden wagon as Da pulled her
and Bridget over the cobblestone street. A shrill whistle cut
through the darkness.

"Hurry, Oskar," called Mama.

*Tugging harder, Da weaved through the people running
toward the train.*

Boom! Boom! Boom!

*The wagon tipped over, splintering into pieces. Bridget and
she were tossed high in the sky. She looked down. Below lay
Mama's crumpled body next to Da whose legs were crushed
under the train.*

Irena screamed and woke up.

Mama rushed across the room and sank onto the bed. "Sh-
sh. It's just a nightmare. You're safe."

Irena hadn't known real fear until the night her family had

tried to return to Lithuania. She still had nightmares about the bombs and the train.

In one nightmare, her family boarded the train, and when the bomb exploded, they were tossed onto the tracks with the other bodies she'd seen. In another, her family was huddled in the basement of the department store and the building collapsed on them. Tonight, she had dreamed that she and Bridget were the two curly-haired kids riding in the wagon. When the bomb hit, they had flown into the air and gone straight to heaven. Her nightmares kept changing. But what never changed was the ending—her family had never returned home.

Irena longed to play in the swing that Da had built and sit under the apple tree. She wanted to dangle her feet in the river and let the cool water ripple through her toes as she searched for rocks. She wanted to see Nana and Papa and play with the kittens in their barn. But in Germany, she didn't have a swing in an apple tree or a river to dangle her feet in or grandparents with barn cats to play with. All Irena had were rocks. Lots and lots of rocks that were all the same—gray boring rocks that matched the gray boring days.

After they'd tried to leave, Irena had pestered Mama with questions. "Can we go home on another train?" "Can we ride a bus?" "Can we walk?"

"It's too far to walk," Mama said, but the other questions received her usual, "I don't know."

Tired of hearing Mama's answer, Irena blurted out, "When will you know?"

"When we receive a letter from Mamuska and Tata telling us it's safe."

For several weeks, Mama checked the mail regularly. On the walk there, Mama's eyes glistened with hope, and her step was brisk. But when the small man at the huge desk waved her away, the sparkle in her eyes faded, and she plodded back to the flat, deflated.

Finally, Irena quit pestering Mama about going home. Instead, Irena pestered Mama about playing with Hanna. Irena wanted to tell Hanna the news about the baby. It was almost as exciting as Christmas. But Mama said Hanna was sick, and they couldn't play with her or they might get sick, too.

By August, when Mama had her birthday, Irena still hadn't seen Hanna. Irena was excited about her own birthday. Tomorrow she would be seven. Mama called seven the age of reason. Maybe Mama would let her see Hanna.

On the morning of her birthday, Irena scrambled out of bed early. She didn't want to miss one minute of her age-of-reason birthday. Peeking out the curtains, she stared at Hanna's window. When Hanna didn't appear, Irena gave up and padded into the kitchen. Sniffing, she'd hoped to smell something delicious like chicken and dumpling soup. But she didn't smell anything special, and Mama was sitting at the table.

Irena's stomach growled. Maybe Mama was resting before she started cooking. "I'm hungry."

"I'll warm the porridge for you and Bridget."

Irena sank into a chair. Porridge wasn't special. "What do you think Da will bring me?" He didn't work at the candy factory anymore, so she couldn't expect chocolates.

"He has to work late so don't expect a present."

Maybe Mama would give her a present. "Have you started on my communion dress?"

"Not yet. I'm making clothes for the baby."

Irena frowned. "I need a white dress for communion, and a veil, and—"

Mama let out a sigh. "You'll have to wait on the white dress and communion."

Irena had already waited—seven long years. "You said when I was seven, I could make my first communion and get an amber rosary like yours."

"The war has changed things."

"The war. It's always the war. Can we go to Hanna's?"

"I told you she was sick."

"She can't stay sick forever."

"She has tuberculosis."

Irena tried to repeat the word. "Tu-berc-what?"

"The short term is T.B."

"When will she get well?"

Mama didn't answer, and Irena slumped in her seat and stared at the wall calendar. Tomorrow was Sunday. Maybe they'd do something special when Da was home. "Can we go to church?" Mama hadn't taken her and Bridget to Mass since they'd fled to Germany.

"Church would be good. I'll ask your father tonight."

"I guess I can wait one more day," Irena said, although she didn't feel like waiting. Her whole life was waiting. Waiting to go to school. Waiting to get older. Waiting for the war to end. Then she let out a wail. "I don't have anything to wear to church." In Lithuania, she always had a church dress.

Mama walked to the sewing bag on the floor next to the divan and pulled out Irena's red school dress, the one with the rosebud buttons. The last time Irena had worn it, the dress had been above her knees. Mama held the dress up. "I added a row of lace at the bottom so it wouldn't be too short."

Irena jumped up and snatched the dress from Mama. Right there in the living room, she stripped out of her nightshirt and pulled the dress over her head. She turned and waited for Mama to tie it in the back. Then Irena twirled around the room, her tangled hair flying behind her.

Irena wore the red dress the next day when the entire family went to church. As the organ music floated through the sanctuary, a priest in a white robe with green vestments emerged from the side. He stretched out his arms in a gesture of welcome and chanted.

Irena didn't understand Latin, so she tapped Mama's shoulder. "What's Father saying?"

"August is dedicated to the Immaculate Heart of Mary," Mama whispered. "The priest wears green during ordinary times for hope."

Hope. Irena might not understand the words, but she loved the beautiful rhythm. The sound seemed to weave a web around her, making her feel safe and giving her hope.

Bridget poked her and pointed to the side of the church with the life-sized statue of Mary. At her sandaled feet were rows of votive candles, some of the flames flickering. Irena turned to Mama and whispered, "Can we light a candle for Hanna to get well?"

"Next time."

Irena didn't argue. She was happy there would be a next time.

After church, the family walked toward the open-air market. Halfway there, Da stopped at a vacant lot with grass shaded by an old oak tree. "The perfect spot for a picnic."

Irena loved picnics, especially the food, but Mama didn't have a picnic basket. "What will we eat?"

Mama tapped her pocketbook.

She couldn't have packed much food in there. "I don't want to sit on the ground," Irena said. "I'll get my dress dirty."

Da reached into the pocket of his suit coat and pulled out something wrapped in paper about the size of an apple. Then he took off his coat and spread it on the ground. "You girls can sit on this."

Irena laughed when Mama sat on the coat with them. Unsnapping her pocketbook, she removed a small tin. Irena recognized the oval-shaped tin with the key on top. "Sardines." She loved the salty fish.

While Mama inserted the key and rolled back the top, Da handed Irena what he had removed from his pocket. She unwrapped the paper and stared at a large, white roll with five marks on top that divided it into sections.

"It's called a Kaiser roll," Da said. "The marks make it look like a crown."

Irena had never tasted a Kaiser roll.

Mama finished opening the sardines. "Remember, you're older, so you know how to share."

Irena dutifully divided the roll into five parts, giving one to each of them. That left two for her, which seemed fair because it was her birthday.

Mama distributed the sardines, putting one fish into each bun. Irena bit into the Kaiser roll with the sardine on it and closed her eyes, enjoying the bread with the delicious, salty taste. She couldn't wait to eat the second one.

Opening her eyes, she stared at Mama's round belly. Da always said that Mama was eating for two. Irena handed the extra section of roll to her. "This is for the baby."

As Mama accepted the bun, she smiled. "Thank you. You are growing up."

Da cleared his throat. "I have news. In September, a school is starting for children of guest workers. I thought maybe you would want to go."

"A real school." Irena jumped up and kissed Da. She had been disappointed about not having her first communion or wearing a white dress, but she'd always dreamed about going to school. "This is the best birthday ever."

CHAPTER
THIRTY-ONE

September 1941

rena sat in the kitchen chair, wearing her slip and trying not to fidget. Mama stood behind the chair, brushing her brown hair. "Hold still," said Mama. "Your part will be crooked."

Irena was too excited to sit still. She had yearned to go to school for so long, but for the last week, she worried something bad would happen like last time when the Soviets invaded Lithuania. Only today would she let herself believe her dream would come true.

She had always imagined her first day. She would be wearing a new school dress. Mama and Bridget would be standing at the door, waving goodbye. Sometimes she imagined skipping to school alone. Other times she would be skipping to school, holding hands with a girlfriend.

"My turn." Bridget tugged on Mama's skirt, impatient to have her hair fixed for school.

Irena glared at Bridget. "Wait 'til Mama finishes my hair."

Irena definitely had not imagined holding onto Bridget's hand as she skipped off to school. Bridget was only five. Irena was seven. It wasn't fair. Irena should be the first to go to school. Bridget should have to stay home. But Da said Bridget was old enough for school, so he'd enrolled her, too.

Irena and Bridget had been enrolled in a school for guest workers' children. Da explained guest workers replaced German workers who were off fighting the war. Millions of men fled to Germany and were classified as guest workers like he was. Some men brought families with them, and the children needed to be educated in the German language and culture.

"All done." Mama hugged Irena, giving her an extra squeeze. "Get dressed while I fix your sister's hair."

Irena slid off the chair and sashayed into the bedroom where two dresses lay on the bed. Irena had envied the German girls dressed in their white blouses, navy blue skirts, and long white knee socks. She'd asked Da to buy her a uniform for school.

"German children don't wear school uniforms," Da said. "Those uniforms are for young girls in the Nazi party, *Band Deutschen Madel*."

Even though Irena feared the Nazis, she wanted to belong, to wear the uniform. "Can I join?"

Da frowned. "The *BDM* is the League of German Girls. You have to be German to join."

Irena's shoulders sagged. She would never wear a uniform like those girls. Today, however, she didn't envy the girls in the *BDM*. She had her special dress with the five rosebud buttons and a row of lace around the bottom. She picked up the red dress, slid it over her head, and worked the rosebud buttons into the right holes. When she finished, she twirled around, her pigtails flying behind her.

After she stopped spinning, her eyes landed on the bed where her pink baby-doll dress lay. The high-waisted dress was a little short and even though it fit, she'd given it to Bridget. "It's only fair that Bridget has a pretty dress for her first day of school, too," she'd said to Mama.

When Irena and Bridget were ready, Mama tied on her headscarf. "You don't have to go with us," Irena said. "We know the way." They had practiced the route several times. Walk down the sidewalk in the projects, go under the brick archway, turn right, walk two blocks, and turn left. The school was a single-story, red-brick building with a chain-link fence around it.

"When the baby comes, you'll have to go alone," Mama said. "For now, I'll go with you."

Secretly, Irena was glad Mama walked with them, even though Irena couldn't skip or look around. She had to hold Mama's hand and keep her head down. Today, Irena basked in the crisp fall air and was glad the factories didn't smell so bad.

Along the way, she wanted to look for other girls walking to school, but she kept her head down, staring at her brown lace-up shoes. Last night, Da had given Irena and Bridget a serious talk. He'd warned bad things could happen to nice girls if they misbehaved. Irena wanted to be good, but she didn't know the language, so she hoped she could figure out the rules.

When they made the last turn, Mama stopped. Irena peeked up. Across the street, marching toward the school, were two SS soldiers. When Mama saw them, she always turned and walked in the opposite direction. But if she did that, how would they get to school?

Mama squared her shoulders and tightened her grip on Irena's hand. "Keep your heads down, no matter what." Then she started across the street.

Thump, thump, thump. The soldiers' boots tromped down

SUE STEWART ADE

the sidewalk. The sound grew louder and louder. The pounding made it impossible to think. Mama's hand shook as they stepped over the curb on the other side. They stood, waiting for the soldiers to pass. Irena peeked up. One of the soldiers looked at Mama. Irena couldn't breathe. What if he questioned Mama and took her away? But the soldier tipped his hat at Mama and continued down the street. Irena let out her breath and steadied her quivering legs as Mama led them to the school.

They stopped at the entrance to the red-brick building.

"Irena, be good and watch your sister."

She nodded.

Mama turned to Bridget. "Listen to Irena."

"Yes, Mama." Bridget's tone implied she didn't want to be bossed around.

"When school gets out, I'll be waiting right here." Then Mama wrapped her arms around them. As she pulled away, tears glistened in her eyes.

Mama was crying. She should be happy that they were going to school, but a lump formed in Irena's throat. She couldn't act like a baby and cry. Her eyes would be puffy, and the other students might make fun of her.

Before the tears leaked from her eyes, she grabbed Bridget's hand and shot toward the door of the school. She didn't stop until they were inside the building. She had never been in the school before and didn't know where their classroom was. Holding onto Bridget's hand, she shuffled down the hallway. The wooded floors creaked beneath their feet. When they approached an open doorway, Irena peeked inside. The room had a blackboard and desk in the front and a large wooden cabinet in the back. In the middle were five rows of wooden tables, most filled with other girls who seemed about their ages.

"This must be it." Irena dragged Bridget into the room and stopped at the first table where there were three empty seats

180

next to a tall girl at the other end. Irena wanted to sit in the front, so no one could block their view of the teacher or the board.

Bridget tugged on Irena's hand and pointed to the back row with two empty seats. "Let's sit there."

"The front is better." She tried to pull Bridget, but she didn't budge.

The other girls in the room seemed to watch as Irena and Bridget battled over where to sit. Irena hadn't wanted her sister to come to school with her, but with all these strange faces staring at her, Irena was glad Bridget was there. Besides, Mama had told Irena she needed to take care of Bridget.

Gambling that Bridget wouldn't want to sit in the last row alone, Irena released her hand and slid into the first row near the girl at the end, leaving a chair for Bridget. Irena smiled when Bridget slumped next to her.

After they were settled, Irena glanced at the girl to her right. She had blonde hair plaited into a thick braid that hung down the middle of her back. She sat up straight, her hands clasped together on top of the table.

Irena mimicked her, nudging Bridget to do the same.

A few of the girls were whispering, but most of the thirty girls were quiet. No boys were in the classroom, which didn't surprise Irena. Since coming to Germany, she rarely saw boys her age or older.

Several other girls entered. One of them sat next to Bridget. When no teacher came, Irena mustered up the nerve to lean toward the girl next to her. "Hi, I'm Irena."

The girl continued to stare forward. Maybe the girl hadn't heard her or maybe the girl spoke a different language. Irena pointed to herself. "Irena," she said a little louder.

Without turning her head, the girl whispered back, "Mia."

Mia was the name of the girl at the Registration Department. Was this the same Mia, who had come to their bunk and slept with them? But it had been night, and the room was dark. Irena hadn't seen her well. She thought the girl's hair had been brown, but this girl's hair was blonde.

Irena poked the girl on the arm. Mia turned toward her. She looked like the same girl. "It's me. Remember? Irena and my sister, Bridget."

Mia shook her head, her braid swinging side to side. Irena frowned. She wasn't sure this was the same Mia since her hair was blonde and braided, not dark and frizzy. She had a high forehead, but also a wide nose and plump lips. Irena followed Mia's gaze.

Above the blackboard hung a large oil painting of a man in a brown Nazi uniform with a red armband, white shirt, and matching brown tie. His straight, dark hair was slicked down and parted on one side. Under his nose was a short, thick mustache. It was similar to the picture at the Registration Department, only smaller, and now Irena knew who he was. Hitler. His picture and red flags with swastikas hung everywhere. She fidgeted in her seat as those dark eyes bore into her.

She slid closer to Bridget. Hitler's eyes followed her. She wiggled nearer to Mia. His eyes moved with her. She couldn't get away from those penetrating eyes.

A pretty, young woman entered the classroom. She wore a white blouse with covered buttons and a pleated plaid skirt that swished against her long legs. Her short auburn hair was styled in what Mama called finger waves. She stopped near the front desk. Turning her back to the class, she faced the oil painting, raised her right arm, and exclaimed, "*Heil Hitler!*"

Irena had seen other people make the same gesture. Even Da raised his arm when he entered a store.

The teacher spun around, facing the class. She lifted her hand, palm up, and motioned for them to rise. Somehow Irena managed to stand without her legs collapsing. She sneaked a peek at Bridget, relieved she was standing, too.

The teacher raised her right arm toward the picture and repeated three times, "*Heil Hitler!*"

Irena peeked around. The girls behind her raised their arms, so she raised hers. When they shouted, Irena enthusiastically joined in. "*Heil Hitler! Heil Hitler! Heil Hitler!*"

CHAPTER
THIRTY-TWO

After school, Irena spotted Mama with the other mothers waiting outside the fence. Irena was busting to tell Mama about school. Irena kept her head down and didn't talk until they were safely back in the kitchen. Then Irena burst out. "Guess what?" She didn't wait for Mama to answer. "Our teacher's a woman. Her name is Fraulein Bauer."

Mama untied her headscarf and hung it on the hook next to the door. "The men are off to war, so that makes sense."

"She's pretty, like you and—"

Bridget cut in. "Did you miss us, Mama?"

Mama gave them both a big bear hug. "I missed you bunches and bunches."

Bridget giggled, and Irena soaked in Mama's warmth.

"What did you learn at school?" asked Mama.

Irena stood up straighter. Bridget scurried next to her. They raised their right arms into the air and shouted, "*Heil Hitler!*"

Mama sank into the nearest chair and frowned. "I hope that isn't all you learned."

Bridget climbed onto Mama's lap, but Irena twirled around the kitchen, chattering. "When the teacher said the name of our country, we stood and told her our names. Tomorrow we are supposed to tell something about our country."

"I'll say it has pretty flowers," Bridget boasted.

"I'll say it has rivers and lots of rocks."

"You should tell them about Lithuanian gold," said Mama.

Irena remembered sitting along the riverbank with Bridget while Mama told them the story of the mermaid who lived in an amber castle and fell in love with a fisherman. Sometimes when Mama did the laundry, Irena would scoop up fistfuls of water, searching for Lithuanian gold, but she never found any of the beautiful yellow amber.

She stopped dancing. "When we go home, I'll look for amber. If I find some, we'll be rich and live in an amber palace."

Irena was still dreaming about finding amber the next day when Mama walked them to school. They didn't meet any SS soldiers and at the gate, Mama handed Irena a handkerchief with their lunch tied inside. "Be good and share with your sister."

Irena wanted to race into school, but she remembered Fraulein Bauer's warning. "You're in a foreign country. You must act ladylike at all times so the soldiers don't mistake you for a bad person."

"Like a Jew," a girl behind her had shouted.

Irena didn't want anyone to think she was a Jew. She held onto Bridget's hand and with the other gripped their lunch. She walked as ladylike as possible, taking tiny steps into the building. Her brown hair was in pigtails and she wore her red dress again, as she sashayed down the hall, swishing her full skirt against her legs. Before she reached the classroom, an arm shot out of the water closet and clamped down on her shoulder, pulling her and Bridget inside.

Irena stared at Mia. "Why did you grab me?"

Without answering, Mia stuck her head through the doorway. As she scanned the hall, her long blonde braid whipped across her blue-plaid dress. She was taller than Irena and probably a few years older, but up close, Irena was sure this was the same girl from the Registration Department. "You *are* the girl we met."

Tucking her head inside, Mia pressed two fingers against her full lips. "Sh-sh. Don't tell."

"But your hair was brown." Irena reached out to feel Mia's yellow braid. She stepped away before Irena could touch it. "Bridget, wasn't her hair brown?"

Bridget squinted at Mia and nodded.

Mia frowned. "My hair was blonde. Do you understand? Blonde."

Irena didn't understand. How could Mia's hair change from brown to blonde?

Mia grabbed Irena's arm. "Say it. *Blonde.*"

Irena touched one of her own pigtails. "Is my hair blonde?"

"Don't be a kraut. Your hair is brown."

The room with the bunk beds had been dark. The only light was the moon shining through the window. Maybe Mia's hair just looked brown.

"What color is my hair?" Mia asked again.

Mia had helped them at the Registration Department, and Irena wanted a friend. "Blonde," she squeaked.

Mia let go of her arm. "Smart girl."

Irena smiled at Mia. "How long did you have to stay at the Registration Department until your parents came?"

Mia didn't answer the question. "I live with my aunt."

"What about your parents?" Irena had been scared without Mama and Da.

Mia glanced down. She no longer looked fierce. "I was told they were shipped back to Poland."

"Don't you want to go home with them?" If Mama and Da returned to Lithuania, Irena would go.

"It's safer in Germany."

Irena frowned. Germany didn't feel safe, but she didn't argue with Mia. Irena had learned she wouldn't win.

"I named my baby, Mia, after you," Irena said.

Mia's brown eyes sparkled. "You have a new baby?"

"It's only a pillow, but Mama's going to have a baby and we get to take care of it."

Mia hooked her arm through Irena's. "Tell me about the baby," she said as they walked arm-in-arm down the hall and into the classroom.

Bridget scampered after them. "Wait for me."

When Fraulein Bauer entered the classroom, she wore a black suit with a long, fitted skirt, and her shiny black heels tapped across the wooden floor. She stopped in front of Hitler's portrait and saluted. Irena and the rest of the class automatically stood and raised their arms. They chanted three times, "*Heil Hitler.*" Saluting Hitler didn't seem so strange today.

Fraulein Bauer wrote the word *geography* on the board. Then she pulled down the map above the blackboard, picked up a long wooden pointer from her desk, and circled the largest country on the map. "*Deutschland.*"

The class repeated the word. Irena was surprised Germany was so huge. Her world here was small compared to her world in Lithuania.

The teacher moved the wooden pointer to the adjoining country. The sound of the teacher's words changed. They no longer had the guttural tone of German. Irena heard movement behind her and peeked over her shoulder. Several girls stood. The teacher nodded and spoke to them in a different language. Each time Fraulein Bauer called the name of a country, girls from that country stood. Pierina, the girl who sat next to Bridget, stood when the teacher pointed to the boot-shaped country, Italy.

The teacher must be very smart. She understood all the

languages. Irena fiddled with her rose buttons and hoped the teacher understood Lithuanian because Irena wanted to tell about Lithuanian amber.

The teacher's pointer moved to the country above Germany. "*Polen.*"

Mia stood.

Irena squinted at the map. Poor Mia. *Polen* was such a tiny country compared to Germany. Irena was sure Lithuania would be bigger than Poland and maybe even bigger than Germany.

"*Litauen,*" Fraulein Bauer said.

Irena hopped up and pulled Bridget with her. The teacher pointed to a speck of green. It was hard to believe that was Lithuania. How could her country be so tiny? Heat rose in Irena's cheeks. She wanted to sink into her chair.

She did not like *geography.*

CHAPTER
THIRTY-THREE

October 1941

rena tugged on Mama's hand. "Come on. I don't want to be late for school."

Mama unpinned her apron and hung it on the peg by the door. "What's the rush?"

"I'm teacher's helper today."

"Well, tell your sister to hurry."

Irena dashed into the bedroom and returned, pulling Bridget with her.

Irena and Bridget were the first ones in the classroom, but Irena didn't mind. After four weeks of school, she knew what to expect. When Fraulein Bauer walked into the room, the class rose, saluted Hitler's portrait, and chanted, "*Heil Hitler*" three times. Even Hitler's picture didn't seem scary anymore.

Irena was relieved when today Fraulein Bauer didn't pull down the map and start with geography. Instead, the teacher asked Irena to pass out the slate boards and chalk. Irena moved down the tables, handing them out until one was left, so she and Bridget shared.

"Today we're going to start with arithmetic," the teacher announced.

Irena was good at numbers and felt sorry for the students who had trouble.

Fraulein Bauer wrote a problem on the board. "If you have three sausages and take away two sausages, how many will be left?"

Irena wrote '1' on her chalkboard and held it up for the teacher to see.

Fraulein Bauer smiled and nodded. Irena looked behind her. Other students still had their slate boards on the table. Fraulein Bauer placed a market bag on the desk and pulled out three plump sausages, lining them up on the desk.

Irena's mouth watered. She had eaten porridge for breakfast but hungrily eyed the rolls of sausages.

Fraulein Bauer picked up two sausages and placed them into the bag. "How many sausages are left?"

Every slate board shot up.

"*Gut*." Fraulein Mueller reached into the bag and pulled out all three sausages again. She placed them on the desk and removed a knife from her bag. Irena drooled as the teacher cut each roll in half. "How many sausages do I have now?"

Irena forgot to write the number and blurted out, "Six."

Fraulein Bauer didn't even scold her.

After an hour of addition and take-away problems, Fraulein Bauer said, "Go wash your hands and when you return, we'll sample the sausage."

No one dawdled in the water closet. When Fraulein Bauer handed Irena a thick slice of sausage, she thanked the teacher, "*Danke schön*," and tried to be very ladylike as she walked to her seat. Irena took small bites, but she couldn't resist licking her lips.

Fraulein Bauer slid her chair from behind her desk to the middle of the room. "Story time. Sit on the floor and I'll read you a book about a girl named Heidi."

Irena loved stories, although the teacher said the story was sad. "Heidi lives in the Swiss Alps with her grandfather because her parents have passed away."

Already Irena felt sorry for Heidi. As Fraulein Bauer read the story, Irena started to envy Heidi, running and enjoying the mountain air. Heidi even had a best friend, Peter.

When Fraulein Bauer closed the book, Irena and the other students clapped. "Tomorrow, we'll read more about Heidi."

Irena wished she could be like the Swiss girl who was free to run and play with her animals and friends instead of keeping her head down and worrying about the soldiers.

Next Fraulein Bauer removed her high heels and slipped on a pair of what Mama called practical flats. "Line up at the door for physical training."

Irena stood in line, jigging. PT was one of her favorite times. Twice a day, the class went outside to do calisthenics and race on the track around the grassy field.

When they were behind the school, Fraulein Bauer blew her whistle and led them through a series of jumping jacks and touching their toes before the class lined up on the track to race. Irena was short, but fast. She stood next to Helga, a huge girl whose brown cowlick stuck up on the crown of her head. At first, Irena thought all the girls in her class would be her friends, but most of them stayed with the ones from their country. Others were mean, like Helga, who used her colossal size to pick on smaller girls. Irena referred to her as Helga the Hun.

The teacher blew the whistle, and Irena was off, pumping her fists as she rounded the track. She crossed the finish line first. The Hun glowered at Irena. "*Dummkopf.*"

Irena didn't like being called a dumbhead.

The next day as they raced around the track, the Hun stuck out her foot, tripping Irena. Fraulein Bauer blew her shrill whistle and wagged her finger at Helga, who was banned from PT for the rest of the week.

The teacher was no *dummkopf*.

CHAPTER
THIRTY-FOUR

Harriet waited anxiously outside the school for the girls. She enjoyed how happy they seemed when they told her about their day. Today, however, Irena was scowling, and the hem of her dress was ripped. She mumbled all the way back to the flat before she pushed up her skirt and pointed to her scraped knee. "Teacher cleaned it up."

Harriet listened sympathetically, *tsk-tsking* over the knee. "I can fix the hem."

"The Hun got in big trouble," Irena said.

"The Hun?"

"That's what we call Helga because she's as big as—"

A knock sounded on the door.

Harriet rose and cautiously cracked it open. Audra stood in the hallway, wearing a red sweater over her dress. A chill slivered down Harriet's spine. She hadn't spoken to Audra since the Rokas had told her Hanna had tuberculosis.

"Mama, lift the chain," prodded Irena from behind her.

Reluctantly, Harriet unchained the door, but stood in the middle, blocking the way. "What do you want?" The words spilled out, more venomously than she intended. Her heart broke that Hanna was gravely ill, but Harriet was angry at Audra for exposing her girls to tuberculosis.

Irena wiggled around her. "Is Hanna with you?" She craned her head, looking behind Audra.

Audra twisted one of the pearl buttons on her sweater. "Hanna's...resting."

Irena's smile faded. "Why didn't she come with you?"

"She's too weak." Audra's gaze slid to Harriet. "Could you watch Hanna while I get her medicine?"

Harriet looked down to avoid what seemed like raw pain in Audra's eyes. Irena and Bridget had been vaccinated for T.B. Harriet had not. She couldn't put herself, or possibly the baby, in danger.

When she didn't answer, Audra reached out and gripped Harriet's wrist. "Please, I-I wouldn't ask, but Hanna's been talking out of her head."

Harriet tried to ignore the desperate plea. She couldn't risk it. She just couldn't. She kept her head down and focused on her belly and her baby.

When the silence dragged on, Audra let go of her arm. Her voice changed to a raspy snarl. "So, you know. Who told you? Never mind."

Harriet's head jerked up. "Yes, I know. And I'm sorry about Hanna. But I thought you were my friend."

Audra continued to twist the button. "Hanna's my only child. What would you have done?"

Harriet wanted to say she would have told Audra. But if Irena or Bridget was sick, she would do anything to make them well, and if she needed to hide the fact that one of them had a contagious disease, she might have done the same as Audra.

"Please. It'll be less than an hour. Hanna's sleeping, so you won't even have to go into the bedroom."

Harriet's anger dissipated. She wanted to help, but Audra was asking the impossible. She was asking Harriet to endanger her baby and herself. "I'm sorry," she said and meant it.

Audra's voice changed to the harsh sound she'd used when she'd scolded Irena about opening the curtains. "I gave you things for the baby. And I didn't ask you to pay."

Harriet cringed.

Irena tugged on her skirt. "Please, Mama. I want to tell Hanna about the baby and school. Maybe she can go with us."

Audra patted Irena on the head. "I wish Hanna was well enough to attend school. This new medicine might…" Her voice trailed off. She put out her hands, pleading. "I can't lose another child."

How could she teach charity to Irena and Bridget if she didn't show it? Harriet unpinned her apron. "I'll come." As she hung the apron on the peg by the door, she prayed she wouldn't regret her decision.

———

Irena skipped across the street, hoping Hanna wasn't asleep. Irena wanted to tell her about Fraulein Bauer, Heidi, and the baby. When Irena and Bridget followed Hanna's mother into the bedroom, the blackout curtains were closed, but light from the open door spilled into the room and onto Hanna, propped up in bed by pillows. Her spindly arms stuck out from under her puffy sleeves and her face was chalky. Irena's tongue thickened as she swallowed her cheerful greeting. She closed her eyes. She wanted to pretend she'd never seen this Hanna, the one who looked thin and ghostly.

"You're awake." Hanna's mother sounded so cheerful that Irena opened her eyes, but the bird-like Hanna was still there swallowed up by the bed.

Hanna's mother bent over and kissed Hanna's sunken cheek. "Don't open the window while I'm gone." She turned and stared directly at Irena. "Remember, don't open the window."

Irena couldn't even nod. She stood, frozen, until the door to the flat banged shut. Mama, who'd stayed in the kitchen, had lectured them that they shouldn't get too close to Hanna. Irena inched her stiff legs forward, stopping in the middle of the room. She didn't know what to say to Hanna. She didn't look well enough to get out of bed, much less go to school.

Hanna smiled, but her gray lips barely moved, and her freckles were big muddy spots. She pointed her bony finger toward the window. "Open the curtains."

Irena gripped her hands tightly together behind her back. "Your mother will be mad."

Hanna's voice was barely a whisper. "She won't know."

Irena searched the room to distract Hanna. "Can I hold Gertrude?"

"We're getting a new baby," said Bridget. "Mama showed me how to hold it."

Hanna sat up straighter. "Your mother's having a baby?"

"I get to help take care of her," Bridget said. She raced to the dresser and pulled Gertrude down, cradling the doll in her arms. "You have to hold her head like this."

Irena shifted toward Bridget and reached for the doll. "Hanna's my friend. I get to hold Gertrude."

Bridget turned away, shouting, "I had her first."

Mama called from the kitchen. "Irena, Bridget. Behave yourselves or you'll have to come in the kitchen with me."

Irena quit protesting. She wasn't all that anxious to stay but maybe having them visit would perk Hanna up.

"Mommy was going to have a baby," Hanna said. "It was a boy, but something happened."

A lump formed in Irena's throat. "What happened?"

"I'm not supposed to talk about it," Hanna said. "It makes Mommy sad."

Irena hoped nothing bad happened to their baby.

"I want you to see the pretty lady," said Hanna. "Open the curtains."

Irena put her hands behind her back again.

"She's wearing a beautiful dress," Hanna added.

Curious, Irena glanced toward the window. She wanted to see the lady and her dress, but Mama had impressed upon Irena that she was seven, the age of reason, and she shouldn't do anything that she knew was wrong. If she did, she would have to confess her sin to the priest and do penance. She didn't know what penance was, and she didn't want to find out.

Hanna repeated, "Open the curtains. The lady is right outside."

"You live on the second story," said Irena. "How can anybody be outside your window?"

"I'll show you." Hanna scooted to the foot of the bed. Her legs flopped onto the bare floor. She grabbed one curtain, sliding it open. Instead of wearing her out, when she turned toward Irena, Hanna's eyes sparkled and her colorless lips changed into a radiant smile, making her face almost glow. "See. I told you a pretty lady was at the window."

Irena looked out the window. No one was there. Forcing her feet to move closer, she peered through the glass. She didn't see a woman or a ladder, only her own apartment building across the street. She waved for Bridget to join her.

Bridget scooted next to her, keeping Gertrude out of reach. "I don't see anyone."

"Open the curtains wider," Hanna said. "She has on a lacy white dress."

Irena turned from the window to protest, just as Hanna began to cough. The raspy cough went on and on, frightening Irena. Should she get Mama? But Mama wasn't supposed to be close to Hanna because of the baby. As Irena struggled with what to do, Bridget dropped Gertrude on the bed and patted Hanna on the back until she quit coughing.

Irena worried even more about Hanna. Not only did she look bad, but she also sounded bad. "At church, I'll light a candle for you. I'll pray really, really hard for you to get well and go to school with us."

Hanna gave Irena a weak smile and collapsed onto the bed.

Irena felt sorry for Hanna. "You can pick what to play."

Hanna took several shallow breaths. "Tea party." She took another breath and added, "Sometimes Mommy lets me use a real teapot and cups."

Irena turned to Bridget. "You ask Mama. You're younger. She'll give into you easier."

For once, Bridget didn't argue but scampered into the kitchen. Irena's eyes strayed to the doll. She picked Gertrude up, cradling her. "You're lucky. You have a real doll, not a pretend pillow baby."

"The pretty lady said I can't take Gertrude with me. Will you watch her for me?"

Watching Gertrude would be so much fun. "Where are you going?" Irena asked.

Hanna opened her mouth to answer but started to cough again. The sound was like a rattle with everything inside Hanna being shaken loose. She pointed to her handkerchief on the bed. Irena handed it to her. Hanna spat into the handkerchief. Blood —bright red blood—splattered into the white cloth, and it wasn't the first time. The handkerchief was dotted with brown spots that must have once been blood.

Bridget returned with three tiny cups and a teapot. "Mama even filled the teapot with water."

As Bridget poured water from the teapot into a cup, she whispered to Irena, "Mama said don't get too close to Hanna." Bridget crossed the room and gave Hanna a cup of water.

She propped herself up. "Mommy never lets me use water."

Bridget poured water for Irena and herself then they sat on the bed across from Hanna. Irena held Gertrude on her lap but she couldn't keep her eyes off Hanna's bloody handkerchief.

Bridget quickly emptied her cup. "I need more water."

Irena downed her cup. "I'll pour." She reached for the teapot on the floor.

"I brought the teapot," protested Bridget. "I get to pour."

"You can hold Gertrude." Irena handed Bridget the doll and then poured more water into their cups. She carried the teapot to Hanna, but her cup was almost full. Up close, Hanna looked even worse. Her eyes were like deep sockets sunk into her face, and her once-pretty blonde hair was dull and limp. Her stick-like arms were too weak for her to lift the cup, so Irena held it for Hanna to drink. As she took a sip, the door opened. Startled, Irena jumped back, splashing water onto Hanna.

Hanna's mother clomped across the wooden floor.

"I'm sorry. I'm sorry," said Irena, searching for something to wipe the water from Hanna and her bed. The bloody hand-kerchief was the only thing close. Irena didn't want to touch it, so she lifted the hem of her polka-dot dress and dabbed it with water.

"Clumsy girl," scolded Hanna's mother, pushing around Irena to check on Hanna. "Are you okay, sweetie?" After Hanna gave a weak nod, her mother said, "Now I'll have to change the bed."

From behind, Bridget was tiptoeing across the room. Irena's head jerked around. The curtains were still open. Too late.

Hanna's mother noticed the drapes, too. "Who opened the blackout curtains?"

Irena stepped back. "I didn't."

Bridget stopped next to Irena. "Me, either."

Hanna's mother stomped over to the window and yanked the curtains closed. She yelled loud enough Irena was sure she could have heard from their apartment. "Well, Hanna didn't open them."

Tears welled up in Irena's eyes. She didn't like being blamed for something she didn't do, but she couldn't tell on Hanna. Irena looked at Hanna, waiting for her to fess up, but her eyes rolled back in her head, and she fell against the pillow.

Hanna's mother hurried to Hanna's bed. Her voice was calmer. "Mommy's here now. I'll take care of you."

Hanna's lips twitched into a smile. Her words were slow and labored. "Did you see...the pretty lady...at the window?"

Wringing her hands, Hanna's mother glanced toward the window and then back at Hanna. "Quit talking nonsense. No one's at the window."

Mama called from the kitchen. "Irena, Bridget. We need to go."

Hanna didn't beg for them to stay, and Irena didn't protest.

At home, Mama set her and Bridget on the couch and stood over them ready to scold. "Audra told you not to open the blackout curtains, and you did."

"No, we didn't, Mama. Cross my heart." Irena made an 'x' across her chest. "Hanna opened them."

Mama looked at Bridget, who nodded. "It was Hanna."

"She wanted us to see the pretty lady at the window," Irena said. "She told us she was wearing a lacy white dress, but I looked out the window, and no one was there."

"I didn't see anyone either," said Bridget.

At the mention of the Lady in White, Mama sank onto the couch. Her hand shook as she made the sign of the cross.

"Did you see the lady, Mama?" Irena asked.

"*Nein.*" But Mama didn't sound mad anymore. "Come here."

The girls slid next to Mama, who stretched out her arms, hugging them against her. "You're both good girls."

Irena was relieved that Mama believed her. "Do you think the medicine will make Hanna better?"

Mama didn't answer. Instead, she said, "Say an extra prayer for Hanna tonight."

Irena nodded. "And I told her the next time we go to church, I'll light a candle and pray for her."

CHAPTER
THIRTY-FIVE

The following day, Harriet waved to Irena and Bridget as they ran up the steps and into the red-brick school. The girls hadn't asked why she had on her navy-blue church dress. They were too caught up in their own world.

During the last six weeks, life seemed almost normal. Irena and Bridget looked forward to school. Being outside several hours a day had brought color to their cheeks and walking them to and from school had made Harriet healthier, too.

The nights were no longer filled with fear. The last air raid had been in June, four months ago, when they'd tried to board the train to Lithuania. Oskar still worked long hours, but he was off on Sundays. Although the nights without the air raids gave him some rest, he hadn't regained his easy-going temperament. The lack of air raids and the knowledge that the Germans would defeat the Soviets by Christmas had bolstered Harriet's spirit. Living in Germany was just a short aberration. Soon, they would return home.

Her pressing problem was the baby, due within a month. Even if she received a letter from her parents, she couldn't return now. She was too far along, and the trip would be too hard. Reluctantly, she agreed with Oskar. It would be best to stay in Germany and have the baby here. Then they could go home.

After Harriet left the school, she didn't walk toward the projects. She headed in the opposite direction. She hadn't told the girls or Oskar that she planned to go to church. Last night, when Irena had mentioned church, Harriet knew she needed guidance and wanted to light a candle for Hanna.

As she entered St. Mary's, the same sense of belonging and peace that she'd experienced the first time washed over her. She walked down the side aisle toward the life-sized statue of the Virgin Mary, whose arms were spread wide in welcome. Harriet kneeled at the feet of the Holy Mother and lit a candle for Hanna. After she silently prayed for Hanna, Harriet prayed for her own needs. *Mother Mary, intercede on my behalf with our Savior. I'm with child, and like you, I need somewhere to give birth. Guide me to a place where the baby and I will be surrounded by love and care.*

A hand touched her shoulder. Harriet looked up. Sister Anne Lian, the nun from Lithuania, stood behind her. "I've been praying for you and your daughters. Where are they?"

"In school," Harriet clumsily rose. "I came to seek advice and pray for a sick child."

"What's the child's name?"

"Hanna. She has tuberculosis."

The nun's eyes filled with sympathy. "I'll add Hanna to our prayers." Sister Anne took Harriet by the arm and led her to a nearby pew where they sat. "What about your baby?"

"I hoped the baby would be born in Lithuania. After the Germans drove the Soviets out, we tried to return, but the train station was bombed."

The nun made the sign of the cross. "Thank God for His mercy that you were spared. It is best you don't return. A priest from Lithuania sought asylum here. He said the Germans being in control has changed little. The Nazis have no place for the Catholic Church in their regime."

Harriet flinched at the thought of her beautiful country torn apart by war.

"What plans have you made for the baby?"

"I heard a Polish woman at the market whispering to her friend that all her worries about her unborn child were over. She and the baby would be taken care of by the *Lebensborn* program."

Sister Anne grasped her hand tighter. "Have you gone there?"

Harriet shook her head. "I can't find out much about it and neither can Oskar, but the woman said she would be given extra food and would have the best doctors."

"The secret program was set up by the Nazis mostly for unmarried women. *Lebensborn* assumes guardianship of the babies they deliver. I know a Swedish woman who was persuaded adoption would be best for her baby, so the child could be reared in a proper German home."

Harriet silently considered the nun's words. "I'm afraid to go to a German hospital, and you don't trust this *Lebensborn*. What should I do, Sister?"

The nun didn't hesitate. "Come here."

Harriet scanned the sanctuary, her mouth agape. "To the church?"

"Behind the convent is a small school for orphans. There's an infirmary. I'm a nurse and can deliver your baby."

Harriet trusted the nun. "But I can't leave my daughters alone."

"They can stay at the orphanage and go to school with the other children."

As Harriet left, her heart thrummed with joy. God had answered her prayers. Sister Anne would deliver her baby, and Irena and Bridget wouldn't miss out on school.

Harriet had several hours before she had to pick up the girls, so she headed to the projects. As she neared the archway, the sky darkened. Plumes of black smoke billowed above the rows of red-brick buildings. It seemed to be coming from their flat.

CHAPTER
THIRTY-SIX

Harriet ran toward their flat, her pocketbook bouncing from her arm. She covered her mouth, but smoke filled her nose and her eyes watered. She tried to believe the smoke was from some other building, but each step confirmed that the smoke was spiraling from where they lived.

Her head screamed for her to run away. What was in the flat that needed to be saved? Oskar had his identification papers, and she carried the others in her pocketbook. Her amber rosary. She had received the rosary when she was confirmed. Oskar's pocket watch. His mother had given him the watch after his pa had been killed in the mine. Clothes for the baby. Their ration books. Were any of those worth putting herself and the baby in danger?

Ignoring the warnings in her head, Harriet plowed through the screen of smoke.

"Harriet, is that you?" a woman's voice called.

She squinted through the haze. Coming from the opposite direction was Rosa, her usual afghan covering her legs. She was being pushed in her wheelchair by Jonas, who steered the chair next to Harriet and stopped. His Fedora tilted as he leaned over, struggling to breathe.

"Is it my flat?" Harriet asked, her heart racing.

Jonas shook his head.

Harriet's legs went weak with relief.

Jonas managed to say, "The fire's at Audra's."

Fear shot through Harriet. "Did Audra get out? What about Hanna?"

Tears streamed down Rosa's flushed cheeks. "Hanna... Hanna passed away last night."

"Dear God, Hanna's dead?" Harriet's legs gave way. Jonas lurched forward and caught her. She leaned against him, not sure if her legs would keep her upright. "Poor Audra. What happened?"

"The authorities must have found out Hanna had tuberculosis." Rosa swiped her hands over her wet cheeks. "This morning the soldiers threw everything out of the apartment— their furniture, their dishes, their clothes. They doused it with gasoline and set it on fire."

Harriet stifled a gasp. "Why would they do that?"

"To keep the disease from spreading."

Harriet strained to see past the Rokas. "Where are Audra and her husband? What will they do?"

"They have relatives here," Jonas said.

"It might be too dangerous for anyone to take them in," Rosa said.

Jonas patted Rosa's shoulder as if to console her. "They'll probably go back home."

Home? Audra had said she didn't know where home was.

Rosa looked around. "Where are your girls?"

"School." Harriet swayed again. How would she ever be able to tell Irena and Bridget about Hanna? Harriet knew what death did to a child. She still carried her brother's death with her. She had been eleven when Agne passed away. The girls were younger, too young to face death.

Rosa reached up and took Harriet's hand. "You're pale." She turned to her husband. "Jonas, help Harriet home."

She didn't argue as Rosa dropped her hand, spun the chair around, and rolled ahead of them. Harriet continued to lean on Jonas, unable to stand alone.

Nearing the flat, Harriet's eyes flitted to the fire in front of Audra's apartment. Two soldiers stood nearby, poking the flames with sticks and laughing.

It's only things, Harriet reminded herself. *They can be replaced. Hanna cannot.*

Rosa stopped near Harriet's door. "I'll wait here, Jonas. Help Harriet into her apartment."

Jonas glanced at the soldiers and back at Rosa. "I don't want to leave you alone."

Rosa started pushing her chair. "They probably won't notice me through the smoke, but I'll wait around the corner, out of sight."

After Rosa disappeared, Jonas put his arm around Harriet's waist and led her up the stairs, one step at a time. Something lay on the floor, leaning against their apartment door. When they were closer, Harriet recognized it. Hanna's doll. Jonas picked up the doll. A note was pinned to her white sweater. "For Irena."

Tears trickled down Harriet's face. Irena wanted a doll, but not like this.

Jonas held the doll at arm's length. "The Germans are sterilizing the apartment. Do you think the doll is safe?"

Harriet hadn't thought about that. "Get rid of the doll before the girls see it."

Jonas nodded. "It would remind them of Hanna."

Would that be so bad? Harriet wondered. She unlocked the door, and Jonas took her elbow, steering her into the kitchen. She collapsed onto the nearest chair. "Thank you."

"Do you need anything? Some water?"

Harriet shook her head. "Go to Rosa."

Jonas righted his hat and stepped toward the door, the doll dangling from his hand. Harriet cried out, "Leave it."

Jonas dropped the doll onto the table as if it were on fire, too, and hurried out the door.

Harriet sat in silence, her mind reeling. She checked the clock on the kitchen wall, another thing she had been able to barter for. In two hours, she had to pick up the girls. She needed something to calm her nerves. She wished she had some tea or one of Audra's cigarettes.

Harriet walked to the sink and pumped water into a teakettle to heat on the stove. When it boiled, she poured herself a cup of hot water and sat at the table. She wrapped her hands around the warm cup to keep them from shaking. The doll's innocent blue eyes stared up at her.

Harriet needed to stay busy. She didn't want to think about Hanna, about Audra, about Irena and Bridget—about death. When she was a child, Harriet had ached every time she returned from school and Agne wasn't at the door to greet her.

Finishing the hot water, she carried the doll to the sink. She'd scrub the doll and wash her clothes. If she hung them up now, they would dry by tomorrow.

Two hours later, when Harriet arrived at the school, she still hadn't thought of a way to tell the girls about Hanna. As she waited, she tried to act normal. But what was normal about a nine-year-old child dying?

On the walk home, Irena and Bridget held her hands and kept their heads down, saying nothing. They didn't seem to notice Harriet's church dress, or that she was upset, but as they walked under the archway to the projects, Irena lifted her head and sniffed. "Smoke."

"*Ja,*" said Harriet. The billowing smoke had vanished, leaving behind only curls of gray.

"What's burning?" Irena asked.

Harriet didn't answer. When they reached their apartment, she was relieved the soldiers were gone, and the fire was out.

Irena pointed to the smoldering ashes in front of Hanna's flat and repeated, "What's burning?"

Averting Irena's questioning eyes, Harriet shooed the girls inside and plodded up the stairs behind them. The girls waited outside the door. Harriet's hand shook as she put the key into the lock. Irena and Bridget were young and innocent. Harriet wanted to stall, keep their world from changing, but she couldn't. When she unlocked the door, the girls would discover Gertrude on their bed, and Harriet would have to tell them about Hanna's death. Then their innocence would be gone. Harriet took one last look at their angelic faces.

Click. She turned the lock and shoved the door open.

The girls shot into the apartment. From the bedroom, Irena squealed with delight. "Gertrude."

Irena raced into the kitchen, clutching the naked doll to her chest. "Look, Mama. Hanna left me her doll. She told me she wanted me to watch her."

"She did?" A lump lodged in Harriet's throat.

"Hanna said she was going away with the pretty lady, but she couldn't take Gertrude. Did Hanna leave me Gertrude's clothes?"

Harriet swallowed, forcing the lump down. "I-I washed her clothes." She waved to the line stretched between the sink and the stove. "You can-can dress her tomorrow."

Irena must have noticed the tremor in Harriet's voice. "Is that when Hanna is coming back?"

Harriet couldn't break down. She needed to stay strong for the girls. "You and Bridget sit on the couch. I have something to tell you."

Holding Gertrude, Irena sat on one side of the couch and Bridget on the other. Harriet squeezed between them and forced out the words, "Last night, Hanna went to heaven."

Irena frowned. "Hanna can't go to heaven. That's where old people go when they die."

This was harder than Harriet expected. "Hanna was very sick. She couldn't get well."

Irena's lower lip quivered. "But she didn't die. She's little, like me and Bridget."

Harriet put an arm around each of the girls. "Remember I told you I had a brother?"

Irena and Bridget nodded.

"He was little like you, only four when he died."

Harriet waited as they struggled to understand that their friend was dead. She placed her hand on Gertrude's head. "Hanna left this doll for you to remember her."

Irena shoved Gertrude off her lap and onto the floor. "I don't want that doll. I want Hanna." Sobbing, Irena hopped off the couch and raced into the bedroom, slamming the door behind her.

Bridget slipped to the floor and picked up the doll. "You miss Hanna, don't you?" Bridget patted Gertrude's bare back. "You have us now. It'll be okay."

But how could it ever be okay again?

CHAPTER
THIRTY-SEVEN

"Hurry, Irena," called Mama from the kitchen. "You'll be late for school."

Irena didn't want to go to school, but she plodded into the kitchen where Mama held her coat. Irena forced her arms into the sleeves, and Bridget grabbed her hand, pulling her down the stairs.

The October day was cold. Irena's worn gray coat and the jumper beneath did little to keep out the wind. Shivering, she glanced up at Hanna's curtainless window. Behind the smoke-streaked glass, there was no Hanna. Two weeks ago, an angel had taken Hanna to heaven, yet Irena still expected to see her friend standing at the window, waving. Fresh pain stabbed through her. Nothing was fun anymore, not even school.

Glumly, Irena shuffled into the classroom and sank into her seat. As Fraulein Bauer marched into the room, Irena stood, raised her arm, and chanted, "*Heil Hitler*," but the words were hollow.

She squirmed under Hitler's gaze. His dark eyes stared accusingly at her. *Guilty. Guilty. Guilty.* Hanna was gone, and it was Irena's fault. She had told Hanna that she would light a candle at church for her. If Irena had gone to church and lit a candle, the angel would have made Hanna better. Instead, the angel took Hanna away.

"Irena, do you know the answer?" Fraulein Bauer asked.

Irena hadn't been paying attention. She squinted at the problem on the blackboard. Three apples take away three apples. Three apples had been lined up on the desk, but now no apples were on the desk. She tried to concentrate. She was a whiz at arithmetic and wanted to please Fraulein Bauer, but Hitler's judgmental eyes bore into her. *Guilty*. Irena gave up and shook her head.

Even the story of Heidi was too sad. Heidi's grandfather sent her away from the mountains with her animals and friends. She had to live in the city.

At PT, Irena wasn't excited about racing. The class lined up on the track and Fraulein Bauer blew her whistle. The other students sprinted ahead. Irena tried to push her legs forward, but they were as heavy as wooden logs. Helga dashed across the finish line first. Over her shoulder, she smirked at Irena, who came in last.

When the class lined up to be dismissed, Fraulein Bauer tapped her on the shoulder. "Can you stay and clean the blackboards?"

Irena had helped the teacher before and enjoyed cleaning the boards. The best part was having Fraulein Bauer all to herself. Today, however, Irena suspected the teacher didn't need help but wanted to scold her for daydreaming.

Irena shoved on her coat. "Mama's waiting."

Bridget stepped around Irena. "Stay. I'll tell Mama."

Irena glared at Bridget, but her sister turned and flounced out behind Mia.

Removing her coat, Irena shuffled to the blackboard and picked up the eraser. At least she couldn't see Hitler's picture and his accusing eyes. As she erased the board, she expected

Fraulein Bauer to scold her, but the teacher sat at her desk and waited until Irena was finished before she pointed to the student chair next to her, the one the teacher used when someone was in trouble.

Fraulein Bauer cleared her throat as Irena sank into the chair. "You haven't been paying attention in class."

It was true, so Irena remained silent.

"Can you tell me why?" Fraulein Bauer didn't sound mad, at least not the way Da sounded when he was mad.

Irena hesitated. She wanted to talk about Hanna, but that would make her cry.

When Irena remained silent, Fraulein Bauer said, "I noticed your mother's going to have a baby."

Thinking about the baby made joy spark through her. Then Irena remembered she shouldn't be happy, not when Hanna was gone.

"Does it have something to do with the baby? Are you worried your mother won't have enough time for you?"

"Oh no, ma'am. We get to help take care of her. At least I hope the baby is a girl. I want another sister."

Fraulein Bauer's blue eyes were soft and her words gentle. "You know school is important."

"Yes, ma'am." Irena had wanted to go to school for so long and now she was messing it up.

"You're very smart. I don't want you to fall behind."

Irena's words tumbled out. "My friend, Hanna, died. She was my first girlfriend. Now I don't have anyone."

"I'm sorry about your friend. That's sad." The teacher patted her on the arm. "But you shouldn't think that you don't have anyone. You have Bridget."

Irena frowned. She'd never thought of Bridget as a friend. "Bridget's my sister."

Fraulein Bauer nodded. "But you play together like friends."

Irena disagreed. "When Mama's busy, I have to watch Bridget and show her how to do things."

Fraulein Bauer removed her hand and raked her fingers through her hair as if trying to fix the limp waves. "Let me tell you a secret." Even though no one else was in the room, the teacher leaned in close enough for Irena to whiff her flowery perfume. "I always wanted a sister or even a brother."

"You did?" Irena had not expected the teacher to tell her something so personal.

Fraulein Bauer's blue eyes saddened. "Being an only child is lonely."

"Hanna was an only child. I think she was lonely, too."

"Bridget can't do everything you can do, but you should value her friendship even more because she's your sister."

Bridget's friendship wasn't the same. She had always been in Irena's life. Hanna was someone new. Someone older. Someone special.

From her desk, Fraulein Bauer picked up a slate board. "Would you like to take this home so you won't get behind?"

"May I?" Irena loved practicing her letters. When she wrote, all her worries seemed to disappear.

"I'll let you borrow it and some chalk if you promise to pay attention in class." Fraulein Bauer held out the slate board, enticing Irena.

At school Hitler was always looking down, judging her. At home, she might not feel so guilty. Before the teacher changed her mind, Irena grabbed the board and chalk and dashed out the door.

CHAPTER
THIRTY-EIGHT

Saturday, a shaft of light landed on Irena lying in bed. She opened her eyes. Today she'd play with Hanna or at least wave to her from the window. Then Irena remembered she would never be able to play with Hanna again. Rolling over, Irena closed her eyes. She didn't deserve to be happy, not when Hanna was gone.

The bedroom door opened, and footsteps crossed to her bed. "Irena, are you sick?" Mama sounded worried.

"I don't know." Her head ached when she tried to push thoughts of Hanna away, and her stomach hurt when she ate.

Mama felt Irena's forehead. "You aren't warm. Get dressed. You'll feel better after you eat breakfast. I have something important to tell you."

Irena didn't want more bad news. "Is it good?"

Mama smiled and looked happy. "Yes, very good."

In the kitchen, Irena slumped in her chair and ate her porridge. Everything tasted bland.

"Tell us the good news, Mama," Bridget said.

Mama put down her spoon. "When I'm ready to have the

baby, we're going to the convent, and Sister Anne is going to deliver the baby."

Irena remembered the pretty nun. "I thought we got to help with the baby."

"You can help *after* the baby is born."

"Can we come to the church to see you and the baby?"

"You won't have to come. You get to go to church with me for a week or two."

Irena frowned. This was not good news. "Why can't we stay here?"

"Da has to work, and you're too young to be alone."

"No, we aren't. We can take care of ourselves, can't we, Bridget?"

"I wanna go with Mama."

Bridget wasn't being a friend. Irena didn't want to live in some place different, some place she didn't know, some place that might be like the Registration Department, and Mama wouldn't be with them. She would be with the baby. Irena tried again. "I don't want to miss school."

"You won't have to. Behind the convent, the church runs a school for orphans. You and Bridget can go to school with the other children."

"Orphans!" Irena rose and stomped toward the bedroom. "We're not orphans, and I'm not going."

CHAPTER
THIRTY-NINE

November 1941

Harriet was awakened by a warm liquid trickling down her leg. No, not the baby. It was too soon. She wasn't ready.

She clamped her mouth shut, afraid she would cry out and wake Oskar lying beside her or the girls across the room. She should have gone to church sooner, but each day she'd delayed. She thought Irena would be excited about staying at church and playing with the other children. Instead, when she heard 'orphanage,' she'd become upset.

Harriet didn't want to take Irena away from everything familiar, not when she was grieving. In Irena's mind, she'd lost Hanna and now she was losing her school and this place to live. Harriet understood how difficult grief was and had given Irena more time.

The baby, however, seemed to have other plans. Maybe Harriet had been too hasty. Her water hadn't broken this early with Irena or Bridget. The warm liquid on her leg might not be water. The baby had definitely turned. He or she might be putting pressure on her bladder, making her lose control.

Harriet wanted to stay in the warm bed. She patted the damp sheet. She wasn't imagining it. What if her water had broken? She needed to check. She scooted to the edge of the bed and sat up. Her bare feet hit the cold floor. Her ankles were swollen and her back ached. She planted her hand on the crook of her back and stretched, hoping to ease the pain.

Yesterday, she had a spurt of energy. She'd just overdone it —dusting and sweeping the two rooms, washing the sheets, stringing them up around the kitchen, and packing the suitcase. She also had a spurt of energy before the girls were born. She wouldn't be able to rest until she checked the wet liquid between her legs.

A chamber pot was under the bed for the girls if they needed to potty during the night. Harriet had used it a few times, but squatting was difficult now and without light, she wouldn't be able to see into it. She'd have to go out down the hall to the water closet.

Drawing her thin nightgown tightly around her, Harriet hoisted herself up and fumbled into the kitchen. She unhooked the chain on the door and waddled down the hall, her bare feet softly *tap-tap-tapping*. She didn't want to wake the brothers across the hall. Opening the door to the dark water closet, she reached overhead for the string dangling from the single bulb and pulled. Light flooded the small room.

She sank onto the bowl, not bearing down hard. Water gushed out. She spread her legs and checked, praying the baby's head was not coming. Blood swirled in the water. Sweat beaded on her forehead.

She hurried back to the bedroom and shook Oskar, who was asleep. "Wake up."

Groaning, he rolled away from her.

She raised her voice but tried to sound calm. "Oskar, it's the baby."

He bolted up. "Now?"

"I-I think my water broke."

He sprang out of bed. "What can I do?"

"The suitcase is packed and under the bed. Dress the girls while I get ready."

Throwing on his clothes, Oskar pulled out the suitcase and dashed across the room to take care of the girls while she slipped on her green dress. Her shoes were next to the dresser. She wiggled her toes inside. Her feet were too swollen to slide into them. After several tries, she jammed them on. She took a step and winced.

Irena and Bridget were in the kitchen and ready to go by the time Harriet walked to the door and put on her coat. Oskar shooed the girls down the stairs and put his arm across Harriet's back, steadying her.

They would expect Oskar at the factory. He'd never missed before. "What about work?"

He nudged her toward the stairs. "I need to be with you. I told them about the baby."

Relieved, Harriet took one step at a time as she silently said a prayer of thanks that she was married to a man who put her and their family first.

Outside, the full moon illuminated the empty street through the projects. She lowered her head against the fierce November wind. Each step hurt her feet. She couldn't walk all the way to church in these shoes. They would have to turn back. She'd deliver the baby at the apartment. Oskar could help. But what if something went wrong? Her water had gushed out, and blood had been in the stool. If something wasn't right, she wouldn't know what to do, nor would he.

Gritting her teeth, she plodded forward. She swiped at something cold on her nose. The front of her coat glistened with white. Snowflakes. The first snow of the year. The girls held out their mittened hands, enchanted by the snow landing on their palms.

Harriet's mother had said on the day Harriet was born that it was raining, and a calf had been birthed. Now she would have a story to tell the baby. You were born on the first snowfall of the year, November 5, 1941.

The snow distracted her from the urgency of the baby until her stomach cramped. Pain ripped through her. Bending over, she cupped one hand under her belly and with the other held onto Oskar.

She couldn't go into labor, not outside in the cold.

Oskar put his hand on her shoulder. "What can I do?"

She tried to breathe through the pain. She inhaled through her nose and exhaled short puffs from her mouth. Breathe… one, two, three. Breathe…one, two, three. She continued the pattern until the pain let up enough for her to straighten.

"Are you in labor?" Oskar asked.

It felt like labor, but she didn't want to believe it. "I hope not."

When the cramping subsided, they walked under the archway and turned in the direction of the church. The moon in the west was still slightly visible even though in the east the sun peeked above the horizon. A truck with workers riding in the bed rumbled down the street, followed by a black motorcar. Other people headed out as if it were a normal day. Nothing seemed normal to Harriet.

Her feet ached. Her body cramped.

Oskar prodded her on. "We have to keep moving."

He was right. She calculated about ten or fifteen minutes before another pain would hit. Her labor with Irena had taken six hours, and with Bridget, three hours. The church was at least an hour away. Harriet wouldn't be able to walk that far— not in these shoes, not in the wind and snow, and not in labor.

A terrifying thought flickered in her mind. An air raid. Fear rippled down her spine. If there was an air raid, she couldn't run. She wouldn't be able to make it to a shelter. She would be left outside to have the baby in the cold. The poor thing would certainly die and maybe she would too.

Fortunately, not a single air raid had happened since June, when they'd tried to return home. She forced her cramped feet to move faster. With each step she silently prayed, *Please Lord, give me strength.* She repeated the words, *give me strength, give me strength*, until they shielded her, blocking out the cold, the snow, and some of the pain.

When she reached the corner near the market, another pain hit. Certainly not fifteen minutes or even ten since the last one. She leaned over and breathed through her nose and exhaled three short puffs.

Irena ran to her side. "Mama, what's wrong?"

Harriet couldn't answer. *Breathe…one, two, three.*

Irena cried out. "Da, something's wrong with Mama."

Breathe…one, two, three.

"It's the baby coming," Oskar said.

"Now?" Irena's question echoed Harriet's fear.

"Stay with your mama." Oskar dropped the suitcase and rushed down the sidewalk.

Where was he going? Why was he leaving? At the next corner, a bus pulled over and stopped. The door slid open and Oskar stood on the sidewalk, gesturing.

As Oskar raced back, the pain let up. "The bus will take you."

Her prayers had been answered. She wouldn't have the baby outside in the cold.

Oskar led her to the bus with three other passengers in the back and settled her into a seat near the driver. He picked up the suitcase and gave her a small peck on the cheek. "Come on, girls. We'll meet your mama at the church."

Terrified of being alone, Harriet clawed at Oskar's coat. "Aren't you coming with me?"

He turned to her. His face, red from the cold, grew redder. "I only paid for you."

Harriet understood what he was not saying. *I don't have enough money for all of us to ride.*

Irena broke loose and latched onto her arm. "I'm staying with Mama."

The bus driver turned to Oskar and said something in German before he closed the door. As the bus roared away from the curb, Oskar lifted Irena and then Bridget onto the empty seat across the aisle before he sank next to her.

Harriet whispered, "What did the driver say?"

"That he would take all of us. Just don't have the baby on his bus."

She wasn't planning to have the baby on the bus. Then another contraction made her double over, and she wasn't so sure.

The bus seemed to take hours, although it was probably no more than fifteen minutes before it screeched to a stop. Oskar sprinted to the door of the convent. He quickly returned and helped Harriet off the bus as Sister Anne approached, wheeling a chair toward them.

Harriet sank onto the chair and gave Sister Anne a weak smile. "Thank you."

The nun patted her on the shoulder and turned to Oskar. "Follow me. I'll take the girls to the orphanage, and we'll go to the infirmary."

Sister Anne pushed Harriet into the school and down a long hall. She stopped at a ward filled with beds of sleeping girls. "This is where Irena and Bridget will stay."

Then Sister Anne whisked Harriet down the hall to a small room with dark gold walls that were bare except for a brass crucifix hanging directly across from the single bed. Harriet eased onto the bed. Another contraction hit. She tried to breathe through the pain. Why did she think once she made it to the church, she would be all right? She still had to deliver the baby.

But Sister Anne was beside her, holding her hand, coaching her when to breathe and when to push. Another nun came into the room and did whatever Sister Anne asked, fluffing Harriet's pillow, laying a cold rag on her forehead, wiping the sweat from her face, and helping Harriet sit up to push.

She stared at the crucifix, which gave her strength, but after two hours, she was exhausted. She wanted to give up and sleep. But her body jerked her awake, and Sister Anne kept coaxing. "One more push. Just one more."

Harriet gave one more push. The most wonderful sound filled the room. *"Wah! Wah!"* The baby—her baby—was alive and crying.

Sister Anne held the bloody baby by the ankles, dangling it upside down. "You have a girl."

Harriet collapsed onto the bed and closed her eyes. "A girl."

It seemed like only moments later that Sister Anne nudged her awake. Her baby had been washed and swaddled in a blanket. Harriet stretched out her arms, eager to hold her daughter. The nun laid the baby in her arms.

Harriet gazed down at her. The memory of the pain, only minutes earlier, slipped away. Her body had split open. She had experienced the most excruciating torture of her life. Yet as she ran her finger over the soft skin on her baby's forehead, the memory faded. It had been the same with Irena and Bridget.

Harriet lifted her eyes to Sister Anne. "How can I forget the pain so quickly?"

"The miracle of childbirth. It's God's plan."

The baby found Harriet's finger and clutched onto it.

The world was at war, yet Harriet gazed down at their beautiful baby girl, a special gift from God.

CHAPTER
FORTY

rena lowered her head and gripped Bridget's hand as she pushed against the winter winds. Today was the first time she and Bridget would attend their regular school since the baby had been born. Irena was excited to see Mia and Fraulein Bauer, but it was scary walking to school without Mama, who'd stayed home with the baby. Irena heeded all Mama's warnings—head down, don't talk, and don't draw attention to yourself.

Shivering, Irena sucked in a breath of cold air and tried to be brave as they crossed under the brick archway and turned away from the projects. Each step made her heart thump louder than her boots on the brick sidewalk. What if she got lost? What if she ran into soldiers? She peeked up. No soldiers were in sight. She let out her breath. It turned into steam, rose, and disappeared.

She and Bridget had been absent from school for more than three weeks. Irena wanted to return, but she was worried. How would Mama take care of the baby without her and Bridget to help? They didn't feed the baby. Mama had to do that because milk ran right out of her breasts. But Mama let Irena and Bridget hold the baby, if they were careful with her head. Irena liked to coo and make the baby smile. Sometimes she helped Mama put her to sleep. At night the baby slept in bed with Mama and Da, but when Betty was older, she would sleep with her and Bridget.

The baby's real name was Elizabeth. Mama was so grateful to Sister Anne and the other nuns that Mama asked them to name the baby and be her godparents. Elizabeth was a pretty name, but it was too big for such a tiny baby, so she'd quickly become Betty.

When Betty was born, she weighed less than two kilograms. The nuns insisted the baby stay until she was 'fattened up.' They must have wanted to fatten up Bridget and Irena, too. Every day they ate three meals and drank a glass of thick, creamy milk.

At first, Irena was homesick and would ask what the baby weighed. But when Elizabeth had been fattened up, Irena was sad to leave. She liked the school at the orphanage even more than her regular school. She had made lots of friends because she and Bridget seemed to have a magical status.

Some children at the orphanage had parents, or at least they said they did, but they didn't know where they were. Others knew their parents had gone to heaven. But none of them had what Irena and Bridget had—a mother, a father, and a home.

The teacher at the orphanage was Sister Francis. Each school day didn't start by saluting Hitler's portrait. The classroom didn't even have a picture of Hitler. Instead, a picture of Mary cradling baby Jesus hung on the wall. Irena took comfort in staring at Mary and Jesus, more than at Hitler.

The school day started with attending Mass. Irena liked the school and Sister Francis, but she couldn't concentrate on learning any more at the orphanage than she'd been able to do at her regular school. All she thought about was Hanna.

After the teacher caught Irena daydreaming several times, she was sent to Sister Anne. The nun usually smiled, but the day Irena was sent to her office, she was not smiling. Sister Anne took Irena's hand and marched her into the church through the side door that the priest and nuns used. They sat in the pew near the front, where Irena had first met her. "Your mother told me you recently had some bad news."

Irena lowered her head and nodded. Thinking about Hanna made the food in her stomach slosh.

"Can you talk about it?"

Irena pressed her hands against her stomach. "My friend Hanna went to heaven."

The nun lifted the large crucifix on a chain around her neck and kissed it. "I'm sorry you lost your friend. Was she Bridget's friend, too?"

Irena had never thought about Bridget missing Hanna. "I guess. But Hanna liked me better. She gave me Gertrude, her doll."

"Gertrude must be very special."

Irena had always wanted a doll, but she admitted, "It makes me think of Hanna."

"Is that a bad thing?"

Irena fought her tears. She would be embarrassed if she cried in front of Sister Anne. "It makes me sad."

"You don't want to forget your friend, do you?"

Irena raised her head and shook it so hard her pigtails flopped back and forth. "I just want her to come back."

The nun's blue eyes clouded. "My parents went to heaven when I was just a little older than you. I prayed hard for God to send them back."

The food stopped sloshing in Irena's stomach. She sat up straighter. "Did He send them back?"

"No." Sister Anne gazed up at the domed ceiling above them. "God has His plan, and we have to accept it, even if we don't like it." Sister Anne looked at Irena again. The nun's blue eyes seemed peaceful.

Irena craned her head up, hoping to see something that would give her peace. All she saw was the peeling plaster on the ceiling. She slumped lower in the pew.

Sister Anne must have noticed. "Are you sad because you feel guilty about your friend's death?"

Irena's throat hitched. Sister Anne knew her secret.

The nun put her hand on Irena's shoulder. "Can you tell me about it?"

God already knew and Sister Anne talked to God, so Irena couldn't keep the secret from her. Admitting her guilt to Sister Anne was hard. Irena took in a shallow breath. "I-I told Hanna I would come to church and light a candle for her...so-so she would get better."

Irena clasped her hands in her lap and took several more breaths. She didn't want to confess the rest, but Sister Anne stayed silent, waiting.

Irena gulped and blurted out, "When my family came to church on my birthday, I asked Mama to light a candle and pray for Hanna. She said I could light one next time, only we never came to church again...until the baby was born."

Sister Anne didn't look angry or disappointed. "Did you pray for Hanna at home?"

"Oh, yes, Sister, every night."

"Your mama told me about Hanna and lit a candle for her. All the nuns prayed for her."

"But she didn't get well."

The nun patted Irena's hands clenched in her lap. "My child, I suspect you did all you could for your friend."

Mama and Fraulein Bauer had said similar words, but Irena still felt guilty.

"Would you like to light a candle for Hanna now?"

A flicker of hope stirred inside. "Will Hanna come back from heaven?"

"No, but we can pray for Hanna and give her peace."

Sister Anne reached into the pocket of her robe and pulled out a coin. She held Irena's hand and led her to the statue of Mary. Irena dropped the coin into the box and lit a candle. Kneeling together, they prayed for Hanna.

After that day in church with Sister Anne, Irena didn't feel so guilty. She was sad and missed Hanna, but it didn't crowd out all her other thoughts. Irena paid attention in class and even raised her hand when she was sure she knew the answer. Fraulein Bauer would be pleased by how much Irena and Bridget had learned while they were gone.

As they reached the steps of the red-brick building, relief washed over her. They had made it to school without Mama. Irena wanted to race up the steps to get out of the cold and to tell Fraulein Bauer about her new baby sister. But Irena needed to set an example for Bridget. As ladylike as possible, she led Bridget up the stairs and into the school.

When they reached their classroom, Irena was glad the two seats at the first table between Pierina and Mia were empty. As Irena and Bridget slid into their seats, Pierina smiled but stared straight ahead. Mia looked different. Her hair was still blonde, not brown, but her long braid was wrapped into a bun at the nape of her neck, making her look older.

Irena was busting to share her news. "We have a new baby sister. I can't wait to tell Fraulein Bauer."

Mia frowned. "Fraulein Bauer isn't..." She stopped mid-sentence and sat up straighter as a large-shouldered woman, in a black wool dress with a jacket, entered. The woman's dark hair, streaked with gray, was parted in the middle and pulled into a tiny bun. She wore black, lace-up shoes with thick heels that clomped across the wooden floor. Stopping at the teacher's desk, she pivoted toward Hitler's gilded-framed picture and raised her arm.

All the girls stood, except Irena and Bridget. Mia elbowed Irena, who hoisted herself up, pulling Bridget with her. They raised their right arms and repeated three times, "*Heil Hitler.*" Saluting now seemed odd and didn't bring comfort the way praying at the orphanage had.

The thick woman walked to the teacher's chair and sat in it. Irena scooted over and whispered to Mia, "Why is she sitting at Fraulein Bauer's desk?"

Mia kept her hands folded on the table and stared straight ahead. Maybe she hadn't heard. Irena elbowed Mia and whispered louder, "Where is Fraulein Bauer?"

Mia still didn't answer. Irena kicked Mia's leg under the table.

Suddenly, a long wooden pointer smacked the top of the table between her and Mia. Irena jerked back and looked up. The large woman was towering over them, close enough for Irena to see a swastika pin on the lapel of her jacket. "Is there a problem?"

Mia shoved her hands under the table, out of reach of the wooden stick. "No, Fraulein Mueller."

The woman's dark eyebrows lowered as she glared at Irena. "And who are you?"

Irena struggled to speak. "Irena Golcvegaite. This is my—"

The woman cut her off. "Can she talk?"

Bridget didn't wait for Irena to answer. "I'm Bridget and we have—"

Again, the woman cut in. "School is a privilege, especially for children like you. There is no talking in my classroom. Do you understand?"

Her classroom?

The woman raised the wooden pointer and smacked it down between Irena and Bridget. "Do you understand?"

Nodding, Irena slid her hands onto her lap, safely away from the wooden stick. But she didn't understand. Why had this woman sat at Fraulein Bauer's desk? Why had she said this was her classroom? And where was Fraulein Bauer?

CHAPTER
FORTY-ONE

December 1941

T he following week, Irena sat in the first row, her hands folded on the table and her eyes focused on the door. Anticipation shivered through her as she waited for Fraulein Bauer to return. Irena's hopes were crushed by the heavy footsteps clomping down the hall. Fraulein Mueller marched into the classroom. She wore the same black dress with the swastika pinned prominently on the lapel of her jacket. The class rose—even Irena and Bridget—raised their right arms, and chanted, *"Heil Hitler."*

Then Fraulein Mueller pulled down the world map above the blackboard. "We'll begin with geography."

Irena fidgeted. Geography was her worst subject, but she unclasped her hands and poised her arm to shoot into the air. Last week, she had not answered a single question, not even when Fraulein Mueller called on her. Today, Irena wanted to show this woman that she was not a *dummkopf*.

Fraulein Mueller picked up the long wooden pointer. "Who can list the Axis powers?"

Irena's hand shot up. Then she jerked it down. She had studied hard at the orphanage and didn't think she would be behind, but who or what were the Axis powers?

Beside her, Mia raised her hand. When Fraulein Mueller called on her, Mia stood. "The Axis powers are Germany, Italy, and Japan."

"*Gut*." Fraulein Mueller didn't smile but tapped the pointer on the map. "Who can locate the Axis Powers?"

Irena squinted at the map. The large blue country in the middle of Europe was Germany and the green boot to the right was Italy, Pierina's homeland, but where was Japan?

The teacher called on Pierina, who walked to the map and wielded the long pointer to Germany, Italy, and then a group of islands in the Pacific.

Irena frowned. She thought 'axis' had something to do with a wheel and expected the Axis countries to form a circle.

"Who can tell me why the Axis powers are fighting?" Fraulein Mueller asked.

Irena cringed. The Axis powers were about the war. School had always been a place where she had been able to forget about the war and feel safe. Fraulein Mueller was ruining it. She was taking away those precious hours of not thinking about Nazis or air raids or killings.

Fraulein Mueller barked out another question. "Who are the Allied powers?"

Mia's hand shot up. Fraulein Mueller called on another girl who answered, "Great Britain and France."

Fraulein Mueller's chest puffed up, making her swastika pin more prominent. "Which of these Allied countries has been conquered by our *Wehrmacht*?"

The German military was still fighting Great Britain, so the answer must be 'France.' Irena hesitated. She wanted to answer, but she wasn't sure she was right, so she kept her hand down.

From behind her, a deep voice boomed, "France."

"*Sehr gut*, Helga." This time, Fraulein Mueller smiled.

Even Helga appeared smarter than Irena.

"What other countries has Germany conquered?"

Irena listened to the list. She heard her beloved Lithuania. A wave of homesickness washed over her. She wanted to go home. She looked up. Fraulein Mueller glared at her as if she expected some kind of answer. Above the map, Hitler stared down at her. Irena's stomach knotted. The walls closed in. She had to get away. She forced her hand into the air.

The teacher pointed the wooden stick at her. "Can you tell us a country?"

Irena shook her head. "I have to use the water closet."

Fraulein Mueller's mouth flattened into a straight line as she gave a curt nod.

Irena scurried out of the room, fleeing from Fraulein Mueller, from Hitler, and from all the talk of war.

The school days took on a sameness, one after another, until the second week in December, when Fraulein Mueller stumbled into the classroom, appearing rattled. She still wore her black wool dress and clunky shoes, but the swastika pin on her jacket was crooked, and her tiny bun drooped onto her neck. As she pulled down the map, her hand shook. Irena wondered what could have rattled Fraulein Mueller.

"Who can tell me what happened five days ago on December seventh?"

Irena couldn't think of anything. Even Mia didn't raise her hand. Fraulein Mueller pointed the wooden stick to a large black dot in the Pacific Ocean. "Japan attacked the island of Hawaii, a territory of America. How does that affect Germany?"

When no one answered, Mia raised her hand and rose. "Japan is an Axis power."

"*Ja,* go on."

Unable to add more, Mia sank to her seat.

Fraulein Mueller placed her hand over the swastika pin on her jacket. She must have realized it was crooked because her fingers worked to right it. "Yesterday Germany declared war on America. Remember the date: December 11, 1941." Fraulein Mueller turned her back to the class and raised both arms toward Hitler's picture. As if in jubilant adoration, she exclaimed, "*Sieg Heil*! Hail Victory! Now Germany will rule the world!"

———

On Sunday, Mama stood at the stove, stirring the potato dumpling soup. Irena's mouth watered as she sat at the table, cradling Betty in her arms. Across from them, Bridget sat on Da's lap, giggling as he ran his scruffy whiskers across her red cheek.

Sunday was Irena's favorite day. School was replaced with family and sometimes church. Irena missed the nuns and her new friends at the orphanage. She'd liked attending Mass each day and longed for the peace it had given her. But the wind rattled the windows, and the snow splattered the glass, so they wouldn't be going to Mass today.

At least Da was home. Mama used to let her and Bridget sometimes stay up to see him, but that ended now that they had to get up early for school.

Da stopped teasing Bridget and looked across the table. "Irena, what did you learn at school this week?"

Talking about school and the war made Irena's stomach hurt. She looked down at Betty in her lap. "Nothing."

"Yes, we did." Bridget hopped off Da's knee. "We learned about the Axis powers."

Wanting to distract Bridget, Irena offered, "You can hold Betty."

Bridget pranced to the empty chair next to Irena and held out her arms for the baby.

"What about the Axis powers?" Da asked.

Irena slid the baby into Bridget's arms to keep her from answering, but it didn't work.

"They're Germany, Italy, and..." Bridget turned to Irena. "What's the other one?"

Irena didn't want Da to think Bridget was smarter than she was. "Japan."

"Yes, that country," Bridget said. "And Hitler declared war on America."

Mama's spoon clattered to the floor. She turned from the stove. "That can't be true. The German troops will be home by Christmas and the war will be over."

"Is so true." Bridget sounded insulted that Mama didn't believe her. "Teacher said so. Tell her, Irena."

Instead of answering, Irena tickled Betty. The baby's legs flailed in the air. "Look. Betty's kicking."

Da wasn't distracted. "I overheard the guards say Japan had bombed Hawaii, a territory of America."

Mama set bowls of potato dumplings on the table. "But why would Hitler declare war on America?"

"Maybe because America declared war on Japan, and Japan is an Axis power." Da lifted the baby from Bridget. "Sit down and eat, Harriet."

Mama sat and said the blessing, but when she finished, she didn't eat. She continued to talk to Da. "How can America send troops here?"

"I doubt if they send troops across the ocean, but they could send bombers."

"We don't need more bombing. I can't bear the thought of living with this fear much longer."

"Don't worry, Harriet. We haven't had an air raid for six months, and if we have one, we'll go to the new air-raid shelter. It'll be safer than the basement."

"Will Germany be bombing America?" asked Mama.

Irena lowered her head and tried not to listen to Mama and Da talk about the war. She scooped up a spoonful of soup. The dumplings tasted doughy and lumped in her stomach.

CHAPTER
FORTY-TWO

December 1941

On Monday, Irena sat behind the long wooden school table, her hands folded in front of her, her eyes focused on the door as she prayed for Fraulein Bauer to walk into the classroom. Footsteps clomped down the hall and pickle-faced Fraulein Mueller marched into the room. Irena stood, raised her arm, and chanted, "*Heil Hitler!*"

Irena slouched into her seat. She had been back at school for more than three weeks. How long would Fraulein Bauer be gone?

The class began as usual with geography, but Irena perked up when Fraulein Mueller announced she was going to read a book to the class. Irena loved to listen to Fraulein Bauer read. Irena had told her friends at the orphanage about Heidi, who was an orphan like them and lived with her grandfather in the mountains.

Irena sat on the floor and scooted close to the teacher's

chair. She wanted to find out what happened to Heidi after she left her grandfather to live in the city. Fraulein Mueller held up a book with a red cover. Pictures of fat men with high fore-heads and long, hooked noses were on the front. The book was definitely not *Heidi.*

Fraulein Mueller cleared her throat. "Today I'm going to read *Don't Trust a Fox.* Who are the people on the front?"

Irena and Bridget kept their hands folded in their laps. So did Pierina and Mia. Fraulein Mueller pointed to Helga, who answered, "Jews."

"*Sehr gut.*" Fraulein Mueller lifted the book higher. "Study these pictures. If you see a Jew, you must report him."

Irena stared at the ugly men. She had never seen anyone who looked like that and would have no trouble spotting them.

Fraulein Mueller read the scary book. "Like a fox, he slips about, so you must look out!" No wonder the Germans didn't like the Jews. They were sneaky.

In the afternoon, Fraulein Mueller announced, "Today we're going to discuss our winter holiday. What do we cele-brate on December twenty-fifth?"

Mia was a front-row-raise-your-hand student. Not Irena. She only raised her hand when she was sure of the answer. Irena's hand shot up.

Fraulein Mueller aimed the wooden pointer at her.

The answer was so easy. Irena stood and boomed, "Christ-mas, the birth of Jesus."

Fraulein Mueller puckered her lips and emphatically shook her head. "No, no, no." Each 'no' was punctuated by the pointer moving up and down. "We do not celebrate Christmas in Germany."

Irena sank to her seat. Her face burned. Behind her, Helga and her friends snickered. Last year Irena's family had not attended midnight Mass, but they had celebrated Christmas with the twelve dishes, straw, a tree, and presents.

A student at the back of the room answered, "On December twenty-fifth, we celebrate *Julfest.*"

Fraulein Mueller's pursed lip relaxed. "*Ser gut.*"

Irena didn't think it was very good. She had never heard of *Julfest* and whatever *Julfest* was, it couldn't be better than celebrating Jesus' birth.

Fraulein Mueller pointed her stick at the class again. "Who knows what *Julfest* is?"

Mia raised her hand and stood. "*Julfest* is our Winter Solstice."

"And how does your family celebrate Winter Solstice?"

"We light the men—I mean, we have a light tree." Mia slumped into her seat.

Fraulein Mueller's mouth drooped. "And what do we put on top of the *light* tree?"

Irena remembered the beautiful star on their tree in Lithuania, but she tucked her hands into her lap. This might be another trick question.

A girl from the back answered, "A *sig rune* that looks like a swastika."

Irena had never seen a sun wheel that looked like a swastika.

The teacher nodded. "What else do we do for *Julfest?*"

One girl's family displayed a winter garden with figurines of deer, rabbits, and a mother with a baby. Another classmate hung up stockings for Odin, who rode down on his white horse and left treats. And a third girl's family sang songs.

Fraulein Mueller put down the pointer. "Today we're going to sing a beautiful Winter Solstice song, *Hohe Nacht der Klaren Sterne.* Some of you might know the words."

Irena had never heard of Winter Solstice, so she expected the words to the song to be new, but when the teacher's voice boomed through the classroom, Irena recognized the Christmas carol and joined in. *"Silent night! Holy night! All is calm, and all is bright.*

"Round yon Virgin, Mother…" Irena stopped. The class was singing different words. She thought they were *"Only the Chancellor steadfast in fight, watches o'er Germany by day and by night."*

When the class again reached the refrain *Silent night! Holy night!* Irena sang, too. Then she waited, hoping the next words would be *Sleep in heavenly peace.* Instead, Fraulein Mueller's voice reverberated above the others. *"Adolf Hitler is Germany's wealth. Brings us greatness, favor, and health."*

The following week, before Fraulein Mueller dismissed the class, she announced, "Because of *Julfest,* school will be closed until next year."

The room buzzed with excitement. As the students gathered their coats and hats from the hooks near the door, Irena whispered to Bridget. "If you want to celebrate Christmas, you better not tell Mama or Da about *Julfest.*"

CHAPTER
FORTY-THREE

Sunday, December 21, 1941

rena sat on the kitchen floor, wiggling her feet into her galoshes. She didn't want Da to change his mind about taking her with him to cut down a Christmas tree.

Bridget hopped off the couch and ran to Da, who was putting on his coat. "Can I come, too?"

Da patted her head. "Maybe next time."

Bridget crossed her arms over her chest. "That's not fair. Irena always gets the extra sausage because she's the oldest."

Irena jumped up. "No, I don't." But Irena felt sorry for Bridget being left behind. "You can play with Betty all by yourself."

Bridget glared. "She's too little to play."

From the bedroom, Mama walked into the kitchen and put two fingers to her lips. "*Sh-sh*, Betty's sleeping."

Bridget stomped to Mama. "Irena gets to go with Da to cut down a light tree. I wanna go, too."

"It's too far for you to walk," Mama said. "Da and Irena will find us a Christmas tree."

Maybe Bridget had just slipped about the light tree. Irena rushed across the kitchen and nudged her sister. "You can play with Gertrude while I'm gone."

Bridget turned her back on Irena and followed Mama to the couch. "In Germany, they don't put up Christmas trees. They put up light trees."

"What's a light tree?" asked Mama as she took her sewing out of her bag.

Irena had to fix things. "It's just a different name for a Christmas tree, isn't it, Bridget?"

"No, it isn't," Bridget said. "They don't even celebrate Christmas in Germany."

Now Bridget had ruined everything.

Mama picked up her yarn and the tiny hat she was crocheting for Betty. "Why do they need a light tree?"

"Teacher said they celebrate *Julfest* with a light tree. On top is a light wheel. To me, it looks like a swastika."

Mama's fingers weaved the yarn around the crochet hook, working faster and faster as she talked. "Winter Solstice is an old pagan holiday that honors the sun god." She stopped and pointed her crochet hook at Bridget. "In this house, we will have a Christmas tree and celebrate Jesus' birth."

Relieved, Irena tugged on Da's hand. "Let's go."

"It's cold out there." Rising, Mama walked to the pegs by the door and removed her gray scarf. She wrapped it around Irena's neck. "This will keep you warm." Then Mama handed Da and her each a tied handkerchief with a chunk of bread.

Outside, the ground was blanketed with snow and the cold air stung Irena's cheeks. She pulled the gray wool scarf onto her face. The scarf blocked the stinging air and smelled like Mama.

Da carried a hatchet and Mama's shopping bag, so he didn't

make her hold his hand or tell her not to talk. She enjoyed running beside him, kicking up the snow with her galoshes. They passed the general store where Mama bought their food and the cobbler where Da had his boots resoled. He led her down a street with shops she'd never seen before. Her mouth watered for the baskets of bread in the bakery, and the three bottles of milk, almost as tall as she was, displayed in Schmaltz Brothers' window.

Too quickly, Da strode through the town and stopped near a downed oak tree. He swished his gloved hand over a log, sweeping off the snow before he lifted her. "Sit here and rest." Reaching into his coat pocket, he pulled out a cigarette and lit it. He leaned against the partial trunk of the dead tree, smoking.

Irena was hungry. She pulled out the handkerchief Mama had given her and popped the crusty bread into her mouth. She chewed slowly to make the taste last longer as she gazed at the gray, cloudy sky. In the distance, a giant steeple rose so high that the top was hidden under the clouds. "What's that?" she asked.

"St. Nicholi, the main Lutheran church in Hamburg. It used to be the tallest building in the world."

No wonder it seemed to reach right up to heaven. "You're Lutheran. Can we go there?"

"Another time. It's too far to walk. The city center is about fifteen kilometers from here."

Fifteen kilometers sounded like a long way. "Is that farther than walking to the Catholic Church?"

"A little. The church is toward the city. The forest is in the opposite direction, away from the city. We live between the two."

Irena didn't complain about it being too far to walk. She was afraid Da might not bring her again. After Da finished smoking, he flicked the cigarette butt into the snow, where the embers slowly smoldered. "Let's go cut down a tree."

Irena rose from the log and trudged behind Da over flatter ground covered with snow. In the distance appeared several red-brick buildings surrounded by barbed wire. Irena slipped her hand into Da's. "What's that?"

Da's voice was barely audible. "A camp."

"What kind of camp?"

He cleared his throat. "A place where they take Jews." Da picked her up and set her on the other side of him, so she wouldn't walk next to the barbed wire. "Keep your head down and don't look."

She wondered if these Jews had hooked noses and fat bellies like the ones in the book Fraulein Mueller had shown them. Irena lowered her head but peeked around Da. Near the last building huddled four men. Their heads were shaved, and they wore gray-striped trousers. On their shirts were yellow stars.

Fraulein Mueller said the Jews were greedy and hoarded everything. These Jews didn't wear coats and looked as if they were starved. One man's bald head popped up. He turned in their direction and limped toward the fence.

Da picked up his pace, but the man reached the fence several meters ahead of them. With his gnarly fingers, he clawed up the barbed wire. "*Bitte helfen Sie!*"

Ignoring the plea for help, they kept walking. The man dropped from the fence and rushed ahead, climbing up another barbed section. This time as they passed, the man thrust his hand through the holes in the wire. "*Bitte helfen Sie!*"

Da seemed startled and stumbled. Slowly, he righted himself, picked her up, and hurried away. Irena was glad to leave the camp behind.

When they reached the forest, Da stepped inside. The thicket of trees surrounded them, protecting them from the cold. He set her on the ground, and as they walked, he identified the trees—oak, spruce, and beechnut.

Irena spotted a grove of pines that looked like Christmas trees. "Can we cut one of these?"

Da nodded. "Norwegian pines. Good choice."

Da handed her the market bag and pointed to the ground. "Pick up pinecones for decorations while I cut down the tree."

Irena listened to Da's rhythmic chopping as she gathered the pinecones. Finishing, she yelled, "I don't see anymore."

"Walk around, but don't leave my sight. Look for more pinecones or try to spot some blueberry bushes. They're low to the ground and won't have berries. When we come back in the summer, we'll know where to find them."

Irena wandered around until she discovered what she thought might be a blueberry bush. Squatting down, she reached beneath the bush, hoping some berries would be left. Something sharp poked through her glove and pricked her finger. She let out a cry.

Da rushed to her. "What's wrong?"

She removed her mittens and held out her hand. "Something stabbed me."

Da examined her finger and then bent down under the bush to scrape away the undergrowth. Straightening, he held up a spikey brown pod. A wide smile spread across his leathery face. "It's a beechnut."

The brown sphere didn't look like any nut she'd seen. "I'm not sticking that in my mouth."

Da squeezed the dry pod, popping it open. Tucked inside were three fuzzy nuts. "These can be roasted and eaten like chestnuts. Look for more while I cut down the tree."

Irena searched for the pods. When she found one, she carefully picked it up and thought about how good it would taste. Her stomach growled. She had already eaten her bread.

She returned to Da. "Stand back, Irena. The tree is about to fall."

He swung the hatchet several more times against the tree.

Crack! The tree toppled to the ground. He propped the pine against the trunk of another tree while he rested.

"Da, don't forget to eat your bread."

He must not have heard her because he didn't reach into his pocket.

"If you don't want your bread, I'll eat it," Irena said.

He whipped out his empty handkerchief and swiped it across his brow. "I ate it while you were gathering pinecones."

He must have eaten fast because, although she hadn't always seen him, she'd heard his constant chopping.

"Let's go." He sidled under the tree until it rested on his back. He rose from his squatted position, braced the tree on his back, and headed out of the forest. At the clearing, Irena's eyes followed their path of footprints in the snow leading to the camp. She was nervous about going by the camp with the Jewish men. Da must have felt the same way because he turned in the opposite direction.

The route took longer, but Irena's head was filled with decorating the Christmas tree, celebrating the birth of baby Jesus, and tasting warm roasted beechnuts.

1942

During the first two years of the war, British bombings of Germany were no more than nuisance raids. One German was killed for every five tons of bombs. [1] In 1942, the British introduced two new airplanes—the Lancaster, which carried twice the bomb load, and the Mosquito, which flew higher and faster than most German planes.

The British commander, Sir Arthur Harris, switched from dropping explosive HE bombs to mainly incendiary bombs. One firebomb was a thermite stick similar to a mini-missile that would strike and burst into flames. A second firebomb, weighing thirty pounds and filled with a liquid mixture of Benzol and rubber, was able to set fire to the surrounding ten meters.

The British targets also changed. Cities with centers of industry surrounded by dense populations were bombed. "The idea was that even if the factory itself was not destroyed, the homes of those who worked in them would be." [2]

CHAPTER
FORTY-FOUR

January 1942

Humming softly, Harriet sat on the green chair with Betty sucking at her breast. This was her favorite time of day. The house was quiet, the girls were tucked in bed, and soon Oskar would be home from work. But for now, Harriet and the baby were alone.

Harriet ran her finger over the few wisps of brown hair on her crown, across the baby's wide forehead, and down her petite nose. Others might have seen the imperfections—her forehead too high like Oskar's, her belly too round, her legs and arms too scrawny—but not Harriet. Betty was a beautiful gift from God.

All the worries about the baby had been senseless. Harriet should have trusted that God had a plan. Her baby was born in a convent, and the nuns had named her after Elizabeth of Hungary, whose all-saints' day was in November. Elizabeth was one of Harriet's favorite saints because she was associated with roses, built a hospital for the needy, and fed the poor.

Harriet gazed down at Betty. Her eyes were closed, but when Harriet tried to release the baby from her nipple, she squirmed and latched on again. Harriet didn't mind. She liked to keep Betty awake for Oskar. No matter how tired he was, whenever he saw her, his gray eyes lit up.

Even with the little they had, Betty's first Christmas had been special. Harriet had crocheted green sweaters for the three girls, and since she no longer traded tobacco rations with Audra, she had splurged and bought Oskar a tin of tobacco. He had secured an orange, which he stuffed into Betty's stocking; however, everyone enjoyed the sweet juicy fruit. Harriet had even dried the rind for a zest.

With the Christmas tree gone, the living room looked bare. Irena and Bridget had decorated the tree with pinecones and a paper chain that they'd wound around the branches. Harriet had suggested they make stars for the tree, but Irena protested, "If someone sees our tree decorated with stars, they'll think we're Jews."

"I don't want to be a Jew," Bridget said.

Harriet worried about what the war was doing to the girls. She prayed the cruelty would not change their sweet nature. The German troops had not come home by Christmas, and no one seemed to know when they would defeat the Soviets. She would just have to have faith and hold on a little longer. The war would be over soon.

Eeeoooeeeoooeee.

Harriet bolted up, yanking Betty from her breast. The baby wailed in protest as Harriet raced into the bedroom to get the girls. The British hadn't bombed Hamburg since last summer when the family had tried to return home. The government had built air-raid shelters throughout the city and told people they were not allowed to stay in their basements. If the Germans found them there, they would be shot.

Eeeoooeeeooooeee.

Maybe this was a practice drill like the one they'd had in the fall when they were first assigned a shelter. Oskar had been home for the drill. But what if this was a real attack?

Betty was screaming. Irena and Bridget were under the blanket, crying. Their assigned shelter was blocks away. How could she dress three children and herself, go out into the bitter January night, and run to a shelter that was at least ten minutes away? She would have to hold the baby and also Irena's and Betty's hands. It sounded impossible, but she had to do it. Oskar said they could not stay in the basement.

Eeeoooeeeooooeee.

Harriet patted Betty on the back and pulled the blanket off the girls. "Put on your shoes and coats. We have to go to the air-raid shelter."

Irena screamed and grabbed the blanket, burrowing under it with Bridget. Harriet didn't yell at her. She wanted to nuzzle under the blanket, too. But she couldn't. Soon the planes might be here. Leaving their flat and running to the shelter didn't make sense. It was too cold outside. The shelter was too far. The girls were too young to run that far. They'd never make it before the planes. They'd be in the street with no protection.

Eeeoooeeeooooeee.

Harriet lifted the blanket, keeping a tight grip on it. "Girls, get your shoes on. We'll go to the basement."

Irena sat up and rubbed her eyes. "Da said we can't stay here."

Silently, Harriet counted to three. "When Da is here, he'll take us to the shelter. For now, we'll be safe in the basement, just like always."

Going to the basement seemed to appease the girls. They put on their shoes and Harriet wrapped the blanket around their shoulders. She led the way down the steps, carrying Betty, who was still crying, while the girls trailed behind them.

When they neared the basement door, Irena cried, "I left Gertrude."

Harriet turned as Irena threw off the blanket and scampered up the steps.

"Come back!" yelled Harriet, but Irena disappeared up the dark stairs.

Harriet latched onto Bridget's hand and led her into the empty basement. The three other families must have gone to the shelter. Spreading out the blanket, Harriet laid it on the floor for Bridget and slipped Betty into her arms. "Watch the baby. I'll get Irena."

Harriet raced up the stairs. Before she reached the first-floor landing, the door to the building opened. Cold air rushed in, along with a shadowy figure. Maybe it was Oskar. She started to call out, but what if the person running upstairs wasn't Oskar? What if it was a soldier or a thief?

Irena was upstairs, alone. Harriet bolted to their flat. The door was ajar. She barreled in and thudded against a man. Oskar. He was carrying Irena.

Her relief was short-lived as he barked, "Where are Bridget and Betty?"

Harriet struggled to breathe. "Basement," was all she was able to say.

Oskar put Irena down. He gripped Harriet's shoulders and shook her. "Don't you understand? You can't stay here. If they find you, you'll be shot." Each word was a bullet shooting down her confidence.

———

Irena gripped Da's hand and ran through the dark street toward the shelter. She usually enjoyed being the oldest and managing without help, but now she wished Mama or Da would carry her, but Mama held Betty and Da carried Bridget, so Irena had no choice. She had to run. Her heart pounded against her chest, keeping rhythm with her bare feet slapping against the brick pavement.

In the darkness, she couldn't see the other people rushing to the shelter, but she heard them. Men barking out orders. Women screaming at their children. Babies crying. And above all the noise, the siren.

Eee ooo eee ooo eee ooo eee ooo eee ooo eee ooo eee ooo eee.

"It's the *Fliegeralarm*!" yelled Da.

The second siren warned only minutes were left before the attack. Her legs ached. She couldn't keep up. She begged Da to slow down, but he wouldn't. He was mad at Mama for not taking them to the shelter. Irena had told her they were supposed to go, but Mama wouldn't listen and had taken them to the basement.

Tromp! Tromp! Tromp!

German soldiers ran from building to building, pounding on doors and yelling for people to leave, quickly. "*Schnell. Schnell.*"

Bang! Bang!

Irena jerked at the gunshots. Da said that they would be killed if they stayed in their building. The shots must be a warning. The soldiers wouldn't shoot people for not leaving their flats during an air raid, would they?

Eee ooo eee ooo eee ooo eee ooo eee ooo eee ooo eee ooo eee.

Just before her legs gave way, they reached the slope to the underground bunker. At the door, a civil defense worker in a green helmet and uniform checked their papers. Da pulled out their *Platzkart* to show they were assigned to this shelter. Irena had seen the civil defense worker who had only one eye before.

Da said Mr. Werner had been a soldier and had lost his eye in the Great War. Now in his left socket was a milky white sphere.

With his good eye, Mr. Werner squinted at the papers and waved them in. Da motioned for Mama to go first. Irena clutched Da's coat and shuffled behind him. She had been in the tunnel-shaped shelter for the practice drill, but that had been in the evening. Now it looked scary. The concrete-block walls glowed an eerie green from the iridescent stripe painted on the sides of the walls. A light bulb hung from the low arched ceiling, and the wooden benches on each side were already filled with what must be a hundred people. Their basement had only six other people and smelled of coal and cigarette smoke. This shelter was musty and stunk like Papa's barn.

Da led them to their assigned places on the bench near the door. During the drill, Irena and Bridget had sat on the benches. Now the space was only large enough for Mama and Da because people had brought suitcases, rucksacks, and boxes stuffed with valuables they didn't want to leave. Irena had wanted to bring Gertrude and her heart-shaped rock, but Da said they didn't have time to find them.

He set Bridget on the floor, and Irena dropped next to her. The shelter was cold and under her coat, she only wore her nightshirt.

Eee ooo eee ooo eee ooo eee ooo eee ooo eee ooo eee ooo eee.

The last ones to enter the bunker were the Rokas. Mr. Roka was so tall he had to duck as he carried his wife and set her on the bench across from them. Since they were also from Lithuania, Mama always stopped and talked to them when they were outside.

The couple looked different now. Mr. Roka didn't have on his Fedora, and his black hair made a bowl around his head. Mrs. Roka wasn't wearing her tinkling earrings, and her braid, which was usually coiled in a topknot, lay on the shoulder of her red coat like a fox's tail.

Irena didn't know what was wrong with Mrs. Roka, except she couldn't walk. Mr. Roka had to carry her to the shelter. Her legs were always covered with what Mama called a granny-square afghan. Even now as she sat on the wooden bench across from them, her legs were hidden beneath the colorful yarn blocks.

Irena had asked Mama why Mr. Roka didn't go to work with the other men. Mama shrugged and said someone had to take care of his wife and they didn't have any children to help.

Eee ooo eee ooo eee ooo eee ooo eee ooo eee ooo eee ooo eee.

When the siren stopped, Mr. Werner bolted the door. If others were outside, they would have to find another shelter. Da said that in the last two years, more than a thousand bomb shelters had been built in Hamburg. One near the port was a *hochbunker,* a high bunker above the ground large enough to hold a thousand people. Women rolled their baby prams right inside. Too bad Mr. Roka wasn't assigned to the *hochbunker.* Then he could push his wife in her wheelchair instead of carrying her.

After making his wife comfortable, Mr. Roka struck a match against the concrete block wall and lit the candle inside a metal can on the floor. The wick flared, and the candle's yellow flame danced, sending shadows flickering against the green walls.

Irena tugged on Mama's coat. "Why did he light a candle?"

Mama glanced at the flame. "To test for oxygen. If the flame goes out, too much oxygen has been used. Then you and Bridget need to climb up on our laps."

Irena wanted the candle to go out so she could crawl onto Mama's lap, but that would mean they didn't have enough oxygen. Irena opened her mouth and gulped in as much air as possible before it ran out.

Mrs. Roka reached across to Betty. "She's so beautiful. May I hold her?"

Mama smiled and handed the baby to her. At first, Betty squirmed, but then she settled into the crook of Mrs. Roka's arm. Mama and Mrs. Roka continued to talk about the baby. Other women had brought their knitting or crocheting. Some men played cards.

Bridget fisted her hand. "Let's play rock, paper, scissors."

Irena wanted to go back to the flat, climb into her warm bed, and go to sleep, but she played the game, mostly losing. She was distracted by the flame, flicking and flaring until it went out.

Irena jumped up and climbed onto Mama's lap. Bridget hopped onto Da's lap. Mr. Roka lifted the tin can, set it next to him on the bench, and relit the candle.

"What if the candle goes out again?" Irena asked.

"Then everyone has to stand on the benches," whispered Mama.

"Why?" Irena wanted to stay on Mama's lap.

"Because oxygen rises and—"

The roar of airplanes drowned out Mama's words. The noise was deafening. Irena covered her ears and buried her head in Mama's lap. The rumbling grew louder. Not two or three planes like the air raids when they'd hunkered in the basement. Lots of planes thundered over them.

Toddlers and babies screamed. Betty wailed, and Bridget joined in. Irena tried to be brave, but inside she was shaking. She was going to die. She slid her arms around Mama's waist and screamed.

CHAPTER
FORTY-FIVE

The next morning, Irena curled under the blanket and tried to sleep. The family had stayed in the bunker for what seemed like hours. When the all-clear siren sounded, they trudged out into the cold to return to their flat.

At bedtime, Irena kept her clothes on. "When the siren goes off, I'll be ready."

"The planes won't attack two nights in a row," Mama assured Irena as she kissed her cheek.

Mama was wrong. This time, when the siren sounded, Da was home and helped Mama with the baby. No one helped Irena. She slipped on her coat and felt for the heart-shaped rock she'd put in the pocket. As she rushed to the bunker, she held onto Da's hand and clutched the rock, but her insides were still shaking.

The third night, the entire family went to bed dressed in their clothes. That night the sirens were silent, but the fourth night was another air raid. Now, when Irena kneeled beside the bed to pray, she added, "No more air raids."

Her prayers seemed to be answered. For the rest of January,

the British planes did not attack. That's when Mama announced that school would start again. Irena had mixed feelings about returning to school. She liked helping Mama with the baby, but Irena also wanted to learn. If only Fraulein Bauer would be their teacher again, then school would be fun. All Fraulein Mueller talked about was the war and the Jews.

Mama didn't give Irena and Bridget a choice. The day school started, Mama knotted two pieces of hard bread into a handkerchief, bundled the girls up, and shooed them out the door.

Irena hoped school would be different. But nothing had changed. Fraulein Mueller marched into the classroom, pickled-faced as usual, and turned to Hitler's picture. The class automatically stood, raised their arms, and chanted three times, "*Heil Hitler!*"

Dropping into her seat, Irena waited for Fraulein Mueller to pull down the map for geography. Instead, she opened her desk drawer, took out a large box, and displayed it to the class.

Irena sat up straighter. Maybe something fun was in the box.

"During *Julfest*, I reviewed Fraulein Bauer's records. It seems she was lax in keeping up with your cranial charts."

Placing the box on the desk, Fraulein Mueller lifted the lid and removed two attached metal headbands that looked like a medical instrument. The teacher held up the strange device. "This is a craniometer."

Irena shifted uncomfortably. This did not look like fun.

"Who can tell me the name for the study of the skull?" Fraulein Mueller asked.

The teacher called on one of Helga's friends who sat near the back. "Phrenology."

Fraulein Mueller pinched her lips together and frowned. "Phrenology studies the bumps on a person's head to reveal character traits. Craniometry is the scientific study of the size and shape of the head to determine ethnic and racial groups."

The teacher twisted a dial on the side until the two metal headbands separated into a sphere. "Germans, the superior race, have round heads." She patted her head to show how round it was.

Fraulein Mueller's head did not look round. With her hair pulled into a bun, her head seemed rather pointed in the back. Of course, Irena wasn't about to say that to Fraulein Mueller.

"Jews, Romas, and other inferior animals have odd-shaped skulls, such as this." Fraulein Mueller again whirled the dial on the side of the headband until the craniometer was flatter and wider. She held it up for the class to examine. "Memorize this shape. Recognize those among us who do not belong and report them to me."

Irena's hand crept up the back of her head, checking the shape of her skull. She hoped it was round.

Fraulein Mueller returned the craniometer to the box and removed a second instrument. "This is a caliper that measures the nose. Can someone tell me what a Jewish nose looks like?" Fraulein Mueller pointed to the back of the class.

"Large," a girl answered.

Fraulein Mueller nodded. "What else?"

Another student said, "Hooked."

"Yes." Fraulein Mueller arched her thick brows. "And?"

The room fell silent.

The teacher stomped to the blackboard and drew the number six. "Lots of people have large noses, and lots of people have hooked noses, but a Jewish nose is bent at the point. It resembles the number six. We call that nose a Jewish six."

Irena's nose began to itch. She wanted to scratch it and make sure it hadn't morphed into a Jewish six.

"As I call your name, proceed to the desk. I will calculate the size of your head and nose."

Irena fidgeted. One by one, the other girls' names were called. They walked to the front, sat in the chair facing the blackboard, and were measured. When it was Mia's turn, Fraulein Mueller spent a long time calculating the size of the Polish girl's head, which was small, and her nose, which was large but did not resemble a six. Mia couldn't be a Jew. Fraulein Mueller said Jews were *dummkopfs*, and Mia was the smartest girl in the class.

Fraulein Mueller must have said something to upset Mia because, after she returned to her seat, tears puddled her eyes.

"Bridget Golcvegaite."

As Bridget marched to the front of the classroom, Irena prayed that her sister's head would be round and her nose would be small, the way they were when they left the apartment that morning.

"Irena Golcvegaite."

Her prayer was answered. Bridget had passed. Irena rose and squared her shoulders. As Bridget walked to her seat, Irena smiled at her sister, thankful she had not been classified as inferior. Bridget smiled back, only it looked more like a smile of sympathy.

Irena's false bravado slipped away. It was true. Her head was too small and her nose too big. She wilted into the chair next to the desk. Fraulein Mueller clamped the craniometer onto her head and adjusted the bands. Irena sucked in air, hoping her head would remain round.

After the teacher finished and recorded the numbers on the chart, she picked up the caliper. The pinchers looked like something Mama used to prune flowers.

The teacher placed the prongs on each side of Irena's nose, making her nostrils twitch.

"Stop moving."

Irena froze, terrified Fraulein Mueller would pinch off her nose.

The teacher checked the numbers on the chart. "Your nose seems adequate. Your head meets the guidelines."

Irena slunk to her seat. She had not been labeled the worst of the worst. A Jew.

CHAPTER
FORTY-SIX

April 1942

T he last week of April, Irena and Bridget clattered up the stairs as they returned from school. As usual, Mama stood at the door, but she put her fingers to her lips. "*Sh-sh*. Betty's sleeping."

Irena tugged on Mama's hand. "We have to go—now."

Mama frowned. "Go where?"

"On the way home from school, a truck with a loudspeaker repeated, *Raus! Raus! Schnell! Schnell!*"

Mama moved to the closed window and peeked out the curtains.

Maybe Mama didn't know those German words. "Out! Fast!" Irena shouted.

"I don't hear anything."

Bridget ran toward the bedroom. "Betty has to come, too."

Hurriedly, Mama crossed the kitchen and stopped Bridget

from opening the door. "Betty's been fussy all day. I told you not to wake her."

"We have to go." Irena shook her finger at Mama. "Da will be mad at you, like when you took us to the basement during an air raid."

"Irena, this is different. I—"

"*Raus! Raus! Schnell! Schnell!*" A loudspeaker blared from outside.

Irena fisted her hands on her hips. "I told you, Mama."

"I'll get Betty." Mama lifted her headscarf and sweater from the hook and hurried toward the bedroom. "Maybe I can carry the baby without waking her."

Betty wailed down the stairs. Irena made faces at her, which usually made Betty giggle. This time, she only cried harder.

Outside, Irena barely noticed the warm spring breeze against her cheeks. She kept her head lowered and remained silent as they followed the throng of people under the archway and out of the projects. The cobblestone street was crowded with onlookers lined up three rows deep. Mama found a space and squeezed in behind a thick woman in a black coat and plaid headscarf.

Irena stood on her tiptoes, but she couldn't see around the woman. The air crackled with excitement and fear as boots thundered in rhythm down the cobblestones. Curious, she inched away from Mama and peeked around the wide woman.

Row after row of Germans in Nazi uniforms marched like waves of wooden soldiers, their legs kicking straight out. The clomping of their boots was deafening. Other soldiers shouted and used their rifles to shove people back onto the sidewalks.

A single word rippled through the crowd, *Hitler*. In the distance, the familiar chant rose, "*Heil Hitler! Heil Hitler! Heil Hitler!*"

Irena and Bridget automatically raised their arms and shouted, "*Heil Hitler!*"

The woman in front of Irena raised her arm and joined in. Others nearby shouted, too.

Irena nudged Mama, who was cradling Betty. "Raise your arm."

"I'm holding Betty."

"Everyone's saluting." Irena grabbed Betty's arm, lifting it into the air with hers. At school, she saluted Hitler's picture, and when Da entered a store, he saluted. But why was everyone saluting now?

She dropped Betty's arm, but continued to scream, "*Heil Hitler!*" The chant exploded to a crescendo.

"There he is!" someone shouted. People leaned forward and pointed to a line of open-topped black cars rolling down the street. In the first car, stood two SS men on running boards, their heads swiveling as they eyed the crowd.

Moving around the woman, Irena barely breathed as she inched forward, trying to catch a glimpse of Hitler. Behind the first car, a sleek black convertible with a V-shaped chrome grille and red leather seats cruised down the brick pavement like a hungry animal. On the passenger side stood a man in a brown uniform with brass buttons. His straight hair was slicked down, his tie was knotted, and under his nose was a thick, black mustache.

The man raised his arm. The crowd went wild, roaring the salutation in unison, "*Heil Hitler!*"

Irena's throat caught. Was this Hitler? Was *De Führer* in Hamburg riding in a car down the street toward her? She couldn't believe it. This was more exciting than seeing Father Christmas, but Hitler didn't look the way she'd expected.

At school, the oil painting of Hitler above the blackboard towered over her. She'd imagined Hitler as a giant of a man. The man standing in the convertible with the red interior was short, and he puffed out his chest. Size didn't matter. Da was short, and he was great.

The car rolled closer. Fear sniggled down her spine. What if it was Hitler and his eyes locked on hers the way they did in the picture at school? What if he pointed his raised arm at her and accused her of not paying attention at school? His bodyguards might snatch her and drag her away.

Being in the presence of such a powerful man unsettled her. She wanted to scurry behind the large woman and hide. But her legs wouldn't move, and her arm remained raised. She held her breath, waiting for the car and the man to come closer, close enough for his eyes to see her. The car crept forward. The passenger side of the black convertible was only meters away. Her mouth dropped open. It was Adolf Hitler. If she sprang forward, she would be able to touch his car, but guards on the street and running board protected it—and him.

Hitler's head swiveled from side to side. Breathlessly, she waited for him to turn and find her, but his eyes swept over her, and the big black car rolled down the street, leaving her behind. The roar of the crowd died. The excitement fizzled. Irena's body slumped. Her arm hung limp at her side. She was relieved the soldiers hadn't dragged her away, and yet she felt a sense of rejection and disappointment. Hitler had looked over her head, smiling at the other people screaming his name in adoration, but he had not looked at her.

———

Harriet held Betty in her arms and stood on the crowded sidewalk, watching Hitler in his sleek black Mercedes recede in the distance. Smoke swirled from the exhaust like the tail of a prowling panther. Relieved that Hitler and the hoopla were gone, Harriet sucked in a lungful of air. The pungent odor of gasoline choked her, causing Harriet to cover Betty's mouth to protect her from the vitriolic smoke.

Betty stopped fussing and blinked up at Harriet. Her long

lashes framed her innocent brown eyes. Trustingly, she latched onto Harriet's finger. At that moment, Harriet was over-whelmed by the magnitude of motherhood. Her responsibility was to protect her children. Somehow, she'd let her guard slip. She'd been so busy with Betty that Harriet hadn't worried as much as she should have about what Irena and Bridget were learning at school.

Their arms had shot into the air before the others, and they'd yelled, "*Heil Hitler!*" Irena had even raised Betty's arm toward *De Führer*. Harriet didn't like some of the comments the girls had made when they returned from school, telling her about a Jewish six and saying the Germans were the master race, but Oskar had warned her to be cautious about what she said around the girls because children were encouraged to turn in their parents if they were disloyal to the *Reich*. But she could no longer ignore what was happening to her sweet girls.

Oskar admired Hitler and had convinced her that fleeing to Germany would keep their family safe. When the German troops ousted the Soviets from Lithuania, she had been jubilant. But her admiration for Hitler had been short-lived after Audra told her of German atrocities.

The stories were not hard to believe. She had peered out the train window at the camp in Poland with barbed-wired fences. At the Registration Department, she'd witnessed Nazis with their snarling dogs and guns, and her children had been ripped away from her. She had walked by Jewish stores defiled with graffiti.

She'd made excuses and turned a blind eye. It had nothing to do with her and her family. But seeing Irena and Bridget stand at attention and regale Hitler—the man who had twisted Christmas into the pagan holiday *Julfest*, the man who had rejected Christianity and started his church with him as the head instead of the Pope and God—made her realize she could not ignore what was happening. This Nazi ideology, with its master race, was affecting her family and changing her precious little girls.

The crowd thinned. People trudged back to their homes and their lives. Harriet touched the girls' heads signaling them to follow her. After several steps, Bridget tugged on Harriet's sweater. "Irena's not coming."

Harriet glanced back at Irena, wistfully gazing down the empty street like a puppy abandoned by her master.

A lump formed in Harriet's throat. She forced out the words. "Get your sister."

Bridget scampered back and returned, dragging a scowling Irena. "Wait 'til I tell Da you didn't salute Hitler. You're going to be in big trouble."

Harriet hoped that wasn't true. She hoped Oskar would be as upset as she was about how the girls were being indoctrinated at school.

That night, Harriet put Betty to bed, but Irena and Bridget were wound up, so Harriet allowed them to wait for Oskar. As soon as she unchained the door, Irena shot out of the kitchen chair. "Da, we saw him. We saw Hitler."

Bridget jumped up. "He rode in this big, long car."

Oskar tossed his hat on the kitchen table and pulled out the nearest chair. "I know. Hitler came to the factory."

Irena's eyes widened. "You got to see him? Did you talk to him?"

Oskar shook his head.

Her mouth drooped, and then she pointed an accusing finger. "Mama was bad. She didn't raise her arm and salute Hitler. She didn't make Betty do it either."

Oskar looked at Harriet as if searching for some clue as to how he should respond. She cradled her arms and rocked them.

Oskar cleared his throat and addressed Irena. "Well, if your mother was holding Betty, it would have been hard for her to raise her arm."

Irena stuck out her bottom lip. "She should have saluted him."

As Irena continued to jabber about the parade, Harriet walked to the stove and heated the leftover cabbage soup. She was relieved. Oskar understood and would help her. Together they would combat whatever Nazi ideology the school had implanted in the girls.

Harriet carried Oskar's soup to the table. "Why did Hitler come to the factory?"

"To inspect the plant and to increase our bomb production."

"Why do they need more bombs?" Harriet's temples throbbed. "In a few weeks, the weather will be warm enough for the German troops to move toward Moscow. Once the Soviets are defeated, the war on that front will be over."

"Moscow will not be that easy to take. Germany invaded the Soviet Union in June. The German soldiers were not equipped with warm clothes and supplies to last the winter. We don't have a lot of troops left. Many men froze, dying without—"

"Time for bed." The girls had heard enough about the war. They didn't need the gruesome details about men freezing or being blown up. She shooed the girls into the bedroom, listened to their prayers, and tucked them into bed.

Returning to the kitchen, she slumped in the chair across from Oskar. He must be stressed too because while she was gone, he'd rolled a cigarette. "What should we do, Oskar?"

He lit the cigarette before he answered. "About what?"

"The girls and what they're learning in school. You heard the way Irena went on and on about Hitler. At the parade when Irena and Bridget saw Hitler, they resembled tiny robots, yelling and saluting him."

"They're only doing what they've been taught and what's expected of them to survive."

"But you should have seen Irena. After Hitler left, she seemed so-so rejected." Harriet reached across the table and clasped his hand. "We have to do something about what they're learning. It's changing them."

Oskar slipped his hand from hers and puffed on his cigarette.

Harriet was trying to understand this adoration for Hitler. "I hear *Heil Hitler* everywhere—when friends meet on the street, when I enter a store, but I don't know German. What does it mean?"

He tapped his ashes into his empty soup bowl. "*Heil* means salvation and formerly was used for the relationship between man and God. The adjective 'holy' comes from the noun."

Her temples pounded. "This is worse than I thought."

Oskar picked up his cigarette. He drew in a deep breath and exhaled, waving away her concern as easily as he waved away the smoke. "It's not used that way now, Harriet."

She didn't argue, but she had been at the parade. She had seen the girls. She had heard the crowd's fervent cheering. All of them had been praising Hitler as if he were a god—as if he were *their* god.

Oskar repeated his previous warning. "Be careful what you say to the girls. They might repeat it at school."

Irena had tattled to Oskar. What if she told her teacher? Harriet pressed her hands against her pounding temples. "I hate this war. When will it be over?"

"I don't know. Now that America has entered, it's not so one-sided. Before, America gave the British money and supplies. There are rumors that America might send fighter planes."

The pounding in Harriet's head worsened. "You said

Hamburg has the best flak defenses in Germany. Surely those German guns can shoot down a few American planes that cross the ocean."

"Hamburg has a ring of batteries around the city and four massive gun towers in the center. But even if only a few planes make it through the defense, their bombs could be deadly. You saw what happened at the train station."

Harriet wanted to believe they were well protected. "We haven't had any air raids in the last three months, not since those nights in January. I'm more worried about you. Do more bombs mean you have to work longer hours?"

"It's not just me, Harriet. It's everyone. The German guards are grousing because they are working almost sixty hours a week. But so far, they haven't mentioned more hours for us. I think it's because a few days ago, they brought in a crew of laborers from the work camps."

"Work camps?" Harriet's tone was cynical. "If they're work camps, why do they need barbed wire?"

"Germany has different kinds of camps, depending on the crime. Work education camps are to discipline Germans. Other camps are for foreign prisoners. The men in those camps are slave laborers."

Harriet crossed herself. "Are the men at the factory Jewish?"

Oskar smoked and was silent for so long that Harriet thought he might not answer. Finally, he tapped his cigarette out in the bowl. "The men have red badges with the purple letter *P*."

Harriet tried to remember the German classification of badges. The yellow star of David identified Jews and a pink triangle was for homosexuals. Wasn't purple for Jehovah's Witnesses? But Oskar had said the badge was red. "Are they political prisoners?"

Oskar shook his head. "I didn't say anything because I

didn't want to upset you. I know your parents still have relatives there."

A searing pain flashed through her head. "Is the purple *P* for Poland?"

Oskar nodded. "Yes. The men are Poles."

CHAPTER
FORTY-SEVEN

May 1942

rena sat at school, her back straight, her hands folded in her lap. Today was the last day before summer vacation. In the afternoon, the class would celebrate by doing calisthenics and German folk dances. First, though, the students had to pass their recitations and spell Hitler's full name.

Irena fidgeted as Fraulein Mueller called each girl to her desk. Irena wasn't worried for herself. Printing the name *Hitler* was easy. Bridget, however, sometimes reversed the letters.

"Bridget Golcvegaite," Fraulein Mueller said.

Irena reached over and squeezed Bridget's hand as she slipped out of her seat and flounced up to the teacher's desk. Last fall, Irena had not wanted her sister to start school with her. Now sometimes the only good part of school was Bridget sitting beside her. But what if she didn't pass?

Bridget sat in the chair next to the teacher's desk, facing the blackboard. Fraulein Mueller asked several questions in

German. Irena couldn't hear the answers, but the teacher's head bobbed up and down. Then Fraulein Mueller handed Bridget a pencil and pointed to the paper lying on the desk.

Irena sent her sister a silent message. *Concentrate, Bridget. We have to stay together.*

Just like in practice, Bridget scribbled the name. Fraulein Mueller examined the paper. Irena held her breath.

"*Sehr gut,*" Fraulein Mueller said.

Irena let out a whoosh. Bridget had passed. They wouldn't be separated next year.

"Irena Golcvegaite."

Irena rose and walked forward, whispering her congratulations to Bridget as they passed. Then Irena hurried to the chair next to the teacher's desk. Fraulein Mueller rattled off something in German. She spoke too fast, but from the tone, it was evident that Irena was being scolded, probably for whispering to Bridget.

Fraulein Mueller pointed to the paper on the desk. "Spell *Adolf Hitler.*"

Was this a trick? The other girls had gone through their recitations first. Tugging on her pigtails, Irena gazed at the paper. Her mind went blank.

Fraulein Mueller's voice rose. "Write *Der Führer's* name."

Irena stared at the blackboard and rolled her eyes up to the gilded-framed picture of Hitler, hoping somehow the spelling of his name would come to her. Instead, Hitler pinned her with his powerful gaze. Seconds ticked by. Her mind remained blank. What was she going to do? Words from the rosary floated through her head. *I believe in God, the Father Almighty...and in Jesus Christ, his son...born of the Virgin Mary.*

Mary. Picking up the pencil, Irena prayed for the saint's help. The blankness lifted. She carefully printed 'Adolph Hitler,' and then checked to make sure she had crossed the *t.*

She handed the paper to Fraulein Mueller, who gave a curt nod.

Irena wanted to cheer. She and Bridget had passed.

In the afternoon, Irena reveled in being outdoors and doing PT. Fraulein Mueller started by leading them in jumping jacks as she shouted, "Strengthen your body so when you become young women, you'll be able to bear a child for Germany and our glorious *Führer*."

Irena stopped in mid-air. Mama had told her how a baby comes out of a woman's body. Irena didn't want that to happen to her, even for *Der Führer*. Irena glared at the teacher. Behind her, a huge weather balloon floated toward the school. Dangling from the bottom was something that resembled a long tube sock.

Irena pointed to the sky. "Look."

Fraulein Mueller continued doing jumping jacks, but other girls also noticed the balloon with the dangling sock. The sock detached and dropped on the grass near Fraulein Mueller. It burst into flames.

"Fire!" Irena raced toward the small grass fire to put it out while the teacher rushed in the opposite direction toward the school.

Maybe she was getting water, Irena thought. Helga stormed past her toward the fire. The Hun reached the fire first and stomped her large shoe on the flames licking through the grass. Irena was next, followed by Bridget and several other girls. They surrounded the fire, jumping up and down on the flames. Within minutes, the fire was out, leaving black smoke rising from the scorched grass.

Helga slammed her hand against Irena's back. "Nice work, *dumpkoff*."

Irena lurched forward, almost falling. Maybe Mama was right. People weren't all good—or all bad.

CHAPTER
FORTY-EIGHT

July 1942

Harriet swiped her hand across her sweaty forehead as she stood at the sink, peeling carrots. The window was raised, but instead of cool air, gusts of hot wind ruffled the blackout curtains. Irena and Bridget sat at the table, sipping glasses of carrot juice.

Irena pushed her drink away. "Are we going to the store today?"

Harriet turned from the window. "It's too windy."

"You never let us go outside," complained Irena. "First, it's the Nazis. Then it's too cold. Now it's too windy. The wind won't hurt us."

"It's not the wind. It's those balloons like the one that started the fire at your school. This summer hundreds of them have flown over Hamburg."

Irena jumped up and stomped her foot on the floor as if extinguishing flames. "I can put out the fire."

Harriet shook her finger. "You will do no such thing. Those weather balloons are dangerous."

"Helga and I snuffed out the fire at school."

"You were lucky. Some balloons carry jars that explode on impact."

Irena slumped into her seat. "Where do the balloons come from?"

"Across the English Channel. The British Women's Royal Army launch them when it's windy enough to float to Germany."

Irena perked up. "Women? That's clever. I want to do something to help Hitler win the war."

Hitler again. During the summer, Harriet tried to combat what was drilled into them at school. She read the parables to them and had the girls memorize simple verses from the Bible. This week they were learning the Ten Commandments. Irena, however, still idolized Hitler.

"Finish your juice," Harriet said. "Carrots are good for your eyes."

Irena rested her hands on her chin and stared at her glass.

"Can I have your juice?" Bridget asked.

Without grumbling, Irena slid her glass to Bridget.

Harriet smiled. Maybe her teachings were working.

Then Irena groaned. "Carrots, carrots, carrots."

Irena's sharing must be because she was tired of carrots. The potato crop was slim this year, but carrots were bountiful. Harriet served raw carrots, cooked carrots, and juiced carrots.

A knock sounded on the door. Harriet unchained the lock, and Oskar walked in. Her voice trembled, "What's wrong?"

"Do we have electricity?" Before she answered, he stepped to the light switch next to the door and flicked it up. Nothing happened. "The electricity must be out all over town."

Harriet gripped the counter. "What's going on?"

"The factory doesn't have electricity, so they sent us home."
Oskar took off his hat. "It's those blasted balloons again."

Irena ran to Oskar. "Did they start a fire at the bomb factory?"

Oskar patted her on the head. "Not all balloons start fires. The balloons today had metal tails dangling below them. They hit electrical lines and shorted them out."

Irena's eyes widened. "Wow, those British women are smart. I want to be just like them."

Mama frowned. "I didn't see any balloons near here. Why is our electricity out?"

"The balloons must have struck enough power lines to knock out the transformer."

"Mama won't let us go outside," whined Irena. "Da, will you let us play outside?"

"I thought I'd go to the woods and check on those blueberries."

"Take me, take me," pleaded Irena.

Oskar turned to Harriet. "Can you get along without Irena for a few hours?"

"*Ja*. But what about the soldiers?"

"They'll be too busy repairing the lines to worry about us today."

Bridget stretched out her hands, palms up. "Can I go, too?"

Harriet gasped. The palms of Bridget's hands were orange.

Irena's eyes widened. "You can't go. You're sick."

"She's not sick," Harriet explained. "She ate too many carrots."

Irena checked her own hands. "My palms aren't orange. I can go."

Bridget pleaded, "You want me to go, don't you, Sissy?"

Irena did not want her to go. "Mama needs someone to help her with Betty."

Betty took a nap in the afternoon, but Harriet held her

tongue, hoping Irena would do the right thing and say she wanted Bridget to go.

A tear trickled down Bridget's cheek. "I never get to do anything."

"Bridget's six, now," Harriet reminded Irena.

"It's too far," Irena said. "She'll slow us down."

Oskar stroked his chin. "We'll need lots of hands to pick the blueberries. Bridget, you can come, too."

———

Irena swung the large metal bucket while Bridget skipped next to her, swinging the smaller one that Da had made. Irena's feet were squeezed into her brown lace-up shoes, but even her cramped toes and having to drag Bridget along didn't dampen her mood. After days of being cooped up inside, the warm sunshine soaking into her skin felt wonderful.

Irena stopped skipping and waited for Da. "Will we find mushrooms, too?"

"Not today. September or October."

"Can I go with you to pick mushrooms? I can tell the poisonous ones," Irena boasted.

Da cocked his head. "You can?"

"Fraulein Mueller showed the class pictures of bad mushrooms. She said they were like the bad people."

"Who are the bad people?"

Irena stared up at Da, surprised he didn't know. "The Jews."

He frowned and continued toward town. He was right about the soldiers. They were busy helping the Civil Defense Workers restore the electrical lines and didn't look their way.

On the other side of the city, Da stopped near a downed tree. Irena climbed onto a large trunk and pulled Bridget beside her. Da stood and took a rolled cigarette from his shirt pocket and smoked half of it. Before Irena was rested, Da said, "Let's go."

She didn't complain. Jumping down, she trekked beside him and Bridget until the camp with barbed wire came into view. Irena pulled Bridget back and whispered, "That's the place where they keep the bad people."

Bridget's eyes widened. "The Jews?"

Irena nodded.

As they approached the camp, at least a hundred shirtless men in striped pants were lined up in straight rows outside the barracks. In front of the men stood four guards. Two held dogs on leashes while the other two aimed rifles at the men.

Irena swiped the sweat from her brow. A wave of sympathy for the skinny men standing in the scorching sun rippled through her. Then she remembered Fraulein Mueller's words. "The Jews are the cause of this war."

Irena hated the war. She couldn't play outside. She couldn't sleep without worrying about the bombs. She couldn't even go to church and pray for the war to end. She pushed her sympathy away. The Jews had caused the war. They should be locked up.

Near the corner of the camp, Da tossed his cigarette butt outside the fence. "Keep your heads down." He gripped Irena's hand. "Hold on to Bridget." His stride lengthened as he hurried along the outside of the fence.

"*Halt*," shouted a guard.

Irena wondered which poor Jew the guard was yelling at, but she kept her head down as she and Bridget ran to keep up with Da.

"*Halt*." The guard's voice sounded angry.

Irena peeked up. Two guards were outside the fence, heading toward them. Da was looking down at his shoes. Irena tugged on his hand. He lifted his head and skidded to a stop. One guard raised his rifle and pointed it at Da.

The other guard approached them. He had big fish lips that

smacked when he talked. "Why did you drop your cigarette near the fence?"

Da's face turned red. "It was only the—"

The fish-lipped guard, who had enormous hands, cut off Da's words as he wrapped his thick sausage fingers around Da's neck. The guard lifted Da off the ground and pressed him against the barbed-wire fence, choking him.

Da's feet dangled in the air as he struggled to get free. Fish Lips kept him locked in his meaty grip. He jerked his head toward the corner of the camp where Da had tossed his cigarette. "I should kill you for that."

The other guard raised his rifle and aimed it at Da. Irena's bucket clattered to the ground. "Don't kill him!" She tugged on Da's hand, trying to free him.

Bridget dropped her bucket and cried, "No!"

The guard with the rifle growled, "Get those girls out of the way."

Fish Lips turned his head and glared down at her. Irena's mouth went dry. She felt as if those massive sausage fingers were strangling her. His eyes flicked to Bridget and softened.

He straightened. His fingers opened, and he released Da, who dropped onto the ground and righted himself. "You're a lucky man. You would have been shot, but you have two daughters. It seems they want you to live."

Da rubbed his neck. Without speaking, he picked up the buckets, grabbed her and Bridget's hands, dragging them away.

When they were halfway between the camp and the forest, Irena couldn't control her fear. Her body began to shake. Da stopped and wrapped his arm around her.

Irena sobbed, "He was going to kill you."

"He—he was only trying to scare me."

Bang!

Irena jumped at the gunshot from the camp. Da clutched her

tighter and pulled Bridget next to him. He held them close so they wouldn't be able to look back.

She was still shaking when they slipped into the cool woods, sheltering them from the sun and the soldiers. Da led them to the bushes covered with plump blueberries. They started picking and didn't stop until they'd filled their buckets and their bellies.

Irena wasn't in a hurry to leave. She didn't want to walk by the camp and the guards. But Da nudged her forward through the woods and back out into the bright sunlight. Irena blinked and waited for her eyes to adjust. The image she saw was Fish Lips with his fingers around Da's neck, choking him.

"We'll go back a different way." Da's voice was barely a whisper.

As Irena followed behind Da, she thought about the good people and the bad people. The guards who had threatened to kill Da were bad. But what about the people inside the camp? Were they bad, too?

At school, Fraulein Mueller made it sound easy to tell the good people from the bad people, but trying to figure it out on her own made Irena's head ache.

CHAPTER
FORTY-NINE

November 5, 1942

H arriet sat in the green chair, humming softly as she cradled the sleeping baby in her arms. Her light brown hair was combed into a topknot and tied with a red ribbon. Careful not to wake her, Harriet untied the bow and ran her fingers through the fine hair. Today was Betty's first birthday.

Harriet should lay Betty in bed for the night and begin praying, but Harriet lingered over this precious time and was weary of saying prayers that were not answered. She had prayed and prayed for the war to end, but God seemed deaf to her pleas.

In August, Harriet had turned twenty-seven and Irena had turned eight. They had lived in Germany for more than two years. In the fall, school had resumed, but Irena and Bridget didn't seem as happy to return. Harriet didn't want them to be indoctrinated by Hitler's philosophy, but she was careful not to criticize the Nazi regime. Oskar's words had been chilling.

"I've heard of children turning in their parents for questioning the *Reich* and the *Führer*." She didn't want to believe Irena or Bridget would intentionally do that, but they might accidentally repeat something they'd overheard.

Bridget's reluctance to return to school had more to do with her hands still being orange from all the carrots she had eaten. Now the carrots were gone, and since Betty was one, their rations had been cut.

In October, Oskar had taken Irena and Bridget to the forest to forage for food. They'd returned with a handful of precious mushrooms that Harriet made into mushroom gravy. She'd used margarine and water, but the mushrooms gave the gravy a rich earthy flavor. *Next year the mushrooms will be more plentiful.* What was she thinking? Surely the war couldn't go on for a third year. How could they continue with so little? Harriet would breastfeed Betty as long as possible, but without the extra nutrients, she suspected her milk would dry up.

Betty's birthday renewed Harriet's longing for home. Her parents had not seen their new grandchild. Possibly, they didn't even know they had a new granddaughter. Harriet had written letters months ago but hadn't received a reply.

She had shared Betty's momentous birthday with the nuns. Harriet's feet had ached, and her bunion had throbbed from walking to the convent, but the Sisters had doted on their godchild, taking turns holding her and saying how cute she was. They even complimented Irena and Bridget on what grown-up girls they'd become.

Before Harriet left the convent, Sister Anne had slipped her more than the usual few coins. "Buy something for our baby."

Harriet was touched by the word 'our.' She gazed down at Betty sleeping so peacefully and thought about everything she needed. She was already pulling herself up and soon would be walking. Harriet ran her finger over Betty's soft feet. She'd buy her a pair of shoes. If enough money was left, Harriet would purchase flour and bake a birthday cake. She didn't have eggs, and she'd have to sweeten it with honey, but a cake would be a treat for the whole family.

Betty let out a soft coo, and her dainty lips turned up into a smile. What was she dreaming about? It took so little to make Betty happy, and Irena and Bridget, too. But what kind of childhood was this for the girls—staying inside most of the day and at night worrying about the bombs?

Even now, holding the baby, Harriet had one ear tuned for the sound of the air-raid siren. She lived in constant fear that she would have to bundle up the girls and run out into the cold to seek shelter from the bombs.

The holidays would be bleak this year. She wouldn't be able to save enough food for the traditional twelve dishes on Christmas Eve, but she'd make beetroot soup, Oskar would still cut down a tree, the girls could make decorations, and she would sew them new dresses. She had time to work on their dresses before Oskar returned.

Harriet carried Betty into the bedroom, checked on the girls who were asleep, and then tiptoed back to the living room with her sewing. Folded inside was the red satin dress she'd finished for Irena. Harriet certainly hadn't minded cutting up that horrid red flapper dress that she'd been given at the Registration Department. Tonight, she would stitch the puff sleeves onto Bridget's matching dress. Pieces of Betty's dress had been cut out, and enough scraps were left to make a doll dress for Gertrude.

As she pushed the needle in and out of the red satin, memories of those first days in Germany when she'd been separated from Oskar and the girls drifted back. By the time she unchained the door and let Oskar in, she chastised herself for railing against God for not answering her prayers. Betty's first birthday and Oskar's return reminded her that God had answered the most important prayer of all. Her family was alive and together.

As she collected her sewing, Oskar stayed in the kitchen, working the handle on the pump until water splashed in the sink. He washed his hands and pumped more water to wash his hands again. When water splashed into the sink a third time, Harriet laid down her sewing and walked into the kitchen. "Is everything all right?"

Oskar didn't look up. He kept pumping water and washing his hands.

Tentatively, she touched his arm. "Oskar, what is it?"

He turned toward her with a hollowed-out stare that seemed haunted. She squeezed his arm. "Oskar, you're scaring me. What happened?"

He shook his head. "I can't talk about it."

"Why not?"

"It's better you don't know."

Since moving to Germany, their marriage had been rocky. She'd wanted to return to Lithuania while he struggled to make a life for them in Germany. They had not been sharing the load, but pulling the cart in different directions. If he opened up to her, they might find their way back to each other, but if he kept himself closed off, they would become strangers living together but emotionally unconnected. She could not let that happen.

She framed his face in her hands and looked into his haunted gray eyes, trying to reach him. "How can I help if I don't know what it is?"

He pulled away. "You can't. No one can."

She tried again. "Sometimes just talking helps."

"Not about this."

She took his hand. He didn't resist as she led him to the couch. She sat, and he collapsed next to her, clenching his hands together. Tears streamed down his cheeks.

"Tell me." Her voice took on a commanding tone, one that

she used with the girls, but until now had never used with Oskar.

Her desperate determination must have reached him because he began to speak. Once he started, the words gushed out like water splashing from the primed pump. "Between breaks, a guard brings a bucket of water to the workers so we won't have to stop production. Today, that peacock, Hans Weber, toted the water bucket and passed by Luka."

"The man from Lithuania?"

Oskar nodded. "Luka's been secretly talking about sabotaging the bombs."

A new fear spread through her. "You haven't done that, have you?"

Oskar shook his head. "But I had to stand up for Luka. I told the guard he'd skipped him. The peacock rammed the butt of his rifle into my stomach. 'Keep your trap shut or next time I'll skip you.' I knew then that his actions were intentional.

"When both guards' backs were turned, Luka sneaked to the bucket and gulped down a ladle of water. He was a few steps from his workstation when the peacock raised his rifle and shot Luka in the center of his forehead. He crumpled to the floor, his body twitching. The peacock raised one finger. 'A point for me,' he bragged."

Oskar wrung his hands. "I had to work next to Luka, his blood pooling on the concrete floor and his vacant eyes staring up at me."

Harriet fought the scream lodged in her throat. She couldn't let Oskar see how much his words had shaken her.

He continued to wring his hands. "When it was time to leave, the peacock pointed his gun at me and the man next to me. 'Dump him outside,' he ordered. We lugged Luka's body behind the building and laid him on the frozen ground next to the trash. I removed my hat and the other man mumbled a few words. Then…then we left him there."

Oskar hung his head. "I should have done more, Harriet, but I couldn't. I just couldn't." He stared at his hands and wiped them on the sofa. "I still feel his blood on me."

Harriet imagined the horror, but for her, the worst part was that instead of Luka, Oskar might have been shot. She couldn't open her mouth, afraid she would scream and rant at the senselessness of all the killing.

Oskar seemed to think the same way. "I don't know how the war can go on. The Germans are battling the British, the Americans, and the Soviets. When will Hitler stop? How many more men will be killed before this bloody war ends? And for what? Greed? Is that what it's about?"

These were questions Harriet had asked herself. Now Oskar was voicing his doubts about the war and Hitler. She wanted to return to Lithuania, but when she talked to Sister Anne today, the nun told her that the Germans were slaughtering Jews in Lithuania, and it wasn't safe for anyone there. "Stay until the war is over," the nun had advised.

Harriet wanted to discuss leaving with Oskar but now was not the right time. He was slumped on the couch as if he were defeated. As a child, Harriet had listened to her parents and tried to do what they wanted. After she married Oskar, she had listened to him and tried to do what he wanted. But when she was pregnant, she'd found the courage to insist on returning to Lithuania. That hadn't turned out well, but Oskar hadn't blamed her.

This war had not only changed their lives, it had changed her. It had made her stronger. The war had also changed Oskar, not just his opinion of Hitler. Oskar seemed more than willing to ask her advice and listen to her. She had always drawn her strength from him. Was it possible that Oskar drew strength from her?

She leaned into him and laid her head on his shoulders. He put his hand in her hair and stroked her short locks. His fingers shook, and he let out an audible moan as he wrapped his arms around her and pulled her against him so tightly she could barely breathe.

For a long time, he just held her. When his heart quit beating against her chest, she tilted her face up to his, questioningly. His lips found hers—soft, caressing, desiring. This part of Oskar had not changed. He was still the virile man she had married. He no longer reminded her of woods and chocolate. He smelled of sweat and oil from the factory. She breathed him in and relaxed.

He deepened his kiss and groaned. She knew he wanted more, and so did she. She closed her eyes and let him take her with him, away from their problems, away from the terrors of war. They were just two people who could be anywhere, stripped naked and bound by their need and their love.

1943

No minutes were kept at Bomber Command Headquarters in England, but this letter dated May 27, 1943, written by Sir Arthur Harris to his six group commanders and labeled 'Most Secret,' survived.

The importance of HAMBURG, the second largest city in Germany with a population of one and a half million...needs no further emphasis. The destruction of this city would...reduce the industrial capacity of the enemy's war machine. This, together with the effect on German morale, would play a very important part in shortening and winning the war.

The 'Battle of Hamburg' cannot be won in a single night. It is estimated that at least 10,000 tons of bombs will have to be dropped to complete the process of elimination.

INTENTION: To destroy HAMBURG. [1]

After the attack of Pearl Harbor, America entered the war, but it took eighteen months for American planes to join forces with the British and bomb Germany. The British bombed at night to avoid casualties. The Americans bombed in the daylight because they were morally opposed to bombing civilians and believed in the daylight they could see their targets clearer and would have fewer casualties.

The Battle of Hamburg, Code name Operation Gomorrah, was ten days of bombing that was highly successful partly because the British introduced 'windows,' bundles of paper strips coated with metal foil that were dropped from the windows of airplanes. Within twenty seconds, bundles of the 2,200 metallic strips twisted and fluttered into little clouds. These clouds appeared on the German radar as the echo of one bomber and would remain effective for at least fifteen minutes. [2]

On the fourth and fifth day of Operation Gomorrah, the target was the overcrowded working-class districts. In just over half an hour, approximately 100,000 incendiary bombs fell onto the city. Leonard Cooper, flight engineer in a 7 Squadron Lancaster, stated, "We could definitely smell...well, it was like burning flesh." [3]

Bill McCrea, a British bomber stated, "The (last) raid was a shamble...We should never have gone because this electric storm came through England the previous day...They said it would have cleared Hamburg in 24 hours—well, it hadn't." [4]

CHAPTER
FIFTY

January - July 1943

rena pushed open the blackout curtains in the bedroom. Large snowflakes flicked against the glass. "It's snowing," she called to Mama in the kitchen.

"You better stay home from school."

Irena didn't protest. She loved learning, but school always started the same. The class rose, saluted Hitler's portrait, and repeated three times, "*Heil Hitler.*" Geography was next. Fraulein Mueller would pull down the map and point to all the countries that belonged to Germany in 1943: Austria, Czechoslovakia, Poland, Norway, Denmark, Belgium, Netherlands, Luxembourg, France, Estonia, Latvia, and Irena's own beloved Lithuania. In vocabulary, Fraulein Mueller taught the class new words like *panzer*, the German tank, and *radar*, a radio and ranging device that spotted incoming airplanes.

Even the arithmetic problems were related to war. "If the

British RAF had five Halifaxes and the German *Luftwaffe* shot down four of them, how many British fighters would be left?"

Irena had no trouble solving the take-away problems, but the teacher never explained that if the Germans were shooting down so many British bombers, why had the air raids increased?

Irena turned away from the window and crossed to the dresser for Gertrude. She loved the new red dress Mama had made for her doll for Christmas. It matched the ones Mama had sewn for her, Bridget, and Betty. When they had tried them on, Mama called them quadruplets.

Irena reached for the doll perched on top of the dresser, but her fingers hit the hand mirror. Pulling it down, she peered at her reflection. She started to slip the mirror back when her eyes landed on her nose. Had it grown? Was it beginning to hook? She placed the mirror under her nose and studied it until she was sure that her nose was definitely not a Jewish six. After listening to Fraulein Mueller talk about the Jews and seeing their pictures in the books she read to the class, Irena was sure she would not be fooled by a Jew.

The next day and the next were cold, wintry days that turned into cold, wintry weeks and months. Then one morning, Mama said that it was spring, and they had to return to school. Irena didn't want to leave Mama and the baby, but at least she would see Mia. However, when Irena and Bridget walked into the classroom, Mia's seat was empty. All week Irena expected Mia to return, but each day Mia wasn't there.

After two weeks, Fraulein Mueller introduced a new girl to the class. "This is Nina Strola." Nina had short, curly blonde hair and kept her head down as if she were too shy to look at the class.

Fraulein Mueller pointed to the rows of tables. "Take a seat."

Nina darted to the empty chair next to Irena and plopped

into Mia's seat. Irena expected Fraulein Mueller to object. Instead, the teacher turned her back and wrote the weekly spelling words on the blackboard.

When the class lined up to leave for the day, Irena lagged and inched toward the teacher's desk. She took a steadying breath. "Nina is sitting in someone's seat."

Fraulein Mueller's thick brows bunched together. "That is not your business."

Irena shuffled her feet. She couldn't give up. When Mia returned, she might have to sit next to Helga the Hun. "Where will Mia sit?"

The teacher puffed out her chest, making her swastika pin more prominent. "Who?"

Fraulein Mueller must not have heard her. Irena spoke louder. "Mia, the girl who sat next to me."

"You are mistaken. No girl sat next to you."

Irena stared at Fraulein Mueller. Had the teacher gone crackers? Irena protested, "But—"

Fraulein Mueller interrupted. "No girl sat there. It was a Jew."

Irena couldn't believe she had been duped. How could Mia be a Jew? She was smart and kind and Irena liked her, even if she was a Jew.

That night, Mama again tried to explain it to her. "Every nationality has good people and bad people, even Lithuanians and Jews."

That only confused Irena even more.

When summer arrived and school was out, Irena thought life would be better. But nothing changed. The days were hot with little rain, and they couldn't play outside. When Mama took them to the store, they had to keep their heads down and be invisible.

On the last Saturday night in July, the twenty-fourth, Da announced, "Tomorrow, we'll pick blueberries."

That night Irena drifted off with visions of blueberries dancing in her head.

Eeeoooeeeooooeee.

Irena woke, screaming, but she had to get up or she might be left behind. Mama carried Betty, and Da held Bridget, so Irena gripped Da's hand as he guided them through the dark, crowded street. Near the bunker, the clouds parted, revealing the moon and a myriad of twinkling stars. Just as Bridget and Mama walked into the bunker, a flare shot up in the sky. Irena tugged on Da's hand, stopping him at the top of the ramp. Airplanes. Irena counted one, two, three. Something shiny fell from the rear of the planes.

"Look, Da." She pointed to the sky, glittering with what seemed like hundreds of fireflies. Suddenly, the entire sky glowed as a multitude of firebombs rained down on the city. The sight was beautiful and terrifying.

Da pulled her down the ramp and squeezed through the closing door. He dropped onto the bench with Mama, who held Betty on her lap. Irena plunked next to Bridget on the concrete. The floor was cool, but the crowded bunker was hot and smelly. Mr. Roka, perched on the bench with his wife across from them, lit a candle. Da whispered to Mama about the planes and the firebombs. His words were cut off by loud whistling. Irena covered her ears to block out the planes that sounded like a hive of angry hornets.

Someone chuckled. "The whole RAF must be attacking." No one else laughed.

Irena didn't know how many planes were in the British Royal Air Force, but it sounded like hundreds were flying over.

Boom! Boom! Boom!

She jerked as the floor beneath her shook. Bridget and the other children screamed. Many of the women cried out.

Boom! Boom! Boom!

Irena was too scared to stay on the floor. She scrambled

onto Da's lap and leaned against him, wanting his solid body, but he was quivering, too. In previous raids, the bombs sounded far away, and days later, Da would report the bombs had hit a factory or a shipyard or oil tanks. Tonight, the explosions sounded as if the planes were dropping bombs near their shelter. Didn't the British know this was where workers and their families lived?

Boom! Boom! Boom!

"The *Luftwaffe* will stop them," cried Da, but the bombs kept coming.

Mama prayed to Mary, repeating the rosary. The flame on the candle flickered and went out. Mr. Roka reached down and moved the candle, placing it next to him. Children on the floor scrambled onto the benches. Irena closed her eyes and prayed that she and her family would live.

For the next thirty minutes, hundreds and hundreds of explosions shook the shelter. Sweat rolled down her face. She couldn't breathe. She opened her eyes and searched for the candle. It wasn't lit.

"Everyone up," shouted Mr. Werner, the civil defense worker.

Da lifted her off his lap, and Irena pulled Bridget up with her. They stood on the bench and wrapped their arms around each other. Da helped Mama, who was holding Betty, climb onto the bench. This was a new level of terror. They'd never had to stand on the benches before, but they'd never been trapped in the shelter this long before, either.

Irena glanced across at Mr. and Mrs. Roka still sitting. Why didn't they get up? She started to nudge Da, then stopped. If Mrs. Roka couldn't walk, she probably couldn't stand. Da must have noticed because he whispered to the man standing next to him, wearing a sleeveless T-shirt. "Let's help her."

Da and the man jumped to the floor. Facing each other, they

locked arms to form a chair. "Jonas, move your wife here. We can hold her higher."

"*Danke*." Mr. Roka put one arm behind his wife's back and scooted her forward. At the edge of the bench, he gave a slight push. His wife dropped onto Da's makeshift chair. The men's arms sank but stayed locked together. As they lifted the 'chair,' it tilted toward Da, and the afghan covering Mrs. Roka's legs slipped off.

She lurched forward, trying to catch it. "No, no." The colorful afghan slid off her legs onto the floor.

Irena gaped. Mrs. Roka's legs were short, no longer than her own, and withered. The useless limbs dangled beneath her like a stringed puppet, but on her feet were beautiful red velvet slippers. Mr. Roka slid off the bench and retrieved the afghan. Hastily, he wrapped it around his wife's legs. She smiled at him, but her smile didn't disguise the humiliation in her eyes. Then Mrs. Roka's eyes focused on Irena.

Embarrassed to be caught staring, Irena gazed down at her own dirty feet. She'd always envied Mrs. Roka's shoes and thought it would be fun to ride in a wheelchair, but seeing the withered legs made Irena's heart hurt.

For the next hour, the men shifted Mrs. Roka from one to the other. Irena became light-headed and wobbled. When the whistling stopped, she let go of Bridget. "Is it over?"

"I hope so." Da handed Mrs. Roka to her husband. "They've been dropping bombs for hours."

Fifteen more minutes passed before the all-clear siren signaled the raid was over and the door to the bunker opened. Air gushed in. Irena jumped down and sucked in a deep breath. Smoke clogged her lungs. Coughing, she covered her mouth and darted out the door.

Her eyes watered as she blinked through the smoke. In the distance, flames shot up from what looked like one big fireball. The entire city of Hamburg seemed to be burning.

Across the street, a small fire sparked in the dry grass. Down the block, other fires glowed, their lights flickering like lanterns in the night. As Irena waited for her family, her foot slipped on something lying in the street.

Squatting, she picked up a small strip of black paper about the size of the ruler at school and examined it. Lights from the fires reflected against it, making it shine. She ran her fingers over the silvery underside. On the ground were hundreds of the strips twinkling like shiny Christmas lights. She scooped up a handful and ran to Da as he walked out of the shelter with Mama and Betty. Bridget trailed behind, clinging to Mama's skirt.

"Look what I found." Opening her palm, she showed Da the fistful of strips.

He picked one up and ran his fingers over it. "It feels like aluminum foil." He let the paper slip through his fingers. Reaching down, he took her other hand. "Let's go home."

Irena was too tired to ask more questions, so she dropped the strips, letting them flutter to the ground.

They trudged toward...home? Da had never said *home* to refer to where they lived in Hamburg. He said *flat* or *apartment* or *projects*. Home was Lithuania.

Irena tried to picture their old apartment. She remembered the fragrant smells from the kitchen and the warmth of the bedrooms. Mama and Da had one bedroom. She and Bridget had the other, and they didn't have to share a bed. Irena squeezed her eyes closed. She could feel Mama pulling up the covers as she tucked her into bed. An intense longing surged through Irena as she remembered being snuggled up in her own bed at home. She never felt that way in Germany and had almost forgotten the feeling. When Mama pulled up the covers in Lithuania and kissed her on the cheek, Irena had felt safe.

CHAPTER
FIFTY-ONE

July 25, 1943
Day two of Operation Gomorrah,
the ten-day strike against Hamburg

The next morning, Irena lay in bed, her nightshirt soaked in sweat. She hadn't slept. The whistling flares, the rumbling planes, the exploding bombs still swirled in her head.

Careful not to wake Bridget, she padded into the kitchen. Mama and Da were at the table. Betty sat on Mama's lap, slurping oatmeal from Da's bowl.

Irena's stomach growled. She dashed to the stove and peeked into the pan. Empty. She sighed. Then she remembered today was Sunday, and Da was taking her blueberry-picking.

She darted to the table but didn't sit. "I'll get dressed so we can go pick berries."

"Don't be in a hurry, sleepyhead." Da pushed the bowl of oatmeal toward her. "We left some for you."

Betty screamed in protest, her sticky hands grabbing for the bowl.

The oatmeal smelled tempting, but Irena shoved it back. She wanted to save room for all those juicy blueberries. "You said we'd get an early start."

"Last night changed that," Da said.

Irena panicked. "We're still going, aren't we?"

"Later, when it's cooler and they've had time to—"

Mama nudged Da with her elbow. "Are you sure it's safe?"

He cleared his throat. "The fires should be out, and the Allies never bomb in the daytime."

By three o'clock, Irena had pestered Da until he gave in. Bridget seemed content to help Mama with Betty.

The joy over berry picking was flattened by the remains of last night's attack. Bombs had cut deep craters in the road, and apartment buildings were still burning, sending curls of smoke into the air. Inches of soot covered the street, littered with hundreds of what looked like foil strips.

Irena reached down and grabbed a handful. She wiped off the soot and rubbed the slick foil between her fingers. They looked like the ones she had seen last night. "Da, what are these strips?"

"I don't know. Somehow, the British dropped tons of bombs on us and the Germans couldn't stop them."

She discarded the pieces, letting them flutter onto the brick pavement. "I can't wait to eat those plump blueberries."

"The berries might not be plump this year."

As they walked, Irena mulled over Da's words. "Is that because of the war, too?"

"No, because we haven't had much rain. Without enough moisture at the right time, the blueberries are small, or sometimes they don't produce at all."

Irena wiped the sweat from her brow. Da was right about the heat. The afternoon was a scorcher. She hoped he wasn't also right about the blueberries. She closed her mind to all the destruction and held onto the image of being in the cool forest, picking plump blueberries, and filling her bucket and her belly.

As they approached the small business district, a thick cloud of smoke engulfed them. Coughing, Irena covered her mouth with her hand. Her eyes watered as she squinted through the haze at the businesses. Some of their windows were shattered, leaving glass lying on the sidewalk.

In the last block, Da inched toward a crowd that had gathered. They paused behind the on-lookers. Four civil defense workers were digging in the bricks. Irena shifted for a better view. Sticking out of the rubble was a man's arm in a torn brown sleeve with a red band. The hand had long, slender fingers that pointed to the sky.

Frantic to free the man, the civil defense workers clawed at the bricks. A bear-like worker tugged on the man's limb, wiggling it back and forth. Grunting, he dug in the heels of his boots and pulled. The surrounding bricks gave way, and the arm popped out.

Irena gasped. The arm wasn't attached to a body. It just dangled in the air until the worker must have realized what he was holding. Then he dropped it, bent over, and vomited.

Da stepped in front of her view. "Come on, Irena."

She was too shocked to move. Da took her hand and led her by the gutted telephone exchange and police station, destroyed except for three empty cells with warped bars and the doors hanging open. Her body shook, so she fixed her eyes on the tall, needle-like tower that rose in the distance. "St. Nicholi is still standing."

Da said reverently, "At least they didn't destroy the cathedral."

At the edge of town, an alarming buzz began—planes. Irena dropped her bucket and clutched Da tighter. "The bombers are coming!" she shouted.

Da gazed up at the thick clouds and continued walking. "The British won't attack during the day. We shoot down too many of their planes."

She picked up her bucket, but the roar of the engines grew louder. She tugged on Da's shirt sleeve. "Don't you hear them?"

"The siren didn't go off. It's probably German planes surveying the damage from last night."

Irena continued to scan the sky. The clouds parted, and rays of sunshine broke through. She shaded her eyes with her hands. A squadron of planes forming a 'v' flew overhead. She liked to wave to the German planes flying low.

When several planes in the rear of the formation dipped down, she raised her arm. Her hand stopped in mid-air. The wing tips were red, and instead of the iron cross on the under-side, these planes had blue circles with white stars. "Da, why do the planes have red, white, and blue on their wings?"

His head jerked up. "American airplanes."

CHAPTER
FIFTY-TWO

July 25 - 26, 1943
Operation Gomorrah (Sunday and Monday)

arriet lay under the bed, pressed against the floor with Betty and Bridget. Her breath came in uneven gulps. A little more than an hour after Oskar and Irena left, planes roared over the projects. They didn't have time to run to the shelter. Even the basement was dangerous. "Let's play hide-n-seek," she said and grabbed Betty.

Bridget must have heard the planes because she grabbed Gertrude from the dresser. "Irena would want me to protect her doll."

The three of them wiggled under the bed. For almost half an hour, the bombs whistled and exploded. She worried about Oskar and Irena. Were they safe? And why hadn't the sirens gone off?

Finally, the booming stopped and the planes faded away. Harriet's heart raced as she peeked from under the bed, straining for sounds that the Allies might be returning. When the silence continued and her heart slowed, she pulled the girls from under the bed. Bridget jumped up and headed for the kitchen.

"Let's stay in the bedroom." Harriet didn't add because sometimes the planes return. For the next half hour, she sat on the double bed, worrying about Oskar and Irena, while Bridget played with Betty and Gertrude.

Footsteps padded up the stairway. Harriet rushed to the kitchen and unchained the door, throwing it open. Irena, with only one pigtail left in her hair and smelling of smoke launched herself at Harriet.

"It was awful, Mama. In town—"

"Harriet." Oskar stood in the doorway, his smoke-streaked face glistening with sweat. She released Irena and rushed to Oskar. Her family was safe.

Bridget led Betty into the kitchen. "I watched Gertrude for you."

Irena didn't get mad at Bridget for playing with her doll. Instead, Irena said, "A man was trapped under a pile of bricks. They were trying to get him out and—"

"Irena," Oskar's voice boomed. "We're just thankful your mama and sisters made it safely to the shelter and back."

Irena stuck out her lip. "I want to tell them about town."

Oskar shook his finger at Irena. "I don't want you scaring your sisters."

She skittered around as if itching to talk, but Oskar's reprimand made her stop. Harriet wet a rag and washed Irena's face. "Now go play in the bedroom."

"Did you bring blueberries?" Bridget asked, turning and heading to the bedroom.

"No blueberries," Irena answered as she followed her sisters.

Harriet shut the door and rinsed out the rag for Oskar. He

thought she had taken the girls to the shelter. He'd be furious if he found out they'd stayed in the apartment.

Turning from the sink, she handed Oskar the rag. "Here. You smell awful." As he washed the soot from his face, she asked, "What didn't you want Irena to say?"

He wiped off his face and told her about the fires, the charred trees, the bombed buildings, and the arm. After he finished, she asked, "Where were you and Irena during the attack?"

"We ran to a round silo in town that's used for a shelter."

"Did you hear the siren?" she asked.

"No, but the planes were flying low enough that we could see them. I don't understand why the radar didn't detect them."

Harriet was glad he didn't ask if the sirens had gone off here. "I thought the British stopped bombing in the daytime," she said.

"These weren't British planes. They were American."

Harriet felt as if all the air had been sucked out of the room. They had considered America might bomb Germany, but she never expected it to happen. "We've been here almost three years, and the war is escalating."

"Hitler must have been mad to declare war on America."

Harriet nodded. "Hitler's fighting the whole world. How can he win?"

Oskar threw the rag onto the table. "I'm not sure I want him to win."

Harriet glanced over her shoulder to make sure the bedroom door was closed, so the girls wouldn't overhear what Oskar said. He'd voiced his displeasure about Hitler before, but she didn't know he felt such antipathy.

Oskar lowered his voice. "Luka is gone, but other men at the factory want me to sabotage the bombs."

Harriet was too stunned to reply.

"I can't get the images of the destruction from the bombs

out of my mind." He stretched out his arms. "What should I do, Harriet?"

She took his hands. "If they find out, you'll be shot like Luka."

"But if I do nothing, evil wins."

———

That night, Irena, still dressed in her clothes, tried to sleep, but pictures of the bombed town ran through her head—the fires, the hole, the arm...the fires... Her eyelids closed. She jerked awake, listening for the wailing sirens. But on Sunday night, July 25, the British did not attack Hamburg.

On Monday, Irena walked into the kitchen, yawning. Da was still home, and the two tin buckets were in the center of the table. "Are we going berry picking?"

Da nodded.

"What about work?"

"On Sunday, the Americans knocked out the power lines at the factory."

"I'll get ready."

"It's too hot. Late afternoon will be better."

Irena didn't argue. Her joy of berry picking had fizzled. "Will there be more raids today?"

"Surely the bombing is over." Mama tied her apron and picked up a potato. "I'll make some soup."

"Can I help?" asked Irena. She liked cooking with Mama.

"Get out the bowls and spoons."

Irena stayed in the kitchen, enjoying the aroma of the boiling potatoes and onions while Bridget and Betty played near Da on the couch. When the soup was ready for the noon meal, Mama said, "I'll fill the bowls, and you can put them on the table."

Irena carried the bowls of soup to the table, walking slowly, making sure not to spill a drop. She set the first bowl at Da's place and the next ones at Mama's and Bridget's. "This one's for me." She lifted it to her nose and sniffed.

Eeeoooeeeooooeee.

The bowl slipped from her hands. Potato soup sloshed onto her brown polka-a-dot dress as the bowl crashed to the floor and shattered.

Da jumped up from the couch, grabbing Betty, who was screaming. He handed her to Mama and then hoisted Bridget into his arms.

Eeeoooeeeooooeee.

Da threw open the door. "Let's go."

Irena stared down at the ruined bowl and soup. Her head screamed for her to run. Her stomach yelled for her to stay. The warring voices split her apart like the pieces of pottery scattered on the floor.

"Come on, Irena," yelled Da.

Her feet wouldn't move. Da set Bridget down. "Hold your mama's hand. I'll carry Irena."

Mama hurried out of the flat with Betty and Bridget. Da lifted Irena into his arms.

Eeeoooeeeooooeee.

Irena let out a loud cry and covered her ears with her hands. Not again. She couldn't go through this again, but Da whisked her out of the flat and raced through the street. She was still crying when they entered the shelter. Instead of sitting on the floor, Da set her in the space next to Mama.

When the bombing began, Irena cried harder. Mama put a comforting arm around her and whispered, "You're the oldest. Be strong for your sisters. If you're afraid, they'll be afraid."

Bridget sat at her feet, holding Betty on her lap. Both were crying. Irena dug her nails into her fists and forced back tears.

Across from them, Mrs. Roka smiled at her. "Such a pretty face, just like your mama's."

Irena liked being compared to Mama. But as the bombers continued rumbling overhead, Irena couldn't understand how Mrs. Roka could keep smiling.

She couldn't even walk, yet Irena should quit acting like a baby. It was just a broken bowl and spilled soup. Much worse could have happened.

But much worse was happening. Hamburg was being bombed night and day.

CHAPTER
FIFTY-THREE

July 26 - 27, 1943
Operation Gomorrah (Monday and Tuesday)

M onday night Irena kneeled with Bridget on the floor, praying harder than ever for the bombing to stop. When Da tucked them in, Irena asked, "Will they bomb us again tonight?"

"I don't think they have any bombs left." Da leaned over and kissed her forehead. "The last bombing was probably a mistake. The British must know only workers and their families live here."

But shortly after midnight, the siren howled.

Eeeoooeeeooooeee.

By the time the family scrambled outside, the planes were already rumbling toward the projects. Irena didn't need any coaxing to hurry. She had seen the destruction and death from the bombs. As she ran, something landed on her shoulder. She hoped it was rain. The night air shimmered with heat, and she wished for cold raindrops to cool her.

Something landed in her hair. Not looking up, she tucked in her chin and raced ahead. At the top of the ramp, she paused, waiting for her family. Searchlights cut across the night sky. Swirling in the air like giant snowflakes were hundreds of foil strips.

A beam lit up a plane. Her heart pounded. Then her family came into view. She waved and darted down the ramp.

Her family and others piled in after her. Several minutes passed before Mr. Roka, carrying his wife, ducked inside. The benches were filled. The Rokas had no place to sit.

Da stood. "Jonas, set your wife here." He motioned to the space next to Mama, who was holding Betty.

"*Danke.*" Jonas slid his wife onto the bench above where Irena was sitting on the concrete floor. Usually, she leaned against Da, but she sat up straighter, afraid to bump Mrs. Roka's legs.

The warning siren ceased.

Boom! Boom! Boom!

Betty and the other toddlers continued to cry. The shelter was so crowded that the candle flickered and fizzled out. Bridget climbed onto Mama's lap with Betty. No space was left for Irena.

Mrs. Roka smiled at Mama. "I'll hold the baby."

Mama looked down at Betty, who was still crying. "Are you sure?"

Nodding, Mrs. Roka held out her arms.

Mama shifted Betty to Mrs. Roka and then patted her empty knee for Irena. After climbing onto Mama's lap, Irena angled her body to help calm Betty as she searched for a distraction to keep her from crying. Irena glanced at Mrs. Roka's colorful afghan, imagining the red velvet slippers beneath.

Betty lurched toward Irena, shifting Mrs. Roka's afghan and revealing white satin slippers.

Irena pointed to Mrs. Roka's feet. "Look at the pretty shoes."

Betty continued to squirm as Mrs. Roka asked, "Which shoes do I have on?"

"How many pairs of shoes do you have?" Irena asked in amazement.

Mr. Roka, standing near his wife, chuckled. "She has lots of shoes."

"Are they all so beautiful?" Irena asked.

Mrs. Roka laughed. "Of course. Why have ugly shoes?"

Irena's only pair were her sturdy brown lace-ups that were worn out and hurt her feet, but Mrs. Roka didn't walk in her shoes.

In less than an hour, the all-clear siren sounded. The door opened, letting smoke-filled air roll into the shelter. Coughing, Irena slipped off Mama's lap. She held her arms out for Betty, who jumped into them.

Blinking, Irena carried Betty up the ramp. The night air was hazy, and Irena waved her hand to clear away the smoke. Along the street, several fires crackled in the grass.

Heat from the fires and the heavy night air made Irena feel as if she were walking in an oven. Da would help the Rokas, but she was too tired to wait, so she trudged toward the projects, dreaming about curling up in her own bed.

Betty wailed, "Wah-wah."

Irena was hot and thirsty, too. "We'll get water soon." She weaved through the crowded street, thinking about that cool drink.

Then she heard them. Planes. Irena's head jerked up. Beams from the searchlights rotated across the sky, illuminating a single airplane. From the opposite direction rumbled several others.

Lights streaked through the sky as bullets *ra-ta-tatted* toward the lone plane. The single aircraft flew erratically, then spiraled downward.

Eeeoooeeeooooeee.

Another attack. Her heart *ra-ta-tated* with the guns. Some people in the streets sprinted toward the projects; others scrambled toward the bunker. Irena wanted to go back to their flat, but the basement wasn't safe, and she didn't want to be separated from Mama and Da. Turning toward the shelter, she gripped Betty tighter and fought through the crowd.

Eeeoooeeeooooeee.

Smoke clung to the air. Carrying Betty made it impossible to run, but Irena shuffled as fast as she could. The buzzing planes and whistling bullets grew louder. Foil strips fluttered around her like glittering snowflakes. Nearby fires snapped and popped. Her eyes stung from the smoke. A few meters ahead stood Da, waving them forward.

When she reached him, he snatched Betty and ran toward the ramp. Irena followed.

Boom!

The impact lifted her off her feet and into the air.

CHAPTER
FIFTY-FOUR

July 27, 1943
Operation Gomorrah (The firestorm)

rena winced as she ran her hand over the lump on the side of her head. Voices faded in and out. She blinked, trying to focus. She was in the bunker, sitting on Mama's lap. Da was perched on one side of her and Mrs. Roka on the other. Bridget was settled on the floor, holding Betty. "What happened?"

"The blast knocked you down, and you hit your head." Mama probed Irena's scalp for injuries.

As Mama touched the bump above her ear, Irena winced. "I heard the all-clear siren. Why are we still in the bunker?"

"This is a second wave of British planes," answered Da.

Mrs. Roka whispered, "I hope Irena doesn't have a concussion."

Boom! Boom! Boom!

The bombs and the pressure in the shelter made her head hurt more. Mrs. Roka's soft hand squeezed Irena's as she glanced down. "You have little feet like mine."

Mrs. Roka's feet and shoes were so fascinating that for a few minutes, Irena forgot about the pain and the bombs.

Boom! Boom! Boom!

She screamed, her head throbbing more with each boom.

"Be a brave girl and tomorrow your mama might let you come over. I'll show you all my shoes."

Irena wanted to see the shoes, and the Rokas lived near them. She swiped her wet cheeks with the backs of her hands and tilted her head. "Please, Mama."

"*Ja,* we'll go."

Mama must have wanted to see the shoes, too, because Irena didn't have to beg.

The bunker vibrated. What seemed like a blast of air slammed against her chest. She couldn't breathe. Mrs. Roka put her hand on Irena's back and leaned her over. "Open your mouth and stay bent down." Mrs. Roka's head was almost in her lap.

Irena's chest heaved as she gulped in air and imitated Mrs. Roka. Mama showed Bridget and Betty how to breathe.

They'd never had trouble breathing before when the candle was lit. Irena stayed bent down, staring at her bare feet and thinking about the red slippers. Then the booming stopped, but the bunker continued to shake.

"What's happening?" Mama asked.

"The bombs are too close to hear," Da whispered. "We can only feel them."

The pressure built. Wave after wave pounded against Irena. She couldn't hear, she couldn't think, she couldn't breathe.

She lost track of time, but the bombing must have been less than an hour because the candle was still lit. When the door opened, Irena didn't jump off Mama's lap but carefully slid down. She winced. Her head ached, and she had trouble balancing as she wobbled up the ramp behind Da, who was carrying Bridget.

The air swirled with smoke. Coughing, Irena covered her mouth and plowed forward. She slid on something in the street, almost falling. Probably more foil strips, although it felt as if it were a whole puddle of them.

In the distance, flames from a round yellow ball flared, lighting up the sky and the street. Lying on the brick pavement were black humps. People—lots and lots of people. Their clothes and skin had been burned off. Trickling down the street like rain after a shower was blood. Her feet were in a pool of blood. She screamed and choked on the smoke.

Da pulled her against his side. "A child should not see such things."

Shaking, she stood there, unable to close her eyes.

"Harriet, hand me the baby. Then lift Irena onto my back."

Da juggled Bridget and Betty as Mama lifted Irena. She hooked her arms around Da's neck and wrapped her legs around his waist.

Da returned Betty to Mama. "Hang on." Da carried Bridget in his arms as he balanced Irena on his back. She squeezed her eyes shut, but she could still see the dead.

At home, Mama wet a rag and wiped the smoke from Irena's face and the blood from her feet. "I'll wash you better in the morning. Get a drink and go to bed."

Irena curled in bed with her arms around Betty and Bridget, trying to create a safe cocoon. Betty went to sleep first, followed by Bridget. Irena closed her eyes. Her head hurt, but it wasn't the dull throbbing pain keeping her awake. It was her feet. She rubbed and rubbed, but she couldn't get the feel of blood off them.

Eeeoooeeeoooee.

Irena shot up, the siren making her head ache more. Betty screamed, but Bridget moaned, "Not again. Let's go to the basement."

Irena tugged on Bridget's hand. "We have to go to the shelter."

Bridget didn't budge. "Mama, let us stay here before."

"Come on, girls," said Mama. "Da and I will carry you."

Bridget refused. "I'm staying here."

Eeeoooeeeoooee.

Irena's head pounded. She longed to go back to bed. She didn't want to stay in the bunker for the third time in one night, but she remembered the gutted buildings and the man's hand in the rubble. "I saw a man covered with bricks after a bombing. They pulled on him so hard his arm popped right off."

Bridget shot up, her eyes wide. "Just his arm?"

"Irena," scolded Da. "Don't scare your sister."

Too late, she remembered her promise to Da, but she'd take her punishment as long as Bridget was safe from the bombs.

After Mama picked Bridget up, and Da grabbed Betty, Irena ran down the stairs. She fisted her hands and raced through the crowded street to the bunker. Her bare feet slapped against the cobblestones as her pigtails flopped behind her.

Eeeoooeeeoooe.

The high-pitched screech of the air-raid siren sent chills slithering down her spine. She wasn't going to make it. She squinted through the fog of smoke. Her eyes burned. "Mama, Da, where are you?" The fierce wind carried away her words.

Screams filled the darkness as footsteps pounded against the pavement. She pumped her legs harder. She had to reach the shelter before the bombs hit.

The sky rumbled. Her head jerked up. Airplanes. Lots of enemy planes, one after another cut through the clouds.

Boom! Boom! Boom!

The ground rolled. In the distance a bomb exploded. A yellow ball of fire illuminated the night sky. Lying in the street were mounds of soot from the previous raid. Her foot hit something solid. Her arms shot out to break the fall. Her knees slammed against the jagged stones, ripping her skin as her hands landed on the black soot. Only it wasn't soot. None of the black mounds lying lifeless in the street were soot. She screamed. She had tripped over the charred remains of a child no bigger than she was.

Other bodies littered the street. One woman kneeled beside a man, probably her husband. She seemed unwilling to leave even as the planes swooped overhead.

Irena forced herself up. In the next block, a boy wandered aimlessly. "Help me. Somebody help me."

Irena turned in his direction. Then she heard her family calling for her. "Here," she shouted, not moving until they caught up with her. She clung to Da's shirt as he led them to the shelter. Then she sank to the floor, gasping for air.

When Mr. Werner closed the door, the bench across from them was empty. Where were Mr. and Mrs. Roka? They'd made it to the bunker during the last two bombings, so they couldn't be among the bodies lying in the street unless they'd been hit now.

Irena pointed at the bench. "The Rokas aren't here. Who will light the candle?"

Mr. Werner struck a match and lit the candle. Pounding from outside shook the door. Mr. Werner pushed it open. Ducking, Mr. Roka squeezed inside—alone. He sank onto the bench next to Da.

Irena blurted out, "Where's Mrs. Roka?"

"She wouldn't come." He put his hand on his forehead and looked down as if he'd done something wrong. "I pleaded with her. She said it was too much for me to carry her a third time. I tried to change her mind, but she begged me to go. She said she wouldn't be scared if she knew I was safe."

Da put his hand on Mr. Roka's shoulder. "She'll be all right. The bombs have never hit the projects."

Mr. Roka raised his head. He stretched out his arms, palms up. "What could I do? She wouldn't come. I pleaded with her."

Da didn't answer as Mr. Roka repeated the same words as if trying to understand why he was sitting here and his wife wasn't with him.

Irena pointed to the candle. "The flame's out."

Da nudged Mr. Roka. He looked down, but he didn't reach for the matches. Several minutes passed. Finally, Mr. Werner struck a match and lit the candle.

Mr. Roka continued repeating, "What could I do? She wouldn't come." He only paused to ask, "How long has it been?"

Each time Mr. Werner answered, "Twenty minutes...thirty minutes...forty minutes." After sixty minutes, the siren sounded, and the door opened.

Bolting up, Mr. Roka struck his head on the door jamb. He seemed unphased as he leaned down and raced out of the shelter. Da carried Betty and Irena rode piggyback. By the time they climbed the ramp, Mr. Roka was merely a tall shadow, jogging left and right through the dead people lying in the street.

Irena didn't look down at the burned bodies and the blood. She stared ahead at Mr. Roka until he disappeared in the thick smoke. Closing her eyes, she thought about something pleasant. Tomorrow she would visit Mrs. Roka and see her shoes.

Irena wiggled her toes, hoping her feet were the same size as Mrs. Roka's. Maybe she could even try her shoes on. If they fit, Mrs. Roka might give her a worn pair, but Mrs. Roka couldn't walk, so the soles wouldn't be worn out. She hoped it would be the red ones. She imagined twirling like a ballerina in her red velvet slippers.

Cries cut through her daydreams. Her eyes opened. People screamed, "Projects...fire!"

A chill shivered down her spine. Da ran faster, almost jogging.

Mama pointed ahead. "There it is."

Irena stretched up. Her eyes burned as she squinted through the heavy smoke. Their building was still there. She sagged against Da. He ran forward into a blanket of heat and smoke that swallowed them.

Irena pressed her mouth against Da's back. Her eyes burned. She blinked, trying to see across the street where Hanna had lived. All that was left was a large hole filled with burning bricks. Nearby, people stood holding each other and wailing. Irena hoped no one had stayed inside. She gasped. "Mrs. Roka!"

"Harriet, take the girls," Da said. "I'll check on Jonas and his wife."

Irena slid down Da's back. "I'll go with you."

She didn't wait for an answer but sprinted after him. The bump on her head throbbed, but she ignored the pain. When she neared the Roka's, more than a dozen people stared at the building—or what was left of it. Only the back wall of bricks remained. The roof and everything inside had collapsed into a deep crater.

Da worked his way through the people, and Irena ducked behind him. Mr. Roka stood in front of the smoldering ashes, struggling to get closer. Two men, one on each side, gripped his outstretched arms, holding him back. He twisted and turned like a crazed animal trying to get free.

His knees buckled. He fell to the ground. He lifted his head and howled. The guttural cry rose and fell like the burning flames.

Tears streamed down Irena's cheeks. She lowered her head and stared at her bare feet. Mrs. Roka was going to show Irena her shoes tomorrow. But Mrs. Roka with her bright smile, soft hands, and red shoes was gone.

Pain balled in Irena's belly. It rolled over and over, growing bigger and bigger until it was too big to keep inside. She opened her mouth and screamed, "Noooooooooo!"

CHAPTER
FIFTY-FIVE

July 28 - 30, 1943
Operation Gomorrah
(Wednesday, Thursday, and Friday)

The next morning, Harriet had barely fallen asleep when she was awakened by pounding on the door. A man's voice yelled, "Oskar, we're leaving in fifteen minutes."

The bedsprings squeaked as Oskar sat up on the edge of the bed and buttoned his work shirt. She reached over and touched his arm. "We spent all night in the bunker." She panicked, afraid of another raid. "Stay here, please." She hated the needy tone in her voice, but she'd lain awake for hours, reliving the horror of last night. Blood running in the street, buildings burning, charred corpses, and most of all, Rosa. That sweet lady, dead. Harriet's heart hurt for Jonas and the others who had lost loved ones.

Her hand slipped from Oskar's arm as he stood and pulled up his suspenders. "I have to go."

Defeated, Harriet asked, "When will it end?"

"It can't go on much longer. After last night Hitler must realize it's insane to fight the Soviets, the British, and the Americans."

Harriet hoped the girls were asleep and didn't hear Oskar defame Hitler. She, too, wanted to rail against Hitler and the senseless killing, but the girls must not hear them criticize *Der Führer*. When Oskar went down the hall, she shuffled into the kitchen, opened the tin of oats, and poured them into a pan of water. By the time he returned, the porridge was ready. His shaved face and clean clothes didn't seem to revive his spirits. He ate a few bites and shoved the bowl away. "If there are more attacks today, promise you'll take the girls to the shelter."

"I promise." As she said the words, her stomach knotted in panic.

After Oskar left, she pumped water into the sink. She would boil water for the washtub when the girls woke. For now, she wiped a washcloth over her skin, scrubbing away whatever soot and smoke were left. Her arms turned pink, but no matter how hard she scrubbed, she could not scrub away the images from last night or quit thinking about Rosa.

It had been the third air raid of the night. All the other nights, Rosa had let Jonas carry her to the shelter. Why hadn't she gone one more time?

As Harriet dried off her face and pumped water into the kettle, Irena screamed. Harriet set the kettle on the stove and rushed into the bedroom. Irena was sitting up in bed, sobbing. Bridget and Betty were crying, too. Harriet sank onto the bed and drew them into her arms. "My poor babies," she said as she gently rocked them back and forth.

Irena pulled away, sniffling. "I-I'm not a-a baby."

Harriet leaned over and kissed her cheek. "No matter how old you are, you'll always be my baby."

Tears welled up in Irena's eyes. "We were going to visit Mrs. Roka and see her pretty shoes."

Harriet blinked back her own tears. "We'll pray for her, and when we go to church, we'll light a candle."

"Can we go today?"

"Right now, you need to wash. You smell like smoke."

"Can I take a bath?" Irena asked.

"*Ja.*" Harriet released the girls and trudged into the kitchen. She pumped the handle to get more water to boil. A few drops dribbled out of the spicket. She worked the handle. Nothing happened. She tried again. Still no water.

Irena walked into the kitchen. "Is the water ready?"

Harriet continued pumping. "I can't get any more. You'll have to use the water in the sink."

Irena looked into the sink and turned her nose up at the gray water. "How can I get clean in that?"

Harriet moved to the stove. "I'll heat some water and add it."

After the water boiled, Harriet poured only a small amount from the kettle into the sink. She didn't know how long the water would be off, and they would need drinking water. Harriet ran a washcloth over Irena's face, touching the bump above her ear. She jerked away.

"Does your head still hurt?" Harriet asked.

Irena nodded.

"This afternoon, we'll take the buckets to town and get drinking water."

"Let's go now," said Irena. "It'll be cooler."

"This afternoon will be better. I have to wash Bridget and Betty." Harriet wanted the workers to have time to clean up the bodies and blood from the street. The girls didn't need to see that. *She* didn't need to see it again.

In the afternoon when they left the apartment, a heavy cloud of smoke hung in the air, blotting out the sun. The heat was stifling. Harriet held Betty while Irena and Bridget carried the buckets and stayed by her side. With each step, Harriet's stomach lurched. Little had changed since last night's bombing. If anything, the sight was worse. Blood and bodies covered the street, but the blood had dried on the cobblestones, and the bodies were covered with buzzing flies.

The girls might have nightmares from seeing the decaying corpses, but they needed water. Changing directions, she turned at the next corner. No bodies lay on the cobblestones, but the buildings along the street were smoldering, and layers of soot covered everything.

Betty's face was flushed from the heat. She wiggled to get down. "Me walk."

Harriet had made the girls wear shoes, and even though her feet hurt, she had slipped on shoes, too. She set Betty on the ground and took the buckets from Irena and Bridget. "Hold your sister's hands and don't let her wander off."

Harriet followed behind the girls as Betty toddled between Irena and Bridget. With each step the smoke thickened. Harriet's eyes watered. Not wanting the girls to breathe in all the smoke, she called, "Turn at the next corner."

The block was worse. Tall, six-story apartment buildings that lined the street had been gutted, leaving only the warped shells of their skeletons standing. A crowd watched the smoldering fire, while others wandered aimlessly.

A woman with singed hair curling around her black-streaked face rushed to Harriet, grabbing her arm. "Have you seen my Henry? I have to find Henry."

Shaking her head, Harriet pushed the girls behind her. The frantic woman released Harriet and darted away, weaving through the crowd, calling, "Henry."

Harriet wanted to flee too, but where would she go? The devastation was everywhere, plus they needed water. She pointed to another side street. "This way."

She led, and the girls followed. They passed a scorched tree with a small boy in knickers. His face was pressed against the charred trunk, and his shoulders shook as if he were crying.

Irena tugged on her arm. "That might be Henry?"

Harriet stopped near the boy. "Even if it isn't Henry, maybe we can help him." She crept toward the boy, not wanting to startle him.

Behind her, Irena shouted. "Betty, come back."

Harriet whirled around. Betty had broken loose from her sisters and darted across the street. Harriet ran after her as she scampered toward a pile of charred rubbish. Catching up with Betty, Harriet grabbed her hand, but Betty dug in her heels and pointed to the black heap. "Baby."

Harriet picked Betty up, but she tried to squirm free. "Baby. Baby."

Harriet glanced down. A burnt suitcase was open with clothes spilling out. In the ashes next to it was a baby doll, its glassy eyes staring up. "I'll get it." Harriet stooped to pick up the doll. Her hand froze. Beside the doll were the charred remains of a child no bigger than Betty. Harriet stifled a scream as she grabbed for Irena's hand. "Bridget, hold on to Irena."

Turning, Harriet rushed the girls back to the flat and dropped the empty buckets next to the door. They had not found more water.

That night, the girls were in bed when Oskar returned to the apartment. Covered in soot, he dragged across the kitchen and sank into the nearest chair. Harriet wet a rag from the water in the kettle and gently washed his face. "I went out for some water. It was...awful."

Her hand shook as she told him about the blocks of burning buildings and the people wandering around looking for loved ones. She didn't tell him about the baby. She couldn't, not without breaking apart.

After she finished his face, Oskar leaned his elbows on the

table to prop up his head. His words were flat, barely a whisper. "When I made bombs at the factory, I thought being killed by a bomb would be a fast death. Boom and you're gone." He threw up his hands, imitating an explosion. "But today they shut down the factory because we had no electricity or water. They drove us to another section of town, similar to what you described. I had to retrieve the corpses from last night's bombing."

"Oh, Oskar." She put her hand on his shoulder, her heart breaking for him.

"I loaded body after body into a truck. After a while, I stopped counting."

She wrapped her arms around him and was hit by the odor of alcohol. Shocked, she stepped back. Oskar rarely touched liquor because his pa had been an alcoholic. "Have you been drinking?"

"They handed out liquor. I took some, hoping to numb the pain. It didn't." Oskar looked up. His eyes were bloodshot.

"You need sleep." But no amount of alcohol or sleep could erase the pain she saw in his eyes.

That night she lay in bed with her clothes on, listening for the planes. After no sirens sounded, she dozed off and slept fitfully until she was awakened by Oskar getting dressed for work.

She rose and padded into the kitchen. She pumped the handle on the well. Nothing came out. "When will we get water again?" she asked, as Oskar trudged into the kitchen.

He shrugged. "The cleanup will take weeks."

"Weeks? How can we live for weeks without water?" She thought about the little boy at the tree and the people searching for loved ones. She ran her hand through her dirty hair. She didn't like the way it smelled, but she and her family were alive.

Before Oskar left, he again made Harriet promise to go to

the shelter if they were attacked. She agreed, but no air strikes happened that morning. In the afternoon, hours before Harriet expected Oskar home, he knocked on the door. When she opened it, he burst in, covered in soot. Setting down a bucket of water, he grabbed her, pressing her against him as if he thought he would never see her again. "Thank God you and the girls are still here."

Puzzled, she pushed away. "Of course, we're here. Where else would we be?"

He sank into a chair. "They took us to clean up the—" Oskar stopped when the girls rushed into the kitchen, and Betty climbed onto his lap. "Today, trucks with loudspeakers drove through the streets, ordering all women and children to evacuate Hamburg."

"But how can anyone leave? The train tracks are gone and most of the main roads are blocked."

"Groves of people are leaving the city, walking."

"Where are they going?" Harriet asked.

"To the country. It might be safer there."

Ever since they'd come to Hamburg, Harriet had wanted to leave. But where would they go? Lithuania wasn't safe, and they didn't have relatives or friends in Germany who would take them in. At least here, they had a place to live, together.

Irena moved close to Oskar and held her nose. "You stink."

Oskar didn't explain, but Harriet suspected the workers had been given alcohol again.

He pointed to the bucket he'd set near the door. "I brought water." Then, reaching beneath his shirt, he pulled out a loaf of bread. "The relief workers handed out food."

Harriet ladled water for the girls. "Drink slowly or you'll get sick."

When they'd quenched their thirst, she sliced some bread and handed each a small piece. Usually, she insisted they eat at the table, but she wanted to talk to Oskar. "Take your bread to the bedroom and play."

"Can we have a tea party?"

She gave Irena and Bridget each a teacup. "Be careful with those." Harriet was thankful they seemed to forget everything that was happening around them as they rushed into the bedroom, giggling.

Harriet sat at the table, and Oskar waited until the girls closed the bedroom door before he began. His voice was so low Harriet strained to hear. "It must have been an inferno. The dry weather and the winds aided the bombs, causing a firestorm. Blocks and blocks of buildings burned."

"Where are they taking the dead?" Harriet asked.

"They dug a mass grave at Ohlsdorf Cemetery."

Harriet made the sign of the cross and said a prayer for their souls. "How many died?"

"I don't know. Whole families burned, their bodies melted together."

———

That night, Irena kneeled beside the bed and added to her usual prayers. "Take care of Mr. Roka and Henry and the little boy at the tree." After she finished, she crawled into bed and asked, "Will we be bombed again tonight?"

"What more can they bomb?" Da answered.

But when Da and Mama climbed into bed, they wore their clothes, too.

Eeeoooeeeoooee.

Irena, Bridget, and Betty woke screaming. Irena continued to cry as she ran to Da, stretching out her arms for him to take her.

"Da's too tired to carry you," said Mama. "You'll have to walk."

When Irena didn't move, Da grabbed her hand, pulling her outside. The bodies on the street were gone. Irena tried to keep up with Da, who was rushing to the bunker before the planes started dropping their bombs.

Eeeoooeeeoooee.

No planes were in sight when she and her family raced down the ramp and into the shelter.

By the time the door closed, Mr. Roka hadn't come, so Mr. Werner lit the candle. Irena sat on the bench next to Da, listening for Mr. Roka to pound on the door. Instead, she heard buzzing. Airplanes. So many they shook the shelter.

Irena nudged Da. "What about Mr. Roka?"

Before Da could reply, Mr. Werner fixed his one eye in their direction. "He left. Said there was nothing for him here."

Irena fought back tears. All of her connections to Mrs. Roka were gone.

"Where did he go?" Mama asked.

"Maybe Lithuania. He has relatives there." Mr. Werner puffed out his chest. "The Germans are in charge now, so he'll be safe."

"If it's safe there, maybe we should leave," Mama said.

"No." Da's voice was firm as he reached over and took Betty from Mama's arms. "At least here we have a place to sleep."

"Sleep? How can we sleep when we're being bombed every night?"

Da didn't answer as he bounced Betty on his knee, trying to quiet her.

After almost an hour, the all-clear siren blared. When they rose, Da carried Betty and Mama held Bridget's hand. Irena stayed seated, gripping the bench. She didn't want to leave.

Bridget waved at Irena. "Come on."

Irena clutched the bench, tears rolling down her cheeks.

Mama dropped Bridget's hand. "Go with Da. I'll get Irena."

Mama walked to her. "What's wrong?"

Irena burst into tears. "I don't want to see dead people."

"I didn't hear bombs exploding or feel pressure, did you?"

Irena choked back sobs. She hadn't heard explosions or had trouble breathing. Mama pried Irena's fingers loose from the bench and pulled her up the ramp. Beacons crisscrossed the sky, lighting up the street. No foil strips covered the brick pavement. No fires burned. No bodies lay in the street.

Leaning against Mama, Irena plodded toward their apartment. She wanted to think about something besides bombing and blood and Mrs. Roka. She wanted to think about something pleasant, like her birthday. In a few days, she would be nine years old.

CHAPTER
FIFTY-SIX

August 2 - 3, 1943
Operation Gomorrah
(Monday night and Tuesday)

B *oom. Crackle. Boom.*
Shortly before midnight, Harriet was awakened by the loud noises. The girls woke screaming. Harriet understood how they felt. She wanted to stay in bed, not run to the shelter and sit in the bunker for hours, but she had no choice. If they stayed, they might be killed.

Boom. Crackle. Boom.

She shook Oskar, lying next to her.

He rolled over. "It's only thunder."

"Listen," said Harriet to the girls. Rain splattered against the window pane. The girls quieted and Harriet sat up.

"Where are you going?" Oskar asked.

She ran her fingers through her stringy hair. "To catch some rainwater."

Irena jumped out of bed. "I want to go, too."

"Bring the buckets. I'll get some containers."

In the kitchen, Harriet filled the laundry basket with various pans and bowls while Irena grabbed the buckets. They groped their way down the stairs, pushed open the door, and stepped into the rain. Water splashed onto Harriet's face and arms, shocking her. Beside her, Irena dropped the buckets and giggled with delight.

For days Harriet had been weighed down by oppressive heat and air raids. Now she reveled in the cold water sluicing through her hair and soaking her thin nightgown. Laughter bubbled up inside her. She stretched out her arms, threw back her head, and opened her mouth. Rain splashed onto her tongue and rolled down her parched throat. She combed her fingers through her matted hair, fanning it out.

"Look at me," cried Irena.

It was too dark to see. Then several large lightning bolts zigzagged through the sky. Like stage lights, they spotlighted Irena twirling around with carefree abandon. Harriet joined her, and together they danced in the rain and celebrated. They were alive. Her family had been spared.

Crackle. Crackle. Boom. Boom.

Harriet stopped whirling and glanced up. More lightning streaked across the sky. A bolt shot out of a dark cloud, splitting it open. Inside was a blue inferno.

Boom. Boom. Boom.

Harriet jerked. The thunder sounded like bombs. She moved to Irena, who had stopped dancing. "Heat lightning. Go inside."

They didn't gather the containers but raced up the steps to the apartment. Harriet pulled a towel from the cupboard and dried off Irena. Then Harriet stepped out of her wet nightgown, letting it puddle onto the floor. As she wrapped the towel around her hair, the air-raid siren screeched through the kitchen.

Eeeoooeeeoooee.

The towel slipped from her head. She leaned over and grabbed the nightgown. Wiggling into it, she shivered against the cold wetness. The bedroom door flew open. Oskar in work pants and an undershirt raced into the kitchen carrying Betty. Bridget trailed behind.

A flash of lightning outlined the blackout curtains. Oskar skidded to a stop. "It can't be an air raid. The British aren't crazy enough to attack in a lightning storm."

Eeeoooeeeoooee.

The siren continued to squeal. Oskar rushed to the window. Before he could raise the curtain, the drone of airplanes filled the kitchen.

"Oskar, it's no mistake." Harriet grabbed his arm. "Let's go."

He didn't budge.

"Irena, take Bridget's hand. I'll carry Betty." Harriet lifted the baby from Oskar and pulled him out of the apartment, following the girls clambering down the stairs.

When Harriet stepped into the rain, she didn't revel in the cold wetness. The wind plastered her wet hair against her head. She tucked Betty close to her chest and lowered her chin. Fighting the wind and rain, Harriet plodded toward the shelter, dragging Oskar with her. Rain rolled down her forehead, blurring her vision. She couldn't see where to step, but she slogged on, her bare feet splashing in the puddles.

Boom. Crackle. Crackle. Boom.

The booming was constant. Was it thunder or bombs? It didn't matter; both were deadly. Pushed by her fear, she held onto Betty and Oskar. She didn't stop until they reached the bunker. Irena and Bridget ran down the ramp, but the overhead rumbling made Oskar balk. He pointed to the sky. "Look!"

Harriet shielded her eyes from the sheets of rain. In the distance, a fleet of planes descended. "Why are they flying so low?"

"They're trying to stay out of the storm clouds."

It didn't work. More than a dozen planes flew directly into a huge cumulous cloud and disappeared. Lightning cracked, illuminating the inside of the cloud. The planes were in the eye of the storm. Eerie blue flames of electricity snapped and popped. The outsides of the planes glistened with crystals of ice.

Tha-ump. Tha-ump. Tha-ump.

"Hear that?" asked Oskar. "It's our anti-aircraft cannons." Shells, one after the other, shot into the air and exploded. The deadly artillery opened like umbrellas of fireworks and showered glittering shrapnel down on the planes.

Oskar put his hand on Harriet's shoulder. "It won't be so easy for the British to bomb us tonight without casualties. The Germans have brought additional cannons to reinforce the flak."

The sky lit up. Half a dozen German fighter planes, which Oskar called *Messerschmitts*, swooped in from the opposite direction. Their guns sprayed a barrage of bullets at the British planes. "Tonight, the British have to fight the weather, the *Luftwaffe*, and heavy ground artillery," Oskar said.

"Surely they'll turn back," Harriet said as she tugged on Oskar's arm.

"I don't think so. The British seem set on one goal—to destroy Hamburg."

CHAPTER
FIFTY-SEVEN

August 3 - 8, 1943
Operation Gomorrah, the aftermath

H arriet sat across the table from Oskar, neither one of them speaking. She stared at the calendar. Sunday, August 8. Today was her twenty-eighth birthday. This wasn't the way she expected her life to be. Since July 25, she'd lost track of the attacks. Before, the bombing had only been at night. But in the last week, they had been bombed day and night. Sometimes three or four raids back-to-back.

She lived in constant fear. In the daytime, she was afraid to go out because the Americans would attack. At night she lay awake because the British would attack. Hamburg was decimated—water lines busted, electrical lines down, homes and apartment buildings gone, factories and refineries burning, and thousands of people dead. Yet, the Allies continued to bomb.

Then, for the last five days, since August 3, the bombings had stopped. Life, however, was harder. They had no water, no electricity, no gas, and little food. Harriet's days took on a new routine. She woke the girls early so they could walk to the nearest water station, stand in line, and fill their buckets before the supply ran out. Then they'd look for the Emergency Relief Service and stand in another line for food. Harriet was thankful for whatever the civil defense workers handed out, which was usually bread.

She looked across at Oskar as he tapped some tobacco into a thin paper, rolled it into a cigarette, and lit it. He smoked almost every day now. The bomb factory had been severely damaged, but he continued to work for the Decontamination Service to clean up the city. Each day the workers were trucked to a section of the city where they searched through the rubble for charred bodies. The bodies continued to be hauled to Ohlsdorf Cemetery and stacked into one of the four mass graves dug in the shape of a cross.

One night Oskar had come home from work carrying a gas mask. Harriet was horrified. "Are the Allies going to gas us?"

"I hope not," said Oskar, as he set the mask next to the door. "They issued us gas masks to block out the smell of the bodies."

A few days later, when Oskar returned to the flat, he staggered into the kitchen wearing his gas mask. As he removed the mask, the kitchen was filled with the smell of liquor. "Have you been drinking again?"

Oskar gave her a vacant stare. "They give us tobacco and soak the filters in our gas masks with rum or cognac."

Swigging liquor or smoking cigarettes would not make Oskar forget. At night, the nameless dead haunted him and he would pace the living room. He grew thinner, his rib bones sticking out. Working at the bomb factory had been physically draining, but cleaning up the city after the bombings was eating away his soul.

Irena walked into the kitchen, and Harriet was relieved

when Oskar lifted his head and teased her. "Who is this big nine-year-old girl? She can't be our Irena."

"It is." She pointed to the wall calendar. "I won't be nine until tomorrow."

"Tomorrow I work, so today we celebrate your mama's birthday and yours. What would you like to do?"

"I want to go to church to see Sister Anne and light a candle for Mrs. Roka. Then I want to go berry picking, and I want to—"

"Slow down." Oskar put up his hand. "Sunday is supposed to be a day of rest."

Irena looked across the table. "Mama, it's your birthday, too. You want to go to church, don't you?"

"*Ja*. We need to thank God we're alive."

Oskar hesitated. "I'm not sure we can get to the church. Many roads are blocked, and water is so scarce they haven't put out all the fires."

"So we try," Harriet said.

On the way to church, a path wide enough for foot traffic was crammed with hundreds of people. Most were walking in the opposite direction, carrying battered suitcases. Some were pulling carts piled with their possessions. Others shuffled by with nothing but their ragged clothes.

The fires along the street had been put out, which only made the damage look worse. Hamburg had been a vibrant city. Now it was a charred wasteland—leafless trees, scorched grass, and heaps of blackened bricks. On a chimney where a house had once stood was a chalked message. "Where are you, Ingrid?" Harriet hoped Ingrid had been found.

A few blocks from the church were soldiers, pointing their guns at a half-dozen men wearing striped pants and shirts. The prisoners, loading bricks from a collapsed building into a wheelbarrow, had shaved heads, and on the pockets of their shirts were prominent yellow stars. Their limbs were gangly, and the skin on their faces was stretched so tightly that their bones protruded.

Unable to take her eyes away, Harriet slowed and nudged Oskar, who was carrying Betty. "Do you work near here?"

He shook his head but didn't speak until they reached the church. "The trucks take us to the dead cities."

Harriet didn't ask why they were called dead cities. She knew. When she and the girls searched for food and water, they passed other burned-out parts of the city, and she could hear it. The silence. Even the wind seemed to still. The only sounds were the swarms of buzzing flies and scampering rats. She lifted Betty from Oskar. "I'll take the baby to the convent."

Irena tugged on Harriet's arm. "I want to see Sister Anne, too." Before Harriet could protest, Irena added. "Remember, it's my birthday tomorrow."

"All right. Bridget, go with your father and wait in church."

At the convent, a nun directed them to the parish hall, which had been turned into a make-shift hospital. As soon as Harriet opened the door, she was hit by an antiseptic smell. Rows of cots spread across the room, filled with injured men, women, and children. No privacy curtains separated the canvas beds. Some patients had their heads wrapped in bandages. Many had ugly red burns exposed on their chests and limbs. Several had their arms or legs in slings. Others had only stumps. Three nuns and a doctor in a white lab coat hurried down the rows attending to the patients.

Harriet pressed Betty against her chest and scooted in front of Irena to block the view, but she couldn't block out the smell and the moans of pain.

The familiar clicking of rosary beads made Harriet look up. Sister Anne approached. She wasn't gliding as usual. Her steps were labored, her face lined with worry.

The nun stopped in front of Harriet and gripped her hand. "I've been praying for our Betty and your family." She swiped her sleeve across her brow. "Are you all right? Do you have a place to stay?"

Harriet turned Betty to the nun. "We're fine and so is our flat."

"Our prayers have been answered." Sister Anne glanced over her shoulder at the filled ward. "There's no mass today. Everyone is needed here, but ask God to show mercy and compassion for those who need His healing touch."

A man called out, pleading, "Sister, help me."

"I have to attend to my patients."

Irena stepped around Harriet and said, "We're going to pick blueberries this afternoon. Maybe I can bring you some."

Sister Anne caressed Irena's cheek. "My child, it's not safe to go near the forest. I heard it's still burning."

When they left, Harriet led Irena into the church and kneeled at the feet of Mary, expecting to find peace. Instead, the images of those injured stayed with her. Harriet struck a match and handed it to Irena. "You can light a candle for Mrs. Roka."

Irena shied away. "It might burn me."

Harriet lit the candle. When the yellow flame spurted and jumped to life, Irena jerked back. After experiencing the firestorm, it was only natural for her to be afraid of fire. Harriet had a different reaction. The flickering flame dancing on the candle was warm and inviting.

As she prayed the familiar words of the rosary, the knots in her shoulders relaxed. The heat of the flame caressed her face. A warmness moved inside her. The destruction and pain had been too much to take in. Her feelings had shut down. Now warmth spread through her body and eased the numbing cold. It was as if she was filled with new life.

As she finished the last decade of the rosary, an image of Mrs. Roka drifted into her mind. She was smiling, her white teeth beautiful, and she wasn't sitting in a wheelchair or being carried. She was walking, almost floating, the way Sister Anne usually did, and on Mrs. Roka's petite feet were her dainty red slippers.

Harriet felt a tap on her shoulder, and the image of Mrs. Roka disappeared. "Let's go, Mama."

As the family stood on the church steps, Irena pointed to the steeple rising above the city. "Look, St. Nicholi. Da, you said you'd take me to your church. Can we go today?"

Oskar lifted his head. "It's a long way."

Irena pleaded. "I want to see the beautiful stained-glass windows."

"Mass was canceled. Maybe they'll have a service," said Harriet as she slipped her arm through his. The girls followed and didn't complain about walking so far. Maybe they were too shocked by the destruction. Huge department stores were piles of rubble. The buildings still standing had broken windows and doors hanging on hinges. They turned the corner at the block where the church stood. Oskar jerked to a stop.

Only the spire and the back portion of the nave were standing. The frames that had once held stained-glass windows were vacant eyes, with nothing behind them but smoke.

A tear trickled down Oskar's cheek. "St. Nicholi is gone."

"Why would they bomb a church?" Irena asked.

"Lots of bad things happen in war," he said.

Harriet used to think she and her family would be safe from the bombs if they hid in the basement of their apartment building. But she had seen how bombs destroyed entire buildings. Then she thought her family would be safe if they made it to the bunker. Now she knew until the war ended, her family would never be safe.

CHAPTER
FIFTY-EIGHT

Fall 1943

arriet's daily routine started with a quest for water. She would prime the pump in the kitchen and pray for water to flow out. When nothing came, she and the girls would search for the nearest Civil Defense Station, handing out water and sometimes food. After almost six weeks, one morning in early October, she pumped the handle, and a trickle of brown liquid dribbled out. Her breathing quickened. She pumped harder. More brown streamed into the sink. She worked the handle up and down until the water became clear. Raising her hands, she shouted, "We have water!"

Irena barreled into the kitchen. "Can I take a bath?"

"*Ja,* I'll get the water ready."

Harriet filled the kettle with water and put it on the stove. Then she remembered there was no gas. Maybe the girls would enjoy a cold bath. They did not, nor did she. Her good mood flattened even more later in the day when trucks drove through the projects, their speakers blaring.

"What are they saying?" Harriet asked Irena.

"Boil all drinking water."

Harriet added another task to her daily routine—hauling water outside, building a fire, and boiling the water until it was sterile. Keeping Betty out of the contaminated water was difficult. If she was thirsty and a bucket of unsterilized water was sitting by the door, she would sneak a drink.

"It'll make you sick," Harriet scolded.

Betty, almost two now, would give Harriet an impish grin. "Me thirsty."

After several weeks of boiling water, the trucks rolled through the projects. Irena translated again, "Boil order over." She and Bridget jumped up and down. "Do you think that means we can go back to school?" Irena asked.

"I'm not sure the school is still there," Harriet said.

Irena's eyes widened. "We have to see."

The next day Harriet carried Betty and walked with Irena and Bridget to check on the school. The girls kept tugging on her arm, urging her to go faster. They broke loose at the sight of the red-brick building still standing.

Irena pressed her nose against the fence. "At least it didn't get bombed." She pointed to a note on the door. "Closed."

On the trip back, Harriet was the one pulling them. Her worries about the school's influence on the girls had been solved. Irena and Bridget would be home with her and not at school learning more of Hitler's propaganda.

By the end of October, Oskar returned to the armament plant, although it was running at eighty percent of its previous capacity. One night when Oskar returned from work, he flicked the switch next to the door. The lights turned on. Blinking against the brightness, Harriet bolted to the window and shut the blackout curtains. No air raids had happened in September and so far, none in October; however, the fear of another raid never went away.

One morning as she mopped the kitchen floor, she glanced at the calendar, November fifth, Betty's second birthday. Betty, Bridget, and Irena were in the living room, playing with clothespins. Harriet dropped onto the kitchen chair. Tears welled up in her eyes. Her shoulders shook as she fought back sobs.

Irena tiptoed into the kitchen and put her hand on Harriet's shoulder. "Don't cry, Mama."

Harriet blinked away her tears. "Today is Betty's birthday."

Irena ran to Betty, pulling her up. "Yeah! Let's celebrate."

Harriet gestured around the apartment. "With what? We don't have money to buy shoes or material for a dress or flour for a cake."

"Bridget and I will be really, really nice to Betty. I'll let her play with Gertrude."

Harriet swiped her wet cheeks and forced a smile.

"I know," said Bridget. "Let's play dress-up."

Bridget and Irena loved to dress up in Harriet's clothes. Until recently, she hadn't minded, but her dresses had become so thin that she'd stopped letting the girls play in them. "My dresses are too big on Betty."

Frowning, Irena slumped onto a chair. Then she jumped up again. "Betty, you can wear our clothes, and we'll dress up in Mama's."

Betty clapped her hands.

Harriet hesitated. "It's Betty's birthday, not yours."

Irena pleaded, "If Bridget and I dress up, it'll be more fun for Betty. Tell her, Betty," prompted Irena.

"Please," said Betty.

"We'll put on a show for you," added Irena.

Harriet paused. The girls had such little enjoyment, and she could always mend her dresses. "Okay, but don't wear anything good." Not that any of Harriet's dresses or the girls' were good anymore.

The girls' joy was contagious. Harriet's spirits lifted as Irena and Bridget rushed into the bedroom, pulling Betty with them.

Fifteen minutes later, Harriet called, "Do you need help?"

Irena and Bridget shouted, "No!"

Harriet waited at the table until Bridget opened the door and waltzed into the kitchen, wearing Harriet's belted green dress. Flipping up the skirt, Bridget stopped in front of Harriet and curtsied.

The bedroom door opened again. "Go on," Irena urged as she pushed Betty out the door. She pranced into the kitchen wearing the full-skirted dress that Bridget had been given at the Registration Department. The dress was too long, and Betty tripped on the hem, but Bridget caught her before she fell or ripped the dress.

Last, Irena strutted into the kitchen, wearing Harriet's purple paisley, which had been stretched out during pregnancy, and her high heels. Irena swished the skirt and clomped around the kitchen, wobbling. Harriet opened her mouth to scold, but Irena stopped and curtsied. Her face glowed with a smile of happiness that Harriet hadn't seen for months. Harriet smiled, too, as she clapped her hands.

The girls continued to play with the clothes and had so much fun that Bridget announced, "I want to play dress-up on my birthday."

As Harriet started supper, she half-heartedly turned the knob on the stove. To her surprise, she smelled gas. She struck a match to light the pilot. It sputtered and then flared. She whooped with joy. She had not been able to cook on the stove for almost three months. She didn't have anything special to fix, so she peeled a potato and made potato soup with water.

But she and the girls slurped up the warm soup as if it were a royal feast.

Harriet felt a ray of hope. Maybe the worst was over. No bombing had occurred since August. They had water, electricity, and gas. That night, Harriet closed her eyes and drifted off, dreaming of going back to Lithuania, only to be awakened by the all-too-familiar air-raid siren.

Eeeoooeeeooooee.

As they raced into the dark night, the cold November air jolted her back to reality. She and her family were still caught up in this nightmarish war. The next night Oskar came home with the news that the air raid had been merely a couple dozen Mosquitoes. "A nuisance raid to disrupt the city."

"It was more than a nuisance raid to me," Harriet said. "I foolishly thought the war was about to end. But at any time, we could be bombed again."

A few days later, Oskar reported more bad news. "The city has large outbreaks of typhus and diphtheria."

"I'm not surprised. We've been living in unsanitary conditions for months."

"I don't want the girls to contract it," Oskar said.

"I check their heads regularly for lice. What can I do about the other diseases?"

"Immunizations are being offered to guest workers' children."

"Do you think the girls should get the shot?"

Oskar nodded, "I do."

The girls did not, but Harriet ignored their protests and dragged them to the clinic for the vaccinations. Betty was too young, but at least Irena and Bridget were inoculated.

On the way home from the clinic, Harriet didn't feel the relief she'd expected. With diseases running rampant through the city, new food shortages, and more bombing, she realized that the worst might not be over.

CHAPTER
FIFTY-NINE

December 24 - 25, 1943

H arriet scooted a kitchen chair over to the cupboard and opened the door. A few cans of food and tins of staples. Tonight was *Kūčios,* Christmas Eve. Oskar couldn't cut down a tree because the fires had ravished the forests, and she couldn't fix the traditional twelve dishes.

She reached to the back of the first shelf and then the second shelf, feeling around. Nothing. No use checking the third shelf. She never put food there. Yet, a small voice urged her hand up.

She slid her hand to the back. Nothing. As she pulled her hand out, she touched something and cried with joy. The night they tried to return to Lithuania, she'd left a can of tuna for the next poor family. She never expected that poor family would be hers.

When Oskar came home, he lifted his fist with a few pieces of straw. Harriet ironed the traditional white tablecloth and covered the blades. Then she placed the fish on the table. The girls smacked their lips and licked the oil from their fingers as they ate the tuna with bowls of potato soup.

Afterward, the girls wiggled with excitement, impatient to select a straw that would predict the coming year. Oskar was first, pulling out a thick blade. "I'll be rich and happy." He chuckled. "I'm already rich in blessings." He looked around the table, smiling at her and the girls.

Harriet reached under the tablecloth and pulled out a straw. She sank against the chair. The straw wasn't bent. Irena and Bridget pulled out long straws, which meant they would have long lives.

Last year Betty had been too young, but this Christmas, she eagerly reached her pudgy fingers under the tablecloth. She pulled out a thick, stubby straw and waved it in the air.

Harriet gasped. The straw was short, not even a third of the length of the others.

Irena figured it out. "Our straws mean long lives. Does Betty's straw mean a short life?"

Harriet grabbed the straw from Betty's clutched fist. "These things aren't always true."

"That's what you said the Christmas yours was bent." Irena leaned over and tickled Betty, who laughed. "But we have a new sister."

The next morning, Harriet laid out three red dresses. She did not have enough material to make new ones for the girls, so she'd sewn a green ruffle around the bottoms and added green bows at the collar. The girls squealed in delight. Donned in red and green, Irena and Bridget sang Christmas carols. Their sweet voices made Betty clap and brought tears to Harriet's eyes and more smiles to Oskar's face.

1944

The deaths from Operation Gomorrah were ten times more than any previous raid and caused approximately one million German civilians to flee the city. Five thousand more people died from Operation Gomorrah than from the nuclear bomb dropped by America on Nagasaki. [1]

Before 1945, probably the biggest single event in Germany was the mass migration of refugees from Hamburg. The residents of small towns knew only what they read in newspapers or heard on the radio. Now they had first-hand facts. Nobody was safe, and what happened in Hamburg could happen to them.

One of Hitler's last instructions to all his troops stated, "not to give up under any circumstances but...to continue to fight against the enemies of the Fatherland." [2] Hamburg's gauleiter disobeyed these instructions. He handed the city over to the British Second Army without firing a shot. It was an admirable example of common sense.

The scenes that greeted the British troops as they marched into Hamburg were shocking. Even battle-hardened soldiers were appalled. Tommy Wilmott sums it up succinctly. "All I remember about Hamburg was the smell. The smell from Hamburg was awful. The smell of death." [3]

CHAPTER
SIXTY

January - April 1944

O n January first, Harriet looked forward to the new year and prayed that in 1944 the war would end, but that night, they were awakened by the air-raid siren.
Eeeoooeeeoooee.

They raced into the cold and fled to the shelter. No bombs were dropped, just another nuisance raid. No other attacks happened in January or February, only more bitter winds and freezing snow. When March came, the weather let up, and the Allies attacked again. Little additional damage was done to Hamburg. Almost everything had already been destroyed, but each bombing brought back Harriet's fear and dashed her hopes of the war ending soon.

After months of wintery gray skies on the first Sunday in April, the sun popped out. Irena and the girls were itching to leave the flat, so the family took a walk.

The three girls held hands, skipping ahead while Harriet

hooked her arm through Oskar's. She had an extra bounce to her step as she enjoyed the first signs of spring. Black branches on some of the charred trees were filled with green leaves. Grass peeked out of the scorched ground. Clumps of daylilies and lilacs dotted yards where houses once stood. Harriet expected the air to be filled with the fragrant scent of flowers. Instead, even after eight months, the stench of decay still hovered over the city.

She didn't pinch her nose. She was used to the odor, just like she was used to the empty buildings lined up along the street, like rows of tombstones marking where someone had once lived.

When they reached shops that had been a vibrant part of Hamburg, Harriet paused and stared at the ruined businesses. She imagined them as they had once been—Gueten Bakery with its wonderful aromas of bread, Woolworth's with its sewing notions, and Schmaltz Brothers with their three bottles of milk in the window.

Irena let out a scream. Harriet turned from the boarded-up business and rushed to the girls. "What's wrong?" she asked as she picked up Betty.

Squealing, Irena and Bridget grabbed Harriet's skirt as they pointed to a pile of red bricks. A pack of rats was gnawing on something bloody and unrecognizable.

Harriet's stomach roiled. "Let's go, Oskar."

As they turned toward the projects, Irena gazed up at Harriet. "When will it be like before?"

Harriet's steps no longer bounced. She was weighed down by all the loss. "I don't think it will ever be the same."

Irena seemed to mimic her teacher's words. "Germany is a superpower, and its people are the master race. They can rebuild. They can do anything because Hitler is the leader."

Harriet shot Oskar a glance. His jaw clenched, but he

remained silent until they were back in the flat and the girls were in the bedroom, playing dress-up.

Harriet primed the pump and filled two glasses of water. She placed them on the table and wearily sat. Oskar, agitated, paced the kitchen. "Hitler, Hitler, Hitler. Irena seems to think he's invincible. Our great *Führer* didn't even show up for the reopening of the factory."

"But he always comes in April around his birthday." Harriet picked up her glass of water.

"Not this year. He doesn't want to face the reality of Hamburg's destruction. Last year the Germans surrendered to the Soviets in Stalingrad. Now the Italians have changed sides."

Harriet knew the Soviets had defeated the Germans, but she hadn't heard that Italy had joined the Allies. She slammed her glass of water on the table. "How much longer can Germany go on?"

Oskar shook his head. "Hitler will never surrender."

Harriet had expected the war to end last August when the Allies had destroyed most of Hamburg. She gripped her water glass, steadying her shaking hands. She didn't know how they could continue, but what else could they do, except go on?

The following Friday, Harriet's mood improved when she took the girls out for a walk, but that night Betty woke fussing and holding her throat. "Hurt. Hurt."

Harriet looked into Betty's mouth. Her throat was red and swollen. Harriet put Betty in bed with her and Oskar so the other girls would not get sick.

On Saturday, Betty remained in bed all morning, and at lunch, she refused to get up and eat.

Harriet boiled water and grated some ginger. After the pungent tea seeped, she carried Betty to the table and held her on her lap. She took a few sips, but the tea didn't help. By evening, her face was flushed, and her forehead was hot. "I better put her in bed with us again, Oskar."

That night Betty was fussy, and Harriet walked the floor, trying to soothe her. On Sunday when Betty was fitfully sleeping, Oskar took Irena and Bridget outside to give Harriet some rest. But Harriet didn't rest. Betty woke crying and nothing Harriet did helped.

When Oskar returned with the girls, Harriet was sitting in the chair with Betty languid in her arms. Oskar kneeled in front of them while Irena and Bridget stared over his shoulder. "Is she better?" Oskar asked.

A lump lodged in Harriet's throat. She shook her head. In the last few hours, Betty's fever had spiked. Memories of holding Agne before he died haunted Harriet.

Oskar laid his hand on Betty's forehead. "You better take her to a doctor tomorrow."

The doctor had been too late to save Agne. She couldn't let that happen to her baby. "She can't even swallow water. We have to do something today."

Betty didn't stir when Oskar put his finger in her mouth and opened it wide enough for him to peer inside. "It looks bad," he agreed. "But where can we take her on a Sunday?"

Harriet had been praying for help. The nun from Lithuania and the other Sisters were Betty's godparents. They might have an answer for her. "Sister Anne is a nurse. She might have some medicine or know what to do."

"I'll watch the girls if you want to take her today."

Irena and Bridget didn't beg to go. Their wide eyes and solemn faces showed they were worried about Betty, too.

At the convent, Sister Anne led Harriet into the small green room with a single bed and gold crucifix on the wall. Two years ago, Harriet had stared at that cross and prayed to deliver a healthy baby. Betty had been born healthy, but now she lay in Harriet's arms, too weak to lift her head. Harriet stared at the cross, praying again for her baby's health.

The Sister waved to the bed. "Hold Elizabeth on your lap so I can look at her throat."

Opening a glass jar, the nun removed a tongue depressor and peered into Betty's mouth. The nun's eyes widened. She stepped back. "You must take Elizabeth to the hospital immediately."

Harriet lowered her head, too embarrassed to admit she didn't have the money. "Do you have medicine here that would help?"

Sister Anne's voice was firm. "Elizabeth's too sick. She needs to be treated by a doctor."

The nun's tone alarmed Harriet. She lifted her eyes. "What's wrong with Betty?"

"Pray we are not too late."

Harriet latched onto the nun's arm. "Please, Sister, tell me what's wrong."

Sister Anne's voice trembled. "I-I think she has...diphtheria."

Harriet's hand flew to her mouth. "Oh no. Isn't that what they call the Strangling Angel?"

CHAPTER
SIXTY-ONE

April 1944

rena's heart thumped. She kept her head down as she walked between Da and Bridget. Betty was sick—so sick that Da didn't go to work, and Mama had stayed with Betty all night at the hospital. When they arrived, Mama met them in the waiting room. She said only Da could visit Betty. After he left, Irena drilled Mama with questions. "Is Betty's fever down?" "Can she eat?" "When can she come home?"

"Does she want to see us?" Bridget asked.

Mama's lips turned up in a weak smile. "Maybe tomorrow she'll be better."

The next day at the hospital, Mama didn't even try to smile, and her eyes were red as if she'd been crying. "You can see your sister today."

Irena danced with joy. She and Bridget could see Betty. But Mama, who sat in the chair in front of them, did not look happy. Irena stopped dancing. "Is Sissy better?"

Grasping their hands, Mama lowered her head. "I'm afraid we might...lose her. So you need to say goodbye."

"Goodbye?" asked Bridget. "Where's she going?"

Mama didn't answer. She only squeezed their hands, but Irena bit her lip to keep from crying. She didn't want Betty to die. Irena knew how awful it was to lose someone. Every day, she missed Hanna.

"Before you see Betty, you need to be prepared. Her mouth is..." Mama dropped their hands and shook her head. "She doesn't look the same."

In the hospital ward, Irena's nose turned up at the smell of medicine. On both sides of the center aisle were cribs filled with sick children. Mama led them past the other sick children to Betty, whose crib was at the far end. Even though Mama had warned them, when Irena peeked through the slats of the wooden crib, a girl, who did not look like Betty, lay curled on her side with her back to them. The girl resembled a lifeless puppet.

Irena whispered uncertainly, "Betty, is that you? It's Sissy."

The girl rolled over. Irena fought back a scream. It was Betty, only her eyes were blank, and her mouth was crooked. One side turned up as if the marionette had pulled the string too tightly. The other side drooped down.

Reaching for Bridget's hand for support, Irena struggled to say goodbye as Mama asked, but the word stuck in her throat, so Irena repeated what she said in her prayers. "If you get well and come home, you can play dress-up or do whatever you want. Just please, please get well."

Bridget didn't say anything. She only lifted her hand and waved goodbye.

Betty's limp wrist waved back as her crooked mouth turned up in a grotesque smile. Her voice was weak. "See nice lady?"

Irena looked around. Only Mama was standing behind them. "You mean Mama?"

Betty barely raised her finger and pointed over Irena's shoulder. "Lady at window."

Turning, Irena squinted at the window. Nothing was there except the light which spilled into the ward. "There's no lady at the window."

Betty sucked in a breath and struggled to speak. "Dressed...in...white."

Before Hanna had died, she'd seen a lady dressed in white at the window. Irena ran across the ward and yanked the curtain closed. Then she rushed back to Betty. "The Lady in White is gone. She's not coming back."

Betty's twisted mouth drooped. "Me like her."

Reaching through the slats, Irena grabbed Betty's hand, holding onto her so the Lady in White couldn't take her away. "Promise you won't look out the window."

Betty withered. Her eyes rolled back in her head as she became that puppet again.

An hour later, a tall, thin doctor with a whiskery chin arrived to examine Betty. When he finished, he addressed Da, who translated for Mama. "The doctor said she's weaker. It won't be long. He said we need to make preparations for when she...she passes."

Mama fell against the crib. Da put his arm around her to hold her up. "Harriet, you need to rest. Take the girls and go home."

"I don't want to leave," protested Mama.

"The girls can't stay overnight. Come back in the morning."

Mama protested, but eventually, Da convinced her she couldn't do anything for Betty by staying and Irena and Bridget needed her.

When they left the hospital, Mama didn't turn toward the projects. She headed to the convent to see Sister Anne. The nun welcomed them with an anxious smile. "How's Elizabeth?"

The nun's smile slipped as Mama said, "The doctor doesn't think Betty will..."

Sister Anne opened her arms, and Mama collapsed into them. Irena and Bridget clutched Mama's skirt and cried, too.

Finally, Mama pulled away. "We made it through the bombings and firestorm. Why is this happening now?"

"I have no answers." Sister Anne lifted the crucifix around her neck. "Hold on to your faith and pray."

Mama removed her handkerchief from her sleeve, dabbing her eyes. "I don't think I can bear it if she..."

"The nuns and I will hold a prayer vigil for Elizabeth. She's God's child. We will ask for His loving intercession so that our beautiful baby who was born here might live to love God for many years." Sister Anne looked down at Irena and Bridget. "You must pray, too, and be good. Don't cause your mother and father any worry."

Irena nodded, but Bridget hid behind Mama.

At the flat, Mama led them into the bedroom. The three of them kneeled beside the bed and silently prayed for Betty. Then Mama rose. "Your sister should have something nice to wear...I'll make a dress."

Mama pulled the sheet from her bed. "This should be enough material." She carried the sheet, along with one of Betty's old dresses and her sewing bag, into the living room. She laid the sheet on the floor and placed Betty's dress on top to trace around it. Next, she cut out the pieces. "If I work hard, I might finish the dress tonight."

Irena didn't feel like playing, so she and Bridget sprawled on the floor while Mama sat on the green chair, sewing. At first Mama's hand shook, but with each stitch, her hands grew steadier.

Irena wanted to do something for Betty, too. "Can I help?"

"Get my button jar. Find four identical buttons for the front of the dress."

Irena ran into the bedroom, returning with the glass jar of buttons. After she spilled the buttons onto the floor, she and Bridget raked their fingers through them, looking for four matching buttons.

They found four white buttons and placed them in a row to show Mama. She shook her head. "They're too big."

They rummaged through the buttons again and lined up four metal buttons. "What about these?" Bridget asked.

"Too heavy," Mama said.

Irena and Bridget hunted through the buttons. "Nothing looks right," Irena said. "We need pretty buttons, like the roses on the dress you made for me when I started school."

"I wore that dress to school, too," said Bridget.

Mama put down her sewing and walked into the bedroom. She returned with the red dress she had made for Irena. "I stored this away for Betty for when she...for when she started school." Mama picked up the scissors. Tears rolled down her cheeks as, one by one, she snipped off the buttons. When she finished, she laid the four rose petal buttons, which had faded to soft pink, onto the front of the white dress. "Perfect."

Irena and Bridget sat cross-legged on the floor while Mama continued to work. The rhythm of Mama's sewing was hypnotic. The needle went in and out, in and out, making tiny stitches. As Mama worked, she fervently recited the rosary. When she finished the prayers, she started again.

Irena silently added her own promises to God. "Please God, if you make Betty well, I'll always be good. I'll never get mad at her or Bridget, and I'll mind Mama and Da, no matter what they want me to do."

Mama stopped stitching and held up the bodice, making sure the shoulders were straight. "It will do." Mama's eyes filled with tears. She gathered Irena and Bridget into her arms. The three of them clung to each other, crying.

When they were spent, Mama wiped away her tears. "I have to finish tonight."

As Mama stitched the sleeves onto the dress, Irena again settled next to Bridget on the floor, watching the needle go in and out. When the first sleeve was finished, Mama held up the dress again. The tears started.

And so it went. Mama would stitch a piece, examine it, and then break down crying. The three of them would hold each other and cry together.

Finally, Mama said, "Girls, go to bed. I'll stay up and hem it."

Irena started to argue, but she remembered her promise to God and Sister Anne to be good. Irena lay in bed, but she couldn't sleep. It wasn't fear of an air raid that kept her from sleeping. It was fear that Betty would never lay in bed between her and Bridget again.

CHAPTER
SIXTY-TWO

H arriet sat in the living room working on the dress. Her fingers automatically guided the needle up and down, making tiny stitches as she hemmed the skirt. She was determined to finish the dress for Betty.

Last were the rosebud buttons. After Harriet sewed the four buttons down the front, she held up the white dress with the cap sleeves and a full skirt. Instead of satisfaction, she felt empty. She ached to hold Betty in her arms, to caress her soft skin, feel her fine hair, and smell her little-girl scent.

Two years wasn't enough time to give Betty all the love Harriet had for her. Closing her eyes, she tried to picture Betty, not as she was now, but the way she had been before diphtheria had disfigured her. She remembered the day Betty had taken her first step. Her hair was tied in a topknot that was lopsided and as she let go of Harriet, Betty's mouth rounded in surprise.

Harriet opened her eyes. The white funeral dress slammed her back to reality. She had followed Oskar to Germany to protect their family. All the months and years of living in fear of the Nazis and Brownshirts and bombings, all the shortages of food and water and clothing had been bearable because she had her family. Now, those sacrifices seemed meaningless. A part of her family was being ripped away, and no matter how hard she tried or what she did, without Betty, her family would never be whole again.

Rising, Harriet shuffled into the kitchen to heat the iron. As she waited for it to get hot, voices swirled in her head, telling her she was fortunate. She still had two daughters, but Irena and Bridget could not replace Betty. Irena was stubborn and independent; Bridget was sweet and a follower; but Betty had come into their lives during the war and had brought them unexpected joy.

At the hospital when the doctor said that Betty would not make it, Harriet had leaned on Oskar. At the convent when she had told Sister Anne the bad news, Harriet had clung to the nun. When she returned home, she'd cried with her girls. Now she was alone. She opened her heart to pour out her sorrow, but it was too big, too painful. Sinking to her knees, she wailed to God, "Why? Why are you taking our Betty from us?"

Harriet had asked Sister Anne the same question. She had answered that Betty's life was in God's hands. The nuns were praying and Harriet prayed, too. She beseeched God to spare her child. She listened for an answer, but He was silent.

I can't do this. I can't. How can I go on living after my child is gone?

She knew what death was like. She had experienced it with her brother, Agne. She had held him in her arms until his body had turned blue, and he'd been taken from her. She had thrown a handful of dirt onto his coffin. She had prayed for his soul. She had picked golden rods and laid them on his grave, but no matter what she had done, nothing ever filled the hole in her heart.

Shaking away the memory, she spit on the iron. When it sizzled, she picked up the iron and carefully laid it on the dress, moving it back and forth. She couldn't, wouldn't, open herself to the wrenching pain of death again. Pushing the iron over the dress, she tried to remove the wrinkles in the skirt and the pain in her heart. She ironed the dress over and over until the wrinkles were gone and her heart was numb.

After Agne died, Harriet's mother had been different—stoic and aloof. Harriet thought her mother blamed her because Harriet had brought home the measles that had killed little Agne. But her mother was distant from her dad, too.

Tata explained, "I think your mother is afraid to love you or me. She's afraid something might happen to us and she couldn't go through another painful loss."

But Harriet's mother had gone through more losses. She'd become pregnant again and had buried a second child. When the third baby was born, her mother refused to hold him. In a few hours, he died, too.

How long did Betty have? Was she already gone, or did she have a few hours? Harriet had stayed up all night, sewing. As the sun peeked in around the blackout curtains, she felt an urgency to be at the hospital. She had to see Betty. Maybe it wouldn't be too late. Maybe Harriet could hold her baby in her arms—one last time.

She raced into the bedroom. "Hurry, girls, get up."

Irena rubbed her eyes. "Did you finish the dress?"

"*Ja*. Maybe Betty will be able to see her dress."

Irena trudged into the kitchen. The dress lay on the table. "It's so pretty."

Bridget raced into the kitchen. "She'll look like an angel."

"I don't want Betty to be an angel," Irena snapped. "I want her to be my sister."

"No bickering. Let's go." Harriet got the girls ready, folded the dress into her market bag, and herded them out of the flat, not knowing what awaited them at the hospital.

When they arrived, she rushed into the children's ward. She ignored the other sick children in cribs with parents sitting by their sides and searched for Oskar. He was stretched out in a chair, sleeping next to the crib. She couldn't see Betty because he was blocking the view.

With the girls following, Harriet tiptoed down the center aisle. She stopped next to the crib and gasped. She expected Betty to be lying down. Instead, she was standing, her hands gripping the rails. And she was smiling. Not that twisted, grotesque smile that drooped down, but her beautiful, sweet smile with both sides turned up.

Harriet reached out her arms. "My baby."

Betty shook the rails. "Mama."

Harriet dropped the bag with the funeral dress. Tears of joy rolled down her cheek. She lifted Betty from the crib and wrapped her arms around her. Irena and Bridget grabbed onto their sisters' legs.

Incredulous, Harriet placed her hand on Betty's soft cheek, ran her fingers through her hair, and breathed in that little-girl scent she thought she'd never smell again.

The commotion woke Oskar. "What's going on?"

Harriet turned to him. "It's Betty. What happened?"

He sat up straighter. A broad grin spread across his face. "I thought it might have been a dream. Last night I drifted off. Right before sunrise, when I awoke, Betty was standing in her crib saying she was thirsty. I gave her some water, and she was able to swallow it."

Harriet continued to stroke Betty's hair. "But her mouth. It-it looks normal. What did the doctor do?"

Oskar shook his head. "I haven't seen him since yesterday when you were here."

A few minutes later, the doctor hurried to where they were gathered. He bent over the empty crib and stroked his whiskery chin. When he looked up, he saw Betty. His hand slipped from his chin and his mouth flapped open. He gazed down at his chart, flipping through the pages. Then he stepped closer to Betty and pressed his fingers around her mouth.

Harriet was flooded with gratitude. She searched for the German word for thank you. "*Danke, danke.*" Then she turned to Oskar. "Ask him what he did?"

Oskar spoke to the doctor and translated for Harriet. "He said he hasn't been here."

Harriet held Betty as the doctor examined her. When he finished, Oskar translated. "Her fever is gone, and the swelling in her throat has shrunk."

The doctor seemed to frighten Betty. She clung to Harriet. "Home."

"Oskar, see if she's well enough to leave?"

After the doctor answered, Oskar reported, "He doesn't know. He said he can't explain what happened."

"Nice lady," Betty answered. "She say…no die until fifty."
l

The doctor pulled on his goatee as if he still couldn't believe what he was seeing.

Harriet hugged Betty as she spoke to Oskar. "Tell the doctor anything is possible if you have a convent of nuns praying for you."

CHAPTER
SIXTY-THREE

June - December 1944

H arriet sat at the kitchen table to write a letter to her parents. The yellow glow of the kerosene lamp cast its beam on the single sheet of paper. She picked up her pencil and dated the letter June 1944. *Dear Mamuska and Tata.*

She had so much to tell them. Two months ago, the doctor had said they would lose Betty to diphtheria, but God had answered Harriet's prayers and those of the Sisters. Now Harriet was convinced God would answer her other prayers— the war would end, they would return to Lithuania and be reunited with her parents. Almost four years had passed since she had seen them. She had written several letters but had received no reply. Still, she held out hope that they were alive.

In November, Betty would be three. How could she explain her recovery, except it was a miracle? Betty had been weak when they brought her home from the hospital, but each day she grew stronger. Harriet was cautious and probably hovered over her a little too much, but she didn't want Betty to relapse.

After Harriet finished the letter, she slid it into the envelope but didn't seal it. When Oskar came home, he might have news about the war's end, and she could add the date of their return.

Last fall, after the armament plant had reopened, Oskar's hours had been shortened. The factory didn't have enough raw materials to produce as many bombs as before, plus the shift ended earlier because headlights on the trucks taking the workers home after dark were an easy target for the bombs.

Rising, she pushed back the blackout curtains in the kitchen. It was dark and Oskar wasn't home. What if there was another air raid? This year Hamburg had experienced only a handful of raids, and those were nuisance raids. Then, for the last five days, from June eighteenth to June twenty-third, Hamburg had been bombed four times. Two of the raids had hit oil refineries. She didn't know what last night's attack had destroyed, but she was worried that if an attack happened tonight before Oskar returned, she would have to take the girls to the shelter—alone.

Five minutes later, Oskar's footsteps sounded on the stairs. She opened the door, but he didn't go to the sink to wash up. "I have bad news."

She sank onto the chair. Was it her parents? Was that why she had been thinking about them tonight? Oh God, she hoped they weren't dead.

Before she could ask, Oskar blurted out, "The Germans are going to be defeated."

She was confused. "But that's good news. It means my prayers have been answered and the war will be over."

Oskar wasn't smiling. "For us, it's not good news. The Soviets have invaded Lithuania. They're driving the Germans out of our country."

Harriet bolted up, jostling the table and almost toppling the kerosene lamp. "But—but the Germans won't let the Soviets take over Lithuania."

"There's not much Germany can do. They don't have enough troops in Lithuania to stop them."

Harriet's skin was clammy. "But Germany can bring more troops."

"Hitler is fighting too many countries. There are no more soldiers to send."

The solution seemed logical to Harriet. "He can conscript more men."

"Thousands of men have already been killed. The only ones left are boys as young as Irena and men over fifty."

The reality sliced through Harriet. She had never imagined the Soviets would seize Lithuania again. For the last three years, her country had been part of Germany. But if the Soviets controlled Lithuania, it would change everything. "Are you sure?"

"I heard the guards at the factory talking. They want Germany to pull out of Lithuania and defend their own country."

"We don't need German troops here. The British and Americans are bombing us, but they aren't marching on German soil."

Oskar rubbed his temples and didn't meet her eyes.

Harriet's stomach rolled over. "What—what aren't you telling me?"

"In early June, I think around the sixth, Allied forces began retaking France."

"How? France is separated from Great Britain by the English Channel and from America by the Atlantic Ocean."

"The Allies landed amphibious transports with thousands of combat soldiers on Normandy and several other beaches. Along with heavy air strikes, the Allies are pushing the Germans back and marching toward Paris. If they free France, they'll set their sights on taking Germany."

Harriet grasped for some hope. "If the Allies free France, maybe they'll send troops into Lithuania and free our country, too."

Oskar shook his head. "That won't happen. The Soviet Union has joined forces with America and Great Britain. The Soviets are now part of the Allies."

Harriet clutched her stomach. "If the Soviets take Lithuania and Germany doesn't stop them, then our country is lost and...and we won't be able to go home."

Harriet's fears became a reality. In July, Oskar returned from work with the news that the Soviet Union had recaptured Vilnius, the former capital of Lithuania, and in August, he reported the Soviet Union had recaptured Kaunas, their hometown. Lithuania was once again under Communist rule.

On August ninth, Irena turned ten. When she asked when they were going home, Harriet's heart broke. She and Oskar had not told the girls Lithuania now belonged to the Soviets, so she quickly changed the subject.

Germany was losing the war, and in December, Harriet resigned herself to another bleak Christmas. The forest had burned so there would be no tree, and they had little money, so again this year there would be no presents or special food.

The week before Christmas, the girls began whispering and staying in the bedroom. On Christmas Eve, Irena burst into the kitchen. "Mama, Da, sit on the couch. We have a present for you."

Harriet and Oskar exchanged puzzled looks as they moved to the couch. Irena raced back to the bedroom, and when she returned, she had a pillow tied to her stomach and a folded sheet draped over her head and shoulders. Walking next to her was Bridget, wearing Oskar's hat.

Irena stooped over and held onto Bridget's arm. "Joseph, you have to find a place for me to have the baby."

"All the inns are full, Mary. I don't know where to go?"

The bedroom door opened, and Betty crawled into the room. "*Ba-ba.* Go to stable."

Betty crawled back into the bedroom and closed the door. Joseph knocked on the door and led Mary into the bedroom.

Harriet and Oskar wildly applauded. Bridget peeked her head out the door. "It's not over." She led Irena, who was no longer wearing a pillow under her sheet, from the bedroom. In her arms was Gertrude, wrapped in a blanket.

Behind them walked Betty, carrying the button jar. "Present for baby."

As the girls took their bows, tears streamed down Harriet's cheeks, and even Oskar choked back a sob.

Bridget ripped the sheet from Irena and plopped Oskar's hat on Irena's head. "Now I get to be Mary."

For the rest of Christmas Eve, the girls repeated the play, changing parts and finally asking Harriet and Oskar to join them.

On Christmas morning, Irena tugged on Harriet's hand. "Wake up. It's Christmas."

"We have another surprise," said Bridget. "Go into the other room."

Harriet and Oskar waited on the couch. When the bedroom door opened, the girls pranced out wearing their red dresses trimmed in green. Irena stood where the Christmas tree usually was and sang, "*O tannenbaum, o tannenbaum.*" Even though *Oh, Christmas Tree* was originally a German Christmas carol, Harriet recognized the tune and understood the words.

As Irena finished singing, Bridget shoved her aside. "My turn." She opened her mouth and sang, "Silent night, holy night." Harriet was glad Bridget sang in Lithuanian.

Before Bridget finished, Betty stepped in front. "Me, me."

She cradled her arms and swayed back and forth. "Away in manger, no bed for baby."

After the girls took their bows, Harriet and Oskar joined in and sang the familiar Christmas carols. Christmas would have been unimaginable if Betty had not lived, but thanks to God, their daughter's beautiful voice was singing praises on Christmas morning.

The family had endured four long years of war. Harriet worried about what effect the war was having on her daughters, but even with all the hardships, the girls seemed to find a bit of joy, and Harriet's voice rose as she sang, "Joy to the world."

Her family had survived, and on this Christmas Day, her heart swelled.

CHAPTER
SIXTY-FOUR

December 31, 1944

rena rubbed her eyes as she lay with Bridget and Betty under a blanket on the living room floor, trying to stay awake to celebrate New Year's Eve.

"Be sure to keep Betty covered," said Mama who sat next to Da on the couch.

Irena slid more of the blanket over Betty. She had recovered from diphtheria, and Irena didn't want her to get sick again. "Is it midnight yet?" she asked.

Da flipped open his pocket watch. "Not yet." He turned the watch to face her. "When both hands reach twelve, it'll be midnight."

Irena wanted to stay awake, but it seemed so long. She tried to think of something fun. "What did you do in Lithuania to celebrate New Year's Eve?"

Da and Mama exchanged odd looks that Irena didn't understand. They used to smile when she talked about Lithuania, but something had changed. Whenever she mentioned home, they quickly changed the subject like Mama did now. "We can start our own traditions here. We'll—"

Eeeoooeeeoooeee.

The wail of the air-raid siren sliced into Irena's veins making her turn ice cold. She threw off the blanket and ran for her coat. Without complaining, she bundled up and rushed out into the cold December night. Since October, the attacks were no longer nuisance raids. The Allies had resumed bombing oil refineries, factories, and sometimes apartment buildings.

At the shelter, Irena huddled on the floor with Betty on her lap and tried to block out the rumbling planes and whistling bombs shaking the shelter. On the bench across from them, where the Rokas had sat, was a washerwoman. Her dark hair was rolled in rags, and her black coat with wide padded shoulders was missing a button. Beside her sat a short, bald man with a white fringe of hair above his ears. The woman's eyes were closed until the man shouted, "It's midnight." Standing, he raised his empty hand and made a toast. "Happy New Year."

No one echoed his flat words.

The young woman beside him jerked up. One by one, she yanked the white cotton rags from her hair and combed her fingers through her long, wavy locks. Then she opened her mouth and sang, "We'll take a cup o' kindness yet, for days of *auld lang syne.*"

The transformation was remarkable. The woman was almost as pretty as Mrs. Roka, and her voice was so beautiful that the drone of the planes seemed to fade, and a hush fell over the crowded shelter. At first, a few voices joined in. Da sang and Mama hummed. Then other voices were added until the entire shelter was filled with music. Irena wanted to sing, but she didn't know the words.

As the last notes drifted away, Mama's eyes filled with tears.

"The song was so pretty. Why are you crying?" Irena asked.

Mama wiped the sleeve of her coat across her eyes. "*Auld Lang Syne* is a Scottish ballad about old friends who're gone and happier times."

Irena looked around the shelter and remembered Mr. and Mrs. Roka, Hanna, and Mia. She fought the tears in her eyes, too.

The bald man plopped onto the bench. "Not much to be happy about this New Year."

Irena clutched Betty closer. She didn't agree. The Strangling Angel had spared Betty.

The woman who had sung flipped her wavy hair across her worn coat. "We survived, didn't we?"

1945

After WWII, the Soviet Union's borders roughly followed those established by the Nonaggression Pact in 1939–41. The Soviet Union claimed the Baltic states. Lithuania remained part of the Soviet Union until March 11, 1991, when it was finally granted independence. [1]

CHAPTER
SIXTY-FIVE

January - March 1945

S urvived. Like the washerwoman reminded them, Irena and her family had survived four long years of air raids. Now was the fifth year, and the raids kept coming. Mama recorded each one on the wall calendar. One in January, two in February, six so far in March. Each time Irena was awakened by the blaring siren, scenes of Hamburg on fire would haunt her.

Holy Week was at the end of March and on Good Friday, Mama walked into the kitchen carrying Betty's white dress with the rosebud buttons.

Irena sat at the table with her head propped up on her elbow. "Is Betty going to wear that for Easter?"

"*Ja,* but I want Betty to look nice for the nuns." Mama examined the hem. "She hasn't grown much since last year."

Mama often saved an extra spoonful of food for Betty. When Irena's stomach growled, she envied her little sister, but then she remembered the Strangling Angel and didn't want her to take Betty away, so Irena sneaked food to Betty, too.

Mama ran her finger over the hem. "If it doesn't fit, I can let down—"

Eeeoooeeeoooee.

Betty, who had been in the bedroom sleeping, let out a scream. The dress slipped from Mama's hands. Irena jumped up to grab it from the floor, but Mama shooed her and Bridget toward the door. "Leave it. Put on your coats. I'll get Betty."

Usually, Da took charge, but he was at work. Mama rushed into the bedroom and picked up Betty, who was still crying. As Mama hurried to the shelter, Irena and Bridget didn't run ahead. They stayed close to Mama in case she needed help, but she got them safely to the shelter.

They were one of the last families to arrive, yet half of the seats were empty because most of the men were at work. Mama sat on their usual bench, settling Betty on her lap. Irena and Bridget plunked down on each side of her. When the planes roared overhead. Irena squeezed her eyes shut, waiting for the rumbling to fade away. Instead, the noise increased, followed by whistling.

Boom! Boom! Boom!

The bombs sounded close, like the ones during the firestorm.

Boom! Boom! Boom! Boom! Boom!

The ground beneath the shelter shook. Irena's eyes flew open. She put her hands on her legs to stop them from jumping, but they continued to jerk. She threw herself against Mama. Irena just wanted the war to stop. "When will it end?"

Mama handed Betty to Bridget and reached for Irena, who crawled into her lap, sobbing. Mama ran her fingers through Irena's hair and whispered in her ear, "You're the oldest. Be brave for your sisters."

Mama had told her this before, but Irena was tired of being

brave. She wanted to be little again and believe that Mama and Da could keep her safe.

Boom! Another bomb exploded, shaking the earth so hard Irena expected the ground to split open and suck them up. *Boom! Boom!* They sounded close. What if the planes dropped bombs on Da's factory?

She choked back her cries. "I'm—I'm scared for Da."

Mama wrapped her arms tightly around her. "God will look after Da."

Irena wanted to believe the way Mama did. Her faith was so strong. Irena started to pray, but the booming of the bombs filled her head, scattering her thoughts.

A tense hour passed before the all-clear siren sounded. Irena stood and plodded up the ramp. Explosions echoed in her ears. She was surrounded by smoke. Her eyes watered as she squinted through the gray haze. No bodies lay on the street and no blood trickled through the cobblestones. The attack must have sounded worse than it was.

When they arrived at the flat, Irena was too upset to play. She lay on the couch anxiously waiting for Da. When his footsteps thudded up the stairs, she jumped up and raced to the door. Opening it, she launched herself at him. He caught her, teetering until he balanced both of them, before he collapsed in a chair at the table. He kept his arms around Irena. "That was quite a greeting."

Irena's words tumbled out as she tried to tell him about the air raid and the shelter and the bombs.

"Slow down," Da said.

Irena took a deep breath. "Mama led us there. She was so brave, and we helped her with Betty."

Mama wiped her hands on her apron. "Where did you go during the air raid?"

"They herded the workers into the warehouse where they store the bombs."

Mama's hands flew to her mouth. "You could have been blown up."

"They painted a big red cross on the roof of the warehouse so the Allies think it's a hospital," explained Da.

"That was clever." Irena felt a swell of pride. "Hitler sure fooled them."

Da's arms tensed around her.

"I'm just glad you're home," said Mama.

That night, Irena kneeled on her knees by her bed and folded her hands. "Please, God. Watch over our family. Stop the bombing—"

Eeeoooeeeoooeeeooo.

Her prayer was interrupted by the siren. God had not answered her.

Irena and her family stayed in the shelter for hours. On Saturday, the family was exhausted. Da dragged himself to work while Irena sat at the table, nodding off, and Bridget lay stretched out on the couch. Mama was on her hands and knees, scrubbing the floor. "Staying busy keeps me from worrying." Mama had been doing plenty of scrubbing lately.

Irena's eyes closed. The siren jolted her awake.

Eeeoooeeeoooeeeooo.

She rushed for her coat. "Come on, Bridget."

As Bridget hopped down, Irena opened the door. "Let's go."

Mama grabbed her coat. "Wait."

Irena and even Bridget often ran ahead. "But Mama—"

"We need to stay together."

Irena wasn't as scared when Mama walked beside her, and they arrived at the shelter before Mr. Werner closed the door.

In the evening, Irena curled up in the green chair, her eyes drooping. She was too tired to play with Bridget or hold Betty, who was on the floor, whining for Irena's attention.

"Go to bed, Irena," said Mama who was sitting on the couch, crocheting.

Irena kept her eyes on the door. "It's dark. Da is usually home before now." She was worried that he might have been blown up in the warehouse of bombs, but she didn't say this in front of Betty or Bridget. "Please, let me stay up. I'll help with Betty."

Irena picked her sister up and paced around the room, making a big circle from the door to the table to the couch. She kept her head cocked, listening for steps on the stairs. When Betty nodded off, Irena put her to bed and returned to pacing.

It seemed like hours before footsteps thumped up the stairs. Irena beat Mama to the lock and unchained the hook. She threw open the door. "Da, you're safe."

Da shuffled in and slumped into a kitchen chair. "The factory and the warehouse were spared."

Irena climbed on his lap and leaned against him. He smelled bad, but he was here, solid beneath her.

"Bombs struck the power station near us and knocked out the electrical lines."

Mama put her hand on Da's shoulder as if she, too, needed to touch him. "How could you work without electricity?"

"We didn't. They marched us to the power station and ordered us to dig it out. They only let us leave when it was too dark to see."

Irena sat up. "You said the trucks shouldn't be out at night because the headlights would be a target for the bombs."

Da cleared his throat. "I guess your Hitler doesn't think that's a problem anymore."

Irena frowned and slid off his lap. She stood up straight and automatically repeated the words she had memorized in school. "Our Führer is a great soldier and tireless worker. He delivered Germany from misery. Now everyone has work…" She stopped and didn't repeat the last two words, "bread, and joy."

CHAPTER
SIXTY-SIX

April - May 1945

Harriet swished the broom across the wooden floorboards, working off nervous energy. She glanced at the wall calendar. Today was April twenty-eighth. For weeks, Irena had asked when Hitler was coming to town. She expected him to parade through the streets as usual, but Hitler had not come to Hamburg since it had been set on fire.

For the last four and a half years, Harriet had prayed for the war to be over. The end was near, but their lives were in limbo. The plan had always been to go back home, but the Soviets controlled Lithuania and returning was too dangerous. But if her family didn't live in Lithuania, where would they live?

She continued to sweep, chiding herself for worrying too much about what would happen *after* the war. The war wasn't over, and who knew how long it might drag on. Right now, her family needed to survive whatever was about to happen in Hamburg.

Harriet paused at the wall calendar and counted the *Xs* recording the bombings. During the two weeks after Easter, the Allies had bombed Hamburg six more times. Harriet wondered if their plan to end the war was to bomb Hamburg off the map.

Each night Harriet went to bed expecting to wake to more bombing. Each day as she swept, she checked the calendar. Two weeks passed. The last attack had been April fourteenth.

As Oskar predicted, the Allies had liberated France. Then they freed Belgium and Luxembourg. According to Sister Anne, the Allies had reached Germany, and the Soviets were marching toward Berlin, but Oskar had heard the troops were headed toward Hamburg.

Harriet swished the broom faster. What would happen if fighting broke out here? Would the Allies go door-to-door, ferreting out people, taking them prisoners or shooting them? And what would they do to the refugees?

That night when the girls were in bed, Harriet voiced her questions to Oskar. Like other nights, he shook his head and mumbled, "I don't know."

Not knowing what was about to happen frightened Harriet, but Oskar's sullen behavior was even more frightening. He had no plan. Since coming to Germany, he had obeyed orders and did what the Germans demanded. She'd spent the last four and a half years figuring out how to survive—stretching their food, providing clothing, and keeping the girls safe.

The next morning, after Oskar went to work, she fed the girls and began her usual routine. As she swept, Oskar's footsteps thudded up the steps. Why was he home so early?

She stopped sweeping and opened the door. His hat was askew, and lines furrowed his forehead. The broom slipped from her hand. Oskar looked the way he had on their last day in Lithuania when he'd rushed home and announced the Soviets were invading. Was it happening again? Were the Soviets about to attack Hamburg? Her heart pounded. "What's wrong?"

He stepped over the broom and slunk into the living room. His breathing was heavy. He sank into the chair, taking several breaths before he answered. "The Allies are across the Elbe River, overlooking Hamburg. They opened fire, shelling the Phoenix Rubber Works."

Harriet picked up the broom and held onto it for support. "Will the troops cross the river and attack Hamburg?"

He ran his fingers through his messed hair. "All I know is they shut down our plant and told us to leave. We waited for transports, but no trucks came."

Harriet tightened her grip on the broom. "How did you get home?"

"We walked." Oskar raised his head. "On the way, we passed shop owners boarding up their businesses and a man running down the street yelling, 'The enemy is coming.'"

Harriet leaned the broom in the corner and turned to Oskar. "How much time do I have to pack?"

"Pack? Where would we go?"

"The Soviets are butchers. We can't stay here."

"It might not be the Soviets, Harriet. Another rumor is the troops are British."

Harriet's legs went weak with relief. "Thank God. The Soviets have already taken our homeland, so we can't go back. I don't want them—"

"What?" cried Irena.

Harriet glanced over her shoulder. Irena stood in the doorway of the bedroom. All of the sparkle in her eyes was gone.

"Why can't we go back home?"

Harriet and Oskar hadn't told the girls that the Soviets had driven the Germans out of Lithuania. She'd planned to talk to them when the time was right. But no time seemed right to tell them they couldn't go home again.

"Where-where will we go?" Irena asked.

Oskar didn't answer, so Harriet tried to keep Irena from worrying. "We're not going anywhere, at least not now. Play with your sisters."

Irena didn't move. Her hands fisted at her side. Tears ran down her cheeks. "I'm ten. Old enough to know."

Harriet's heart ached for Irena. "*Ja*, but your sisters are not."

Irena sucked back a sob and slammed the door behind her. Harriet winced. "She's not happy about staying here."

"I'm not happy about staying, either," admitted Oskar. "But what choice do we have? We can't return to Lithuania. We don't know anyone in Germany to take us in, and it's too dangerous to hide in the forests like others are doing."

"But the fighting in the city could go on for months."

"I doubt it. On the way here, we passed German soldiers, mostly old men and young boys. They won't be able to put up much of a defense."

"If we're staying, we need to prepare." Walking to the cupboard, she pulled out the ration book and handed it to Oskar. "Go to the store while there's food left, and it's still safe."

Oskar slipped the book into his shirt pocket and rose.

"Be careful." Harriet followed him to the door and hooked the chain behind him.

Instead of silence, the girls' angry voices rose from the bedroom. She had enough problems without them being out of sorts. She crossed the kitchen and opened the bedroom door.

"Get away, Betty." Bridget pushed Betty off the bed. She fell and hit her head against the floor, letting out a loud wail.

Rushing across the room, Harriet picked up Betty and examined her head. "Bridget, you could have seriously hurt your sister," scolded Harriet.

"We're playing school and she's too little."

Was Bridget acting out because Irena had told her they

couldn't return to Lithuania? But if that were true, Bridget would have asked about it. Harriet sighed. "I'll take Betty into the kitchen with me."

Betty turned toward Irena. "Me stay."

Irena reached for Betty, who jumped into her arms. "I'll take care of her, Mama," Irena said as she carried Betty to the opposite bed.

Bridget whined. "Now I don't have anyone to play with."

Before Harriet could answer, Irena said, "That's because you were mean to Betty."

Bridget crossed her arms. "She was bothering us."

"You used to be little and bother me," said Irena.

Harriet backed out of the room, grateful that Irena was taking charge. In the last few months, Irena seemed to have grown up. She rarely fought with her sisters, and since Betty had come home from the hospital, Irena worried over her like a little mother. Still, Irena was a child and once the war was over, Harriet wanted Irena and her sisters to have a normal childhood, if that was possible.

Harriet, however, couldn't stop her own worries. What if the Allies came to the flat while Oskar was gone? How would she protect the girls and herself? The door was locked, but that wasn't enough to keep them out. If she blocked the door, the extra resistance might dissuade the soldiers. She scooted the table across the kitchen and shoved it against the door. It needed to be heavier. She piled two chairs on top. It wasn't much, but it might help.

An hour later, Oskar banged on the door. "Let me in."

Wiggling the table, Harriet reached over and unlocked the chain. Oskar squeezed inside. She waited for him to chastise her for such a lame idea. Instead, he said, "I'm glad you barricaded the door. At least you have some protection if..."

Her mind didn't register the rest of what he said. In his

arms was a half-filled market bag with a loaf of bread sticking out the top.

"How did you get so much?" she asked as he set the bag on the counter.

"The shopkeeper is afraid when the Allies come, they'll confiscate everything in his store, so he's selling as much as he can."

Reaching into the bag, Harriet removed two potatoes. "Does he know when they'll attack?"

"No one seems sure what's going on." Oskar took off his hat and hung it on the hook by the door. "The shopkeeper said Hamburg is surrounded by enemy troops and fighting could break out any day, but one man said the Germans blew up part of the autobahn so the Allies can't advance, and another swore he saw a German staff car waving a white flag."

Harriet's hand fluttered to her chest. "A white flag?"

Irena must have heard Oskar because she barged into the kitchen. "Does a white flag mean victory?"

Oskar shook his head. "A white flag means surrender."

"Have the Germans surrendered Hamburg?" Harriet asked.

"I hope so," said Oskar. "Too many lives have already been lost."

Irena glared at Oskar. "Hitler would never give up."

The color in Oskar's cheeks rose. "Let's hope Hitler doesn't sacrifice every man and boy in Germany for his so-called master race."

CHAPTER
SIXTY-SEVEN

The next day Irena and her sisters stayed in the bedroom, playing house. When Bridget became bored, she suggested, "Let's play going home."

The game had been Irena's favorite until yesterday when Mama and Da said they couldn't go back to Lithuania. Irena had stomped into the bedroom, ready to tell Bridget and Betty, but the words stuck in her throat. Never going home was too painful to say aloud. Maybe pretending to go home would take away the ache in her heart.

Once their pretend train arrived in Lithuania, Irena said, "Let's go to the river."

Irena scattered the rocks from her jar onto the floor. Then she, Bridget, and Betty lined up on the edge of the bed, dangling their feet over the side and swishing their toes in the pretend water. Irena pointed to the floor. "There's a rock."

The girls scooted off the bed and walked along the river bed, picking up the rocks and putting them back into the jar.

"Let's pick flowers," said Bridget. The girls skipped around the room as if romping through the meadow. Irena pretended to pick roses, but the game only made her feel worse. She would never go to the river or pick flowers in the meadow or sleep in her old bed again.

For the next several days, Da stood at the kitchen window, constantly peeking out the blackout curtains. "What are you doing?" Irena asked.

"Waiting."

"Waiting for what?"

"For the soldiers to start fighting," answered Da.

"Will they shoot us or put us in one of those camps?"

"Be quiet so I can listen."

At night Irena lay in bed, straining to hear Da's answer as Mama whispered. "What are we going to do?"

All Irena heard was silence.

Waiting was a different kind of fear than the air raids. The air raids lasted for hours and could be deadly. Waiting lasted for days and made her jittery. April ended and May began. The silence continued. The fear intensified.

On their sixth day of waiting, May third, sounds trickled into the apartment. First a few voices and then a low rumble. Da pushed back the blackout curtains in the kitchen. Mama peered over his shoulder. "What is it?"

"People are leaving their apartments."

Irena hopped up from the floor where she had been playing with her sisters, but she was too short to see out the window. "Is it the Soviets?"

When no one answered, Irena ran to the bedroom and slid open the curtains. She expected a scene like five years ago when the Soviets had attacked Lithuania. Then, people fled, taking their suitcases or pillowcases stuffed with their belongings. Here, people flocked from their apartments. They weren't running or carrying their possessions. Their heads weren't bowed in fear. They were smiling and greeting each other.

Irena couldn't figure it out. For days, Da acted as if he

expected something bad to happen, but everyone looked happy. Irena returned to the kitchen.

Mama and Da still stood at the window. "What do you think it means?" Mama asked.

"If the Soviets seized the city, no one would rush out to greet them." Da turned toward the door. "I'll find out."

Irena dashed after him. "I want to go."

Bridget popped up from the floor. "Me, too."

"If you think it's safe, take Irena and Bridget." Mama picked up Betty. "I'll keep the baby with me."

Da agreed, but he made Irena and Bridget hold his hands as they followed the people out of the projects. They stopped on the packed sidewalk near where Irena had stood the last time Hitler paraded through town.

The crowd buzzed with talk of Hamburg's surrender. The drone grew louder. "They're coming."

Irena leaned forward to see who was coming. A tank with a long-barreled gun rolled down the street. Soldiers in khaki uniforms were perched on the top and sides of the tank. "Who are they?" Irena asked.

Da's words seemed to be filled with awe. "The British."

"Is that good?" asked Bridget.

Da squatted down and drew Irena and Bridget into his arms. "It has to be better than the Soviets."

Irena didn't understand how it could be good. "But we lost the war."

Da let go of her and Bridget but stayed eye-level with them. "Germany lost the war. We're not Germans. We're Lithuanians. Don't ever forget where you came from."

The rumble grew louder. Da stood and Irena shrank behind him, peeking out as giant tanks with long cannons roared past. After the tanks were German soldiers, not marching but shuffling. They wore tattered uniforms and dusty boots as they slinked down the street in single file, their capped heads hanging. Alongside the Germans walked several British soldiers, their rifles pointed at the ground.

The line went on and on. Hundreds, possibly thousands of captured German soldiers were paraded down the street. Not one of the Germans lifted his head and looked at the crowd—or her.

Following the prisoners was a convoy of trucks. The flaps on the beds were rolled up, and in each truck at least a dozen British soldiers were standing or riding in the back. Unlike the captured Germans, many of the British soldiers were talking and smiling; a few held their noses.

Irena inched forward. A tall soldier, standing in the truck rolling by, gazed down at her. His unshaven face broke into a wide grin.

Irena shyly smiled back and then frowned as she remembered this was one of the soldiers who had defeated Hitler. Still smiling, the soldier held up his index finger and middle finger, waving them in the air. Several other men in the truck held up their two fingers. "What does it mean, Da?"

Da raised his fingers, too. "It's 'v' for victory."

This didn't seem like a victory parade. No one was shouting or cheering. The British soldiers were eyeing the crowd with curiosity, and the crowd was eyeing the British soldiers with wariness.

At the rear of the parade was a green car with a white star on the door. This must be someone important. When Hitler had ridden down the street in his sleek black convertible, all the frenzied people had raised their arms, shouting, *Heil Hitler.*"

A murmur rippled through the crowd. Irena thought she heard the very name she had been thinking: "Hitler." She slipped her hand from Da's and inched away, trying to hear what others were saying. Murmurs of "Hitler" continued, followed by "Dead."

Was it true? Was Hitler dead? Irena spotted the large

woman with the plaid scarf that she had stood behind when Hitler paraded through Hamburg. The woman asked the same question Irena had been thinking, "Is Hitler dead?"

An old man, hunched over a cane, shuffled closer to the woman. He lifted his head. "Hitler died a few days ago."

The woman yanked off her scarf. "Did the Allies kill him?"

The man straightened. He raised his arm, pointed his thumb and index finger toward his temple like a gun, and pretended to pull the trigger. "Shot himself in the head because—"

"He didn't shoot himself," interrupted a man with a scraggy beard. "He took cyanide. Just swallowed a pill."

"Hitler wouldn't kill himself," said a third man. "He's not a coward."

The woman tossed back her head and ran her fingers through her matted hair. "I just hope he's dead and burning in hell."

The tanks, prisoners, and trucks moved on, winding their way into the city. Walking back to the flat, Irena held Da's hand and tried to make sense of what she had seen and heard. She hoped Hitler wasn't dead. It was hard to believe he was a coward or that he had taken his own life. But it was even harder to believe that the same people who had hailed him as their hero now openly hated him.

CHAPTER
SIXTY-EIGHT

May 9, 1945

After Hamburg surrendered, Da removed the table and chairs from the barricaded door, but the blackout curtains remained closed. "Hamburg has surrendered, but Germany hasn't," he explained.

Each morning, he left the flat to hear news of the war. Before, Irena was tired of war talk, but now she waited in the kitchen with Mama, eager to learn what was going on. One morning in the second week of May, Da opened the door and announced, "Yesterday, Germany surrendered."

Mama seemed hesitant to believe it. "Are you sure the war is over?"

"Japan is still fighting." Da picked up Betty from his chair and sat. "But Germany's surrender was announced on the radio."

Irena hopped off her chair, pulling Bridget with her, who

grabbed Betty. They danced around the kitchen, chanting, "No more war. No more war."

Mama and Da didn't celebrate with them. They stayed at the table, huddled together, their voices low. Irena stopped dancing. "Why are you whispering?"

Da cleared his throat. "For the past week, the Soviet flag has flown over Berlin."

"The Soviets!" Irena slumped into her chair. "They ruin everything." She drilled Da with questions. "Are they coming here? Will we have to salute Stalin? Will they make us speak Russian?"

Da answered each question the same. "I don't know."

Outside, people were shouting, "The war is over!"

Mama hurried to the window and threw back the blackout curtains. Sunshine flooded into the kitchen. "It's a beautiful day. Let's go outside and enjoy our freedom while we can." Mama picked up the brush to fix Irena's hair.

"I don't need pigtails today." She dashed to the door and flew down the stairs, leaving her worries about the Soviets behind. Outside, the spring air caressed her cheeks, and her hair flew behind her. She was free.

The family joined her, and they walked out of the projects toward the neighborhood businesses. The atmosphere was different. No one seemed afraid. People were smiling and hailing their neighbors, not with *"Heil Hitler,"* but with *hallo* and *guten morgen.* Irena and Bridget weaved through the crowd, happy to be free.

They reached the shops that she and Da had passed on the way to the forest. At the corner stood a man with a red accordion strapped to his barrel chest, playing music while people danced in the street. Irena pulled Bridget off the sidewalk and joined in the folk dance they'd learned at school. Irena twirled around. The war was over. They could go outside. They could dance and play. They could do whatever they wanted.

The accordion music stopped, but Irena stuck out her arms and continued twirling. She bumped a man wearing a baggy suit. "Sorry," she mumbled.

The man scowled. "Get away, kid." Stooping, he picked up a fist-sized rock, reared back, and threw it at the store's window where three large bottles of milk were displayed. Irena remembered walking by the store and drooling over those large milk cans.

The store window shattered. *Uh-oh.* The man was going to be in big trouble. Irena looked around, expecting soldiers to march in and haul him away. But the Nazis weren't in charge, and no British soldiers were in sight.

The accordion player struck up another song, but no one danced. The man in the baggy suit rammed his shoulder against Schmaltz Brothers' door, splintering the wood. As it fell open, he stormed inside. His arms, like big windmills, swung around and knocked over the three bottles.

Irena expected milk to splatter onto the floor and splash out of the window. Instead, tiny white granules sifted to the floor. Stooping, the man dipped his finger into a white pile at his feet. He licked it. "Salt." His mouth twisted in disgust. "The Nazis fooled us about everything. I'm tired of having nothing." He charged through the store, snatching up armfuls of cans from the shelves.

Two gray-haired women stood in front of Irena. One had a ragged handkerchief tied around her head. The other wore a print dress with a ripped sleeve. The woman with a headscarf said, "Those Nazis stole everything and left us nothing. It isn't fair."

The other woman pushed forward. "Let's take what we can."

The mood shifted. No one smiled and danced. The crowd was angry and shouting. They lurched forward and rushed the shop.

Frightened, Irena stretched up, searching for Mama and Da. Before she could spot them, the crowd moved, pulling Irena with them. She grabbed Bridget's hand and dug in her heels. But the mob dragged her and Bridget down the street. At the general store, a man raised his heavy work boot, the sole flapping off, as he kicked against the windowpane. The glass shattered. He stepped through the window and unlocked the door. People shoved into the shop, grabbing whatever they could reach.

The remaining crowd whirled to the bakery, its windows boarded up. The people were in such a frenzy that they ripped off the slats and shoved inside. Frightened, Irena clutched Bridget's hand tighter. She wanted the people to go back to dancing and clapping, but the music had stopped, and the air had soured.

A burly man elbowed his way forward. Irena followed, tugging Bridget with her. They cut through the crowd and broke free. Irena took several steadying breaths before she turned to Bridget. "Where's Mama and Da?"

Bridget pointed down the street. "They were in front of Schmaltz Brothers." She stood on tiptoes. "I don't see them."

Irena didn't want to be trapped in the crowd again. "Let's get away from here." They hurried to the next corner, but people were looting in that block, too.

"I want to go home," cried Bridget.

Irena looked around. "I think the projects are this way. Follow me."

Irena fisted her hands and took off. She ran until she could no longer hear the angry shouts of the mob. Then she stopped.

Panting, Bridget pulled up beside her. "Where are we?"

Irena's head whirled around. "Nothing looks familiar. We must have gone the wrong way."

"It's too far to walk back." Bridget sank onto the curb. "Let's wait for Mama and Da."

Irena plopped next to her. "How will they find us?"

Bridget shrugged. "I don't know, but whenever I'm lost, they always find me."

"Maybe we can figure out which way to go." Irena gazed at the empty buildings. Several blocks away were charred warehouses. "Let's go that way."

Rising, they crossed the road and wandered along more streets. "How much farther?" whined Bridget.

"Look!" Irena pointed to the red-brick building down the block. "There's our school."

She darted down the sidewalk and stopped in front of the school.

"Let's go home," said Bridget.

Irena eyed the school. "Maybe we can get inside."

"The school?" Bridget frowned. "Why?"

Irena didn't answer. She grabbed Bridget's hand, yanked her up the steps, and pulled on the front door. Irena's mouth rounded in an 'o' as the door swung open. She held onto the heavy wooden door, waving for Bridget to enter. "Go in."

Bridget shook her head. "You first."

Irena glanced back. The street was empty. She ducked into the building, jerking Bridget with her. The door banged behind them.

Irena blinked, adjusting to the darkness. "Let's find our classroom." She and Bridget tiptoed down the empty hallway.

"It's spooky," whispered Bridget. "Let's go back."

"Don't be a scaredy cat." Irena felt scared, too.

"What are we looking for?"

Irena tried to sound brave. "Something to take."

"There isn't any food here."

"There are books and chalk to play school."

Bridget quit complaining and followed. They stopped at the open doorway of their classroom. The tables and chairs were gone. The only furniture was the teacher's desk and chair in the front of the room and in the back, the wooden supply cabinet with one door hanging open, revealing empty shelves. The other door was closed.

Irena pointed to the cabinet. "Let's see what's inside."

Her heart pounded as she shuffled into the room. When she neared the teacher's desk, her eyes shot up to Hitler's picture, and she raised her arm. "*Heil Hitler.*" She could almost hear Fraulein Mueller bark, "What are you girls doing here?"

Maybe they should go back. Then Irena remembered Fraulein Bauer offering her a chalkboard. Feeling braver, Irena waved to Bridget standing in the hallway. "Come on."

Bridget ambled into the room. She didn't raise her arm.

"You forgot to salute Hitler."

"We don't have to do that anymore," Bridget said. "He's dead."

"You should still do it."

Bridget kept her arm down. Giving up, Irena padded to the supply cabinet. She tugged on the closed door, pulling it open. The shelves were empty. "Someone beat us here. I hope it wasn't Helga."

Bridget agreed. "She's a *dummkopf.*"

Irena slunk back toward the hall. She didn't want to leave without anything. She had another idea. "Let's look in the teacher's desk." She scurried to the desk and one by one pulled open the drawers. "Empty."

She glanced up at Hitler's picture above the desk. The oil painting had always fascinated her.

Bridget tugged on her arm. "Let's go before we get in trouble."

Irena nodded and trailed behind her sister. In the doorway, she glanced back at Hitler's picture. She would never see that beautiful oil painting again. An idea popped into her head. She clamped her hand on Bridget's shoulder and turned her around. "Let's take the picture."

Bridget's mouth dropped open. She pointed to Hitler. "You mean you want to take him?"

"Think about how great it would be." Irena scurried to the teacher's desk. "Help me move this so I can reach it."

Bridget stood on one side of the desk and Irena on the other. "Okay, push." The girls inched the desk backward until it rested below the painting. Irena scooted the teacher's chair next to the desk, climbed onto it, and hopped on top of the desk.

"Be careful," warned Bridget.

Stretching on tiptoes, Irena reached up and grabbed the bottom of the frame. She struggled to lift the picture off the nail on the wall. It wobbled forward. Irena tried to steady the painting, but it was too heavy. The picture slid through her fingers, hit the corner of the desk, and banged onto the floor, where it landed face down.

"It's ruined." Irena jumped from the desk and bent to lift the painting, but it was too heavy. "Help me."

Bridget sidled to the painting and gripped one side. Irena grabbed the other. Together, they stood it upright. The picture was almost as tall as Irena was, but not a hair on Hitler's head or mustache had been scratched.

"Now what do we do?" Bridget asked.

"Take it home and hang it up."

"I don't want it over our bed," said Bridget.

Irena thought about Hitler's eyes staring at her every morning and gulped. "We can sell it and be rich."

Irena hefted one end of the picture, and Bridget the other. Together, they scuttled out of the classroom and down the hall. Once outside, they rested the picture against the building. "I can't wait to show Mama and Da," Irena boasted. "Won't they be happy?"

Bridget frowned. "I don't know if they'll be happy."

"Of course they will. I'm not lugging it back into the school. Let's go."

The projects were several blocks away, but the unwieldy picture made walking slow, especially since they stayed close to the buildings and stopped to cover Hitler with their bodies when someone passed. But the other people were loaded with their loot and didn't seem to notice the painting of Hitler or the girls.

At the flat, they carted the picture to the stairs. Bridget went first, walking backward and guiding the picture, while Irena pushed from below. At their apartment, Irena stood in the hall as Bridget opened the door.

"Let me go in first," protested Irena. "It was my idea." She walked into the kitchen where Mama and Da sat at the table while Betty was on the floor, playing with dishes.

Mama jumped up. "Are you girls all right? We couldn't find you, so we came back to the flat thinking you might be here. Da was ready to go and look for you again."

Instead of answering, Irena slid the picture of Hitler through the door and turned it toward Mama and Da. "Surprise!"

Mama's face paled as if Adolf Hitler had risen from the dead and walked into her kitchen. Da shot out of his chair and marched toward the painting. He grabbed the painting from Irena and heaved it over his head. He slammed the picture onto the floor.

Betty screamed, and Irena jumped back. *Crack.* The frame split. Da picked up the painting and threw it down again. Then he stomped on it with his heavy boots.

Stunned, Irena cowered in the corner, shaking. She had never seen Da so angry. He was like a crazed man. Over and over, he pounded his foot on the frame until it splintered. Then he attacked the painting. He ground his heel into Hitler's face, tearing the canvas into shreds.

When he finished, he pumped his fist into the air triumphantly. "Now Hitler is dead."

CHAPTER
SIXTY-NINE

June - July 1945

rena shrank in the corner, too scared to move as Da destroyed the oil painting of Hitler. When he finished, he turned to her. "Why did you bring a picture of that man into our home?"

Da's harsh voice made Irena quiver. "The—the picture was beautiful, and you always said *'Heil Hitler'* and-and told me not to say anything bad about him."

Da wiped the sweat from his brow and tromped across the room toward her. Irena trembled as he squatted down and gripped her shoulders as if he wanted to shake her. Instead, his twisted face disappeared, and his tone became gentle. "I couldn't tell you how your mama and I felt about Hitler. You might have repeated it at school or somewhere else. Hitler did not tolerate dissent. If the wrong people found out, we would have been severely punished or sent away."

In the following weeks, Irena heard about what had happened to those who were sent away.

She learned about showers that sprayed out poisonous gases and ovens that burned people up. After these awful stories, she understood. Hitler was a bad man, worse than bad. He was evil.

For days afterward, she had nightmares. Her family was at the Registration Department. She and Bridget stood in the shower, waiting for the water. Instead, poisonous gas sprayed out, burning their lungs. Irena would wake up screaming and gasping for air.

Life after the war differed from what she'd expected. The first Sunday the family took a walk, they passed British soldiers and tanks. Irena gripped Da's hand. "If the war's over, why are the soldiers still here?"

"So Nazis don't gain control again," Da answered.

"But they're watching us. We're not Nazis or German."

"The British are sorting out their enemies. They plan to send the refugees back to their own countries."

"Refugees? Who are they?" Irena asked.

"People who fled from another country like us," Da answered.

"When are the Soviets leaving so we can go home?"

Da stared down at his scuffed shoes and kept walking.

In the following days, Irena worried as much as Da about what would happen. Each day he and some of the other men in the projects sat on the stoop of their building and discussed the future while they waited for Big Angelo to report the news.

The brothers who lived across the hall no longer hid their radio. Big Angelo would listen to the news and then stick his head out the open window of his second-floor flat. He wasn't a large man, but he had a booming voice, and he would bellow out the progress from this place called Potsdam, where the Allies met to make a peace treaty.

One night after supper, Mama was on the couch, showing

Irena how to darn, while Da sat in the chair and talked about news from Potsdam. "The Allies want to repatriate all immigrants and refugees."

Refugees? Irena stopped darning the hole in the heel of her sock. What was happening in Potsdam affected her. "What does *re-pa...*what does that word mean?"

"Repatriate means to send a person back to the country where he or she was born." Da's voice rose. "Don't the Allies know what the Soviets will do if we have to return?"

"I don't want our family separated," said Mama.

"The Soviets will do more than separate us. They could—"

"Ouch!" Irena jabbed the needle into her thumb.

"Oskar, you're frightening the girls. We don't know anything for certain."

The following Sunday, instead of a walk, Mama suggested they go to visit Sister Anne. When the nun saw them enter the church, her face lit up with a semblance of her previous glow, but then her smile melted. "I hope you haven't come to say goodbye." The Sister reached for Betty, who jumped into her arms. "I know you're eager to return to Lithuania, but it's not safe."

Mama fisted both hands over her heart. "What have you heard?"

"The Soviets will continue to rule the Baltic countries: Latvia, Estonia—and Lithuania. Men are being sent to Siberia while women and children are left behind, unprotected."

Until now Irena had held onto the hope that the Soviets would leave Lithuania. After hearing Sister Anne, that hope died. But Irena didn't stomp her foot or pout. She understood returning to Lithuania was too dangerous.

On the walk home, Irena shuffled behind Mama and Da, thinking about living in Germany. Every day, Mama took Bridget, Betty, and her outside to run or play or do whatever they wanted. Sometimes when Mama had chores, Da would stay outside and play hide-n-seek or tag with them. Having Da home all the time made summer feel like an extended holiday.

When Irena and her family fled to Germany, she'd been lonely and wanted to make friends, and she had. But Hanna died and Irena didn't know where Mia was. She missed Hanna and Mia, but Irena wasn't lonely, at least not the way she used to be, and she couldn't quite figure out why.

Bridget dropped back, pulling Betty with her, and fell into step with Irena. "We want to walk with you."

Irena looked at Bridget, really looked at her. Not just her brown pigtails and pretty smile, but her heart. All these years in Germany, Irena hadn't been alone. Bridget had been with her.

After the train to Lithuania was bombed, Irena and Bridget had turned their disappointment into one of their favorite games —going home. When Betty was born, Irena and Bridget had stayed at the orphanage—together. And when Betty got diphtheria, Irena and Bridget had clung to each other in fear. But when Betty stood up in the crib with her mouth healed, they had shouted and shared their joy in a way only sisters could.

Sisters. Irena had two sisters. Betty wasn't old enough to play much, but she would grow and the three of them could do everything together. Irena would never be lonely again. She would always have friends. She had her sisters.

CHAPTER
SEVENTY

Harriet stood at the kitchen sink, running Oskar's shirt across the washboard. Her mind drifted back to the river in Lithuania, where she scrubbed the clothes with rocks. The familiar melody hummed through her head. *Swish-swish-swish, slap-slap-slap, click-click-click.* Nearby, Irena and Bridget dangled their feet in the crystal blue water and searched for rocks. Harriet doubled over. She ached to return to those carefree days. She wanted to see her parents and friends. She wanted to breathe in the fresh air and run through the meadow, enjoying the fragrant wild roses and Lithuanian blues.

Irena scampered into the kitchen with Bridget and Betty behind her. "Mama, are you done?"

The memory slipped away. Harriet dropped Oskar's shirt on top of the other wet clothes and picked up the basket. "Lead the way." After years of being trapped inside, she and the girls craved being outside.

Irena grabbed one of Betty's hands, and Bridget grabbed the other. Together, they towed Betty out of the apartment and down the stairs. Humming, Harriet padded behind them. Outside, she was greeted by the sun and a cloudless blue sky.

Even the air smelled different. In the spring, the rains had washed everything clean. The odor of rotting corpses and death that had clung to Hamburg for almost two years was waning. Trees and grass, once dead, had begun to grow.

As Harriet pinned the thread-bare clothes on the line, the girls ran between the buildings, playing tag. Suddenly, the girls stopped and stared toward the street. Harriet turned toward the family trudging past them. The man toted two battered suit-cases. The woman wearing a frayed sweater cradled a crying baby in her arms. Two boys about seven or eight with brown bowl-cut hair wrestled a rickety wagon piled with what appeared to be their possessions.

For the past several weeks, Harriet had noticed other families like this one leaving the projects. A dark cloud hovered in her mind. She'd been hoping for some grand miracle that would allow her family to return to Lithuania and slip into their old life.

She swallowed the lump in her throat. She had to accept that the dream she had held onto for the last five years was not going to happen. Their Lithuania was gone. The tears she had been fighting spilled down her cheeks.

She thought about other people in her life and the choices they'd made. During the Great War when the Soviets had invaded Lithuania, her grandparents had chosen to stay. The Soviets had barged into her grandparents' home and dragged her grandfather away. Not a week went by without her grandmother repeating the horror of that night. Every day she sat by the window, looking out and waiting for his return. When an unexpected horse clomped up the lane or wagon wheels crunched the rocks, she would ask, "Is it him?"

Her grandmother never moved on. She died waiting for news that never came.

Harriet's mother had been a loving woman until Agne's death and the deaths of her two other babies. Day by day, the mother Harriet had known faded away. Harriet had yearned for her mother's attention and love, but she had been stuck in loss, afraid to fully open her heart to the daughter who had survived.

Harriet's eyes flitted back to her daughters. Betty, eager to play, tugged on Irena's hand. As she toddled away, she tripped, falling onto the hard dirt and crying. The clothespin slipped from Harriet's hand, but before she could move, Irena was already at Betty's side, comforting her.

Stooping, Harriet picked up the clothespin. She would always be a little more protective of Betty. After Betty's illness, Harriet understood her mother's loss more. Harriet didn't know what she would have done or how she would have coped if Betty hadn't survived. Each generation had its hardships and decisions to make. Her mother and her grandmother had been given lives they did not want, and they had made choices, right or wrong, that seemed best to them. Their choices caused them to spend their remaining years mourning what they could not have.

It was Harriet's turn. She had been given a life she did not want. She had never wanted to leave her country and come to Germany. She had never learned more than the basic German words because she thought they would return home. Now she had to choose. Mourn the old life that she wanted or embrace the unknown as an opportunity for something new, maybe something better.

Harriet wanted to be a strong woman. Those times when she needed to be strong, she had silenced her fears and stoked enough courage to set an example for her girls. When it was time for Irena or Bridget or Betty to make their own choices, Harriet wanted the girls to have the strength and courage to find their ways.

Now Harriet needed to find her strength. With God's help,

the family had survived the war, but their lives were in limbo, dependent on the decisions that others would make. She had no idea what those decisions would be. But she couldn't look back. She would embrace the future.

That night when the girls were playing in the bedroom, Harriet sat at the table with Oskar discussing their situation. "Do you know what happens now?"

Oskar lowered his head. The blow of not being able to return to their homeland had crushed him. "I'm sorry I brought you and the girls here. If we'd have stayed, maybe-maybe we would have had a chance, but now if we're sent back..."

Harriet reached across the table and took both of his hands in hers. She repeated the words she'd told herself. "Don't look back. You made the best decision you could at the time. We must decide what is best for us now."

Oskar lifted his head. "If the Allies try to make us return, we can leave, hide out somewhere."

She wouldn't have any trouble leaving Germany. Except for the birth of Betty, she had few fond memories here. But she didn't know where they would go.

Oskar cleared his throat. "Even if the Allies decide we can stay, it might not be good."

They had already faced so many problems. What could be worse?

"In Hamburg, thousands of Germans have no homes. Since the fire bombings, many of them have been living in the rubble. Now that Hitler is dead, other Germans are returning to their homeland. The British used all of their resources to win the war. They have little left to provide for their own people and even less for refugees like us."

Harriet expected food, clothing, and other necessities would be scarcer for a while, but she would manage. Oskar, however, seemed to be trying to tell her something else. Something worse.

He squeezed her hands. "I don't think we'll be allowed to live here."

Harriet jerked, pulling her hands from his. She had never considered that if they stayed in Germany, they wouldn't live in this apartment. "I've seen families leaving. I assumed they'd chosen to return to their own countries or to move in with relatives. I didn't realize they were being forced out." Harriet swallowed and took a deep breath. "Where-where would we go?"

"I don't know. I've heard rumors..."

"Tell me?"

"The British are fumigating the camps."

"Yes, you told me German prisoners would be sent there."

Oskar nodded. "But I've heard other rumors. They might move people who can't return to their country there."

"*Us*? They're going to move *us* to one of those camps?" This was a new horror, one she had not expected and could not imagine.

Oskar tried to reassure her. "Only for a short time."

Harriet crossed herself. "Coming to Germany was supposed to be for a short time. It's been almost five years." She glanced around the apartment. She'd thought about sewing flowered curtains for the windows and painting the walls a sunny yellow. The possibility that their apartment might be ripped away was a cruel blow.

She waited for her ragged breathing to calm before she was able to let the idea of leaving their flat seep in. "I never thought of this as home, at least not a permanent one."

"I'm sorry, Harriet." The despair in his voice was heartbreaking. Oskar had endured the work at the bomb factory because he considered it his responsibility to provide for his family. He had labored long hours and done everything he could. She didn't blame him or feel as if he'd fallen short. And she didn't want him to blame himself.

Her thoughts were distracted as Irena shuffled into the

kitchen. She slipped onto Harriet's lap and wrapped her arms around her neck. "We're ready to say our prayers and be tucked in."

Harriet pressed Irena tightly against her chest. She was here. Bridget, Betty, and Oskar were here. Take away one of them and Harriet wasn't sure she could survive. Her family and faith, those were what were important. If they had to leave this apartment, at least they would be together.

She kissed Irena on the cheek and slid her off her lap. "Your father and I will be there in a minute."

After Irena left, Harriet rose and extended her hand to Oskar. "You haven't failed."

He grabbed onto her. "But what about our home?"

She pulled him up. "Home isn't this flat. It's who you live with and what you make of it."

"But we'll have nothing."

"You're here. I'm here. The girls are here. We've been blessed. We survived and we have each other. Don't ever say that's nothing. To me, that's everything."

CHAPTER
SEVENTY-ONE

August 1 - 15, 1945

rena and Bridget sprawled on the cracked dirt in the shade of the apartment building, playing rock, paper, scissors. Da, wearing his battered hat to protect him from the fierce sun, sat on the front stoop talking with three other men about the same thing they always talked about. The war.

The afternoon was a scorcher, but Irena enjoyed being outside instead of cooped up in the flat. Most days as Betty napped, Da would bring her and Bridget outside to play while he waited for Big Angelo to stick his head out of the second-story window and yell the latest peace-treaty news he'd heard on the radio.

Irena and Bridget each made fists, pounded them into the palm of their other hands, and chanted, "Rock, paper, scissors."

Irena kept her hand balled; Bridget pointed her fingers into scissors. Laughing triumphantly, Irena smashed Bridget's scissors. "If grownups played rock, paper, scissors, it wouldn't take f-o-r-e-v-e-r to make a peace treaty," Irena said.

Big Angelo's bellow cut through their laughter. "I have news."

Irena stood and squinted up at the second floor. Big Angelo's head and arms stuck out the open window, his hands waving in the air as he shouted the news. Irena tried to understand what the big Greek said, but Big Angelo had an accent, and her German was limited. Da would explain it to Mama at home.

When they returned, Betty was awake, and Mama had bowls of cold cabbage soup waiting on the table. "What did you find out?" she asked.

Da hung his hat on the hook next to the door, washed his hands, and dropped into his chair. Irena and Bridget cleaned up and then scurried to the table. "It's official," said Da. "The treaty has been signed."

"Finally." Mama slid into her chair, pulling Betty onto her lap.

"Germany will have to pay reparation, and the country will be divided between the Allies—America, Great Britain, France, and the Soviet Union. As we expected, Hamburg is in the British section."

Mama gave Betty a spoonful of soup. "What did the Soviets get?"

"The area around Berlin—and they have claimed the Baltic countries."

Mama dropped her spoon, splashing soup on Betty, who let out a wail. Irena stopped eating. "Does that mean they're staying in Lithuania?"

Da nodded. "The Soviets insist the Baltic countries are theirs. At least America and Great Britain don't recognize their claim."

414

"What about us?" asked Mama. "We fled here to get away from the Soviets."

"They're trying to make all the refugees return to their own countries."

Mama teared up. "I've been expecting the worst but knowing we can't go home is…is hard."

The words hit Irena with such force that her tummy hurt, and she didn't think the ache would go away for a long time.

She glanced at the wall calendar. In a few days, on August ninth, she would be eleven. Today, even thinking about her birthday didn't make her happy. She picked up her spoon, but she didn't feel like eating.

———

The night before her birthday, Irena lay awake, listening to Mama and Da talk in the kitchen. She heard the word *Soviets*. That was never good.

Careful not to disturb Bridget and Betty, Irena rose and tiptoed to the door, cracking it open. Mama and Da sat at the table, their heads together, whispering. During the war, her parents often whispered about things they didn't want her to know. But after Germany's surrender, they hadn't been so secretive.

Opening the door, Irena stepped into the kitchen. "What's going on?"

Mama and Da jerked apart. Da held out his arms. Irena ran to him and climbed onto his lap. He playfully rubbed his whiskery face across her cheeks.

Irena pulled away. "Why were you whispering?"

"A few days ago, America dropped a bomb on Japan," Da said.

Irena scrunched her nose. "The Allies dropped lots of bombs on us."

"This was a different bomb," Da explained. "So powerful it almost wiped out the entire city of Hiroshima."

Images of blood running down the cobblestone street, charred bodies, and flaming buildings flashed through her mind. How could anything be worse than that? "I heard you say the Soviets."

"They declared war on Japan," Mama said.

"The Soviets are getting too big for their britches." Irena huffed. "They took our Lithuania. Do they want the whole world?"

Three nights later, Irena lay in bed, listening to Mama and Da across the room, whispering about being displaced people and about America dropping another bomb on Japan, one of those bad ones. But Japan and America were far away, so Irena cuddled next to Betty and Bridget and fell asleep.

Days passed, and Da continued to listen to Big Angelo yell out the news of the war from his second-floor window as Irena and Bridget rested in the shade. "Do you think we'll go to school in the fall?" Irena asked Bridget.

Bridget shrugged. "I like playing outside better."

"Me, too," said Irena as she ran a twig through the dirt and made a stick figure of herself. "When it gets too cold, we can go back to school. Whose picture do you think will hang in the front of the classroom?"

"Not Hitler." Bridget pointed at Irena. "You stole it."

Irena frowned. She didn't like to remember that horrible scene with Da destroying Hitler's picture. "If it's Stalin, I'm not saluting him."

"Me, either," agreed Bridget as she drew a figure of herself in the dirt. "I hope pickle-faced Fraulein Mueller isn't our teacher."

"She talked about Hitler as if he were God," said Irena, "and she blamed the Jews for the war when it was Adolf's fault."

"You're not supposed to call him Adolf," Bridget said. "That's an insult. You'll get in trouble."

"Adolf. Adolf. Adolf." Irena repeated the name. It gave her satisfaction to insult the former *Führer*. She didn't like being tricked. Maybe Fraulein Mueller and the other Germans had been tricked, too, but Mama and Da hadn't been fooled. They knew Hitler was evil.

Irena would be more careful about whom she trusted. She didn't want to be fooled again. If a teacher or grownup told her something, she didn't have to believe it.

Big Angelo stuck his head out the window of his second-floor apartment. His deep voice grew louder, but he talked too fast for Irena to understand. Then Da and the other two men on the stoop jumped up and slapped each other on the back.

Da turned and ran toward them, a big grin brightening his face. "Did you hear? Japan has surrendered."

Irena's feet were whisked out from under her as Da lifted her and whirled her around. "The war is over!" he shouted.

Her world was spinning. She had prayed for the war to end and had expected to return to Lithuania, but Da said they couldn't. Without all the bombs, it might be okay to live in Germany.

Tightening her fingers around Da's neck, she threw back her head and laughed. After several more circles, Da slowed. Her feet flopped onto the ground. Her legs wobbled. He continued to steady her as she struggled to gain her balance.

The earth beneath her feet shifted, and so did her dream. Da's arms, however, stayed protectively around her, holding onto her until her feet steadied. Then he picked up Bridget and spun her around.

Mama hurried out of the flat, carrying Betty on her hip. "I heard shouting. What's going on?"

Da set Bridget down and wrapped his arms around Mama. "Japan surrendered. The war is finally over."

Irena and Bridget latched onto Mama. The five of them stood together in each other's arms. Irena's head cleared. The spinning stopped. She was right where she was supposed to be.

Bridget stepped back. "Let's play something fun to celebrate."

"Like what?" Irena asked.

"Let's play the train game."

Irena didn't want to return to a Soviet Lithuania. "I have an idea. Let's board the train in Lithuania and leave."

Bridget stared at Irena as if she were crackers. "Why would we do that?"

"Because the Soviets are in Lithuania." Irena took Betty from Mama and set her on the ground. Holding onto Betty's hand, Irena reached for Bridget. "And you and Betty are here."

Bridget waited as if she were considering this. "Okay, but I get to be the conductor."

Irena was the oldest. She should be the conductor. But Bridget was looking up at her with unabashed admiration. "You can be the conductor. I'll be the caboose, and Betty can be the engine."

Bridget lined Betty up in front as Irena shouted from the rear, "All aboard."

They chugged ahead, plowing between Mama and Da.

Da put a staying hand on Bridget's arm. "What's your hurry?"

"We're fleeing from the Soviets," Irena said. "Hop on Mama and Da."

"Where are you going?" asked Da.

"I don't know," said Irena.

Da joined the line, but Mama hung back, her smile waning.

Irena stopped and ran to Mama, grabbing her hand. "Come on, we can't be separated."

Mama's smile returned as she joined them.

"Toot, toot," said Betty.

Everyone laughed as they chugged toward their new life—together.

1945 - 1959

The Allies expected the eleven million people uprooted by the war to return to their own countries. The millions who could not repatriate became Displaced People. The term was not only for Jewish refugees but also for the non-Jewish. Millions of them wound up in displaced persons camps set up by the Allied forces that existed from 1945 to 1959. Some of the DP camps were on the very grounds of the concentration camps.

NOTES

1940

1. Ann Charles, "No Home to Go to: The Story of the Baltic Displaced People," *Baltic Review*, October 11, 2016, https://www.baltic-review.com/story-baltic-displaced-persons/.

1941

1. *Encyclopedia Britannica*, "German-Soviet Nonaggression Pact," https://www.britannica.com/event/German-Soviet-Nonaggression-Pact. Accessed March 30, 2023.

CHAPTER 21

1. Natasha Frost, "The Forgotten Nazi History of One-Pot Meal," *Gastro Obscura*, April 12, 2018, https://www.atlasobscura.com./articles/one-potmeals-nazi-germany-eintopf. 6

1942

1. Keith Lowe, *Inferno: The Fiery Destruction of Hamburg*, 1943 (New York: Scribner, 2007). 54.
2. Lowe, *Inferno*. 51.

1943

1. Martin Middlebrook, *Firestorm Hamburg* (Yorkshire, England: Pen & Sword, 2012). 95.
2. Gordon Musgrove, *Operation Gomorrah* (New York: Jane's, 1981). 171.
3. Lowe, *Inferno*. 179.
4. Lowe, *Inferno*. 259-260.

1944

1. Lowe, *Inferno.* 294.
2. Lowe, *Inferno.* 285.
3. Lowe, *Inferno.* 285.

CHAPTER 62

1. Irena Golcvegaite McCrary, "My Life Story," interview by Sue Stewart Ade, Pana, Illinois, May 3, 2019. "Just as the Lady in White said, my sister (Betty) died when she was fifty years old."

1945

1. *Encyclopedia Britannica,* "German-Soviet Nonaggression Pact."

BIBLIOGRAPHY

Charles, Ann. "No Home to Go To: The Story of Baltic Displaced People." *Baltic Review.* October 11, 2016. https://baltic-review.com/story-baltic-displaced-persons/. Traveling exhibit.

Coburn, Jennifer. *Cradles of the Reich.* Read by Natasha Soudek, Oregon: Black Stone Audio, 2022. Audible audio ed., Run time 11 hr., 10 min.

"Education in Nazi Germany." Accessed Aug. 8, 2021. http://spartacus-educational.com/GEReducation.htm.

Encyclopedia Britannica. "German-Soviet Nonaggression Pact." Accessed March 30, 2023.
http://www.britannica.com/event/German-Soviet-Nonagression-Pact. Accessed 30 Mar.2023.

Frankel, Rebecca. *Into the Forest.* New York: St. Martin's, 2021.

Frost, Natasha. "The Forgotten Nazi History of One-Pot Meal." *Gastro Obscura.* April 12, 2018. Accessed July 7, 2022. https://www.atlasobscura.com/articles/one-pot-meals-nazi-germany-eintopf.

Grant, Rebecca. "Operation Gomorrah." *Air Force Magazine,* March 1, 2007. Accessed May 13, 2020. *http://www.airforcemag.com/article/0307gomorrah/.*

Hilton, Ella E. Schneider. *Displaced Person.* Louisiana State UP, 2004.

Hunt, Irmgard. *On Hitler's Mountain.* New York: Harper, 2006.

Lowe, Keith. *Inferno: The Fiery Destruction of Hamburg, 1943.* New York: Scribner, 2007.

Middlebrook, Martin. *Firestorm Hamburg.* Yorkshire, England: Pen and Sword, 2012.

Musgrove, Gordon. *Operation Gomorrah.* New York: Jane's, 1981.

Scheer, Dag. *When Echoes Speak.* Tipaza, 2021.

AFTERWORD

This book would not have been possible without the support of my husband, Larry, and my family, who have always encouraged me. Thanks to Write Stuff for reading the early drafts, to members of the Iowa classes who stuck with me: Julia O'Donnell, Richard Durisen, Renee Enna, Ellen Smucker, and Gail Funke, to Tim Ellington for making the book better, and to Carol Poe and Deeanna Stalets for the extra eyes I needed.

To my readers, without you, there would be no reason to get up at 5:00 a.m. and write.

ABOUT THE AUTHOR

Sue Stewart Ade is the author of the award-winning novels *Friends Forever* and *Friends Together*. She was compelled to take a brief departure from romantic suspense to record events from WWII that are happening again as the Soviets attack Ukraine.

DISPLACED won first place in Writer's Advice Contest and was a finalist in the Pacific Northwest Literary Contest.

Sue presently lives in Pana, Illinois, with her husband Larry. They have two children, Nelson and Missy, and four grandchildren. Family, friends, and faith are her life.

www.sueade.net

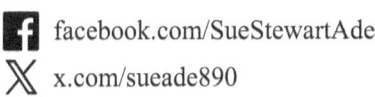

facebook.com/SueStewartAde

x.com/sueade890

ALSO BY SUE STEWART ADE

Novels

Friends Together

Friends Forever

Anthologies

Pumpkin Blossoms in Food & Romance Go Together, Vol. 1

Don't miss out on your next favorite book!

———

THANK YOU FOR READING

Did you enjoy this book?

We invite you to leave a review at the website of your choice, such as Goodreads, Amazon, Barnes & Noble, etc.

DID YOU KNOW THAT LEAVING A REVIEW…

- Helps other readers find books they may enjoy.
- Gives you a chance to let your voice be heard.
- Gives authors recognition for their hard work.
- Doesn't have to be long. A sentence or two about why you liked the book will do.

www.ingramcontent.com/pod-product-compliance
Lightning Source LLC
Chambersburg PA
CBHW030239030726
47493CB00023B/173